THE FELLOWSHIP

By K. Darblyne

ISBN 0-9741034-6-2

Second Printing 2004

Cover art and design by Anne M. Clarkson

Published by:

Dare 2 Dream Publishing

A Division of Limitless Corporation

Lexington, South Carolina 29073

Find us on the World Wide Web

http://www.limitlessd2d.net

Printed in the United States and the UK by

Lightning Source, Inc.

Dedication

Over the years I've taught, served, and worked beside many dedicated professionals in the field of Trauma. Some have been paid for their time and effort, while others have given of their spare hours and themselves on a strictly volunteer basis. Whether paid or not, acting as individuals or highly skilled teams, they all believed in the sanctity of life and the essence that one person can make a difference in the world around us in a time of need. To their compassionate nature and untiring effort, I dedicate this book. May we all come to know the fellowship of their spirit.

ACKNOWLEDGEMENTS

During our lives many people pass in and out of our daily existence, each one leaving an impression on our being in greater or lesser degrees. How we accept or interact with them depends on the circumstances and the time at which we are in our lives. To all those people who have given me encouragement and dirction along the path to my writing, I'd like to say thank you for investing your time, energies, and even an occasional kick in the pants.

The Fellowship is my first novel of **That Healing Touch Series**. It has taken me years to work up the courage to let it go to print for others to see. I can only hope that it will hold your interest as is has held mine.

THAT HEALING TOUCH SERIES

BOOK ONE

THE FELLOWSHIP

By K. Darblyne

Chapter 1

The taxi came to a stop at the entranceway lined with stark wrought iron fencing. It was an eerie sight, as though the early morning fog had swallowed everything just past the ominous looking gates. The driver paused, casting his eyes into the rearview mirror. His gaze now fixed on the silent figure staring out the side window.

This was not one of his favorite areas to take passengers to, especially this early in his shift. It was too far from the downtown area with all of its quick lucrative fares. He cursed himself as he thought of how attractive and stalwart the woman had appeared as she approached his cab. If she had not been a real looker, he surely would have passed on this particular trip.

A smirk came to his face, his words almost inaudible, as if he were thinking aloud in a whisper. "It might not be dollars in my pocket, but is sure is payment for my eyes. After all, she picked ME over the others parked at the taxi stand." This would be payment enough since he knew that in this lifetime his chance of personally attracting someone of her caliber was slim to none.

It seemed like an eternity before he was able to find the words, "You getting out here?"

Still fixed in her position she slowly answered, "No, not here. Take the first road to the left and stop by the reflection pool." The woman was amazed that she remembered the way;

after all, it was a long time since her last visit here. The memories began to flood into her mind. Her eyes became moist, but no tears would come. She knew that they had all been spent on her first visit here some nineteen years ago. She had vowed to herself at that time, crying was a waste of energy that could be put to better use. Energy that could eliminate pain and sorrow…yes, the feeling of loss so no one else would have to suffer as she had and, for that matter, still did.

The cabbie resumed the forward motion following her directives. He could feel the melancholy exuding from the stoic passenger, his heart wanting to offer her support. He resigned himself to the fact that this was not possible.

"Would you like me to wait for you?" His eyes searched in the rearview mirror for hers.

"Yes, thank you. I'll only be a few moments."

She opened the door and climbed out of the taxi. The ride had been long and her body felt relieved to stretch as she walked around to the right side of the reflection pool. The rows of stones materialized slowly, one by one, as her steady gait advanced her down the length of the pool. Then, out of nowhere, it seemed to jump out at her. She stopped abruptly as she recognized her family name in large letters across the top of the marble stone, Trivoli. Closing her eyes and taking in a deep breath she could feel her hands tremble as she reached out to touch the stone, hoping somehow to connect with those of her past. She knelt as she ran her outstretched fingers over the name, Lucas.

"You're not forgotten," she whispered. "You are the guiding force in my mind that enables me to continue on." She bowed her head and shook it slowly; "No one ever needs to feel this pain. No one!"

As if on cue, a gentle wind blew, causing her shoulder length raven hair to caress her face. The woman turned, looking into the breeze and allowed a small lopsided smile to emerge. "You always knew how to comfort me, didn't you?"

If only things were different. If only we could be together

again. Her thoughts raced wildly trying to create images of what should have transpired over the last nineteen years. It tortured her to realize that all of her love and devotion could still leave such a cold, empty feeling.

Bowing her head as though in homage, she quietly whispered. "I promise, I *will* make a difference." Reaching out she gently placed a blown kiss on the cold marble and rose to her feet. Taking a deep breath, she squared her shoulders and turned with almost military perfection. Her walk was purposeful as she returned to the waiting taxi.

She paused half way into the rear seat, turning for one last look. "I promise." The words were barely audible.

The dark hair floated in the air as her head now quickly turned, her intense blue eyes pinning the driver who was staring in utter amazement. His mouth was agape; he could not believe what he saw. Those eyes, they were the bluest he had ever seen. Words…God…his mind and body were failing him as he tried to respond. As his mouth remained open, his ears could hear her say, "Now, to the Emeryville Train Station." Her voice was commanding him.

Slowly he nodded and turned, his body reacting on autopilot as he placed the cab in drive and started the journey. The beautiful woman settled herself for the ride. She looked into the mirror and then to the picture of the cabby on the back of the seat. Her gaze now went back to the mirror.

"Thanks for waiting, Jake."

His eyes darted to the mirror and a warm smile came across his face. "You're welcome."

She had called him by name and it had made him feel good. Yes, he was glad that he had accepted this fare. Now, with every ounce of pride in his cab and himself, he drove on to Emeryville.

****

The ride did not seem as long this time and soon the beaming cabby pulled into the drop off area of the train station. His time in the presence of this alluring creature had come to an end, but he did not mind. After all, she had chosen him to share in her touching farewell, and he was glad that he could be of service.

He got out and held open the door for his passenger. She emerged and stood next to him. He gauged her at close to six foot as he looked up into her bronzed complexion and azure blue eyes.

She smiled at him while reaching with her right hand into her Dockers front pocket. She took his hand and pressed a bill into it. "This should take care of everything. Oh, and Jake, thank you again," her eyes expressed her sincerity.

"Sure, anytime Ma'am," was all he could say.

She hoisted the strap of the garment bag over her shoulder with ease and reached back to grab the small overnight duffel bag off of the seat. She nodded to him and strode over to the entrance of the train station.

He watched her pass through the doors and sighed. She was gone from his sight when he finally opened his hand and looked at its contents. "Wow! A hundred bucks!" His eyes bugged out. Yeah, he was glad she had picked him.

****

She presented her folder to the older man at the ticket window. "Is the train on time?"

"It starts here; it better be on time," he said with a wink, shuffling through her ticket vouchers. "Lets see now, train 6 to Chicago with a final destination of Pittsburgh. Do you have any bags to check in?"

She shook her head, "No."

"Then you're good to go, Miss. We'll be boarding in a few minutes. Have a nice trip." He stapled a boarding pass to the folder and handed it back to her.

She smiled at him and nodded, "Thanks."

The statuesque woman shifted her luggage from one hand to the other and ambled out onto the platform, thankful that she never accumulated many possessions in her life. She detested being tied down to anything or anyone in particular. It just wasn't her style.

****

The train had slowed to a stop and the smartly dressed conductor leaned out of the stairway, looking up and down the length of the train. He descended the steps and yelled, "All aboard!" His eyes fell to her as he held out his hand for her boarding pass. She handed it to him and waited silently.

"You're in sleeper 1304. That's two cars down, just passed the Diner."

"Thank you," she answered, as she found her way down to the appropriate car.

The woman climbed up into the doorway and stopped on the top step. Slowly, she turned around to survey the scene. Taking a deep breath in she muttered what she was thinking. "And so, the journey begins." She turned back to the doorway with commitment to her resolve. Her steps were filled with confidence as she continued into the passageway to find her reserved sleeper area.

The young uniformed man turned to her asking, "Ticket, please."

She handed the folder to him and again waited.

"You're in 6, that will be halfway down on the right." His voice was clear and energetic. "First time on the train?"

"Yes, I thought that I might want to see the country."

He shook his head as he handed the ticket folder back to her, "That you will. Press the call button if you need anything. My name is Carl and I'll be your train attendant for this leg of your trip."

"Thanks," she responded as her hand tried to steady the large garment bag in the narrow aisle.

"Ma'am, you can stow that big piece of luggage on one of those compartments." The train attendant motioned to the metal shelving. "The sleeper will be a little crowded otherwise."

Smiling at him, she nodded in agreement as she carefully placed her piece of luggage on the top shelf, then ascended the narrow stairway. She continued her way down the aisle until she came to the lighted sign suspended from the ceiling proclaiming this berth as hers. The door was open and she peered inside.

It appeared no smaller than the area she was accustomed to be quartered in on board ship for the last year or so. *'Yeah…I can do this for three days with no sweat.'* Her thoughts were of her first night aboard ship and trying to find enough space to relax and stretch out. A tiny smile toyed with her lips as she placed her duffel under one of the seats. *'Well, at least I have a view with this cabin,'* she thought as she made herself comfortable using the seat facing her for a footrest. *'There, that should discourage anyone from visiting.'* Her eyes gazed out of the large window at the landscaped area around the station. It was stark, much like her life with only her goals acting as the mile markers.

'The next few days will surely help me to make the transition into civilian life a little easier. After all, no one will be saluting me from now on,' she reflected. It was her decision not to let anyone know who or what she was on her journey into the next part of her life. Yes, on this trip she chose to use all of her time to reflect on her life and her future goals. She had lived with the past, and now she intended to let it catapult her into the future.

The train began to inch away from the station, the scenery now slowly moving by as she noticed the gentle sway of the car on the tracks. The muffled clickety-clack was a welcomed background noise as she thought of what might await her at her destination.

"Well, perhaps I'll find my destiny in Pittsburgh. Who knows?" Her voice was anticipatory as she let her head lean against the window to enjoy the view, not to mention the ride, alone.

Chapter 2

Small droplets of perspiration showed almost immediately on the woman's brow as she exited her air-conditioned car into the stagnant heat and thick humidity of the inner city parking garage. It was only the last day of June, and already it felt like the dog days of summer. She gathered her small cooler and backpack from the trunk of the car and began her habitual journey out of the garage.

The sun was edging down on the city skyline as the young woman wondered about the night to come. Her thoughts turned to her job and where it would lead her over the course of the next twelve hours or so. Years of experience told her that it would very likely be a hectic night. She could almost predict the jam-packed waiting room as she turned the corner of the building. The large plate glass windows allowed her to see inside the emergency room foyer just as a familiar voice called to her. She turned her attention to the doorway and found the smiling face of one of her co-workers.

"Tell me that you're just coming in, too." Her eyes were beaming as a smile crossed her face.

The freckles on her red-haired friend danced in laughter as she shook her head, "No, as a matter of fact, I'm on my way home to a long cold drink and a quiet night. You would do better to go home, too. It's been a real zoo in there today."

The young woman tossed her head to one side allowing her dampened blonde hair to rearrange itself on her forehead and with hands on both of her hips she demanded in jest, "Now, Dr. Potter, when have you known me to run from work?"

"Never and that's the problem. I think you run towards it, Danni."

"Yeah, I know," the small blonde grinned. "Why don't you have a cold one for me, Jamie, if that'll make you feel any better."

"You bet it will," she responded with her glasses now sliding down her nose from sweat. "Enjoy your night."

"Thanks." Danni pushed the revolving door to gain admittance into the slightly cooler building. She waved at the security guard as she crossed the lobby and walked down the hall towards the Staff locker room. She was eager to get into her almost nightly routine and this night she might even appreciate the artificially cooled climate.

****

The evening was continuing exactly as her friend's day had been…a real zoo.

The E.R. seemed to be a penalty box for the city residents as the heat and humidity brought out the short tempers and the numerous cases of cold beer induced bravado of the struggling working class. Danni felt for these people. She had always associated herself with the poor and oppressed of society, trying as she may to alleviate them of their suffering. This was why she had chosen nursing as her career path. It was a good choice for her as she demonstrated her expertise of nursing principles and kind heart to all her patients.

The customary din of the area was now pierced by a shrill squawking set of tones. Danni's attention was diverted from the computer screen and her charting to the crackling sound her beeper was emitting. "Trauma Team Alert. Helicopter #4 dispatching for a scene run to Fayette County for a head-on two-vehicle MVA. Trauma Team Alert time 2347."

"You'll be able to take that patient when it arrives, won't you, Danni?" the Charge Nurse asked.

"Sure, I'll be done with this last chart in just a few minutes, Karen."

The graying nurse smiled at her and leaned over to speak so no one else could hear, "I tried a new recipe today, and it's in the break room. I think you'll like it. It's nut bread." The older nurse watched the expression on the young blonde as it turned into an all out smile. Trying to prevent her pudgy body from jiggling as she laughed, Karen recalled the addiction that Danni had for food, especially nut bread.

"That's great! Thanks, Mom." Danni sighed. It was a term that most of the younger nurses called Karen. She was like their "Mom". She watched out for them and lent an ear when the need arose. She loved them as she would her own, and they knew that they could go to her with any problem. She was one of the reasons that Danni felt so at home in this environment. Karen made everyone feel like they were one big E.R. family.

Danni finished her charting and made a pass through the break room where she grabbed a small piece of the freshly baked nut bread. She popped it into her mouth and closed her eyes, savoring the flavor. What she wouldn't give for a glass of milk and time to eat some more. The beeper she carried, "Trauma Team Page, interrupted her thoughts. Helicopter 4 inbound with one patient, male, and involved in an MVA rollover. This is a Level I Trauma Team Page. ETA 10 minutes."

She exited the small room and started towards the trauma hall. Rounding the corner into the first trauma room, Danni could see the bustle of activity starting as her back-up nurse, Rosie, made last minute preparations to the room.

"What is this, the sixth in just as many hours? Well, at least they're not coming all at the same time tonight," the auburn-haired nurse grimaced as she pulled the Velcro closure of the leaded apron to adjust to her tall, willowy build.

Danni thought a moment then agreed, "I believe so, but at least we don't have a brand new team to break in for several more hours. Don't you just love the first day of a new teaching year?"

"Yeah, right!" was Rosie's reply. She slowly pondered a thought, and with a wry smile she stated, "Wonder if there'll be any available ones this year."

"Is that the only thing you think about?" The blonde nurse wrinkled her nose at Rosie and proceeded to dress in the fluid proof gown. "I swear you're just waiting to latch on to one."

"Hmm, you never know. I do have my standards to meet. I just don't want *any* doctor, just one who will make a name for themselves."

"Well, your prayers may be answered this year, Rosie." The voice was deep and authoritative as the Chief Surgical Resident enunciated his words to the team members who had assembled outside of the trauma room. "One of the new guys is already making a name for himself before he even starts."

"Come on, David, don't stop there." Rosie was determined to find out what he was hinting at.

"It seems that a certain surgeon left his promising career to take the year of Fellowship here." David pondered. "I don't know why anyone would leave a good job to come here and be subjected to this torture. Long hours and every third night on call wouldn't be bringing me out of private practice."

"He sounds like a man on a mission." Rosie was making eyes as she spoke.

Danni smiled at the antics of her friend, "Almost too perfect for you."

"The name is Garrett Trivoli, one of the Trauma Fellows for the next year. Yep, that'll be my replacement in just about five hours."

"What else do you know about him? Come on, give it up, David."

"Rosie, you are relentless," the Chief Resident sighed. "All I know is for the last three years Trivoli was in the Navy, commissioned as a Lieutenant, and served as a Flight Surgeon aboard several aircraft carriers."

"Oh boy, a Prima Donna that we have to salute," Karen rolled her eyes and laughed.

"I guess we'd better practice our 'Yes, Sir' for tomorrow night," the X-ray tech said as she snapped to attention.

Everyone broke into a chuckle at the antics of the mock saluting being readily passed around the room. The joking came to an abrupt end when the overhead intercom announced, "Trauma in the Department. Trauma in the Department."

"All right, People, we've got a job to do," David regained his composure and awaited the arrival of the Helicopter Crew with their patient.

"Too good to be true," Rosie mutter under her breath. "Probably married, with kids."

"Shhh! Rosie!" Danni scolded her as the stretcher was wheeled into the trauma room. The team immediately began their business as usual with David leading them.

****

The night seemed to fly by as three more trauma patients rolled through the doors, each one allowing a few minutes reprieve upon their dispatch to a floor before the next one came in. Finally, with the last one being sent to a floor for a bed assignment, the chaos subsided and things began to come to a slower, more relaxed pace.

Danni was pleased that all of her patients had lived; though it would be touch and go for a few of them. At least she did not have to think of the devastation to the families that a traumatic death brought with it. If only people would let their true feelings be known, especially to those that they love; it would ease the pain when someone is snatched unexpectedly out of their midst. All too often they wait until it is too late to say words of praise or affection to their loved ones. She had read somewhere that the dead can hear the thoughts of the living. For the sake of all those that had died before they knew they were loved, she hoped this was true.

Danni could see the night sky fading into the light of morning as she passed by the large glass doors leading to the ambulance parking area. They had miraculously survived another night of darkness to revel in the birth of a new day. Her face had a far off look on it as she turned back into the fluorescent lighting of the E.R., her mind preoccupied with the events of the past night.

"Earth to Danni, Earth to Danni." David had come around the corner and stepped to the side so as not to run into the young woman.

"Huh? Oh, sorry." Danni shook the thoughts from her head, causing her short blonde hair to quiver. "I was just…"

"No need to apologize. I just stopped by to say thanks for all your help tonight. Hey, for the last few years, too. You really know your stuff, Danni. You're a real asset to this trauma program. In fact all the nurses are." The Chief Resident reached out and hugged the smaller woman. "Thanks for everything."

She was stunned, and could feel the heat searing through her body as she blushed, turning her face bright red in color. Out of the corner of her eye, Danni could see Rosie mouth the words; *'He's got a crush on you.'*

David released her and turned to see the rest of the E.R. staff silently looking on. He was busted and he knew it. "Everyone, thanks. You're the best."

"Hey David, where's **my** hug?"

"I should have known you would be the one to ask, Rosie." He walked over to the tall woman and gave her shoulders a good squeeze.

"You are so bad!" Danni could not believe her coworkers antics.

She grabbed the Chief Resident's arm in an attempt to pry him away from Rosie. "You better leave before she has you in her clutches."

"Hey, I resent that! So, Doc, what can you tell us about the new Fellows?" Rosie had a one-track mind and right now she wanted to know all she could about any potential available doctors.

"OK, ok, there are three new Fellows starting today. I haven't met them all, but I do know their names." David looked at the crowd and then singled out Rosie. "Two men and a woman; Garrett Trivoli, Nathaniel Hostetler, and Rene Chabot."

"Two men, huh? I always did like men in uniform," Rosie said with a mischievous grin on her face as her thoughts turned to ships and the sea.

Karen now stepped in, taking David by the arm and pushing him along on his way, "Now, off with you, and go be an attending or something will you, please? You're disrupting my E.R." She leaned into his ear, whispering, "Keep in touch, David and good luck."

With that the Chief Resident nodded and waved as he walked down the hall savoring his last few minutes in the program and thinking of all the friends he would leave behind.

****

The daylight shift was slowly gathering at the nurse's station in an attempt to obtain reports on the few patients that were left in the E.R. treatment rooms. It was time for the night shift to begin to wind their activity down and think about home, sleep, and food. The night had been so busy that thoughts of lunch had been put by the wayside. Perhaps this is why there was always an abundant supply of snacks and "finger food" brought in by the staff. They were accustomed to sharing what they had with each other and with the Medical Staff that frequented the area in response to the consults the E.R. Physicians requested on their patients.

Danni could feel her stomach rumbling as she handed the trauma beeper over to her daylight equivalent. John had been a nurse for several years and was capable in his duties. It was his attitude that turned most women against him. His constant discussion of sports or his sexual attributes and exploits made most women feel uncomfortable if they had to be around him for any length of time. Danni was no exception. She thanked the gods above that John rarely worked a night shift, as he had explained that this was valuable copulating time for him. She had learned early in her E.R. career to schedule herself for a daylight shift when it was his day off. Danni secretly thanked "Mom" for teaching her this little trick.

"Everything is stocked and ready for the next trauma patient to arrive. We were alerted for a gunshot victim about ten minutes ago but have had no further updates." Danni smiled at the prospect of changing out of her sweaty scrubs, her shift was now over and on time for once.

John took the smile on her face as an invitation to flirt and asked her quite pointedly, "You off tonight? Maybe you want to meet me after work and we could have our own little sweatfest. I could fit you in early."

"No, thanks, I'll be here working," was Danni's reply. The verbal exchange came to an abrupt end when the piercing tones of the trauma beeper went off.

"Trauma Team Page. Trauma Team Page. Twenty-year-old male with multiple gunshot wounds to the chest and abdomen. Patient is intubated. ETA 1 minute by ambulance to your facility. Level I Trauma Page."

Danni saw John's facial expression change as he took off running down the hall to the trauma room. She raised her eyes to the speaker in the ceiling and whispered, "Thank you."

Rosie came over to where Danni was standing, "Hey, you ready to get out of this zoo?"

"Yeah," she said, turning to go out the E.R. door leading to the Lobby. "It's been a long night and I sure am starving."

"Hey, you two, wait up for me," Karen called out to the pair at the door.

They looked over their shoulder to see "Mom" coming towards them. A split second was all that it took and suddenly they heard a loud bang, as the door in front of them slammed open and a tall athletic body hurtled through pushing between them, eagerly making its way down the trauma hallway.

"Mom, watch out!" They yelled in unison. Each preparing for the impact that they believed could not be averted.

Karen just closed her eyes in anticipation of the impending collision. "Mom" waited, but it never came. Long, dark tresses were flying behind the figure as it moved with catlike grace easily side stepping the older, slow moving, pudgy form of the Charge Nurse by millimeters. She opened her eyes and looked around herself with great trepidation. She was still standing and in one piece.

Danni and Rosie were at her side within seconds, bracing her up. Karen felt like she was going to faint. How could she have not been hit or hurt? Her voice was trembling and soft; "I'm all right, girls. I'm all right."

"I have a good mind to go after that idiot," Rosie blurted out.

"Don't bother, it's probably the first trauma page in her life." Danni was not one to rush in to confrontations. "She'll learn. They should tell these Med Students that they are not the ones who save the patients."

"Do you want to sit down, Mom?"

"No, just get me out of this zoo before it's too late. I just want to go home," the older woman pleaded.

Propped on either side by her co-workers, Karen shakily made her way to the locker room. The night shift was officially over.

Chapter 3

The trauma hallway and room were bursting with activity. The critical nature of the incoming patient was evident. Every level of medical professional on the team realized that it would be a race against the clock to save the young man's life. There would be no time to discuss methods of treatment or to consult with the Attending Physician. It literally was down to do or let the young man die. And by the gods, if Trivoli had anything to say about it, this young man was going to get another chance at life. *'The ball is in my court now! This is what I have been training for my entire career,'* raced through the surgeon's mind.

A feral smile came to the Fellow's face as the overhead loudspeaker squawked, "Trauma patient is in the department. Trauma patient is in the department."

Seeing the blood-drenched, limp body of the young man on the ambulance stretcher, Garrett began firing off orders, letting instinct take control. "I want a quick chest X-ray and abdomen X-ray. Check for pulses. Get me a pressure. Hang all four units of blood and notify the Operating Room that we're coming up **now**. Tell them to have Thoracic Surgery meet us up there. Call the Blood Bank and have them send a ten pack of O positive blood to the O.R. to start, and a four pack every fifteen minutes for the next hour."

Trivoli watched as the team worked to meet all of the demands. The monitor showed tachycardia with multiple PVC's, the pulse was weak and thready; the blood pressure was 70 over 40.

'Not good, not good at all,' Trivoli thought. "Time to move, NOW, to the O.R.," the low contralto voice decreed.

The directive caused the hallway to clear almost immediately, creating an unobstructed path to the elevators. Every hand and foot was in motion to expedite the young lad's way to the operating room, giving him a desperate chance for life. Once inside, the doors closed and the ascent was speedy.

The elevator came to a stop, the doors opening on the Operating Room level.

With the look of a well-rehearsed team, the forward momentum towards the area of bright lights and cold steel resumed instantly. The driven group easily negotiated the sixty feet of hallway and the two left-handed turns needed to bring them to the main entrance of the O.R. where the surgical personnel met them. The exchange of one team with the other was flawless with not an ounce of momentum lost.

The E.R. trauma team now watched their patient being maneuvered swiftly down the hall and into the surgical theater. The concern on their faces could have been construed as a silent prayer offered for the safekeeping of their patient's life, as it teetered precariously on death's doorstep.

A second or two passed before they were able to register what had taken place. They could feel the adrenaline surging through their bodies, their lungs in need of more oxygen. Slowly, each one began to look to the other, searching for reassurance. It felt as though they had been part of some surreal dream sequence of the perfect trauma delivery system. It felt good, damn good! Now, if only the patient would survive.

"Paper work," the stern-looking woman at the desk demanded with an outstretched hand. "Do you have any paper work on the trauma patient?"

The dream atmosphere was now broken by the harshness of reality. John turned his gaze to her and slowly shook his head. "There was no time, no paper work generated. Hell, we didn't even give him a name." He looked down at his watch noticing that only twelve minutes had elapsed since the trauma pager warned them of the almost immediate one-minute ETA.

She looked over the top of her glasses at him and mockingly said, "What am I supposed to call him?"

The other E.R. nurse cleared his throat and softly spoke, "Lucky…call him Lucky Doe." Steve truly believed that, deep in his heart. The ex-paramedic had seen many gunshot victims bleed to death, either enroute to the hospital or upon arrival in the trauma rooms. But this had been different; it had almost a magical feel to it. "I'll let Admissions know." The nurse ran his hand through his thinning, light brown hair in a sort of calming gesture.

"What trauma surgeon is in charge of that patient?" The woman asked the E.R. nurses in front of her. She saw the puzzled look on their faces. "Why am I asking you," she muttered to herself, "first day of…hell, first hour of a new staff year." Her finger slammed down onto the intercom switch connecting her to the surgical arena for that particular patient. "Room One. Do you have the patient with multiple gunshot wounds?"

"Yes!" was the reply heard over the low hum of static noise.

"Your patient will be called Lucky Doe." The woman paused. "I need the name of the operating trauma surgeon please."

There was silence. A moment later the intercom crackled to life. "Trivoli…Trauma Fellow Garrett Trivoli."

The patient had been quickly transferred to the operating table, prepped and draped while the anesthesiologist hurriedly applied his monitoring devices to the young man's body. Trivoli, with eyes never leaving the monitor, donned the customary protective clothing of the operating arena.

"Place him in trendelenberg position and keep the

temperature in this room at 50 degrees," the Fellow directed. "I'll need size 8 gloves, please." She glared at the Scrub Nurse as she held out her hands. "I suspect that this will be the first and last time I have to tell you my glove size."

The nurse was shocked at the display of arrogance in the new Fellow. She readied the sterile gloves for the surgeon to wear. "I'll make sure the word gets around, Doctor," she nodded politely. After her task was done she moved over to the Circulating Nurse and whispered in her ear. "Jeez, not even an hour into the new training year and already an attitude."

"What a demanding bitch." Their eyes met and they subtly nodded, then moved away from one another as the surgeon came toward the patient.

Garrett now stepped up to the table, extending the gloved hand, "Bovie, please."

The surgeons were at the forefront of the battle to save the young life now. There was no time to waste, as Trivoli and Chief Surgical Resident, Rob Kreger would have to quickly find the major bleeders and stop them, if at all possible. It was sure to be a team effort, and one that would not be over any time soon.

****

John and Steve returned to find the E.R. aide, Marianna, starting to clean up the trauma room. They were startled to see the amount of mess that had happened in such a short time.

"I can't believe what a mess you guys make," she teased them.

"Well, be glad that trauma was only in this room ten minutes," John said, "or it would be a lot worse."

"Oh my, guess I'm a little late," Dr. McCormick poked his head into the room.

"Sorry, Doc, the patient is already in the O.R.," Steve apologized to the E.R. Attending Physician.

"All right then, ah...what was his name, do we even know?"

Steve looked straight at the stout, balding physician; "We're calling him, Lucky Doe."

The doctor let a smile slowly crack across his face, "Let's hope so."

"Say, you wouldn't happen to know who the trauma surgeon was?" Dr. McCormick asked, stepping back into the room.

"Trivoli, Trauma Fellow Garrett Trivoli." A large grin appeared on John's face. "Best rush I've ever had compared to a good night of hot, sweaty sex." The nurse looked to the man and winked.

The physician was surprised by the expression on John's face. "Thanks, I'll get the information I need when they're done in surgery," McCormick said as he started to leave.

The nurse's facial expression would not erase itself from Ian McCormick's mind. He knew of John's fanaticism with sports, his appetite for lewd comments and sexual escapades. "Trivoli, hmm...could have been a collegiate sports figure, or maybe someone who cracks comments like John." Then it hit him. That look! It was the one that most teenage boys have after their first sexual encounter, or men when deep in lustful thoughts. The physician looked over his shoulder at John. "Oh, God, he's getting off on men now. For Christ's sake I hope it's only Garrett Trivoli," he mumbled. His pace quickened down the Trauma hall as a feeling of homophobia swept over him.

****

In a combined group effort, the three co-workers and Housekeeping brought the trauma room back to a state of readiness. Now, the nurses would have to try to put together some sort of paper work on Lucky Doe. Everything had happened so fast and simultaneously that it was going to be hard to chronologically come up with the chain of events that took place.

Finally, Steve and John were satisfied with their Trauma Assessment paper work. It was sparse but told the entire eleven-minute story of Lucky Doe while he was in their care. They both knew that once Nan reviewed it, their Manager would be asking why certain things had not transpired in the way of patient care.

Steve hung his head; "Nan's going to be on the war path over this one."

"The patient's still alive," John snapped. "At least I hope he is. If she has questions, let her take it up with the physicians."

"I say, why don't we just let her watch the tape. That should answer any of her damn questions."

John's face lit up; he had forgotten that all traumas were video taped for critical review. "Maybe I should review it myself," he whispered absent-mindedly as he thought of how arousing the ordeal had been.

"Jeez, John, I wish you could keep your mind on work instead of last night's conquests," Steve was now visibly agitated as he left John and the trauma room.

"Oh, but I am," the younger nurse replied as he watched his co-worker walk down the hall.

****

The operating room was quiet except for the rhythmic bleeps of the heart monitor, a constant reminder of the life they were trying to preserve. Surgeons had their own peculiar style of conduct that surrounded them in the operating arena, and Garrett Trivoli was one for intense concentration, solely focusing on the patient. Spoken words were kept to a minimum. Perhaps this is why everyone paid attention when the voice of the Surgeon was heard.

"Vitals, please." The words seemed to be spoken as a directive and not polite etiquette.

The Anesthesiologist surveyed his electronic equipment. "Heart rate, 90. BP 108 over 66. Respiration's 14. Color appears to be good," he reported, looking directly at the patient's face.

Garrett breathed a sigh of relief. The biggest part of the battle was over. Now, only the small skirmishes remained. A fight is still a fight no matter how big or small. The surgeon had learned the hard way many years ago. Some of the most deadly battles were those that could possibly be mistaken as insignificant annoyances. Over the years, Trivoli had learned to let instinct guide the swiftness of response, and to take care that her quest for perfection was not marred by some insignificant oversight that would conquer in any altercation.

"Now comes the tedious part, Dr. Kreger. We run the intestines looking for any sign of perforation or nick," the surgeon looked over at the Chief Resident.

"Doesn't appear to be any injury to it." Dr. Kreger challenged. "I don't think we'll find a thing to worry about."

An eyebrow arched high on the forehead and icy blue eyes shot like daggers. Garrett's voice dropped to a low tone. "This, Dr. Kreger, is my patient. I will do whatever I feel is necessary to assure the success of this operation now and for the future. If you don't agree, then I suggest you assign yourself to a different Trauma Fellow after today."

Beads of perspiration gathered across the Chief's forehead. He let his eyes drop in submission and nodded his head. "I'm sorry," was all he could verbalize. He knew that out of the three Fellows, Trivoli had the skills and surgical expertise that he wanted, but her overall manner with the staff left much to be desired. She seemed to pit herself against them at every turn. He'd have to remember not to pick up those habits.

"Good! Then you won't make that mistake again." Her voice was calloused and cold, rivaling the room's temperature for sending a chill straight to the bone.

His eyes shot up to meet hers and he wondered if he would be able to withstand her condescending attitude for the year to come. He had been told that he could learn many things from this Fellow, but no one had mentioned her brash and arrogant ways.

Painstakingly slow but ever so diligently the two surgeons examined the loops of intestines for damage. They could find no defects but something kept the Fellow on guard, instinct was taking over again.

"Vitals, Please."

The O.R. staff was beginning to hate the sound of the word 'please' coming from the tall surgeon's mouth. It was evident that she had no idea of the courtesy she was extending in the polite mannerism. It came off sounding more like a suffix to the word before it.

"Heart rate 98, BP 100 over 64, respiration's 16," the anesthesiologist reported.

Garrett could not shake the feeling. "Raise the pressure to 120."

The Anesthesiologist pulled a syringe off the tray at his workstation. He uncapped the needle and proceeded to inject one milligram of the drug into the port of I.V. line. "Should take just a few minutes," he reassured the surgeon, "before we can see some results."

"While we are waiting for that to take effect, let's mop up this abdominal cavity of any free fluid."

The Circulating Nurse silently kept watch of each sponge that entered the young man's abdomen and patiently retrieved them as they were discarded.

"Seventeen used inside," she announced, "seventeen out."

"Pressure is now 122 over 70."

"Ok, let us do this one last time." The surgeons inspected each loop of bowel thoroughly, slowly checking for any sign of injury.

"There!" The Chief Resident pointed out. "I see a drop."

Trivoli's eye was caught by the glistening appearance. There, upon wiping the site, one could see another droplet forming within a few seconds. It had paid off. The skilled hands of the Fellow manipulated the area of bowel to reveal a small one-millimeter perforation in the wall.

"1-0 Silk on a curved needle."

Garrett took the needle and put a stitch or two in to hold the area closed. Kreger clipped the silk and proceeded to dab the area; both surgeons waited to see if the stitch would hold.

Rob Kreger silently studied the surgeon across from him and waited for the "I told you so." But it never came. He would have closed without ever checking and risked numerous complications that could have killed the young man on which they worked so hard to save.

Several minutes passed and the evidence was conclusive, the stitch would hold. The surgeons continued their final inspection. Both were satisfied when no other warning signs of injury could be found.

"Is the sponge count correct?" The tall Surgeon waited for an answer.

All eyes were on the Circulating Nurse as she made her final count.

"I don't have all day here, nurse, and neither does my patient." Garrett's voice was antagonistic in nature.

"Yes, Doctor Trivoli, seventeen in and seventeen out." The nurse looked over with eyes turning from shock to that of shooting darts at the brash surgeon. She was an experienced O.R. nurse and didn't appreciate being treated in this manner.

"Great, now let's close and see how he does in recovery." Trivoli motioned for the Chief Resident to do the honors.

Rob Kreger felt a sense of acceptance by the gesture. Here was a surgeon who strived at perfection, and the task of closing was offered to him. It was something that was usually given to first year residents as a practice procedure; but right now it felt very much an honor coming from Garrett Trivoli. No matter how small or monotonous the task, the Chief Resident was sure the Fellow would be meticulous down to the last detail. It was that frame of mind Dr. Kreger kept as he sewed the layers of surgically severed muscle and flesh together.

With the operation over now, Garrett addressed the other participants in the young man's fight to stay alive. "I want to say thank you for the expertise that each of you brought to this arena today, and I will expect nothing less from you in the future. I'm looking forward to working with you again." She turned away from the group of people huddled around the dramatically illuminated form on the surgical table.

"I'll be opting out of her cases for the next year." The Circulating Nurse spoke softly under her breath to the Scrub Nurse who nodded in agreement.

"Rob, page me if anything changes, I'm going to see if any family members are here for Lucky."

Kreger nodded his head in affirmation as he began to take off his gloves and gown. "I'll stay with him in recovery for a while."

Stripping her mask off with one hand, Trivoli gave a small wave with the other hand and proceeded through the door. Above the O.R. desk, the large wall mounted clock read 1458. *'Seven and a half-hours of surgery, not bad for my first day. It will be even better once I have them all broken in, the right way.'* Garrett thought about her empty stomach and remembered that food and drink would be necessary soon. A bathroom break and quick shower might be nice, too.

The family came first, that is if one was found. It was Trivoli's customary ritual to meet and inform the family immediately after any surgery. It was one way that the surgeon could help to put them at ease during their traumatic experience.

Garrett approached the O.R. desk and waited for the Supervisor's attention. "Hello, I'm Dr. Trivoli. Can you tell me if Lucky Doe has been identified yet?"

"Sorry, Doc." The older woman shook her head. "But there is a message for you from Dr. McCormick in the E.R. to call him when you are done."

"Thanks," Garrett motioned to use the phone at the desk.

"Go ahead, it's extension 2744."

The surgeon punched in the numbers and waited for someone to answer.

"Dr. Trivoli returning a call from Dr. McCormick." She paused to listen, then spoke again. "Have him page me at 1048 when he has a moment to talk."

The surgeon replaced the phone, acknowledging the woman at the desk with a slight nod of the head. "I can trust that after today you won't have to call in to my Operating Theater to ask my name, now will you?"

"But Doc, it's the first day of a new year. How am I supposed to know everyone's name?" She looked annoyed at the tall surgeon opposite her.

"Then I can assume that nobody will have a problem knowing me or my name the rest of the year, since I've already told it to you." She challenged the nurse.

The nurse drew in a long breath, her eyes turning into beady little black dots. "Trust me Dr. Trivoli, I'll make sure everyone knows all about you." She let the residual air in her lungs come out of her nose in a snort as she watched the surgeon walk away, muttering to herself, "Damn arrogant Bitch!"

****

The warm water of the shower felt good cascading down the tensed muscles of the surgeon. It was a feeling that Garrett had come to expect at the end of a surgery case, when the focus had been on the needs of the patient, every muscle, every fiber of being standing at attention ready to meet any demand. It seemed such a small price to pay in her quest for perfection. When one knew first hand of the agonizing pain that the patient was experiencing or the torment of their loved ones, perfection was all that mattered. It was never going to be Garrett Trivoli that dropped the ball. The water temperature slowly increased. The soothing rhythm and heat began to loosen her sore shoulders and back. This was indeed a luxury. How many cold or tepid showers had been taken on board ship during the last three years? That never changed the reason Trivoli was in the shower after surgery. It was more than to clean the body. The streams of water diluted the tears that were still felt inside, tears of anguish and loss over past situations and loved ones.

Beep-beep…Beep-beep…Beep-beep!

The reflective ritual dissolving with the pager's cry egged the surgeon to finish. Garrett quickly toweled off and stepped outside of the shower stall. The pager beeped again as the skilled hand of the surgeon picked it up and brought it within range of the clear blue eyes. Recognizing the number, she hastily dressed in a fresh set of scrubs and found the nearest phone.

"Dr. Trivoli here, I was paged." The surgeon waited for the person to come to the phone.

"Dr. Trivoli, this is Dr. Ian McCormick, E.R. Attending," the deep voice said. "How is Lucky Doe coming along?"

"We just finished surgery about 30 minutes ago. Lucky is doing a lot better than initially expected. He sustained several bullet wounds in the abdomen and one in the right upper lobe of the lung. The thoracic team placed a right-sided chest tube and cleaned the wound. The two bullets found in the abdomen shattered the left kidney beyond repair and penetrated the colon near the hepatic flexure. A nephrectomy and resection of four centimeters of transverse colon with therapeutic temporary colostomy was performed. A one-millimeter perforation was found in the small intestinal tract on close inspection and was repaired as well. Lucky Doe is now in recovery and holding his own at this time." Garrett was proud of the work that was done and it showed. After all, it was near perfect for not having people trained to her level of expectation.

Ian was impressed with the concise but thorough report. "I had heard that it was an awesome sight in the trauma room, the team…altogether that is. I wouldn't know first hand, I wasn't fast enough to even see the patient come through my E.R."

Garrett was unsure as to the exact nature of the statement. "Well, sir, I…"

"I guess I'll just have to be a little faster than normal when I know you are on trauma call," McCormick chuckled. "Never saw a first day trauma team move so fast. I understand that there are rumors that you have been secretly rehearsing for the last few years."

"Every day is a rehearsal for the day after it. So, yes, in that respect I have been working up to it."

"Well, Trivoli, it sounds like you did exactly the right things except let me see that patient. You know that it is **my** E.R. that you get to work out of on those traumas." The E.R. Physician stated in a serious tone of voice, "Next time you're down in my E.R. make sure you introduce yourself to the staff. It seems that they don't enjoy being ordered around by the voice of a higher being. You have a fan club with the two trauma nurses, but then again it was only a meager ten minutes of fame."

That last statement shocked the surgeon. "But sir, I wasn't down there… What do you mean by a fan club?"

Ian had found a source of contention in her armor. She absolutely hated to be liked, perhaps seeing it as a weakness in one's character. He thought about that for a moment before goading her. "Doc, don't let it worry you. You did well in their eyes; today you're the hero. Next time you could be the thorn in their side. It's a day to day kind of thing," Ian forewarned the surgeon. "I'll see you around."

"Humph!" Garrett said with disgust as the line went dead. She wasn't here to cater to the whims of the nursing staff. If anything, it would be the nurses who catered to her.

'Well, I can't wait to see what a big hit I'm gonna be with the night crew,' Garrett mused, staring at the phone. The nursing staff had always been a puzzle to Trivoli, whether in the Navy or in the civilian sector. One nurse could accept you as a person and the next would merely look on you as an

intruder in their domain. Funny how you never quite knew which way it would be until you were thick in the middle of some crisis. Hopefully, things will go just as well tonight as it had this morning. After all, they were all there for the same reason. The number one priority in the surgeon's mind was always how successful her skills had been on her patient. Garrett could not see it any other way.

****

'Always put the patient before one's self' was the surgeon's motto. Today was no exception to the rule as Dr. Trivoli stopped in the recovery area to check on Lucky Doe before she found the cafeteria. The patient now had a much better color than the bloodstained pallor of earlier. Checking the chart, one could see that the Chief Resident had only signed out several minutes before.

Garrett was pleased to see that the warning about how a patient was cared for had been heeded. Perhaps this would be a very enlightening year after all. Satisfied, the surgeon continued in the quest for nourishment.

'Perhaps a meal might make me a bit more mellow for the next shift of nurses,' pondered Trivoli. *'I at least owe them that or they'll think of me as some kind of dark ages warlord.'* It was going to be a long time until this night would be over and a hungry surgeon was not always the most tolerant of new surroundings or people.

The time was well after 1800 hours when Garrett was making her way to the cafeteria. The sight of her department head took her by surprise as he came down the hall toward her, still dressed in his lab coat. She would have thought him gone by now. His eyes lifted to settle on her striking figure and a spark of recognition came to his face. He quickly maneuvered the hallway, darting between its human obstacles until he was face to face with the tall surgeon.

"Ah, there you are Dr. Trivoli. I need to talk to you." His voice was calm and unwavering as he motioned toward his office down the hall. "Let's go into my office, shall we?"

Nodding, the woman followed him into the office. The surgeon's mind was racing with thoughts. She was sure that it had something to do with the trauma patient she had operated on all day. Had she done anything wrong? She reviewed her earlier actions, flying through them as she settled herself into the brisk pace of her superior. *'Shit rolls down hill, well I guess I get it straight from the top now.'* She thought about the Navy and its ways, the chain of command and how the orders and discipline came down through the ranks. *'Well, let's see, the ball will start rolling with the Chief of the Service/Attending who will question the Fellow then pass it down to the Chief Resident who will ream out the Resident who in turn will yell at the Intern who will blame the Med Student. Yeah, that seems right.'* It was all coming back to her, the civilian hospital chain of command.

"Dr. McMurray, I…" she started, only to be interrupted.

"Have a seat, Dr. Trivoli," the older man pointed to a chair on the other side of his large desk as they entered the room.

The office was immense, a symbol of his importance in the hospital setting. It was modestly furnished with several photos of the good doctor in his travels, fashionably displayed among the bookcases and on the desk. Garrett's eyes studied them as she sat down in the appointed chair. There was a common person in each of the photos next to the distinguished surgeon; it was a woman who always appeared at his right side, a gentle smile gracing her face.

Noticing her interest in the photo on his desk, he picked it up and began to reminisce. "This one was taken when I was in New Guinea," a smile crossed his face. "We spent two weeks there, my wife and I."

"She's a beautiful woman, Sir." The tall surgeon leaned forward to get a better look. "You must have had some wonderful times traveling with your wife."

"Yes, we did. Heck! We still do." His index finger gently glided over her image under the glass. "Best thing I ever did," he grunted, "I'd do it again." He regretfully put the frame back on his desk, allowing his eyes to linger on it for a brief moment longer. "Well, enough about me. I want to talk about you." His voice was now all business as his brown eyes stared directly at her.

The surgeon felt like she was being dissected right there in his office, his piercing gaze trying its best to cut deep into her soul. Her back stiffened and her shoulders squared in a mock attempt to ward off his insight into her being. She had a thick shell, one that had hardened over the years and she was sure that no one would be able to penetrate through it. It had been her survival tactic and allowed her to move from one station in life to another, never fearing the hurt that life brought with it. After all, it couldn't hurt if it never got close enough to leave any impression on her.

Steel-colored eyes locked onto brown as she asked, "What about me?" She leaned slightly forward as if to challenge the man.

They stayed there for what seemed to be an eternity, until McMurray blinked as he sucked on his teeth making a sharp noise. He sat down in his high-backed leather chair and swiveled it away from her, his mind gauging her boldness. He recounted his first day as a Fellow many years ago. He saw so much of himself in her that it was scary to think about. Right then and there he made his mind up. She was going to learn in the next year what had taken him so many years to realize. Her skills as a surgeon were by far more superior to the other two Fellows. He would teach her what she needed to know to enhance those skills and her life, not to mention the lives of all those around her.

He decided to take a hard line with her and his tone of voice showed it as he began speaking. "Every year I saddle one Fellow and make it their duty to establish a good working relationship with the E.R. staff." He swung the chair around to face her. "This year that person is you." His eyes squinted as he looked at her.

Her mouth opened abruptly. "What?" The puzzlement was written all over her face.

"You heard me. I want you to be the liaison between this department and the E.R., and that means starting immediately."

"Why me? Why not one of the other two?" She paused. "If it's because I'm a woman…" shades of discrimination and sexual harassment ebbed at the edges of her mind.

He looked out of the corner of his eye and pointed directly at her with his right hand as he fished for something out of the drawer to his left. "I don't ever want to hear that in my office again." He pulled three folders out of the drawer and threw them on the desk. "It's all in here," he pointed to them. "Check for yourself if you'd like."

She looked down to see the names listed on the outside of each folder, Dr. Rene Chabot, Dr. Nathaniel Hostetler, and her own, Dr. Garrett Trivoli. Her eyes looked up to his, pleading for some kind of answer.

"Dr. Chabot won't have the time to invest with a family due to deliver in the next few months and Dr. Hostetler, although unmarried, will need to devote all of his time to honing his surgical skills. That leaves only you, Dr. Trivoli. You have no family, your surgical skills are refined and beyond reproach. I've got to teach you something in this program and this is what I have chosen for you. I suggest that you make it your business to be a part of the overall picture in that E.R. and that means spending time with the staff both inside these walls and outside in their private lives, too. I don't care how you do it. Just do it."

The look on his face was one of no nonsense and she knew it. "But…" she grasped at thin air for words.

"No buts, Trivoli. I want to see you be a leader here, not just another blade in the system. I believe that you have a lot of untapped potential. You just haven't figured it out yet." He shook his head as he thought of his recent discussion with several very irate O.R. staff members. "As a surgeon, your main goal is to heal through surgical intervention for the well-being of your patient." He glared at her, his face showing his anger. "Not through the use of confrontation and a demeaning attitude toward your staff. You keep this up, Trivoli, and no one will want to work with you. Then we'll see just how perfect your little world will be when you're all by yourself in that surgical theater."

His face softened and his voice mellowed as he reached out and touched the photo on his desk again. "Besides, you're going to learn real fast that those nurses aren't the enemy. One day that nurse that you threw your weight at today could very well save your butt and the patient's, too." He glanced at the photo, then back to her. "Now, go and think about what I've said."

She immediately jumped to her own defense. "But I'm a damn good surgeon. Why should I…"

"Because YOU," his forefinger shot out, aimed right at her face. "You are a mere cog in this piece of machinery that we call a hospital. The last time I looked, Dr. Trivoli, I was the one writing your ticket in this program. Now, unless you are willing to give up this Trauma Fellowship, I must demand that you learn to become a part of the whole and not cause a hole in any part." He paused long enough for her to digest that last statement. "Did I make myself clear enough?"

Garrett rose from the seat and turned to leave. Reaching for the doorknob she paused and turned to face her new mentor. Before she could speak, she saw McMurray thumbing through her folder. "I'll try not to let you down, Sir, but don't expect me to change overnight. I've had a lot of practice at being as demanding of those that work with me as I am of myself."

"Good! Then you'll learn to accept your own shortcomings at the same time as you do everybody else's. Garrett, learn to get off of the high horse you've imagined yourself on and people may just start looking up to you for **who** you are, not **what** you are." His head never came up from out of its absorption in the folder.

"I'll see what I can do." She exited the office and stopped dead just a few steps down the hall. This was going to be harder than she had anticipated. She shook her head and wondered what freight train had just run through and left a large gaping hole in her plan for the rest of her life. Seething to herself, she named it the "McMurray Special," vowing to never be caught in its path again. She would live with it this time, she had to, and nobody bailed out on the first day of a Fellowship Program. Besides, it was against her nature to give up.

Chapter 4

The bright afternoon sun was filtering in at the edges of the room-darkening blinds as the form began to stir from sleep. The bed was huge compared to the small body that nestled in the middle, with its face buried into the queen-size pillow. The last remnants of a dream still whispered through the fog as one slowly transpired the states of unconsciousness to reality. The dream seemed to have no beginning or end. It was more like fragments of lives through the ages, with the same persons reappearing in different scenarios. It was always the same, never a story or a name. Just bits and pieces of someone's life that had been captured on film yet clipped out for some reason.

The small blonde woman ran her hand through her hair, fighting to come fully into the world of consciousness. Her green eyes opened to a new day as the mind hung on desperately to the last image of her dream; a dark-haired warrior loomed near with a spear clenched in both hands. The image started to fade as the warrior turned to look at her, a twinkle shining in its brave blues eyes. It had not made the transgression into the real world and, for this, Danni was grateful. It was not that the dream had scared her, but that it was always so cryptic in nature. If only she could understand what it was about or what it meant.

Danni flopped over onto her back, her head settling into the soft, fluffy pillow. *'If only there was some sort of reason or meaning to all of these dreams,'* she thought, smiling to herself. *'Or nightmares as the case may be.'* Her face changed rapidly to a smirk.

The images had been with her since she could remember. They had always manifested themselves in the moments just prior to awakening. For this reason, Danni had always believed that she needed to try to remember them.

Her hand reached out, capturing the journal that was kept on the nightstand for this reason. Rolling over onto her elbows she hastily opened the book and seized the pen that was clipped to the page of her last entry. Hurriedly dating the page, she began to follow her routine of describing her dream so as not to miss a single element before it escaped her. She had often thought that one day they would all make sense. Well, perhaps in her mind some little detail would set off a chain of events that would help her make sense of it all. When and if that would ever happen was beyond Danni's control. Now, she just did what she could to preserve them until that time came.

Her task done, she began to emerge from the large bed and slowly shuffled towards the bathroom. Her mind turned to the challenges at hand. Time to shower and start a new day in her life.

The briskness of the water always made Danni think she was off somewhere in the forest, bathing in a refreshing mountain stream. There was an odd familiarity to the chilling response that made her shiver with the initial contact. The thought of the warrior now faded from her mind as her body enjoyed the sensation of the water cascading down her naked form. The long shower ritual would allow her mind and body to join together into a single state of consciousness; ready for whatever the day would bring her way.

****

It was the first of July, the starting date of the new medical staff year. The young nurse began to mentally prepare herself for the grueling night ahead. Another year of training, teaching, and maybe even making a friend or two as she had with David. Her mind thought back to their first encounter several years ago when he had just come to the hospital. That shy, boyish intern over the years had matured into a competent surgeon and, along the way, won a place in many of the nurses' hearts. Danni smiled at the memory, laughing quietly at the numerous times that Rosie had insisted Danni and David would make the perfect couple. She was thankful that the Doctor had never mustered the courage to ask her out. Deep in her heart, she knew that somewhere David would find a mirrored soul that would complement his reserved manner. It just wasn't her. Silently, a prayer rose off her lips for the safekeeping of her friend's soul until that time came.

The locker room door opened, allowing the din from the hallway to break Danni's train of thought. Her eyes moved toward the door, only to see her fellow trauma nurse bounce through the doorway, her face beaming.

"Ah, Danni, my friend, have you heard the buzz in the E.R. about **my** Dr. Trivoli?" Rosie asked.

"I haven't even ventured out through…hey, what do you mean YOUR Dr. Trivoli?" A puzzled look was on her face. She had heard stories that the flirtatious nurse was a fast mover, but could she have already made this supposedly battle-hardened Trauma Fellow surrender to her charm. *No, it's got to be wishful thinking,* Danni shook her head in wonder.

"Unless Garrett Trivoli is bald, fat, over forty with a wife and kids in tow," Rosie stated looking her straight in the eye, "someone's gonna be thanking their lucky stars tonight. The surgeon just doesn't know it yet."

"Well, this I want to see. The poor guy won't know what to think when he sees you across from him in the trauma suite," she teased. "So what's this buzz that you were asking me about?"

"It seems that my Garrett ran the trauma team with all new faces this morning for that multiple gunshot patient like it was a well-oiled machine. They had four units of blood hung, X-rays done, and patient to the O.R. in less than twelve minutes." Her face was registering sheer bliss. "The staff is saying that Trivoli's voice was like a god's."

The blonde nurse was shocked. This was the day every year that never ran perfectly, especially for a Level One Trauma, not at the beginning of the daylight shift. Her interest was piqued; she could not wait to see this surgeon in action. "Did the patient survive?" she asked tentatively.

"Of course," Rosie said with an arrogant flair. "But only after many hours of difficult surgery and painstaking care to prevent any complications down the road to recovery."

"I guess the patient was lucky, huh?"

A broad smile came to the starry eyed nurse, "Funny, that's what Steve named him, Lucky Doe."

Both nurses were finishing their exchange of summer clothing for the traditional hospital scrub top and pants of the trauma team when Rosie grabbed Danni's arm and pleaded, "You've got to change assignments with me. You be the Trauma Nurse and let me back you up as Butt Nurse. O.K.?"

"All right, but why the change?"

"This way I'll be standing next to that dreamy god of a trauma surgeon. Who knows, a little bump here," she demonstrated a seductive hip rotation, "and a little whiff of perfume there," she bent over to show a gaping opening of her V-neck top and the cleavage contained within, "I could be a doctor's wife in no time at all."

Danni gently laughed. "Sure, this should be something to watch and I'll be the one with the front row seat. So…what does this god of yours look like?"

Rosie stopped short, turning to her co-worker with a deadly serious expression on her face, "Tall, dark and gorgeous, of course."

Both burst into laughter as they made their way through the locker room door.

****

Karen was rounding the corner of the desk as the two giddy nurses entered the E.R. triage station. With a look of a mother about to scold her children, the Charge Nurse began to address the unprofessional behavior of the duo. "You girls need to get to work," then with the wink of one eye, "people will think that this is a fun place to be."

"Yes, Mom!" The young nurses said in unison as they quickly turned the smiles into frowns.

The three seriously studied each other for a moment and slowly let smiles shine across their faces.

"Are you all right, Mom? I mean after this morning's near collision on the way out I thought you might call off," Rosie queried.

"No little Intern or Med Student gets **me** rattled." A look of determination was on her face. She was a seasoned veteran and not about to let them get to her.

"That one sure wasn't little, looked more like an 'Amazon' to me. A giant Amazon at that," Rosie remarked. "I still think I'm going to give her a piece of my mind the next time I see her."

Always being the one to seek out peaceful alternatives to a situation, Danni offered, "Why not let me show her the ropes. You know, sort of take her under my wing. Hey, look how David turned out."

"Oh yeah! David was so shy that after all these years he still couldn't get the courage to ask you out." Rosie shook her head, "I don't think this is the cuddly teddy bear type, not that kind of personality at all."

Danni resented the implied comment. "You don't think I can do it, do you?"

"Now girls," Mom jumped in, "let's give Danni's way a try first. If it doesn't change the behavior pattern for the better we can always do something else."

"Yeah, I'll crucify her good."

"My way first, right?" The blonde looked straight into Rosie's eyes. It was a look that meant business.

Slowly the nurse conceded with her posturing. With her eyes closed and her head minutely shaking approval she voiced, "Right."

"Okay then, it's over. Danni, you have one month to get some work in on that Med Student." Karen looked at Rosie. "Agreed?"

"Agreed. You better work fast, Danni. This special project of yours, she is gonna need a lot of work."

"Let me worry about that," her tone was reassuring.

"I bet you brought home strays of all kinds when you were growing up." Karen was chuckling to herself at the thought.

"Well, mostly birds…kittens…puppies," the small blonde winced at the thought of being busted, "and a turtle once."

"Well, now you'll be able to add an 'Amazon' to that menagerie," the charge nurse laughed. "Now, time to get to work," she said making an effort to shoo them on their way.

The two co-workers walked over to the nurses' station and checked the assignment board for their names. As Rosie had predicted, she was assigned the Trauma Nurse position and Danni as her Butt Nurse. She looked over at the blonde nurse with a pouting expression on her face.

"I said I would switch with you," Danni reassured her as she reached up and erased their names, only to write them back in the reverse position.

"Ooh! I'll name our first kid after you," she said rubbing her hands together. "Thanks!" Rosie reached out and gave her co-worker a quick hug.

"Don't mention it. You know that you owe me, don't you?" The blonde shook her head disgustedly, "Now, I have to get a report from John." Her face twisted up and a chill went over her body at the thought. "Well, better to get it over with quickly." The blonde looked around trying to find the disgusting man but he was nowhere in sight.

****

It was another busy day in the emergency room; the hallways were lined with patients on carriages waiting to be transported to various destinations within the medical center. The nurse could hear muffled sounds coming form each doorway she passed on her way to the trauma suites. Years of experience gave her an idea of the ailments or injuries of each patient. Subconsciously, her brain began to register and categorize each one. Soft rhythmic wheezes were at the first doorway. *Room 8: Asthmatic.* She moved a few feet further down the hall to see dimmed lighting and hear snoring sounds coming from the next room. *Room 9: Post-Ictal Seizure.* Danni sidestepped the EKG machine parked outside of the room with bubbly sounding short breaths coming from it and a look of concern came to the nurse's face. *Hmm...Room 10: Congestive Heart Failure.* The last room on the short hallway added a blend of soft groans mixed with angered muttering to the rising din of the department and her self assured confidence but a slight upturn to the corner of her mouth. *Room 10: Orthopedic injury, probably broken.*

It was the usual gamut of complaints typical for July with its mixture of sunshine and oppressing heat and humidity at times. It was no different than any other year. The only thing that ever seemed to change was the cast of characters, both patients and staff.

It's like that movie, "Ground Hog Day", Danni mused. *We just keep doing it over and over again until we get it right...until it becomes the perfect day.*

The young nurse turned at the end of the hall into the trauma area. The area was quiet and had an almost eerie feeling to it. She began to check each room for readiness and also the nurse she was to receive report from, John.

Danni was thankful that it was not busy in her domain, it meant that she would not have to jump right into the middle of a life or death situation without knowing the whole story. It was her belief that each patient treated was not just an injury but also rather a story in itself. In order to heal the wound it was often necessary to reach out to the soul. Her patients always appreciated this effort. It made them feel like they were being treated as a person and not some anatomical practice dummy placed there only for the benefit of the medical community.

Leaving the last of the four trauma rooms, the nurse spied John seated in the conference room sitting intently in front of the television that was used for video taped inservices and the reviewing of taped procedures. She could see his moon-pied facial expression. His eyes were riveted to the screen and she shook her head in disgust. *Good gods, he's got to be watching a porno tape or worse yet, maybe one of his own escapades with some unsuspecting young girl. Ugh!*

Swallowing hard, she walked into the conference room trying not to look at the screen. "Are you ready to give me report, John?" Her tone was very professional. Seeing that he could not tear his eyes off of the action on the screen, she asked, "Can't you watch this stuff in the privacy of your own home instead of here?"

"Yeah! Maybe I can make a copy of this. Thanks for the idea." He looked quickly up at Danni and then right back to the screen. "It will be over in a minute, you just got to see the raw beauty, the magnificent orchestration of the action with only minimal direction. It's literally poetry in motion."

Danni rolled her eyes. *'I don't want to see this!'* Her mind cringed at the thought. *Why did I agree to switch? Rosie, you really owe me big time.*

Static now filled the room as John hit the rewind button on the controls. He slowly inhaled and allowed the trapped breath to emerge as a long drawn out sigh. He was trying desperately to savor the moment. He closed his eyes, a smile appearing on his face. It was as if he was reviewing it all over again on the back of his eyelids.

"John!"

"Shhh…!" He drew his finger up to his pursed lips. "Please, it's not often that there is so perfect a moment."

"Just what is on that tape?"

The male nurse opened his eyes. "You want report, right?"

"Well, yes!"

"Then you need to see this video of the first Level One of the new staff year. It's simply breathtaking." John winked at her, "I know you will enjoy it."

Danni's mind raced, trying to figure out what could possibly be so delightful that John would enjoy in this trauma scenario. *It was probably a big bosom…no, let's not go there,* she immediately halted that train of thought. *I'll hate myself for this, but…* "Okay, show it to me."

Eagerly he pointed the control to the TV and tapped the play button. The clip of video began to play. The patient was hurriedly wheeled into the room and quickly transferred to the trauma stretcher. A commanding voice was snapping out snippets of phrases, directing the flurry of activity for all those in the room. The action was simultaneous and, as John had called it, well orchestrated. Danni's mind was distracted when she caught the appearance of the tall, dark-haired figure at the bottom of the screen. It was her 'Amazon.' She was going to have a lot of work to do with her. The new person wasn't even where she should have been stationed around the trauma patient. Danni made a mental note to go over the correct stations for each rank of medical personnel in the trauma setting as part of her new project. Before she knew it, the patient was being wheeled briskly out of the room. The tape was finished, static noise again filling the air.

"Isn't that voice like a god's?" he said, awestruck. "And that, THAT is what trauma is all about. Yes, sir, I'll work with that Trauma Fellow Garrett Trivoli any day. I might get to like it even better than sex…well, at least here at work."

Danni was shocked that she had been wrong about John. He was always so predictable. No one would believe this; she still didn't believe it herself.

John got up from his chair and handed the trauma pager over to his relief. "If you're lucky, maybe you'll get to see a master in action."

"Yeah, maybe." Danni remarked then asked pensively, "Say, John, what does this Trivoli look like?"

"I don't really know, everything happened so fast. But that voice, I would know it in my sleep." John turned to leave, "In fact, I think I'd follow it anywhere. Have a good night."

Danni ejected the tape from the VCR player thinking about her special project for the month. She did not want to belittle the student but she could definitely see the need for some guidance. A little attention now and she might just become a half-decent doctor or surgeon in the future. *And if done in the proper manner, maybe even someone that she could think of as a friend.* The nurse turned off the TV and headed toward the door.

****

The regular Emergency Room patients kept the staff busy. It was a full house. As quickly as a room emptied out, it was made ready and the next patient was brought in. Since there were no traumas to worry about, Danni and Rosie helped out wherever they could, answering the nurse calls, starting difficult I.V.'s, discharging patients, and assisting with minor procedures. The evening passed quickly. The flood of patients waiting to be seen had dwindled down to only a handful. The hectic pace began to slow down.

"Hey, Danni, I'm going to freshen up a bit." Rosie was motioning towards the locker room. "I want to look nice when those traumas start rolling in. I've got a doctor to impress."

The blonde nurse shook her head and waved her to go on. "I'm going to double check the rooms."

It was almost 11P.M. The time when the hot, humid air kept people awake and irritable. The cycle of trauma would start to be put into motion. It was inevitable. She could just feel the vibes in the air.

Danni did a fast run through of all the rooms in the trauma suite, eventually satisfied that they were all ready for the barrage of traumas that would likely come their way. She turned out of the last room at the end of the hall only to see a tall, dark-haired form emerge from the stairway at the opposite end. The size, the color, and the build - they were all correct; it was her 'Amazon'. *Perfect,* she thought. *I'll start teaching her without anyone else around.* The nurse waited patiently for her student to come within talking distance.

"Hi, my name is Danni, and I'm the Trauma Nurse for tonight." She held out her hand in friendship, which was returned with a gentle nod and a skeptically raised brow. The handshake was firm and to the point. The tall woman started to introduce herself, when Danni held up her hand in a halting motion for the woman to stop. The figure complied, looking puzzled.

"Please, no names. I saw the video of the Level One Trauma from this morning, I thought that I might be able to help you feel a little more comfortable when the next trauma comes in." The nurse took the woman's hand and slowly brought her over to the diagram on the wall. "Here, let me show you the proper placement of the medical personnel in the trauma rooms. Each of these positions has a specific duty to perform without hesitation. In this manner the least amount of time is used to get the most information and procedures done." Danni looked up at the tall woman's face to make sure that everything she was saying was understood. *By the gods, she is beautiful.* Her mouth was agape.

The woman watched in amazement at the expression on the nurse's face. She was taken aback by the friendliness of the young woman, the kindness showed earnestly in her sea green eyes. She had no wish to make the blonde feel embarrassed or uncomfortable, even without McMurray's directive, but she just wasn't sure how much more of this she could take. McMurray's directive came running headlong through her mind. Garrett drew in a breath, trying not to sound annoyed. There was just something about those eyes, perhaps it would come to her later. "So, what and where am I?"

"Well, that all depends on what level of training you possess. Every level is important, but some more than others." Danni was in her reassurance mode. "You don't have to tell me, just go to that spot when the trauma comes in and I'm sure that you will do perfectly fine. Okay?" Her head was nodding in the affirmative manner, hoping for some sign of understanding.

"Yeah, I think that I can follow that pretty well." Her lopsided grin appeared again as she thought about McMurray's talk. She just wanted to tell this impertinent little nurse who she was and be done with it. Resigning herself to her delegated state, she added dryly, "Thanks for the help."

"You're welcome, anytime," was the eager response. Danni thought momentarily and decided to venture into the near collision episode of earlier that morning. "You know, you really have to be a little more careful when responding to the trauma page. You nearly ran a few of us over." She was trying to make a point without causing the obviously over zealous woman any embarrassment.

'This nurse doesn't know who I am.' The woman cleared her throat. It was a stalling technique she had learned long ago to keep her anger in check. "Ah…sorry about that." She hedged a little and then asked, "Nobody was injured, I hope." *There, take that. See, McMurray, I can play nice.*

"No, but you did put the fear of God into Karen, the Charge Nurse. She was pretty shaken up."

"Is she here now? I'd like to give her a piece of my…" she stuttered as a visual image of McMurray crossed her mind, "My apology for any scare that I may have caused." The tall woman was trying to sound sincere but to her own ear it wasn't very convincing.

"I could point her out to you, she is here now." Danni was surprised. This was going all too well. It seemed just too easy. "Or better yet, let me call her back here instead of out in view of everyone."

The nurse picked up the phone, punched in a few numbers and announced over the loudspeaker system, "Karen, will you please come to Trauma Room One, Karen to Trauma Room One." She hung up the phone, turning to smile politely at her new friend. "She'll be back in a moment."

Karen came quickly down the hall. She was aware that the trauma pagers had not gone off, and she was clueless as to why she was being requested. The older nurse stopped abruptly when she caught sight of the tall, athletic woman that only this morning appeared as a train at full speed coming right for her. Karen was amazed at how quickly Danni could tame any wild human, even this one. "So Danni, what can I do for you?"

The young nurse motioned her to come closer. "This nice young lady would like to talk to you about this morning." She looked over at the tall woman only to see her eyebrow raised and contempt seething from her stance. "Go ahead," she encouraged the woman, "I'll just finish up back here a little later." She then proceeded down the hall to the front of the E.R. with a huge grin splashed across her face.

There was a moment of silence before the tall woman spoke. "I truly am sorry for doing that this morning. I'm just not familiar with all of the ways to get to the trauma area yet. I know I had to be there quickly. Again, I am sorry."

"Well, thank you. Apology accepted, I mean since it is your first day and all." The nurse was shocked; this was no 'Amazon' at all. "So, ah…my name is Karen, but a lot of the staff call me "Mom." And you are?" She offered her hand to the tall woman.

"Garrett," she said, grasping the nurse's hand and giving it a firm shake. "Garrett Trivoli, I'm one of the new Trauma Fellows."

The nurse was dumbfounded, "You? You're the Garrett Trivoli that has everyone shaking in their boots and waiting for the lightning bolt to strike them dead if they don't obey your decree within a millisecond?"

Wincing with embarrassment, the surgeon answered, "I'm afraid so." Then, just as quickly, as if to justify her actions, the look on her face hardened. "Why? Do you have a problem with that?"

"No, no problem. She…I mean, Danni knows who you are?"

"No, she didn't let me get a word in edgewise, let alone introduce myself. Is she always that talkative?" Secretively the surgeon thought to herself. *I didn't have the heart to tell her. She was being so nice and polite. I think she was actually trying to help me feel comfortable.*

The surgeon scolded herself for even considering the feelings of the nurse. *When did they ever play a part in **my** considerations?* Then as if to admonish herself, the stoic-looking surgeon spit out. "I don't like a lot of unnecessary talking in my trauma rooms." Her eyebrow rose with the statement.

The two looked down the hallway as they watched the young blonde nurse. As if on cue, she turned, giving a smile and a little hand wave. Garrett returned the wave, as did the Charge Nurse, but at a much slower speed. There was something that made you just want to give in to this imp of a woman, even though it conflicted with your own order of the world. Sensing that she was waving back, the surgeon quickly stopped and shoved her hand deep into the pocket of her starched white jacket.

"Boy, is she going to be surprised." Suddenly Karen's eyes popped wide open, and she began to laugh uncontrollably, " And Rosie's really going to be pissed."

The surgeon looked at the nurse, unsure of what she was laughing at. "Is there a problem?"

"No…no…trust me…she'll get over it." The nurse was still chuckling to herself, "Doc, if it took you almost running me down to save that patient's life, you go right ahead and do it anytime. We thought that you were some Med Student or first year Intern." Tears were now rolling down the nurse's cheeks. "I can't wait to see the look on their faces when they find out who you really are."

****

Danni was proud of herself. She had started to help the new woman without making her embarrassed. *Who knows, she may even turn out as good a surgeon as David. She seems awfully nice.* The young nurse sat absent-mindedly at the desk. She pondered the thought of having a new friend and considered asking her to join in one of the group activities, which was part of the E.R. family outings.

"Well, how do I look?" Rosie was still primping herself as she walked across the room to where Danni was seated.

"I guess, all right. You know scrubs just aren't all that alluring."

"Okay, enough with the smart ass comments." The nurse took the seat next to Danni.

The young nurse sniffed, then sniffed again closer this time to Rosie. "What is that? It is disgusting."

"You don't like my new perfume? That's okay; it's specially formulated for a man's nose. It's supposed to drive a man 'wild' with passion."

"I can't imagine this making anyone passionate." Danni said, wrinkling her nose up at the stench.

"Just wait and see." Rosie was confident in her ability to turn the head of the new trauma surgeon.

"See what?" Karen's face became twisted with the awful smell. "God, can't you people smell that? It's worse than a cheap hooker at the end of a three day convention."

Danni started to giggle, while Rosie let the comment drift by, oblivious to those around her. The only thought in her mind was of Garrett Trivoli.

Then, without warning, the sound of the trauma pager brought everyone to the same mental alertness. Each beep shattered their individual thoughts and turned the attention of all to the needs of the next patient being placed within their care.

"Trauma Team Page…Trauma Team Page. Twenty-eight year old male fell from a second floor window. Multiple orthopedic injuries and paradoxical breathing noted. ETA five minutes. Level One Trauma Page."

Each member of the team went into action. Danni and Rosie scurried to get back to the trauma room while the Charge Nurse grabbed the recording flow sheet before making her way to the trauma area. Quickly, both nurses dressed in the customary leaded aprons and fluid restrictive gowns, gloves, and masks.

Danni retrieved a drug pack from the medication safe in the room, examining the contents carefully. *Paradoxical breathing…huh…chest tube for sure.* She looked over to see her co-worker already setting up a chest tube tray. *Way to go, Rosie.* The rest of the team was now assembling in the outer hall. Each scurried into the position appointed by their medical ranking while desperately trying to finish dressing. Out of the corner of her eye, Danni could see her new friend standing in the hallway finishing the tying of her mask. *I guess I slowed her down a little too much. I'll have to work on that.*

"Trauma is in the Department; Trauma is in the Department," the loud speaker blared.

With the last minute details now complete, everyone's eyes were on the corridor leading to the trauma room. There stood the tall, dark-haired woman, mesmerized by the moment. The Paramedics wheeled in the patient on the stretcher. A condensed report of the patient's condition was exchanged while the patient was transferred to the hospital stretcher. The Medic crew now retreated from the room with their equipment. Rosie filled in the empty space on the left side of the patient as she attempted to find a pulse in the deformed arm. The tall, dark-haired woman now stood at her side, examining the unclad chest of the patient. The labored breathing was evident in both sight and sound.

"Chest X-ray NOW," Garrett commanded.

Danni looked up to see her 'Amazon' in the position of Trauma Surgeon. A troubled look came over her as she quickly glanced at Karen and then back at the dark-haired woman. It unsettled her to see the Charge Nurse start to chuckle.

The Trauma Surgeon examined the patient for any other injuries while the required X-rays of chest, abdomen, and cervical spine were completed.

"The chest is out," relayed the X-ray Tech as she passed by.

The surgeon stepped out of the room and viewed the patient's chest X-ray. There, as plain as anything was a large pneumothorax on the left side. The pressure of the escaped air trapped inside the chest area was collapsing the lung.

"All right, let's prep for a chest tube on the left."

Rosie pulled the stand over into position with the necessary equipment already available.

"Give me a size 8 sterile glove," the surgeon commanded.

Turning with the gloves to see the tall, dark-haired woman waiting to receive them, Rosie blinked in disbelief, then shot a questioning glance across the patient at Danni. The look on Danni's face was one of innocence. Rosie was dumbfounded. Where was her Trauma Surgeon, Garrett Trivoli? Karen caught the exchange and had to keep herself from laughing out loud.

The surgeon glared at the nurse and repeated, "Gloves, please. We don't have all day here, nurse."

Fumbling to get a grip on her emotions Rosie offered, "Yeah, Doc, size 8."

The surgeon smoothly took the gloves and proceeded to check the assembled equipment as the Chief Resident prepped the patient's chest.

"Sir, you have a few badly broken ribs that are making it very hard for you to breathe right now. I'm going to insert a tube into your chest that will make it easier for you to breathe. It's going to hurt a little while I put it in place, but I promise you, it will feel better eventually." The surgeon's voice was full of confidence.

The patient grasped Danni's hand in anticipation of the pain to come. She looked into his terror-filled eyes and softly spoke words of reassurance to calm him. She knew the routine of the procedure well. She had assisted with chest tube insertions hundreds of times over her years as a trauma nurse. First, they would find the level for insertion and then, with a blade, make a small shallow laceration in the skin. The surgeon would probe the opening with a fingertip to make sure it was indeed into the chest cavity. The site would then be widened using small forceps so that the skin would form a tight seal around tube when inserted. This part was what nearly all patients complained of as the most painful.

Looking across her patient, Danni could see the dark-haired surgeon standing with the Trocar clenched in both hands. Danni's mind thought back to her dream, startling the young nurse. Her eyes opened wider as she looked at the surgeon poised, ready to send the long, blunt-tipped rod into the patient's side. The physician looked at the young nurse for approval. Danni took a breath and gave a slight nod of her head. The surgeon began the insertion of the chest tube, her face taut with concentration; the confident blue eyes focused on the job at hand. All of a sudden there was a feeling of déjà vu, as a chill ran down the young nurse's spine. It was an all-too-familiar scene but something was missing. Everything seemed so mechanical and devoid of emotion that it reminded Danni of a cyberspace movie. Her attention turned again to her patient. The chest tube was doing its job. The patient was having an easier time breathing.

The Trauma surgeon expertly stitched the tube in place and assisted Rosie with the dressing of the site. "Karen, can you notify Orthopedics to come down and see this patient, please?"

The charge nurse's voice was loud and clear, "Yes, ma'am!"

"Then secure a C.T. Scanner for this patient. I want a head and abdomen immediately."

Karen watched her two nurses as she answered the demand, "Yes, Doctor Trivoli."

Both pairs of eyes flashed wildly at the tall, dark-haired surgeon, then on to each other, then finally coming to rest on the charge nurse herself. Rosie's mind registered sheer disbelief at the thought of HER Trauma Fellow being a woman. Her hopes of marrying a famous surgeon would be dashed on the rocks, again.

Danni shook her head, letting her eyes close and wondered. *What kind of idiot does this doctor think I am?* Deep in the recesses of her mind she let go of a strangled scream, *Ugh.*

The older nurse just watched the expressions on their faces and knew what each one was thinking.

Chapter 5

The atmosphere in the CT Scanner was quiet compared to the din of the emergency room area. The low lighting gave the room a more casual appearance than the high intensity lighting of the Trauma Suite. The soft melodic hum of the computers after a few minutes was hardly noticeable and became more of a background noise that was very soothing on the nerves. The coolness of the air-conditioning was something that always stood out in Garrett's mind as a reason to linger in Radiology. No, it was nothing like the surgical theater where life and death drama was played out on a minute-by-minute basis, but the surgeon enjoyed it just the same. It was a chance to not only look deep within your patient but also yourself. There you had the time to think about what you had done and properly evaluate the effect that it had on your patient. The surgeon was not as concerned about the patient this time as she was about the events that had taken place in the last hour or so.

Doctor Trivoli rested comfortably in the high-backed chair, letting her long, tapered fingers drape over the arms. Her legs stretched out and crossed at the ankles kept the subtle swaying motion of the swiveled chair from stopping. The back was just high enough to allow the resting of Garrett's head against the very top of it. It could have been a great time for a few moments of stolen shuteye, but the woman was too emotionally charged to allow sleep to overtake her. In this position, she could study the young blonde without the effect of staring. Her head raced with thoughts of what Karen had said to her before the trauma beeper had gone off. Trying as she might she wanted to put some kind of answer to the question she was now plagued with. *Why the disappointment with who I am? My surgical skills are perfect, without a doubt. What more could they ask for?* Finally she disregarded it all with the thought that there was nothing she could do about it, so why let it bother her.

The surgeon studied the young nurse as she monitored the patient's vital signs during the imaging procedure. Her poise demonstrated confidence in both herself and her professional ability. Occasionally, Garrett noticed that a sideways glance was thrown in her direction, as if the nurse wanted to ask a question but then changed her mind. This intrigued and at the same time unnerved the tall woman who prided herself on being totally in control of her emotions at all times. In fact, she was used to being in control period. What was it about this small slip of a woman that made her want to lose all control and just scream out to ask the damn question? She was nothing out of the ordinary: two legs, two arms, two eyes, two ears, and one head. She was not exactly drop-dead gorgeous, but at the same time she possessed an inner beauty that would rival most. Perhaps it was the charisma surrounding the small nurse that made her irresistible to those who came in contact with her. Perchance this was why Garrett needed to know more about this young woman.

Danni was biting on the end of her pen, her nose wrinkled up the harder she thought. Finally, she could wait no longer. The question was out before she could stop it. "Did Karen know who you were before I called her back for your apology?" Almost as a reflex when she heard the words coming from her own mouth, the blonde brought her small hand up in a feeble attempt to halt them.

The words got Garrett's attention. Her head slowly rose off the back of the chair as she watched the stunned blonde try to regain her composure. *So, I'm not the only one trying to figure things out, eh?* "Ah…no," she glared at the petite woman. "Why do you ask?"

The nurse was caught in the middle now. "I was just wondering how Mom was able to call you by name." Inside, she swore at herself and how she must look to the Trauma Fellow.

"Oh, is that all." Garrett decided to add a little fuel to the fire and see if she could get the nurse to really ask what was on her mind. "You know, it is customary for people to introduce themselves…if they are allowed to, that is."

"Well, I didn't want you to feel uncomfortable, like I was making a big issue out of the run-in this morning." Danni was getting a little defensive. "Gods! We thought you were…"

"Some wet behind the ears Med Student. Right?" Garrett finished the sentence for her. Her voice was tense. "Did it ever occur to you to find out just **who** you were talking to before jumping to conclusions?"

"Yeah, I guess so." Her voice trailed off. She thought for a moment then raised her head and looked over at the seated surgeon. "Do you think we could start over?"

An eyebrow raised high on Trivoli's forehead, almost hidden entirely by the dark hair that swept across it. "I guess it could make the year a little easier," a tight-lipped smile appeared on her face, "if that's what you mean. But I thought that you would have known who I was before I even arrived."

"You're expecting too much. The photo identification sheets for all of the new house staff won't be out for at least another week or two. So until then…" the young nurse traveled the short distance over to the surgeon and held out her hand in friendship. "Hi, I'm Danni, and you are…?"

"Garrett Trivoli, one of the new Trauma Fellows." The handshake was returned and the two women began to eye one another up.

"Isn't Garrett a man's name?" Danni asked. "We thought the female Fellow would be the one whose name was Rene."

The light was now coming on. Garrett realized what all the looks and stares were for during the trauma room episode. "You and the other nurse thought I was a man? Or at least supposed to be by name, right?"

Danni looked down at the floor a little embarrassed. "I guess so. I know that Rosie's more disappointed than I am."

"Well, next time maybe you should get all of your facts straight, or do you two just assume everything?" The surgeon eyed the nurse, trying to find her answer from the visibly shaken manner she was witnessing.

"Excuse me, are you implying that Rosie and I…"

"Ah, Rosie, is she the one that smelled like a cheap…I mean, had that terrible perfume on. You know, she should really be more sensitive to the people that she subjects to her aroma."

"Yeah, well, she said that it was specially formulated for a man's nose." Danni was chuckling at the thought. Then, eyeing the tall surgeon she muttered under her breath, "and we sure know that's not your gender."

"I sure hope she didn't spend too much on that. I'd hate to be the cause of her bankruptcy." There, the ice was broken and Garrett was feeling that McMurray would be pleased by her attempt. Her soul contact with the E.R. staff was enjoying her. She could tell by the way that the young nurse was looking at her, green eyes twinkling in laughter. She never had a problem. Winning people over always came easy to her, as long as they did things her way.

"Doc, don't worry about Rosie, she'll get over it. She always does."

"Gee, that's what Karen said when I introduced myself to her."

The nurse shook her head in disbelief. Mom had set both of them up.

Rosie will be fit to be tied. "So, tell me Doctor Trivoli, how did you get the name Garrett?"

The surgeon eyed the young woman. She didn't like talking about herself, at least not in the context of her family life. She never enjoyed bringing up her past. "Why? Does it make a difference in how we treat the patient?"

The blonde looked puzzled. "I was just being curious, Doc." She wrinkled her nose and with a tilt to her head looked over at the tense-looking surgeon. "You don't have to tell me, if you'd rather not."

The raven-haired woman thought about it. It wasn't a bad memory; in fact it was just a story that she herself had been told. *Ah, what the hell! McMurray better appreciate this.* "My parents named me after a dead relative." She looked direly at the petite nurse.

"You sound like you have always had problems with it?"

"Let's just say that it has surprised a few people along the way. People seem to think that I'm something other than who I am."

Danni rolled her eyes with that thought. *Yeah, and who wouldn't want to climb off of their death bed to keep an appointment knowing that it's with such a beautiful surgeon?* Even in the dim lighting, Garrett had a raw beauty in her angular, well-defined features that were outlined by dark-colored hair and eyes that were like giant pools of azure water inviting you in. The dark blue surgical scrubs acted more like a thin veil delicately covering the well-proportioned muscles of the surgeon. The bronze coloring of her skin added to her godlike appearance. The young nurse let her gaze take in all that was offered. "So, I take it that you are Irish and Italian by heritage."

"That's right." Her tone was a reflective one. "But I don't follow any of the customs."

"I'm curious, do you know what 'Garrett' means?" The nurse cocked her head to one side and looked over at the tall woman.

The surgeon thought for a moment and offered, "I have been told that it means brave spear man." She chuckled softly, "I guess that's why I like those sharp cutting instruments, huh?"

The surgeon was now suddenly confused. In fact, the more she thought about it, the more agitated she became at the thought of letting so much of her personal life come to the surface. There was no need for this information to be known. After all, it had no bearing on the patient's outcome or survival rate. How could she let this happen? Garrett closed her eyes, trying to ward off any further investigation of her life from the impertinent nurse.

Suddenly a flash of memory bolted through Danni. The spear held in both hands. It reminded her of her dream earlier today. She shook her head trying hard to get her thoughts in order, to have them make some kind of sense. Could she have had a premonition of the events today? Or could it all just be coincidence? This was something that she was going to have to think long and hard about. *Coincidence, that's it.* There is no life to this woman's eyes. No, sparkle of an underlying soul. Well, at least not to the ordinary person. *I know that it's there; it just has to be drawn out.* Danni looked at Garrett and smiled politely. It was still something to think about.

"Danni..." the Technologist interrupted, "Danni, we're done with the scan."

"Ah...yeah, thanks. Did you see anything?" She tried to regain her composure as she looked nervously at Garrett.

The Radiologist rubbed his chin as he scrolled through the images quickly. "No, no bleed in the head, no fractures either. The abdominal images confirm the broken ribs and chest tube placed within the pleural cavity, but there clearly is no evidence of any visceral injuries at this time." The Radiologist made eye contact with the trauma surgeon who was now standing next to him. "Looks like he got lucky, just a lot of orthopedic injuries."

"Hmm...sounds like he gets a bed on a floor instead of a unit then. Thanks." Garrett shook her head in acknowledgement to the technologist. "Danni, get me the Resident-on-call for Orthopedics? Let's see what they have planned for our patient."

"Sure thing!" The familiarity and the inclusion of the nurse in the patient's care by the surgeon excited Danni. Earlier she had thought there would be no hope of furthering a friendship and now everything was falling nicely into place.

Garrett stood pulling on her long white lab coat. She busied herself looking through the pockets for the key to her call room. The surgeon quickly considered the possibility of actually seeing it and getting some rest, but only after her patient was settled into his room or the operating suite if that was what the Ortho doctors wanted. *'There it is.* She thought as her fingers felt the familiar object.

"Doc, they want him to go to the floor now. They'll operate first thing in the morning." The nurse hung up the phone and began to gather up all the paper work connected to her patient. "Will a room on the orthopedic floor be all right for tonight?"

Trivoli nodded her head in agreement; "I'll want to make sure he gets settled in properly. I'm going up to the floor with you."

"You don't have to, Doc, I've transported lots of trauma patients upstairs..." Her voice trailed off as the fire grew in the steely eyes of the Fellow. "But if you really want to, you're more than welcome."

They seemed to complement each other's action in the care of the patient as they readied him for transfer to the floor. It was obvious to all around them that they worked as a team, the blonde nurse and the Fellow. One anticipated the action of the other without words or looks. If one didn't know better, one would think that the nurse and surgeon had been working together for many years. The two women found themselves completely at ease in the other's company...when they didn't think about it.

****

The charge nurse was amused as she noticed the red scrub

marks on Rosie's neck and arms. She couldn't help thinking about the shocked look on the flirtatious nurse when she realized her hopes had once again run aground. Mom could only hope that Rosie wouldn't take it too hard. "So, Rosie, you're smelling a little better." The older nurse sniffed softly to emphasize the change in her scent.

"It won't do me any good, so why waste it on you people." There was a little bitterness in her tone of voice. "Damn, David." She muttered under her breath.

Karen tried hard not to laugh but lost the battle. "Serves you right, always trying to latch on to some unsuspecting doctor."

Rosie shot an icy glare in her direction but within seconds started to laugh. "That's what I get for trusting people to have the appropriate gender names, I guess."

"You have to admit, Trivoli is a good surgeon. Don't you think?"

"Well, I guess you are right." The nurse self-consciously rubbed the red marks on her neck; "I bet Danni's feeling pretty insignificant right about now at thinking of her as a med student."

"I wouldn't worry about that one. You know she has a way of making things turn out right." Karen settled into her chair and started to view the monitor screen noticing a transfer patient from another hospital. "Looks like we're going to get to see YOUR Garrett Trivoli in action again, Rosie."

"No way," the nurse cringed. It was just too soon. "*Why did I call her that?*" Rosie muttered to herself, knowing full well that Mom wouldn't let her possessiveness of the new Trauma Fellow just drop. It would have to wear off. Somehow she just knew that it would take more than a day or two at that. "Well, I don't have to worry about impressing anyone now. What's coming in?"

"Looks like a head trauma." The Charge Nurse was to the point. "Probably coming in about 20 minutes."

"Great! I hope Danni gets back in time. I don't feel like jumping through hoops every second with that new Fellow."

****

With her patient tucked nicely into his room, Garrett stopped by the nurses' station on the orthopedic floor. She waited patiently for the verbal exchange of information to stop between Danni and the floor nurse before drawing the young blonde's attention. The surgeon invited the nurse. "Care to share an elevator down?"

"Yeah, but I thought you were going to try for some sleep?"

"I can feel the vibes, there's no sleep for me tonight." Her tone was authoritative, as if she could sense something in the air. "Besides, I like talking to you. It's been a long time since I was able to do that. I mean…just talk and not about patients or procedures. It…a…feels kind of nice." *Where did that come from? McMurray, what the hell are you doing to me?*

Danni was taken back by the surgeon's candor. "Sure, what do you want to talk about?"

"Gee, tell me something about you, since you already know my life history." There, she thought, that should break the ice with this nurse. *McMurray, if you only knew what you are putting me through, listening to all of this dribble.*

"Well, I'm a nurse. Surprised, huh?"

The doctor smiled. "Come on, tell me something that I don't know."

"Okay, I'm of French ancestry. My parents named me Danielle, I have two siblings, and that's pretty much my story in a nutshell." The young blonde blushed slightly.

"You don't like talking about yourself, do you?" *Thank the gods, that she is quiet, at least about one subject.*

She wrinkled her nose and looked up nervously at the elevator door as it opened. "No, I don't."

The tall woman waited for Danni to enter the elevator first. She followed, then stood silently until the doors closed. "Sorry." The surgeon feared that she was making the young woman uncomfortable. "I don't mean to pry."

"I know. I just don't think that I'm anything special to talk about. That's all." Her eyes locked onto the cool crisp blue of the surgeon's eyes and Danni could feel herself being immersed into the gentle pools. "If you don't have any plans for this Saturday, we're having an E.R. outing at Schenley Park, Bar-B-Q and a softball game. If you'd like to come, I'm sure you could get to know some of the E.R. staff. What do you say? You could bring your family if you'd like."

"I…I don't really have any family, Danni." The woman's tone was cold and abrupt. "Nor do I want any now or in the future."

"Well, you could still come, or are you on call?"

"No, in fact, I'm off." *Damn, it was out before she could stop it.* The surgeon thought momentarily. "I don't know the city at all, and I don't have a car…" She was trying to regain her sense of control, which was slipping right through her fingers. *McMurray,* she screamed to herself, as if it would help.

"Then, what else would you be doing? It's settled. I'll pick you up and take you with me. How's that?" The young blonde nodded her head in approval.

"Well…if you insist. I guess that would be all right." Garrett was startled. How did this happen? Here she was in a new town, one day into a new job and already she had plans for the weekend with a new friend. She had never found it easy to make friends or to feel at ease so quickly in a new place. The gods knew that she had a lot of practice at new places. She usually accepted her solitude without trouble. But this, this was definitely not her norm. The fact that someone would want to be her friend was a little shocking. It wasn't that she was bad or anything, it just wasn't easy for her to get close to people. She had accepted that many years ago.

"Great!" The nurse was smiling, her teeth showed through the broad grin. There, she had made an offer of friendship and it was accepted.

The feeling of accomplishment suddenly faded with the shrill beeps of the trauma pager. Both women quickly turned sober-faced, reflecting the nature of their jobs. Socializing time was done and all matters turned immediately back to business.

"Trauma Team page…Trauma Team page. Level One Trauma Patient transfer from Uniontown Hospital via helicopter # 3. Twenty-year-old female assaulted with Baseball bats. Patient has sustained head trauma and is intubated. ETA is ten minutes. Level One Trauma Page."

Danni let a long, noisy breath escape her. "Here we go again."

The Trauma Fellow rolled her eyes, "Yeah, I know." She silently thanked the gods for giving her something that would make her feel as if she was in control again. She always felt that way every time she had a patient to worry about. The way she was feeling right now, she would be grateful for every trauma patient that came through the doors.

The elevator came to a stop and both women exited, making their way to the trauma suite. Danni silently offered a prayer for the patient's safekeeping and quickly readied herself to assist in the patient's care. Garrett gowned and prepared mentally for the next battle.

Rosie turned the corner of the hall and smiled silently to herself at the sight of both Danni and Garrett standing ready and waiting. "So, everything alright?" Rosie looked at the nurse as she donned her lead apron.

"Yeah, and you?" Danni returned the cryptic verbiage.

"I'll be okay. You know how fast I bounce back." Rosie winked at her co-worker.

Garrett cleared her throat, "Sorry about the gender confusion."

"Not your fault, Doc." The nurse assumed her assigned position next to the Trauma Fellow. "I think the air will clear on this one."

Garrett smiled under her mask. She sniffed the air lightly and commented, "I think it smells pretty clear already." There was a glare to her eye and sarcasm in her voice.

"Well, you would have liked it if you were a guy. Trust me, Doc." Rosie was being apologetic.

"Trauma in the Department…Trauma in the Department."

The atmosphere hurriedly became sober. Garrett surveyed the room and saw everyone at their stations as the stretcher was wheeled in. The peculiar shape of the young patient's head grabbed the surgeon's attention. It was apparent that the young woman had been the victim of an aggressive attack. Blood was pooled in large clots underneath the short, matted hair. It was impossible to ascertain its true color. The blood was oozing everywhere. The patient was transferred off of the helicopter stretcher as she lay on the long board that was underneath her. The Fellow gingerly started assessing the battered woman's head. The skull felt soft and with no true form. Bone fragments easily moved under her gentle touch. The surgeon swore under her breath at man's savageness to his own kind. It was something that she would never understand.

"X-ray, get a chest, abdomen and lateral C-spine. Karen, call for Neurosurgery and alert CT Scan that we will need a very quick head." The surgeon snapped off her blood-covered gloves and reached for a new pair. The whole time, her eyes kept surveying the patient's body for bruising or any evidence of further trauma. Seeing none, Garrett began to evaluate the woman's body, starting at the shoulders and working her way to the feet. The skilled hands swiftly felt for bony integrity while her eyes scanned areas for asymmetry. The surgeon slowed her assessment when she reached the abdominal area. This was her prime area of expertise. It was an area that could hide injury and she knew it all to well. The painstaking ritual of examining the abdomen for softness or rigidity or rebound tenderness was now addressed. Feeling no rigidity, the surgeon sighed in relief. But the knowledge of protocol dictated that the patient would receive one of two courses of treatment, Diagnostic Peritoneal Lavage often referred to as DPL or exploratory laproscopy surgery while Neurosurgery would operate on her brain and skull. Time was of the essence for this young patient. Trivoli chose appropriately to run to CT Scan for the head and do the exploratory surgery in the O.R.

Garrett looked over at the charge nurse, "Is CT Scan ready for us?"

The nurse nodded her head as she talked on the phone.

"Danni, let's pack her up and move her over to CT." The surgeon was in control. "Neurosurg can see her there."

"Neurosurg will be down as soon as they can. Dr. Shevchik doesn't want you to delay the CT Scan, he will meet you there." Karen bellowed out loud and clear for all to hear as she hung up the phone.

"Okay people, you heard that. Now let's move out." The voice commanded obedience.

Danni hastily transferred the EKG monitor wires to the portable unit. Rosie connected the Bag Valve Mask and oxygen tubing to the small portable tank and turned off the room supply. The young Intern positioned at the patient's left thigh hurried to finish the last of the blood draws from the femoral stick that he had accomplished only to drop one of the tubes causing it to shatter on impact with the floor. All action stopped and an uneasy hush fell over the room, standing out louder than any freight train hurtling noisily down its rickety, old track.

The cold eyes of the surgeon shot daggers at the cause of the delay. All eyes fell on the lowly Intern as he hung his head looking down at the floor where his inadequacy had been made known. The surgeon's eyes fell also on to the floor where, instead of a shattered test tube and wildly patterned blood splatters, she saw the marring of not only her shoes but also of her perfection in treating the patient. How could she make them understand that it had to be perfect…she had to be perfect?

With disgust at her now-failed attempt at perfection this time around, she sighed. Garrett laid the blame on herself for allowing it to happen, for letting an imperfection to slip past her. *You let this happen. You are to blame.* The voice inside of her head screamed at her. She tried to pick up the pieces of her failure as she brushed past the shaken Intern without saying a word. Slowly, the rest of the group followed suit and resumed the effort to mobilize the patient. The Intern stood back against the side of the room, just watching as the stretcher went by.

Within a minute, the entourage of players in this drama made their way into the hall and down to the CT Scanner. The pace was even and slow to accommodate the Respiratory Therapist who was using the Bag Valve Mask to artificially breath for the intubated patient. It was a team effort and everybody knew their station as they entered the scanner. The stretcher was positioned next to the scanner table. The well-practiced maneuver of transferring the patient to the scanner was accomplished with little effort and the team logrolled the patient while the surgeon evaluated the back of the patient. Satisfied that no obvious injuries were there, the Fellow removed the blood stained clothing from under the patient, throwing it to the floor. The spine board was then removed and the patient rolled on to her back to be positioned for the head scan. The Respiratory Therapist connected the endotracheal tube to the ventilator. The doors were closed and the group made their way into the control room for the Scanner.

The technologist was busily typing onto the computer screen the patient's information. With several motions, the screens quickly changed and the machine began to hum as it acquired the images of the young woman's traumatized head. They all watched closely as each image was displayed across the screen. The sight was enough to turn your stomach. The bones of her skull were literally in pieces. The soft tissue was expanding with blood and the brain tissue showed extensive bilateral subdural hemorrhages. The young woman's prognosis was not good at all. *What could she have possibly done to deserve this?* Garret was appalled at the thought. No one deserved this treatment. Her heart ached for this patient and whatever family she had.

The surgeon looked up from the computer screen to see Danni trying hard to keep her emotions in check. She was a professional but that didn't mean that she didn't feel. A tear was gathering in the corner of her eye and slowly spilled over, running down her cheek. The young nurse brushed it away with the back of her hand, hoping that no one had noticed. Little slipped past Garrett without her noticing, though. It was just her nature, being always on top of things as they happened around her.

"Well, what do we have?" Dr. Shevchik questioned as he entered the room. He took stock of the faces as he made his way over to the computer screen. He didn't like the hushed atmosphere and the shocked look on some of the faces. He reached the screen and stood frozen as the technologist quickly scrolled through the images. "Jeez, I don't think we can do much for this one, but let me call my Attending, at home." The Neurosurgeon let out a long whistle. "What the hell did she get hit with?"

Garrett stood next to him. She stared at the patient through the leaded glass in the control booth and said stoically, "Baseball bats."

The Neurosurgeon made a phone call to his Attending and relayed the details of the patient and her injuries. The discussion lasted only two or three minutes before the phone was placed back into its cradle. The man took in a deep breath and announced, "The boss wants to give it a try because of her age. We're going to the O.R."

The team looked at each other and you could sense the small spark of hope that was beginning to take hold. Without any direction, each knew what had to be done and they went into action. Bodies were moving, doors opening, telephone calls to alert the O.R. of their need for a room, all happening simultaneously. She had a chance, slim as it was, but that was not going to stop them. They were here and they were willing to give it their all. Before anyone realized it, the patient was removed from the scanner and transported to the operating room.

The hand off at the O.R. was smooth and orderly. The staff was waiting at the desk when the trauma team came through the door. It was beginning to be an expected site, Trivoli and her crack team whisking in another traumatized patient. The rumors were already starting. This doctor was making a name for herself. No one had ever been so calm and in control as Garrett Trivoli, not on their first day. Although it was the team that accompanied her who was beginning to look battered and beaten up by her all consuming drive for perfection.

Danni and Rosie waited for their portable equipment to be assembled, while they handed over the accumulated paperwork to the nurse at the desk.

"I wish they could all be like that one." The nurse at the desk motioned her head.

Rosie looked puzzled. "Who?"

"You know, that new Trauma Fellow, what's her name, Garnet? She riles the hell out of the staff here. But if I needed an operation in a hurry," she winked at them. "She's got the skill."

"Oh, you mean **my** doctor, Garrett Trivoli," Rosie said with a sense of pride, dripping in sarcasm, while winking at Danni.

The small blonde just closed her eyes, shaking her head slightly and smiled. She could tell that Rosie was over the shock of the mistaken gender and was simply enjoying a good laugh at herself. Danni looked at her watch; it was nearly 3 a.m., the night was going fast. She knew that the surgeon would be tied up in the O.R. for at least an hour or two doing the exploratory surgery and then it would be time for her to round. The nurse made a mental note to page Garrett before she left for home and confirm their arrangements for Saturday's outing. This was one picnic she was looking forward too.

****

The flow of patients into the emergency room had slowed to a stop just like the breeze outside. The heat and humidity clung to the air like the drenched material at a wet T-shirt contest. It was stifling and difficult to breathe. Danni pondered the conditions and mentally considered the change in the patients that would soon be coming into the E.R. The stories would shift from trauma to the elderly who were unable to afford air conditioning and therefore suffered with the weather. Yes, this would be the time for asthmatics and those afflicted with heart conditions. It was almost the end of her shift and the young blonde thought about what she would do on her time away from work.

"Hey Danni, you're coming to the picnic on Saturday, right?" Rosie asked as she looked up from the list she was making.

With her train of thoughts interrupted, she blinked and slowly offered, "Yeah, I'm coming. What do you need?"

"I need a good softball player for my team. You game?"

"When did I ever pass on the annual E.R. Softball challenge with the doctors?" The young nurse sprang into a softball pose. "Those docs won't know what hit them," she chuckled as she completed her follow through.

"Great!" Rosie cautiously inquired, "So, you bringing anyone, my friend?"

Danni wiggled her nose and looked shyly to the floor, "You mean as a date? No…" her head shook slightly from side to side. "But I did ask Garrett, I mean, Dr. Trivoli. I thought it would be nice for her to get to know us outside of the E.R. and have a little fun. She is new in town and all."

Rosie made a face and moaned. "Isn't it enough that we have to put up with her at work?" She eyed Danni. "Well at least she won't be on my team for the softball game."

Karen looked at the young blonde nurse, "Add one 'Amazon' to that list of strays." and shook her head slowly, smiling like a proud mother.

Danni blushed at the attention. Then, as if to change the subject, her eyes narrowed and she nudged the Charge Nurse saying, “Rosie and I should be furious with you. You played us both by not telling us about Garrett before we acted like idiots.”

Startled, Rosie vigorously agreed, “Yeah, why didn’t you warn us?”

Mom just chuckled. “You know, some lessons are better learned by experience than by being told. Besides, I couldn’t help but enjoy the faces that you two were giving back and forth. It was worth every minute.”

“Yeah, well, thanks a lot for letting me make a smelly fool of myself.”

“Gee, I wonder how Trivoli saw it?” Karen mused. “Guess I’ll have to ask her when I see her on Saturday. She is coming with you, isn’t she?”

Danni realized that they had not finished making plans before the last trauma patient arrived. “Ah…I think so. I’ll have to check with her before I leave.”

The Charge Nurse pushed the phone in her direction, “No time like the present. The shift is just about over.”

The small blonde glanced at the nightly on-call schedule that hung on the counter. Finding the notation “Trauma Fellow,” Danni reached for the phone and punched in the appropriate numeric sequence to reach the paging operator. She waited for the computer generated recording and slowly punched in 1048, Garrett’s personal pager, committing it to her memory. She hung up the phone, turned to the older nurse and smiled sweetly. “Satisfied, Mom?”

“You bet!” Mom reached over and fluffed the young blonde’s short hair with a gentle touch, watching as Danni became flushed with embarrassment.

“That’s my girl.”

The phone rang a minute or two later causing all three of the nurses to just stare at it for a moment. Danni answered it with as much professionalism as she could muster. “E.R., Nurse Bossard speaking. May I help you?” Rosie’s eyes bugged out and she quickly clamped her hand over her mouth to muffle the escaping laughter. Danni shot a cold eye toward Rosie as a warning, trying hard to keep a straight face.

The voice on the other end was hesitant but strong; "This is Dr. Trivoli. Danni…is that you?"

"Yeah, I just wanted to confirm our plans for the picnic on Saturday before I left for home."

"I'll be done here in a few minutes. How about we talk over breakfast in the cafeteria?"

"I'll meet you there as soon as I'm off shift. I'm a little hungry anyway."

"O.K. You can help me learn what's edible and what's not. See you soon."

It was a small exchange, but a friendly one. Danni replaced the receiver back into its cradle as a warm feeling ran through her very soul.

Garrett was at the nurses' desk watching the group making its rounds as she answered her page. She was surprised to hear the talkative nurse on the other end of the phone. The surgeon made eye contact with McMurray as she spoke into the receiver, setting up the breakfast meeting with the nurse. Her voice was pleasant and her speech was articulate for being up all night. She was surprising even herself now. It was a long time since her last night on call during her residency. The Navy in some ways had almost been too easy for her.

With the conversation over, she replaced the receiver to its cradle and returned to the rear of the group doing the rounding.

"Was that a date you were confirming on my time, Dr. Trivoli?" The voice was directly behind her as she turned to reference her inquisitor.

"Dr. McMurray, sir," she had to stop herself from saluting. "I was just doing what you told me to."

He looked at her with intense brown eyes. “Then I take it as something to do with the E.R. nursing staff?”

Garrett nodded, “Yes, I’ve been invited to attend the picnic this Saturday. That’s what you wanted, isn’t it?”

“Hmmm…it seems you can do two jobs at one time. There may be hope for you after all.” He turned to leave, then paused saying, “Just remember what job you’re trying to accomplish. Oh, and Trivoli, get yourself a cell phone if you intend on living in a hotel. I don’t like talking to desk clerks.” With that he was off and on his way down the hall.

Her face remained a picture of stoicism. The surgeon could not believe that she was in that direct line of shit rolling down hill again. What was she, the poster child for ‘I need a friend’ or was she just not used to this manner of teaching? *Only 364 more days to go.* She sighed and caught up with the group rounding on the last few patients admitted during the night.

****

The hallway outside of the cafeteria was busy with the traffic of staff and visitor alike. It was a mutual meeting ground where succulence for the body was available without being too pricey. The atmosphere was an attempt at being cheerful but also business-like at the same time. The line for the hot food was already forming at the door when Danni reached the banking machine in the hall. *A quick stop for some money and I’ll be good for the weekend.* She looked around for the tall, familiar form of the surgeon. *Guess I’m here first.* The young nurse stepped up to the machine and submitted her card, punching in a few numbers and patiently waited for the crisp bills to be discharged into her possession. She withdrew her card and quickly counted the new bills.

“Oh, there you are,” Garrett said. “I thought I might have missed you.” She had just gotten off the elevator and was walking across the hall, hoping that she had.

"I needed to get some money for the weekend, you know, with the holiday and all." Danni stuffed the money into her lab jacket pocket. "So, hot or cold?"

The raven-haired woman looked at her perplexed, thinking about the nerve of McMurray to want her to become friends with this non-stop talking machine. "Huh…oh, I don't know. What do you think I should choose?"

"Well, if you are really hungry, hot is always the best." Danni motioned toward the line that started at the door. It was long but she knew that it would move quickly.

They stood in line, in silence. Garrett thought about the events of the night, letting her mind slowly wind down to the more relaxed atmosphere. Her first night here in a new hospital, not to mention new city, was over and all in all she was feeling pretty good about it. It just might be what she had needed all along. For the first time in a number of years, she felt good about her life and the direction it was taking. What she had worked for all those long, lonely years was finally coming to be a realization of her dream, even if she had to do it under McMurray.

Within a few minutes the line had slowly moved to where the available food was displayed behind the glass shields. Steam was coming off of the counter as empty pans were exchanged for freshly made full ones. The aromas mingled together so that no selection could be singled out to tempt the taste buds. The food smelled similar but yet different than Garrett had been used to in the Navy. Danni picked up a tray and some utensils, handing them to Garrett, then repeating the procedure for herself.

"Thanks," an embarrassed grin came to alight on the surgeon's face, then quickly turned into a scowl. "Any suggestions?"

Danni surveyed the selection of hot foods and, after coming to a decision stated, "Your best bet for flavor is to stay away from the scrambled eggs. The French toast or pancakes are always tasty. The sausage patties are better than the bacon."

Garrett was amazed; the small woman was filling her plate as she commented on the food with the expertise of a food critic. This young woman was definitely more than she appeared. The surgeon was finding this new acquaintance to be quite intriguing, if not entertaining. She had never met anyone like this in her life. She followed the young nurse cautiously, choosing the French toast and several patties of sausage from the hot food line. The girl now walked over to the chilled food buffet area and began commentary on the different offerings of seasonal fruit. The surgeon listened intently and watched with awe as Danni placed several choices on her tray. Not being one to enjoy fruit, Garrett just followed along. Next the nurse turned and walked over to the beverage area. "Coffee or Tea?"

"Ah, tea will be fine."

"I like the herbal teas the best," the young nurse picked up several packets of different teas and shuffled through them rather quickly, finally deciding upon a lemon flavored one. She then offered the remainder to the taller woman. "They are all quite good, it just depends on your mood."

The surgeon chose a cinnamon flavored tea and poured hot water into her cup. The nurse slowly walked over to the pastry area and with eyes as big as saucers, considered which one would end her breakfast appropriately. Having acquired her necessary quantity of food, she waited patiently for the surgeon to make her choice. The surgeon placed a small, nut-filled roll on her plate and turned to see the petite nurse carrying what appeared to be enough food to feed a small army. Garrett shook her head and considered her own tray of food. It was nothing compared to the nurse's. *Where does she put it all? She can't possibly eat that entire tray of food.*

They passed through to the cashier line and were looking for a quiet place to eat and share some conversation. They soon found a small table at the rear of the main dining room and made themselves comfortable. The young blonde systematically ate, starting with the hot dishes, pressing onto the chilled fruit choices and lastly the sweet roll that was filled with fruit and dripping with icing. The entire time Garrett just watched. The blonde was still talking about the culinary efforts of the kitchen staff and the numerous selections to definitely choose and those to absolutely bypass. The surgeon was sipping her tea and finishing the last few bites of nut roll when Danni finally swallowed her last mouthful.

"Well, what do you think?"

Garrett looked blankly at the small nurse. *Where did she put it all? I* ***can't*** *believe that she ate every morsel of food.* "Ah…about what?"

"About Saturday, you know, the picnic." Danni was looking intently across the table at the surgeon. "You **are** going to come? It will be fun to get to know some of the E.R. staff, that way they'll get to know you too."

"I said that I would come." Her tone had an air of misgiving in it, then, as if to cover it up, she added. "It will give me something to do."

"So, what time and where do you want me to pick you up?"

"What time do you want to go? I mean, after all, you're the one driving. Mind you now, I do still have to make rounds on my patients."

Danni thought for a moment and offered, "How about 11:30, that way we can be there before the start of the softball game."

"O.K., you can pick me up here at the hospital, outside the front door at 1130 hours sharp." Her voice was good at giving out orders, especially with military time involved. "That way, I will be able to check in on my patients."

"That sounds good to me. Do you play softball?"

"Well, I played in college. Why?"

"It's just that we have this annual game between the doctors and the E.R. staff every year and I thought that maybe you might enjoy playing."

Garrett raised an eyebrow slightly saying, "It's been a long time since I played on a team. I'm afraid I'd be a little rusty."

"That's alright. It's strictly for fun and nothing else." Danni tilted her head to the side and squinted. "We do use it to gloat for the rest of the year, though. Well, that is, if we win."

The two women chuckled softly as friends often do when sharing good times. This was definitely a different feeling from the many shared breakfasts onboard ship for the surgeon. There, friendship was just telling each other about loved ones and that most definitely left Garrett out of the picture. She could not share because she had none. No, all she had to share was pain, suffering, and yes, guilt. Not what anyone would willingly want to share or even listen to. This is why Garrett was so used to her own forced solitude. But this nurse somehow was getting past all of her defenses. Slowly she was worming her way into that lonely world of isolation that Garrett had known for the last nineteen years. A world made up of nothing but her intense focus on caring for the traumatized patient who was entrusted into her care. There, she made little time for herself so as not to allow the torture of her past to haunt her day-to-day life.

The young blonde watched the surgeon as she became distanced in thought. Her heart ached in the worst way to reach out and comfort her newfound friend. It was always so hard to judge what response would kindle the growth of a relationship and which would send it dashing hopelessly to the realms of seclusion. Deciding that it was too soon for Garrett to let her get close, Danni thought that it was best for her to take her leave.

"I've had a good time. Perhaps we can do this again." She was sincere as she rose from her seat.

"Yeah, I think I'd like that. Well, if it fits in with my schedule." She caught herself before it could go any further. "Front door of the hospital at 1130 sharp on Saturday. I'll be ready." Garrett confirmed the arrangements. "Should I bring anything?"

"Don't worry. I'll take care of everything." Danni let her hand rest on Garrett's shoulder then leaned in towards her ear, "It's been a real pleasure to make your acquaintance, Garrett. I'll see you on Saturday."

"Ah...Danni, it's Dr. Trivoli, please. At least inside the hospital."

The young woman's eyes bugged out for a brief second at the recognition of the condescending tone that had just been used toward her. *Now that hurt! I can't believe after all of my trying to help her.* "All right then, I'll see you on Saturday, Doctor Trivoli," Danni drew out the title, nodding in agreement and then walked away from the table.

"Thanks for the company and the invitation." Garrett gave the retreating figure a lopsided grin and admitted, "I'm actually looking forward to this outing." *I'll try anything that will get McMurray off my back.*

Garrett watched as the petite form withdrew. The chipper nurse now seemed upset with something or other. The surgeon shrugged and began to leave the table with her tray in hand. What had changed in just a minute or two? *Nurses...who can understand them?* She quickly and analytically ran over the last few verbal exchanges between them and tried to find a reason. A little voice deep inside of her kept saying, '*you know why she changed.* Then she admonished herself by reasoning out that nurses were used to calling physicians "Doctor" all the time. After all, it was a sign of respect. The scientific mind of the surgeon tried using logic to come to an answer. Her mind ran down a list of things that were logical of a nurse. *They were craving to give aid and comfort to those in need, working long hours and taking verbal abuse from those who were in their care. Basically it all boils down to the ability to care deeply and feel the pain...* Garrett halted her forward motion abruptly. *Nah, she wouldn't be upset with that, would she?* Her eyes darted from one face to another as she watched the people around her, carefully sorting out those of the nursing staff. There was one over there who was laughing at something that had just been said. Then off to the side was another with a look of concern; her arm now encompassed the woman next to her. Wherever she looked, the surgeon saw the emotions of human frailty and strengths etched into the beings of the nurses.

The more she looked into the nameless faces; her words came racing back through her mind. *It's Dr. Trivoli, to you.* Garrett exhaled out of her mouth, cursing at the same time. *What that must have sounded like to that congenial nurse?* "It must have felt like a slap in the face."

Feeling the need to say something, anything, to the nurse to try to soften the blow the surgeon searched the crowded dinning room for Danni. Unable to find her, the depressed woman allowed her shoulders to gently slump in defeat.

Danni had made her way hastily away from the source of her hurt placing her tray on the conveyor belt area. She turned to look back at the table with the raven-haired surgeon. There was so much she could see that was hiding just under the surface of this woman and it made her want to cry. She would have to find a way to break through that tough exterior. *There is an alive and viable person, a real person locked up deep inside. I know that there is.* With that thought, the young nurse mustered up a weak smile focusing on the positive as always. Somehow the night had turned out to be good and breakfast wasn't that bad either. The nurse sighed, letting a smile slowly come across her face. *Yep, adding one 'Amazon' to that menagerie of mine.*

Chapter 6

Cool, crisp air was gently blowing over tense white knuckles wrapped securely around the steering wheel. Saturday traffic in the Strip District was never a picnic no matter what time of year and the steadily rising temperature only made it worse.

Looking down the road to the snarled traffic of the intersection, Danni let go of a short blast of air from her mouth, ruffling the blonde hair on her forehead. "Why did I have to volunteer to get the watermelons at the produce yards?"

She shook her head and glanced at her wristwatch. It was a little after eleven and a growing concern at the stalled traffic in front of her made her contemplate the option of an alternate route to the hospital. Her eyes could barely make out the street sign down the block through the wavy lines of heat rising up from the asphalt of the road surface. The cars in front of her began to slowly inch forward and she gently tugged at the steering wheel, cautiously maneuvering her small vehicle through the gap of pedestrians. Now only a block away from all this time-consuming congestion of both automobiles and humanity she sat waiting for the traffic light to change. Growing more impatient she again noted the time.

"Nothing I can do until this mess starts moving," she sighed. "Looks like I'll just make it, if nothing else comes up."

She looked around at the gathering crowd on the corner and thought about the snippet of a dream she had that morning. It was cryptic as usual. It played again through her mind. There, in slow motion, was the sensation of being pushed from behind that ended in a whirling motion and a view of a rough stick against the outline of clouds. It was, of course, like the rest, making no sense whatsoever. *Maybe someday I'll understand,* she thought whimsically.

The light changed to green allowing movement again to her lane of traffic. The smile on her face began to widen as she anticipated her next destination. For some reason her mind had conjured up the idea of her new friend dressed as a sailor looking out on the horizon waiting for her ship to come into port. The young blonde blinked her eyes and quickly dismissed the idea of Garrett Trivoli in dress whites. *An officer...?* She quickly mauled the thought in her mind. *Yes, but a gentleman?* Danni chuckled to herself and thought of Garrett's womanly attributes. *No,* she mentally perused the tall form in her mind again, *no gentleman there*. Suddenly she could feel her brow furrow.

"Where did that come from?" Danni mentally shook the image from her mind and forced her thoughts back onto the road. "Drive, Danni, drive." Being cautious, she resumed her drive to the hospital.

****

With the preciseness of a military operation, Dr. Trivoli emerged from the doorway of the hospital at exactly 1130 military time. She carried a small duffel bag filled with her clothes from rounding on her patients, a large towel, and a bathing suit just in case the opportunity presented itself. She had forgotten to ask the young nurse if a pool was available near the picnic area. She looked down at the bag. *At least I won't have to skinny dip if there is a pool.*

The sun felt good out here on the driveway. It reminded Garrett of the warm tropical weather in Hawaii. After three years in the South Pacific, she was accustomed to the intense rays of the sun. It brought back memories of lush green foliage and wonderfully colored exotic flowers. She smiled as she remembered her favorite spot. It was on private property, tucked away from the view of the tourist population. She had found it by accident while horseback riding. When she closed her eyes, she could see the waterfall running into the secluded pool. If she concentrated hard enough, she could hear the sounds of the water gently lapping on to the shore. This was a place that made her feel at peace with herself. It was a place that was special to her and she held it dearly in her heart. No words of love were spoken to her there, but if ever there was the possibility, that would be the perfect place to express one's commitment to a life together. The bronzed-skinned woman sighed. *Whom am I kidding? Love? Me? I can't even let anyone get close.*

Annoyed at the direction her thoughts were now turning, the surgeon looked up and down the driveway in search of the friendly nurse. *What's taking her so long?* The tall woman glanced down at her watch. It was 1133 and still no sign of the bubbly, young blonde.

Garrett was in the habit of punctuality and waiting had never been her strong point. It was another one of her perfectionistic qualities, one that she wished everyone had.

She tried hard to keep her mind from drifting and decided to make a quick check of what she needed to address when she came on shift in less than twenty-four hours. The rest of today was going to be for enjoyment and socializing with her new work mates, as it was decreed from McMurray. It would feel good to relax and maybe even have a little fun. The thought of competition excited her. It had been the mainstay of her youth. At least there would be something to look forward to.

"Hey, Garrett! Over here." The small blonde was standing outside of the green Geo Metro with the door open. She waved, trying to get her new friend's attention. *Oh! I forgot, hospital property.* "Dr. Trivoli," she called even louder hoping that the surgeon had not heard her first name called out earlier.

The sound of her name made her look around. There, off to the side, she could see the wild antics of the young nurse trying to get her attention. Garrett allowed the corners of her mouth to slowly turn upward as she waved and made her way across the driveway. "Thought you forgot about me. You did say 1130, right?"

"Sorry, I had a little problem with traffic. Here let me put that into the trunk." Danni accepted the duffel bag from the tall woman and opened the rear compartment, revealing several large watermelons. "Our offering to the picnic. I hope I got enough." She laughed, placing the bag into the little space that was left and closed the trunk lid. "Your door is open."

Garrett looked at the small size of the Geo Metro and thought about her almost 6 foot tall body. *I guess it will be like getting into that damn submarine.* One eyebrow slowly rose. "How far to the park, Danni?"

"Oh, it will only take ten or fifteen minutes, why?" The small blonde was settling back into the driver's seat.

"Nothing, just wondered." The tall surgeon thought about the cramped quarters, gulped, and gingerly tried to fit her long legs into the passenger compartment.

"I moved the seat back to give you more room." Green eyes flicked over to the passenger side as she positioned her hands on the steering wheel.

"Thanks, I think." Garrett was in the seat, her legs more like an accordion with the knees rising just slightly higher than the dashboard. "Airbags?"

"No, the next model year has them. Sorry."

"That's okay, I just wanted to be prepared, that's all." The surgeon was contemplating adding a few more joints to her body. "Okay, I'm in and buckled up."

"Door closed?" Danni threw a casual glance over at her companion then after seeing the nod of the tall woman's head she smiled sweetly and turned her attention to the road ahead.

Garrett could feel her hair rubbing against the padded ceiling of the passenger compartment as the car jerked into motion. With a skipped beat of her heart and Danni's foot on the gas pedal, they were on their way. Headlines began to run through the surgeon's head. *Promising Surgeon Cut Short by Fender Bender.* The woman shuddered at the thought, *Seatbelt, hell, I couldn't move if I wanted to.* The surgeon tried to relax, but it wasn't easy, at least not for the next fifteen minutes or so.

The young nurse sensed her friend's uneasiness and began to ramble on about the passing landmarks and history of that area of the city. "Most people think of Pittsburgh as a Steel Mill town but that's not what the city's like anymore. All of the Steel Plants have been pretty much torn down and replaced with newly developed business parks that are being used by the high tech industries. One of the local colleges, Carnegie Mellon University, is a leader in the developments of the computer industry, especially with their new Robotics Department."

Danni casually looked over to see how the surgeon was doing. It was an attempt to get Garrett's mind off of the incommodious conditions. It was working, as the tall woman allowed herself to become absorbed into the interesting stories that were being conveyed.

"The city used to be known as the dirtiest city in world with all of its mills sending large, thick clouds of coal dust billowing out of their smoke stacks. The old timers even tell stories of not being able to see the sun at high noon for all of the airborne coal dust. But that's not the way it is now, as you can see."

Glancing over at Garrett, the blonde noticed that the surgeon's eyes were riveted on the building up ahead. It was a large, old-style, massive building in foreboding black stone.

She quickly jumped on the fact that it held the woman's interest. "Andrew Carnegie was a coal baron in the rising days of the steel industry. His fortunes have been used to establish the Carnegie Library, that's the big building over there." Danni pointed to it. "He also founded the museum of natural history, too. That's the bigger building in front of it facing out onto the main street."

Garrett eyed it longingly. "I like history."

"Good, maybe we can go together and make a day of it sometime. I'm kind of partial to the Egyptian rooms, myself."

Danni carefully turned down the street at the next corner where a completely different style of architecture was located. It was a dome-roofed building that was almost completely made out of glass with ornate iron work painted white, giving it an almost gazebo appearance. Immediately Danni's tour guide mode started in about it. "That, on your right, is Phipps Conservatory." She smiled at her fond memory of times spent there with her mother.

"Conservatory as in music?" Garrett asked puzzled by the large expansion of domed glass at the center of the architecture.

"It's a botanical garden that changes with the seasons. They have everything from lush, tropical rooms to rooms that take you around the world. The rooms representing the orient have always intrigued me, even when I was growing up. Their sense of serenity is so…peaceful." She laughed at her lack of words, then continued on. "I like to come there to reflect after a particularly bad day."

As they drove past each block Danni came up with interesting little tidbits about their origin or history in the scheme of Pittsburgh's early days. The young woman loved to talk; it was obvious. Her stories were filled with personal insight and observations that held Garrett's attention. So mesmerized was she by the young woman's fluid speech, that she hadn't noticed when they pulled into the parking space.

"Well, we're here." Danni turned to look at her passenger. "You going to get out or are you comfortable like that?" The green eyes flashed as a warm smile was revealed.

Quickly looking around, "Ah…no…I mean yeah, I'm getting out." The surgeon fumbled for the seatbelt. "Damn this!" She took a small, beeper-sized, digital phone off of her belt. "There!" She placed it onto the dashboard.

Danni looked at the phone. "You aren't on call, are you?"

"No!" She struggled with the seatbelt latch. "McMurray insisted that I had to have a phone. Seems the one at the hotel isn't good enough for him."

Danni reached over, laying her hand on top of Garrett's. "Here, let me." The smaller woman deftly released the belt. "Okay, you're free now." She chuckled as she got out of the car.

"Thanks."

The young woman had briskly walked to the passenger side of the car and opened the door for the contorted surgeon. She offered her hand saying, "Need some help?"

Blue eyes looked up and locked onto the shimmering green that seemed to dance in delight. If the eyes were indeed the windows to the soul, then Garrett felt as though she had been privileged with a rare glimpse of this woman's essence. It obviously made her shiver to think about it.

"I guess the air-conditioning is colder than I thought," Garrett offered. She grabbed the small hand saying, "Now get me out of here, huh."

The small woman grasped the hand firmly and positioned herself to help in the extrication of the larger woman from the small enclosure. Slowly, limb-by-limb emerged until the surgeon's entire body was standing outside of the car and extended to its full height. "I should practice my yoga more often."

Garrett looked down at her friend, the lopsided grin showing as she tried to make light of an awkward situation.

"Hey, don't forget your phone." Danni picked it up and offered it to the surgeon. "Small, isn't it?"

"Yeah, I figured I'd have to have it with me all the time." Garrett took the phone and placed it back on her belt.

"Hey, Danni, hurry up. We're about to start the game." Rosie was yelling at the top of her lungs. "What's taking you so long?"

The small blonde turned, held up one finger and yelled back, "Be there in just a minute." She looked at Garrett and asked, "Well, Doc, are you going to play or just watch?" There was a bit of sarcasm in her voice, as if to challenge her friend into the competition.

"If they'll have me, you're on." Her competitive side was beginning to show as the surgeon accepted the challenge. "Let's say we make it more interesting. Loser buys breakfast. Deal?"

"You're on! You know, some people say that I eat a lot," she reminded the doctor. "Let's add to it. Winner picks where to eat."

"All right, that only seems fair."

The two women made their way over to the softball field. Danni gave commentary as well as greetings to everyone they passed on their way. It amazed Garrett how her brief synopsis of each person was always in the positive light. It was as though she only saw the good in people and totally disregarded the bad.

"Hi, Danni, who's your friend? I hope you're not bringing in a ringer, are you?" There was a gentle teasing in the voice coming from the bespectacled, young woman.

"Oh, hi. No, in fact, this is actually someone for your team, Dr. Potter. Let me introduce you to Dr. Garrett Trivoli, one of the new Trauma Fellows. Garrett, this is Jamie Potter, one of the E.R. Attending Physicians."

"Danni!" Rosie yelled across the field, "Danni, are you going to play or be master of ceremonies?"

The nurse shook her head, allowing her short, blonde hair to be tossed from side to side, "Jamie, I trust that you'll do the rest of the introductions." She motioned to the group of physicians assembled together. "I've got to get over there before Rosie strokes out."

She started across the field for several steps then stopped and turned back towards Garrett, "Hey, good luck!" She swiftly resumed her path and was soon welcomed into the rowdy bunch of her coworkers with the rhythmic chanting of "Danni, Danni, Danni!"

Garrett let a smile come across her face. "Is she that good or does she just do wonders for the team spirit?"

Dr. Potter pushed her glasses up and said, "She is the best shortstop the nurses have ever had, one heck of an all around player and a great morale booster at that. Have you played before, Garrett?"

The surgeon smiled as she thought of the wager. *So, you think you're gonna win...huh?* "Ah, when I was in college I played some."

"Any position in particular?"

The raven-haired woman let her face go into a feral smile. "No, I was always used as a utility player, so anywhere you need me will be fine."

"Come on, let me introduce you to the rest of the team before we get started." Jamie proceeded to go down the bench full of physicians introducing Garrett along the way.

****

It was exactly noon when an official looking pair of men strode out on to the field, one walking to the first base area while the other claimed home plate. The tall red haired man brushed off the plate. He stood looking at one team then the other. "Play ball!" He shouted and stood behind the plate with both hands resting on his hips. He waited patiently for the home team to take the field. The nursing staff huddled quickly and within a few seconds the circle of players and coaches let a mighty roar into the air, "Nurses Call the Shots!" It was as if the huddled bodies had exploded onto the field, each member running at top speed to get to their designated position. Determination was evident in the way they moved the ball around the infield to warm up. They were confident that they would win the game. After all, they had won last year giving them the home team advantage for this year.

"Batter Up!" The umpire yelled.

The first member of the Doctors team picked up a bat and settled into the batter's box. It was Dr. Potter. Her stance wide, bat raised high as she waited for the first pitch. Nan, the manager of the nursing staff had the honors of delivering the ball high and inside.

"Ball one."

"Come on, Nan, let her hit it. She'll never get it out of the infield." Danni teased from the shortstop position. Her body was ready for action as she balled her right hand into a fist and hit it into her glove.

Nan concentrated. She released the ball. The arc was perfect in height. Jamie gripped the bat, sucking in a breath, and timed her swing to meet the ball as it crossed the plate. Crack! The sound was solid as the ball ricocheted back on to the playing field. It was low and fast dropping to the ground a few feet in front of Danni. Reacting to the ball, the short stop charged into it and caught it on the first bounce. With lightning speed, the young woman had retrieved the ball from the pocket of her glove and fired it at the first baseman who caught it with ease. Rosie stepped on the bag with ball in glove. "OUT!" cried the umpire. The nursing staff on the sideline went crazy, chanting "Danni, Danni, Danni!"

Danni dusted off her hand and settled back into her position on the field. "One down, two more to go, Nan." She held her finger up in the air to remind the team of where the play would go. Satisfied that everyone knew, she readied herself for the next batter.

The tall surgeon sat watching from the bench. She was impressed with the small nurse's athletic ability. She marveled at the level of intensity that the young blonde had for whatever she was doing. Garrett could tell already that this woman put her best effort into everything that she did. No matter how insignificant the activity, she gave it her all. *She has every right to be confident. Too bad she thinks she is going to win.* The woman thought about her own ability as a slow smile began to take shape on her face.

Their turn at bat was over before Garrett had realized it. She was caught in the middle of daydreaming by someone shaking her shoulder.

"Garrett! Dr. Trivoli!" Jamie shook a little harder.

"Huh…oh yeah. Sorry, I was thinking about something." The surgeon was obviously startled.

"Here's a glove for you to use. You okay with playing center field?" The doctor pushed her glasses up.

"Sure, no problem." Garrett accepted the glove and slid her left hand into it. "Thanks, it's a good fit." She looked at Jamie and grinned. Her body reacted to the familiar feel of the glove. The familiarity of the game was all coming back to her as she stood and began trotting out to her position. It had been a long time, but it was like riding a bicycle…past abilities learned always came back.

"Batter up!"

A tall blonde male strode to the plate. John stood adjusting his batting glove and surveying the field. He stepped into the batter's box and dug his left foot into the dirt. His hands wrapped tightly around the wooden bat as he raised it onto his right shoulder. Slowly and deliberately he took several practice swings into thin air as his eyes looked over the possible targets that would allow him to get on base. Satisfied that he had found the weak link in the Doctors' team, he brought his focus onto the pitcher and waited for the ball.

Ian McCormick looked around the playing field. His team was ready and so was he. The E.R. Physician started into his routine of concentration that ended with a deep expiration. His fingers gripped the softball that was nestled in his glove. The slow motion of the wind up began as he brought the ball out of the glove. The forward momentum of his left foot was in complete opposition of the backward movement of his right hand. His weight now shifted forward as he delivered the ball, stepping forward with his right foot. The tips of his fingers allowed the ball to roll off with a gentle backspin. The arc was high and perfectly gauged in distance to come slicing right through the middle of the strike zone on the tall nurse.

"CRACK!" the sound echoed into the sidelines.

John swung the bat with a slight up swing on his follow-through. The ball was literally screaming for the outfield. It was a good solid base hit, if not more. John took off running, letting the bat drop to the ground. The nurse was fast and he knew it. His head turned toward center field as he rounded first base. The ball was in its descent heading into the gap between left field and center.

Karen stood in the coach's box watching the movement of the outfielders in reaction to the descending ball. Her arms frantically were waving the base runner on for additional bases. The nurses on the sideline were cheering for their coworker while watching the ball soar into the outfield. The first ball to the first batter and already they had the possibility of being on the scoreboard. They watched as John rounded second base and headed for third.

The left fielder was now calling for the ball as he stood waiting patiently for it to drop. The young physician had made a small miscalculation and, trying to readjust, attempted to catch the ball with his gloved hand extended over his head. The ball struck the tip of the glove and veered off towards center field.

Seeing that the speedy nurse was now stepping on the bag at third base. Mom screamed, "GO HOME!" Her arms waved wildly as her face grew beet red from yelling. John put his head down in a determined run for the plate. The nursing staff was going crazy with excitement, jumping and shouting words of encouragement.

Garrett saw what was happening, her long legs moved swiftly to cover the ground between her and the deflected ball. She was no longer thinking, just letting her natural ability take the reins. Seeing that she would not be able to reach it before it struck the ground, she positioned herself to catch it off of the bounce. The glove took the abuse of the hard hit as the ball slammed into it. In a smooth motion, the surgeon had excised the orb and cocked back her arm to throw it into the infield. Her mind had quickly calculated the speed of the runner. He would be at the plate before the standard relay from the outfield to the second baseman could turnover to the catcher. With that in mind, Dr. Trivoli took aim and let her arm fire the ball into the catcher. It would be a long shot, but she had done it before. Garrett's follow-through carried her into a forward momentum, her face strained with determination.

Dr. Porter threw off her facemask. Her peripheral vision allowed her to follow the base runner as he drove with abandon towards her at home plate.

Jamie's focus was on the play being made from the outfield. She concentrated on the ball and realized it was coming directly into home. Her feet went into a readied stance as she braced herself for the impact of the runner. She held her glove in position to catch the ball as it got closer. Her eyes grew bigger as she sucked in a large gulp of air. It was going to be close.

"WHAM!" the ball embedded itself into the padded glove. The catcher felt the impact and swiftly brought the arm in a sweeping motion across the baseline in front of the plate. She caught John as he was sliding between her feet. The kinetic energy that was transferred from the forward charge of the nurse to the stationary doctor sent the young woman into the air and rolling backwards. Glasses flew and red hair was wild as it tumbled out of the cap that was thrown off in the collision. Both teams went suddenly silent, fearing injury to one or possibly both players.

The umpire stood waiting for the dust to clear. He quickly surveyed the scene seeing John an inch away form the plate and Jamie sprawled out with the ball still tightly held in her glove. "YOU'RE OUT!" His hand motion was strong and animated for all to see.

The team of nurses stood in shock. Karen just kept blinking and shaking her head in disbelief. Danni couldn't believe her eyes and slowly turned to stare out at the tall woman in centerfield. Rosie suddenly was without words.

"She said she played a little in college," muttered Danni under her breath, "…as a utility player. I never expected this."

"Well, thanks a lot, Danni. It appears that you gave them a ringer." Rosie was finally able to vocalize.

"I wonder if she can bat?" Steve weakly voiced, not really wanting to know the answer.

Nan thought about the skill and strength that the throw had needed, "I don't think I want to know. Figures that she'd be perfect."

The once over-confident team was now lost in the beginnings of despair. Danni quickly took stock of the team's shattered confidence and stepped in to put a stop to the defeatist attitude that was taking it over. "Ok, she just got lucky. That's all! We still have two more outs before they get up to bat again. We can still score. It's only the first inning, guys, we can do it."

Rosie began to help out, "Yeah, come on! We can beat them. We did it last year, didn't we?"

The rest of the team chimed in with words of encouragement as John slowly came over to the sideline. "What happened?" he asked.

"You tried for one too many, that's all," Marianne the E.R. aid answered.

"Who threw that ball?" John demanded.

Rosie and Danni looked at each other and spoke at the same time in an accusing tone.

"YOUR Dr. Trivoli!"

"YOUR 'Amazon'!"

Karen heard the exchange and busted out in laughter. It was contagious; soon the whole team was caught up in it. The two nurses looked at the rest of the team in amazement, then at each other, immediately exploding into a giant belly laugh themselves.

Dr. Potter was painstakingly taking stock of her body parts, making sure that no injury was apparent before trying to get up. Assured that she was neurologically intact and uninjured otherwise, the catcher slowly pulled herself to her feet, searching for her glasses. Ian had rushed in, securing the glasses and started to walk toward his shaken colleague.

"Jamie, you okay?" He grabbed her hand and placed the glasses into it. "Here, put these on."

"Thanks, I'm fine. Honest, nothing is damaged." She looked over to the sound of hysterical laughter coming from the nurses' sideline. "They laughing at me?" she asked puzzled.

"I don't think so. Must be something they said." Ian offered as he dusted the catcher off. "That was some play. Great catch for a woman!" he teased. His head turned to the tall woman in centerfield. "Great throw from one, too!"

Seeing that no player had been hurt in the collision, the umpire pulled a small whiskbroom from his rear pants pocket and began to sweep off the plate. Satisfied in its cleanliness, he stood back and yelled, "BATTER UP!"

****

The sun, now gravitating toward the western horizon, followed its path as the game waged on. The competitors each determined not to accept defeat, as they took turns to advance their side's odds of winning, but to no avail. It was the top of the fourth inning with no score for either side. The nurses had taken up their positions and awaited the first batter.

John adjusted his facemask as the approaching figure made her way to the batter's box. It was the center fielder, Dr. Garrett Trivoli. Standing outside of the box, she swung several bats together in a looping arc around her head as an attempt to loosen her shoulder muscles. After choosing one bat and discarding the rest, the surgeon squared her shoulders as she stepped into the lines of the batter's box. John looked up at the tall figure saying, "Well, Trivoli, let's see what you can do with a bat." His tone was one of scorn.

The surgeon let one eyebrow arch high as she cast a downward glare at him. She took in a large breath and cleared her throat. Her attention now turned to the woman on the mound. She settled into a comfortable stance and waited for the first pitch. The arc of the ball was high as she watched it go by.

"Ball one!" The umpire noted.

John threw the ball back to Nan. He turned toward Garrett and spit the tobacco juices from the chew placed in his mouth, attempting to intimidate the physician. It didn't work. The surgeon remained aloof to any attempts to unnerve her concentration. The catcher resumed his position. He waited until the pitcher released the next ball before asking, "So, what college did you play for, anyway?"

Garrett was undistracted, her eye steady on the approaching ball. The subtle cocking of the bat in anticipation of the impending swing was evident. The powerful arms tugged at the bat as it was whipped in a thrusting arc, colliding over the plate with the sphere. Her body twisted with the momentum of the swing. The bat was dropped one-handed to the ground as her long legs began the forward driving motion toward first base. She watched as the ball sailed over the right field hedges. The base umpire signaled a home run and Garrett slowed to a trot, making sure to touch all the bases on her way back to home plate. The doctors were jumping, cheering, and several were waiting at the edge of the home plate area to shake the trauma surgeon's hand in congratulations.

John positioned himself in the front of the line reaching for Garrett's hand as she stepped onto the plate. His eyes searched hers, "Honestly, where did you play?"

The surgeon looked the nurse straight in the eye, "U.S.C. '82 through '85." A smirk remained on her face as she withdrew her hand and continued into the throng of well-wishing physicians.

John was annoyed by the smile and began to wonder why it would be important for him to know exactly what years she played at U.S.C., absent-mindedly he continued to walk in a daze toward the pitching mound.

The young woman at shortstop watched as John neared the mound. Thinking that a conference was necessary to calm the jittery pitcher down, Danni ventured over to the mound. *Time for damage control.*

"What's wrong, John?" Nan saw his puzzled look.

"I'm not quite sure, but I think I should remember something."

"Hey, guys, come on. It's only one run. We can get it back." The young nurse was as positive as ever. "What's up with John?" she addressed Nan directly the closer she got.

"I don't know," Nan shrugged her shoulders. "He keeps trying to remember something."

Suddenly, John's head snapped upright, his eyes bugging out as his color drained to a pasty white. "Oh, my God! Do you know who that is?"

The two women nodded in unison. "Dr. Garrett Trivoli, John," Danni answered. "She told me herself."

John shook his head vigorously, "No! That is Garrett Trivoli, four time NCAA Most Valuable Player for the championship U.S.C. women's softball team 1982 through 1985."

Their eyes grew large and their mouths fell agape as Rosie and Karen now joined the huddle of players at the mound.

"Hey, what's wrong with you guys?" Rosie asked. "You trying to catch flies out here?" she chuckled.

Nan looked at Rosie and Karen. "Our own shortstop gave the doctors a real ringer!"

All eyes slowly turned to Danni. Feeling the intense stares, the young nurse wrinkled her nose, "How was I supposed to know? I just meet her two days ago. She didn't tell me. We all thought that she was a man until yesterday morning. How was I to know that she was an NCAA M.V.P. during her college years?"

Mom closed her eyes and shook her head slowly.

Rosie's face grew red with anger as she spat out, "YOUR 'AMAZON'!" She turned and stomped back to first base.

"Jeez, Danni!" John was obviously upset.

"Well, you're the walking book of sports trivia. Why didn't you know it sooner?" The young blonde was trying to defend herself. "Awe, let's just play ball. She's only one person, for crying out loud, not the whole team."

The short stop took in a deep breath and exhaling loudly turned to walk back to her position. She readjusted the glove on her left hand and began to smack her balled right fist repeatedly into the pocket of the well-used glove. *How was I supposed to know?* The nurse kicked the dust as she took her cap off and wiped her forehead with the back of her arm. She attempted to rid her hair of its excess moisture by tossing her head from side to side. Reaching her position, she looked over to the sideline and searched the crowd of physicians. There, at the end of the bench sat her 'Amazon'. *So, what other talents are you hiding, Dr. Trivoli?* Danni slapped her cap against her leg and shook her head. She threw her cap onto her head and adjusted it as she stole another look at her 'Amazon'. *I wonder...just how long will it take me to find out?*

****

The little softball game was drawing the attention of other people in the public park. It started as just a few passers-by stopped to watch the friendly rivalry and increased into small gatherings of rooting and cheering fans as favored sides were chosen. Each spectacular play or hit only added to the enthusiasm of the spectators as the game progressed on. The teams were definitely unknowns to the applauding fans, but the caliber of play was far above that of a pick-up game at an annual picnic.

Softball may not have been their profession of choice, but the ability to act as a team was part of the daily routine of every player on the field. It was their teamwork at the hospital that made them a strong, cohesive unit on the playing field, each one giving their strengths to obtain the common goal. This game was an extension of their work camaraderie. They all seemed to pitch in to get the job done, whether it was making the play at a base, catching a fly ball, or advancing one base at a time to score a run. Whatever it took, they would pull together as one to do it.

It was the bottom of the sixth inning with the score tied at one run each. The nurses were at bat with the intent to score at least one run. Karen had pulled out all of the tricks that her 50 years of playing experience had taught her. If they could not score the long ball hits into the outfield then they would find another way to advance the runner around the bases. The first batter for this inning was Rosie, the first baseman. Karen motioned for the tall nurse to come over to her before stepping into the batter's box.

"Rosie, I want you to watch those balls carefully. No reaching for anything, got it? I want Ian to have to throw as many balls as we can let him," the coach instructed. "I want to tire out that arm of his. Remember what I said in the huddle?"

Rosie nodded, "Yeah! 'Everything gets hit on the ground,' just like you said."

"Right! Now let's get you on base."

The nurse shook her head and proceeded over to the batter's box.

"Play Ball!" the umpire bellowed.

With bat at the ready, Rosie stood there looking, as the first two pitches were high and inside. The next pitch was a perfect one, right through the strike zone, as was the one after it. The count was 2 balls and 2 strikes on the batter. The nurse readied herself mentally. The pitch came over the plate just as she liked it, low and inside. Without warning the bat was slicing through the air in a slightly downward swing as it impacted the cowhide cover of the ball. The sphere took off in a lurch, diving into the ground several feet up the third base line. The nurse ran for first base as if she had been shot out of a cannon, making it there just before the throw from the third baseman. The leading run was now on base.

Danni was the next in line to advance the lead runner. She waited as she was instructed until her count was 3 and 2. The pitch was perfect, right down the middle. Mentally she chastised herself for wanting to really swing at this one. She knew what was expected of her and resigned herself to following Karen's wish. Her hand slid up the rear of the bat as she leveled it into the bunting position. She held it there across the plate and waited for the ball to strike the wood. "Thunk!" The sound was not the usual one for her at bat, but she would do what was planned to get the runner around the bases. The ball dropped lifelessly and rolled slowly, staying in the playing field. Danni hesitated to start her run to first base in a delaying tactic for the catcher to get to the ball. It was only a second or two, but that was all her tall teammate needed to get to second base. The small nurse dropped the bat and quickly sprinted to first base. The ball was still rolling in the dirt as her foot touched the bag. The team now had two runners on base with nobody out.

The next batter was Marianne. She stood at the plate with all the determination of a major leaguer, waiting for her pitch to cross the plate. Seeing the ball come into her sweet zone, the batter flexed what little muscle there was on her slender frame and brought the bat around. It was not a hard hit by any means, as the ball lazily bounced back to the pitcher. Ian looked nervously over at third base before catching the ball. Rosie was already a step away from the base. Knowing the speed that the nurses' shortstop was capable of, the only possible play would be to first base. The throw was uneventful, arriving ahead of the runner. The batter had done her job, that being to advance the runners on base even though she was sacrificed as the first out.

Karen grabbed the next batter as she stepped on deck. "Nan, we need a base hit down the right field line. Do you think you can do it?" The coach's eyes narrowed. "She's a left hander out there. It will give Rosie enough time to take home."

Nan looked nonchalantly across the playing field; "You got it, Mom!" Her voice was full of determination. She turned and proceeded up to the plate.

The infield began to move a little closer as Nan stepped into the box. Her bat was held tightly, as her knuckles began to turn white. She waited until she found what she was looking for, a high and inside pitch. Her arms kept the bat close to her body as she swung it into the ball. Contact being made, the ball ricocheted over the head of the first baseman and dropped into a gap in right field. Rosie was anticipating the hit. She immediately bolted toward home plate at the sound of it. The ball bounced and was caught by the right fielder who immediately threw it in to the pitcher. With the ball in hand, Ian called for a time out. They were now down by one, with runners on first and third, and only one out.

The nurses were jumping and celebrating on the sidelines. They had put their faith in Karen to lead them to victory and it was paying off. Danni stood on third base clapping wildly. She winked at Mom as they celebrated with a high-five hand slap. Karen tried to calm herself, knowing full well that the game was not over yet. Anything could happen, especially with another inning to go. "Let's see what you got now, Docs," the older nurse mused. Mom leaned into Danni saying, "The top of the order is up, so be on your toes. YOU are going to be the insurance run for our win."

The young nurse nodded her head in agreement; her green eyes twinkled at the thought. "You bet, Mom!" *I can taste that breakfast already and I know just where I want to eat it, too.* Danni noticed that the color was draining out of Karen's face, "Mom, what's wrong?"

The coach's mouth dropped open and she pointed towards the mound. "No, they," she took in a breath, "they…they…wouldn't." She stammered out.

The young nurse quickly turned to see what was bothering Karen. There, walking on to the mound was Garrett Trivoli. They stood helpless as the watched Ian throw the ball with a flick of his wrist in Garrett's direction. Jamie patted Dr. McCormick on the shoulder as they walked off of the mound together. Ian headed to the bench as a young emergency medicine resident ran out to center field. Jamie adjusted her facemask into place and stooped down into the catcher's position. Garrett was mentally preparing for her new role as a pitcher.

Danni turned to look at Karen, her eyes as big as saucers. "I…I…" she started to apologize.

Karen just gritted her teeth saying, "Your 'Amazon'!"

The young nurse balled her hands into fists, bringing them down onto her hips. Taking a deep breath she tried to calm herself. *I'll get to know you better than I know myself before this year is done. You just wait, Garrett, just wait and see.* Her eyes were locked on to the tall, dark-haired surgeon.

"Batter up!" The umpire cried.

John sauntered into the batter's box. He looked directly at the surgeon as if to challenge her. He positioned himself and waited for her to make the next move.

Karen yelled at Danni, "If you hear the sound of a hit, you just put that head of yours down and run like hell for home."

The petite woman standing on third base nodded her head in acknowledgement. Determined more than ever, she positioned herself to charge at home plate at the first sound of a hit.

John watched the first pitch as it crossed the plate. It was high and inside, ball one. The next pitch was coming right through the strike zone. John quickly swung the bat in a powerful arc, impacting the ball with a loud noise. "Wham-boing." John hurriedly took off running for first base.

The young blonde nurse charged off of third base determined to capture home plate, her gaze locked onto her goal.

Garrett watched as the ball veered off from the impact where it had caused the bat to break into pieces. The momentum of her body kept her moving toward the advancing base runner in an attempt to divert a disaster. The young nurse was unaware of the danger about to descend upon her. After several long swift strides the surgeon thrust her body into the air, reaching out with her long arms to grab the small nurse from behind, twisting to pull her effectively out of the path of the rampant, odd-shaped, wooden fragments of the bat.

"Hey, what the..." the shortstop was confused. One minute she had been running toward home plate and the next she was being pushed and pulled through the air. Her vision turned skyward with a strange silhouette passing quickly in front of the clouds. *Was that a bird with no wings or what? Why was it so close?*

First Garrett landed on the ground then the bewildered body of Danni followed; the surgeon was cushioning the impact. Both women lay on the ground in a heap, dazed for a few seconds as the ballgame continued around them.

The line drive had gone straight up the middle and was easily caught by the second baseman. With Nan staying on first base, the infielder diverted his attention to third base. He knew that Danni had taken off from the base as soon as the hit was made, she had not waited to tag up after the ball was caught. The ball was thrown to the third baseman who stepped onto the bag. All eyes turned to the Umpire in anticipation of the call.

"You're out!" He yelled as his body animated the call.

Karen ran over to check on her small blonde coworker who was lying with her head on the larger woman's midsection. Rosie was a step behind in reaching the human heap on the ground. The two nurses stopped simultaneously as they overshadowed the reposed figures. Each stole a glare at the other and slowly started to chuckle. It was so cute. The two looked as though they were children who had simply gotten tired out while playing and fell asleep.

"Yep, one 'Amazon' added to that collection." Mom said under her breath.

"Danni! Doc! Are you all right?" Rosie was kneeling down next to the entwined bodies.

Danni was starting to mumble as she squinted up into the sunlight, "Did somebody get the license of that truck?"

"No truck, just me." Garrett offered. "Sorry, but I didn't want that bat to get you in the head." The surgeon was now slowly starting to release herself from the young nurse. "You hurt at all?"

The blonde rolled her head and shoulders as she sat upright. "No, I'm fine, everything feels good." Then, realizing that she had landed on top of the tall surgeon she remarked, "You make a pretty soft cushion, Doc."

The raven-haired surgeon raised her eyebrow at Danni as she dusted herself off. "You're welcome."

Garrett grasped the outstretched hand offered by the shortstop, "Thanks!"

"Same here, thanks!"

They each began to smile as one helped the other to their feet. Blue eyes met green in a gaze of appreciation for the friendship that was both offered and accepted.

"I ought to tar and feather you both for scaring the living daylights out of me." Karen snapped, trying hard not to smile. Inside she was a big softy but, for appearance's sake, she was a stern-faced ogre. After all, wasn't that the way all charge nurses were thought of?

Acting like two pouting children the dust covered figures lowered their heads saying, "Sorry, Mom."

The coach just rolled her eyes and turned to walk away. "Glad I'm not doing your laundry."

Rosie lost it. She could not hold back the laughter as she moved in to help dust off her coworkers. "Don't let her get to you. She was called Mudball in her younger days. She's just mad 'cause you didn't score, that's all." With that, all three burst into laughter.

The revelry was disturbed by the sound of electronic chirping. The cellphone clipped onto the surgeon's shorts had come to life. She retrieved it from its holder and flipped open the cover as she brought it up to her ear.

"Hello, Trivoli here." The gentle laughter still clung to her voice.

"Having a good time, I see. I hope you are throwing yourself into this, Dr. Trivoli. I'd hate to see us not having any ties to the E.R." McMurray was always thinking of how his department interacted with the rest of the hospital.

"Well, actually I seem to be doing just that, throwing myself into the game here." She chuckled as her hand brushed more dirt away from her clothing. "You might say that I'm getting down and dirty with some of the nursing staff." Her eyes began to look around, making sure that no one was listening to her conversation.

"Good then, I like when my surgeons become part of the team." There was a smug sound to his voice.

Garrett's attention was drawn by noises coming from the crowd. She began to search for the source of the raised voices and harsh words that were coming from the group of spectators at the right of home plate. Her gaze came to rest on two men who were visibly in disagreement over something. Each one was in a defensive stance, with angers now turning to rage. Shoves were exchanged as the crowd around them backed away. One of the combatants turned to leave but was abruptly spun around and a fist thrown into his neck. The man staggered slowly, dropping to his knees as he clenched at his throat and gasped for breath. The sound of a shrill, high-pitched wheezing was now evident with each intake for air. The attacker slowly stepped back. Once over the momentary shock of his actions, the man darted into the crowd to get away as the injured man slumped onto the ground. The altercation had lasted only a minute but would evidently take the victim more time than that to recover from the damage that had been inflicted to the limp figure sprawled on the grass.

"Sorry, Sir, we've got a problem here. I've got to go now." The surgeon's voice trailed off as her eyes stared into the crowd. She ended her conversation and automatically closed her cellphone and replaced it into the holder. Her body was starting to go into motion, making her way toward the site of the altercation.

Rosie was still trying to dust off her small friend when she felt the body under her hand tensing up. Danni noticed that the surgeon had gone silent and looked over at her. She followed the direction of Garrett's eyes into the crowd of spectators. The nurse saw the injured man slumping onto the grass.

"Rosie, get the medical bag." Danni yelled as she broke into a run following Garrett's lead in the direction of the injured man.

The nurse quickly pivoted towards Danni's fading voice. Seeing the crumpled body on the ground, Rosie realized the urgency and reacted. Dashing over to the bench, she grabbed the carry strap on the bright orange over stuffed bag and shouldered it. "Mom, we got a man down! We're gonna need some help."

The coach turned in Rosie's direction, throwing the line-up rooster that she had been studying into the air. "Where.... Who...?" her words were sharp. The not-so-in-shape Karen followed after the tall nurse heading into the spectators. There she could see Danni and Garrett kneeling next to a man lying on the ground. She knew by their actions what was taking place. The man was having a difficult time breathing. "Awww, shit! We can't even get away from work at the annual picnic." She took off toward them and she could hear the sound of the man's stridor growing louder with each step.

"Here's the bag. What do you need?" Rosie set the bag on the ground, unzipping it quickly.

"Do you have a trach tube?" The surgeon was removing any clothing around the upper chest area of the downed man.

"Yeah, we do!" Danni assured her. "Give her a scalpel and some Betadine, too," the blonde nurse directed Rosie as she rummaged through the bag.

Within seconds, a small bottle of Betadine was handed to Danni. She quickly opened it and poured it onto the base of the man's neck. Garrett had grabbed the offered 4x4's and wiped the disinfectant off the front of the neck. Rosie offered the surgeon a pair of sterile gloves, which she easily donned. Danni had the tracheostomy tube unpacked and was testing the cuff for leaks with a 10cc syringe as the trauma surgeon made the first incision with the disposable scalpel.

"Karen, could you move a little to the left? You're in my light." The surgeon looked up towards the sun.

"Oh, yeah! Sorry, not used to being out of the trauma rooms, Doc." The charge nurse answered, a little short of breath as she sidestepped, allowing the sunlight to illuminate the man's neck. She grabbed a piece of the discarded 4x4-gauze wrapper and the pencil from behind her ear, settling into the job of charting the aid given to the downed man. She glanced at her watch, making a note of the time on the scrap paper.

"Let's get an IV going, Ringers Lactate, please." The surgeon's eyes flicked to Rosie.

"Sure thing, Doc." The nurse laid the trach tube tie down on the patient's chest.

The surgeon handed the used scalpel to Danni in exchange for the tracheostomy tube. She paused to wipe the trickle of blood from the incision with a piece of gauze before inserting the life-saving apparatus into the new hole in the base of the patient's neck. The blonde nurse connected the syringe to the tubing and inflated the small cuff with air to secure it from dislodging. Garrett held the tube in place as small, skilled hands hastened to attach the tie-down to the tube and around the man's neck. The man was breathing on his own with no sounds of stridor. The color of the man's skin was pinking up again, attesting to the fact that the airway was secure.

"IV's in!" Rosie proclaimed, "18 gauge in the left forearm with Ringers Lactate running at a KVO rate."

"Good, now let's get a set of vital signs." The surgeon continued on with the secondary survey, searching for any other possible injuries to the downed man.

As Garrett reached to examine the torso of the man, Danni took the small cell phone from the surgeon's belt and flipped it up to Karen. "Hey, Mom! Wanna get us a ride to the hospital?"

Karen caught the phone with ease, "Yeah, guess he can't wait until the next inning is over, huh?" She fumbled slightly, trying to open the small phone. Dialing the number, 9-1-1, she waited for the dispatch operator to answer. She gave the nature of the emergency, the location and added that the site was that of the ER picnic. She assured the operator that highly trained personnel were taking care of the victim but that they needed an ambulance to get the patient to the hospital. She ended the call, flipping the phone shut. "They'll be here soon."

"BP is 146 over 92." Danni was taking the stethoscope out of her ears.

"Pulse is 112 and strong, respiration 24 and regular." Rosie looked up at Dr. Trivoli.

"No other injuries found, all bones intact and abdomen soft." Garrett looked up at her makeshift team, "Good work, everyone."

Ian McCormick had ventured over to the group to lend a hand. Seeing that all was taken care of, he stood back and watched the nearly silent exchange of glances between the Trauma Surgeon and the small, blonde nurse. Each one seemed to know what was on the mind of the other with only a word or two being spoken. It was something that he had not seen very often, especially within a few days of meeting someone. The ER attending pondered that thought and placed it into a file deep within the recesses of his mind for future reference.

The sound of the ambulance entering the picnic area was heard in the background, with its short blasts of a siren to clear a pathway up to the ballfield. Rosie replaced the equipment into the orange bag, zipping it shut. She stood up and shouldered it once more. Karen finished her charting and walked over to the paramedic exiting the driver's door. Exchanging a few words with the medics and giving up the makeshift chart in her hand, she waved at Rosie to come join her.

"Thanks for inviting me, Danni." The surgeon looked over at her friend. "You know that I'm going to have to go to the hospital with him, right?"

"Well, don't think that **I'm** handing off to a medic, Doc." Her green eyes twinkled at the thought. "I'm going with him, too."

The surgeon nodded slightly and allowed the faint hint of a smile to come to her face. She was beginning to like this spunky little blonde nurse. Maybe she should give this friendship thing a try.

The patient was loaded into the back of the ambulance with the one paramedic stepping around to the driver's door. The other turned and looked at the two women. "Ladies, if you please." He offered his hand to Garrett.

Garrett raised an eyebrow towards her hairline and met the green eyes of the nurse. Each of them let one corner of their individual mouths curl up into a smirk. Garrett turned to the paramedic, her eyes became steely blue in color, and she began to open her mouth to speak. The nurse, choosing to be a diplomat, spoke up, drawing the paramedic's attention to herself. " Thanks for the offer, but I think we can handle this ourselves," she said, forcing a smile on her face as her nose wrinkled slightly.

The paramedic shrugged his shoulders, "Have it your way then." He stepped into the back of the ambulance. Then, seating himself in the chair at the head of the stretcher, he began turning on the communication radio.

Danni scrambled up into the ambulance, her short legs stretching to reach the top step. She quickly sat down on the long crew bench opposite the patient and slid down its length, stopping at the area of the patient's chest. The surgeon was a step behind her, easily accessing the inside of the ambulance with her tall frame. She obviously had no trouble in closing the double doors at the rear of the ambulance, making sure that they were locked before she slid further up the bench. The nurse began to attach the patient to the electronic monitoring devices onboard in preparation for the ride to the hospital. Seeing that both women were seated, the paramedic signaled the driver to start the journey to the Trauma Center. "Let's make it a nice and easy ride, Pat."

The driver looked up into the rearview mirror and gave a short two-fingered half salute to her partner. "Nice and easy, gottcha!" She paused momentarily to look in the mirror, giving a quick wink and subtle nod. She was going to give the hospital people a ride that they wouldn't forget any time soon. She watched as her fellow paramedic stepped out of her line of vision and back into his seat. Putting the gear selector into drive, she slowly eased out of the grassy area of the park. A devilish grin appeared on her face as her hand slipped over several of the master control buttons on the panel to her right.

Garrett looked over to the monitoring devices, taking in all the information that they offered her about the patient. In this age of technology, these high tech luxuries were standards of care in the larger cities, thereby giving the paramedics the time and free hands to deliver more advanced life-saving care to the patient. It made her think of the times she had served on the community ambulance during her college years. It had been less than fifteen years ago, but it seemed like centuries. Back then, everything was done by hand to obtain the patient's vital signs; except for the cardiac monitor, those big and bulky LifePaks that it took one person alone to carry.

"Little bump," was heard as the driver cautioned the rear passengers. The rig was going over the curb into the parking area for the ballfield. Slowly it crawled forward, the driver's front tire being the first to descend to the asphalt lot. Each tire individually and with no steady rhythm dropped to the level of the parking lot. The constant shifting of the ambulance made for a continuing sway in the back of the rig long after the curb was gone.

The Ex-Flight Surgeon smiled as she remembered the feel of the ship under her body. It brought to mind her days in the Navy. Funny how your mind could be stimulated by something as simple as a gentle rocking motion, she mused, as she thought about her first day onboard ship. The crew had warned her that it would take a few days for her to get her sea legs. Boy, were they right! She chuckled now to herself as she remembered looking like a drunken sailor, staggering from side to side, just trying to walk across the deck that first day.

The touch of the small hand grabbing her leg interrupted Garrett's thoughts. She looked over to see Danni using all of her extremities to try to stop the swaying motion of her petite body. The nurse's head was bobbing back and forth, with a pensive look coming across her face. Small droplets of perspiration were surfacing on her upper lip and forehead. The surgeon placed her hand on to her friend's back in an attempt to steady her, "Are you all right?"

The blonde nurse mustered a slight smile and looked at the doctor, "Yeah, I just forgot how bouncy these rigs are." She swallowed several times, her eyes darting between the paramedic and the surgeon. Her hand left its position on Garrett's leg, slowly bringing it up to wipe the moisture on her upper lip. Nervously she asked "Is it getting warm in here?"

"Hey, Pat, you got the air on?" The medic looked forward into the driver's compartment.

"Yeah, on high, too. It must be cutting out again." She tapped the panel and toggled the switch on and off. "I'll have to let maintenance know about that, sorry," the driver offered. She turned her attention back to the road as a smirk came across her face.

The paramedic looked over at the women shrugging his shoulders; "Not much we can do, sorry. It won't be long 'til we are at the hospital."

The surgeon looked over at Danni, concern showing on her face. She had to get her mind off the ride. "Could you check for bleeding around the cricothyrotomy site for me and give a listen to his lungs, too. You're a little closer than I."

The nurse welcomed the tasks, anything not to think of how sick she was becoming. She looked over to the paramedic, pointing to the stethoscope around his neck, "Do you mind?"

"No, here, you're in a better position than me," taking the stethoscope from around his neck, he handed it to her. He busied himself with the notion of working on his report, while stealing glances at the young nurse as she stood leaning over the patient assessing his lung sounds. He smiled in appreciation of the loose fitting tank top that revealed breasts encased in a sports bra. As if on cue, the ambulance took a series of left and right turns causing Danni to be jostled from side to side. The medic's smile got bigger seeing the mounds of flesh bounce around, disclosing the raised nipples.

Garrett reached out to steady the nurse. A raised eyebrow over her blue eyes pinned a warning stare in the medic's direction, realizing what he was enjoying. It was hard to get a grip on the young nurse; her hands slid on Danni's skin trying to brace her sweaty body. The doctor also was beginning to perspire as she grasped onto the nurse's cloth-covered hips, tugging gently to bring her down into the seat again.

"Hang on!" The driver yelled as she slammed on the brakes, avoiding a near collision.

The ambulance lurched forward to a stop as the momentum of the human cargo continued on. Danni landed face down in the lap of the startled paramedic, with Garrett lying across the bench seat still grasping onto her elastic waist shorts.

Letting go with a string of expletives under her breath, Pat looked into the rearview mirror to check on her passengers.

"You guys okay back there?" She watched as the surgeon slowly raised her head, a stunned look coming across her face.

Garrett opened her eyes to see the exposed buttocks of the nurse delicately outlined by the iridescent thong panties only inches away from her face. Her mouth was agape. The surgeon's mind quickly began to assess the body in front of her, size, color, shape, and asymmetry all being analyzed at the same time. Blinking rapidly, she realized what had happened as she fumbled to push the shorts back over Danni's hips. This only resulted in the young nurse's head being buried deeper into the medic's lap. Finally with no further room to go, the shorts slid into place.

The small nurse brought her head upward, giving a faint smile to the medic. His eyes were bulging out, a surprised look on his face. She began to push herself up off of him saying, "Sorry about that." Her nose wrinkled up as she offered the stethoscope back to him, "You have some really sensitive balls…I mean bells there." She cringed as she attempted to get up onto her feet. "Sprague," Danni pointed to the stethoscope, " they have the best diaphragms, you never have to worry about them getting holes or wearing thin. It's the only one I ever use," she rambled on as the blush grew to a deeper shade of red by the second. "Stethoscopes, that is!"

The surgeon tapped the embarrassed nurse on the shoulder, "How did his lungs sound, Danni?" She was trying to help both her friend and the medic who was starting to hyperventilate, his gaze dropping down to his pants. "The patient, how did the lungs sound?"

"Ah…" she thought for a second, "clear bilaterally with good and equal inspirations." The nurse's color was returning to a more normal shade. She randomly surveyed the electronic monitoring, "Looks like the vitals are all within normal." The patient looked no worse for wear; after all, he had been belted in on the stretcher.

The driver had parked the ambulance and climbed into the back of the rig to examine the condition of her human cargo. There in the captain's chair at the head of the stretcher was her co-worker. She could tell that the man was going to lose it at any moment. She let her gaze drop to where he was staring. His pants where stretched to an expanding point, the zipper threatening to burst apart at any minute.

The hackles on her neck rose as she thought of the mountains of paperwork and endless explaining she was going to have to do to her superiors if this situation suddenly exploded into something even more embarrassing. Thinking quickly, she shook the paramedic's shoulder, "Hey, buddy, can you drive? I think I'm a little too shaken up to get us the last couple of blocks to the hospital." She paused. "Tim, go ahead up front and drive the rest of the way. I'll stay back here."

Slowly pulling himself up, he exited the back of the ambulance through the side door and proceeded to the driver seat. Taking in a deep breath, he released the parking brake and pulled out into the street.

The woman medic did a quick look around at the others. Seeing no injuries, she breathed a sigh of relief. Pat checked the latest vitals on the patient and lifted the phone for radio communication to the awaiting hospital, her attention no longer on her surroundings.

The two women were again resting on the bench seat. Danni nudged the surgeon with her shoulder, "Thanks for helping me out."

"No problem. It was the least that I could do." Making a silly face the surgeon deadpanned, "Silk, huh? Nice color."

Her eyes quickly cast to the ground. The nurse's voice sounded like that of a small child's, "Yeah."

It was only a few blocks to go but it was getting harder by the minute for Tim to concentrate on the road. His throbbing anatomy was causing his mind to battle for control of his actions. How easy it would be to just let his mind go where his body so desperately wanted. The driver's body subconsciously rocked back and forth in time with his pounding heart. Soon the vehicle was exaggerating his pelvic thrusting as his foot pushed and released on the gas pedal.

Sweat pouring from his brow, trying to just get them to the damn hospital. There it was, just a block away. He could see the driveway to the emergency room. Now, if he could just hold out a little longer, relief would not be far away. "Please, God, I know that I'm always asking for this, but just let me keep it up five more minutes. Please!" He implored under his breath as he pulled the ambulance to a stop. He hastily threw open the driver's door and sprinted to the rear of the ambulance.

The heat inside of the patient compartment was getting to be unbearable, with sweat just running down the three women. Pat seemed thankful for the long pants and shirt to help catch the moisture. She looked over to the two women in shorts and sleeveless shirts; they appeared to be a cross between wet T-shirt night and mud wrestling as rivers of sweat mixed with the dirt of the softball field on their skin.

The back doors swung open, allowing fresh air into the now rank-smelling compartment. The woman medic sprang out of the ambulance with clipboard in hand. The play in the springs of the ambulance continued the swaying and bouncing motion as the stretchered patient was moved into the outside air. The doctor and nurse made their way to the back door following the path of the stretcher. Danni hesitated at the doorway, holding her stomach and swallowing hard. Taking a slow deep breath, she followed the group of ill-fated caregivers into the emergency room door.

The Chief Resident, Dr. Maxine Webster, met Dr. Trivoli at the door. Relief was written all over her face when she saw that the injured patient was not one of their own.

"It appears to be a crushed and edematous larynx. We had no choice but to do a cricothyrotomy in the field. Vitals are good. Airway is now clear and patent. The patient is able to breathe on his own."

"We were able to put an 18 gauge angiocath into his left forearm area and establish a KVO line of Ringers," the drenched blonde nurse added to the report.

As they entered the Trauma Room, Tim kept the stretcher in front of himself. Moving the patient to the hospital stretcher, the paramedic appeared to be straining, his neck veins standing out, obviously pulsating. The Chief Resident leaned over saying, "You keep that up and you're going to hurt yourself."

The medic looked up to heaven and whispered back, "If only you knew." Everyone's attention now stayed with the patient as the medic backed out of the room with his ambulance stretcher. Hastily he eyed the open door of the restroom down the hallway. "I'll be right back," he mumbled to Pat.

She grabbed the clipboard, shoving it into his hands and placing it to hide the prominent mound in his pants, "Why don't you go take care of this?" Tim nodded eagerly at her. "And don't come out until your done."

With that, Tim made a beeline for the restroom glancing at his watch. Not five minutes yet and he looked up to the heavens in thanks for time to spare. Immediately his head dropped, bringing into view the growing wet spot on his uniform trousers. Well, at least he was at the doorway of the restroom when the relief came, instead of the room full of hospital personnel. Thankful for that small favor, he looked over his shoulder at Pat. He could already hear the Viagra jokes that would be circulating at the station house, all with his name associated. He continued into the room and closed the door.

Another medic team was coming down the hall. Stopping, they acknowledged the female medic, sweat dripping off her hair as she made up the stretcher. "Say, what's up with the rookie, Pat?" He motioned toward the restroom door. "Something he couldn't handle?"

She paused looking at the closed door. Placing her hands on her hips, she rolled her tongue around the inside of her mouth, "Let's just say that he got something he wasn't expecting by surprise and ah...he's having a hard time containing himself." Her voice began to chuckle with the last few words.

The two medics looked at the seasoned veteran then gave a tiny shrug to each other. "Guess you had to be there," one said to the other as they walked out of the door.

Having relayed all of the necessary information about the patient and the care that was administered until their arrival at the hospital, Danni and Garrett exited the room then leaned up against the wall in the hallway. The nurse closed her eyes, trying to keep the room from spinning. Her face started to lose its color, turning a ghastly shade of pale green. She drew in several long, deep breaths.

"Are you okay, Danni?" The voice was soft and concerned. The smartly dressed Social Worker reached out, placing her hand on the nurse's arm. Her skin felt cold and clammy. "Hey, Doc, she don't look so good."

Dr. Trivoli looked over to the young blonde nurse. Suddenly Danni gulped hard, eyes bugging out, her hand reaching for her mouth as she ran down the hall towards the restroom. Garrett followed after her.

With the perfect timing that only God could create, the restroom door opened just as the nurse reached for the doorknob. Before she knew it, the contents of her stomach were projected over the uniformed man trapped in the small room. Stunned, Tim looked at the petite blonde who was now being held by the tall, raven-haired doctor. Raising his eyes, he looked past the two women only to see Pat sliding to a stop in the hallway.

The Paramedic looked in disbelief, shaking her head and trying to stifle the laughter, "Jeez, Tim, you get it both ways, coming and going." With that out she could no longer contain the laughter. It was several minutes before she could catch her breath to speak. "I'd offer to ride you two back to the park, but I think I had better take Tim back to the station to get cleaned up."

The surgeon pulled at her shirt, wrinkling her nose at the smell. Looking at the medic, she nodded her head in agreement, "I think we could use a little clean up, too." Her eyebrow raised up into her hair.

Feeling better with each second that passed, the nurse kept offering her apologies to the young medic, "I'm really, really sorry. Honest!"

"Let's just pretend that this never happened." He muttered under his breath, "Please God, don't ever let it happen to me, again." The medic was mortified as he exited the restroom. He looked to his partner and cringed. It would take some doing to get over this.

"Well, at least we won't have to explain the wet spot on your pants," the woman medic chuckled, "no one will be able to see it through all that emesis." She grabbed his sleeve being careful not to get any on her. "I know where there is a nice, cold shower and some clean clothes waiting for you, back at the base." Pat turned to the women, "It's been real, guys." She ushered the young medic down the hallway, pushing the stretcher ahead of them. "Next time I sign up for over time, remind me of this run."

Danni turned from washing her mouth out with the water from the sink. Her eyes roved over her tall friend and then her own pathetic-looking body. "Do you think we could get a shower and some scrubs before we head back to the picnic?"

"Yeah, it sounds like a plan to me." Garrett was surprised that after all they had been through today, the nurse was still willing to spend more time with her, even after the embarrassing situations that had happened. Maybe this was what friendship was about. Being able to bare oneself to others and realizing the acceptance in even the worst of conditions by a true friend.

"Do you think the game is over by now? I wonder if we'll get back in time for dinner, I'm famished," the young blonde wore a look of concern across her face. "I wonder who won." It was a non-stop barrage of dialogue coming from the petite woman. "Say, are you up for some fireworks later tonight? I sure am."

The tall surgeon raised an eyebrow and looked in her direction, then just shook her head as they ambled together down the hall towards their respective showers.

Chapter 7

Startled eyes opened wide, trying to acquaint themselves to the darkened room, hands fumbled with the bedding to find a path to her body. The woman's mind raced with jumbled thoughts causing her breath to quicken. The adrenaline rush surged through her body with every beat of her racing heart.

Where, what, who? Desperately her mind tried to make some order out of her surroundings.

The hand finally made its way to her body, finding her midsection. The woman now focused on the hand as it slowly brushed up and down her torso, fingertips deliberately being raked over the curves of the sculptured body. She let the hand sweep a larger area, searching for the distinguishing textures that would tell her what she needed to know. The soft feel of skin followed around the generous curve where puckering flesh stood firmly into a nub. Gliding down across taut, flat muscles, the coarse texture of hair was now at her fingertips. She let out a sigh as her mind told her where she was. Her body now settled into a calming rhythm, as her mind became oriented to both self and place. Her eyelids lowered as a feeling of warmth reached over her being, touching her very soul. She allowed herself the comfort of relaxing down into the plump pillows underneath her head. She was safely floating back into the comfortable sleep that her body needed.

It seemed that sleep had been the only comfort that her mind could accept. It had been used as her refuge from the world of emotions and the few people that tried to lay claim to her body. She was safe and secure in the knowledge that she was alone. After all, it was infrequent that she awoke in the company of someone. Her college days of experiments at finding her sexual stability never brought more than a raised eyebrow to her face. She could never see what all the excitement was about. Then again, you only get out what you invest into it and her fear of hurt never allowed her to invest any more than her body. The story always ended the same way in any of her attempted relationships. The emotionless giving of her body to another in a sexual way was never enough for them. As soon as the fascination wore out, they were gone. There was nothing in her personal life that remained constant, but the feeling of desolation. Her soul was left wandering in that barren world that she had built for it, preserving it for some unknown reason while never really understanding why. She had long ago given up on love of the personal kind. It just wasn't in the hand of cards that the fates had dealt to her. Work was the only thing that gave her any fulfillment in that lonely world. Sleep was something that was best enjoyed alone and therefore, was looked forward to at the end of a day's work, especially one that did not demand her to be on-call.

It was a technique that she had developed early on during her internship days. Not only did it allow her the luxury of a good night's sleep but it kept her mind in balance. The time spent acquiring the knowledge and skills needed to be a surgeon was endless. Nights were often spent absorbing every written word from the standard textbooks and additional reading material that it soon became oblivious as to whether or not one was on-call. She had rationalized if her time were indeed her own that she would be unconfined by structure, as she had known it. Thus became the ritual of sleeping in the buff. It definitely was something that one would only find appealing in the privacy of one's own bed. The simple method had worked for her except for her time in the Navy. Being the only surgeon onboard ship meant that you were always on-call, no matter what. That was, unless you were lucky enough to get shore leave in an exotic port.

Through barely opened eyes, she could see that the golden rays of the morning's first light were creeping into the room. The golden hue stirred memories that her mind associated with the warm glow that she felt. In her state of limbo between deep sleep and the real world, images of the last few months floated around her mind. Never before had she dreamt of a person that was not related to her with such regularity. Her dreams or nightmares as she often referred to them, had always been filled with daily goals and turmoil in her struggle to achieve her career. Her lust for perfection would never allow her time to have friends or even to be friendly with any of her colleagues. She saw them only as people she had to be around to attain her self-driven goals. Her work involved human beings, but that didn't mean she had to socialize with them in order to do it and be the best. Her coldness toward them had always kept them at bay.

The dreams now were like a breath of fresh air. Air that softly swirled causing the short, blonde hair to quiver and carry the fresh scent of a beautiful summer day on it. They had been playing softball when someone in the gathered crowd had been assaulted. Images of the scene blurred as in a fast-forward motion, coming to an abrupt stop as the paramedics placed the man who was now trached on the ambulance stretcher. Her eyes cast about at the odd collection of people that had worked right along with her, never being asked or directed to do so. Each face that she looked at had shown a confident approach to the situation at hand by not letting anyone in the crowd know the severity of the man's injury. They were professionals, whether they were dressed for the part or not. It was like some surreal event before her eyes, the spirit of camaraderie wisping freely between them as it soared amongst the crowd of caregivers, until it approached her and outstretched its arms to engulf her with its embrace. She looked it coldly in the eye and for the first time noticed that it had taken on the face of a human, framed by shimmering flaxen hair.

Then in a rush of fast-forward the events whirled by until they stopped and continued at a normal pace again.

Like the return of the prodigal daughters that they were, Karen met the two lost but not forgotten picnickers with a mother's welcome. "What took you so long? Did you have to rush him into surgery? We were worried about you." Her voice was a mixture of concern and scolding both. "Hey, now give. Why the scrubs?" Her look was stern and skeptical.

Danni dropped her eyes and started to blush. Garrett was quick to come to her rescue. "We got a little dirty and thought that it would be best to clean-up before we came back, Mom. The patient was doing well when we left him." Then, by changing the subject she attempted to take the heat further off of her blonde companion. "I hope we got back in time to eat, did we?"

"Well, you're close but I guess we can find you two some burgers and corn. You know, Danni, we were just wondering where you hid that load of watermelons that you were supposed to bring."

The small blonde breathed a sigh of relief at the direction of the conversation. She winked at Karen and nudged the tall woman next to her. "Come on, Garrett, give me a hand getting them out of the car." She walked over to where her keys had been placed before the start of the softball game.

The surgeon shrugged her shoulders and followed the blonde toward the car. "Yeah, sure."

Once out of earshot of the group of assembled picnickers, the soft and gentle voice of the nurse drew Garrett's attention. "Thanks, Doc. I wasn't quite sure how I was going to answer that. I..."

"What are you thanking me for? I didn't cover anything up. I just choose to be discreet with the information that I shared. I didn't see the need for going into details. Did

you?"

"Hmmm...I guess you're right. Thanks, anyway." She smiled and opened up the trunk of the Metro. "One for you and one for me." She offered the watermelon to the surgeon, closed the trunk and side by side they headed back to the gathering.

The muscular body became accentuated as limbs stretched and retracted causing the woman to roll up on to her side. She positioned herself away from the light that was straining to enter the room through the drawn blinds covering the windows. Settling into a comfortable position, sleep again beckoned the surgeon to retreat into her dreams once more.

"Now let me handle the salesman," the young blonde was drilling the idea into Garrett's head. "Say nothing and be very indifferent to the color and model options. Are you sure this is the vehicle that you want, because once I get the deal ironed out, there will be no going back."

The surgeon looked over at her petite friend as they pulled into the dealership lot. She marveled at the all-business approach that Danni was taking in her behalf. She would have just gone in and asked how much for that one and paid the price. The young woman at her side would hear none of it when Garrett brought up the subject of purchasing a vehicle. She obviously prided herself in the fine art of haggling for a better price. What could it hurt to let her help? "Yes, I am sure."

The nurse put the gear selector into park and pulled on the hand brake, "Whatever you do, Garrett, don't let them know that you are a Physician. They'll never bargain if they know you have the money to spend." She exited the door and walked over to the passenger side of the small Geo Metro to assist the tall surgeon in climbing out of her seat. Coming up to the now-opened door, Danni offered her hand, "Remember to listen to me. If I say we go, then be ready to walk right out of there with me. We are going to have to present a unified front. If you so much as hesitate, they will know that you want the car and never come down in price."

The raven-haired woman stretched to work out the kinks of being confined in such a small space, listening intently to her friend. "All right, I trust you completely with this. Let's see what we can do."

They began walking over to the showroom door when Danni stopped, suddenly grabbing the surgeon's arm, "You did say that you wanted to pay cash, right?"

"Yes, I got the checkbook right here," she patted the back pocket of her jeans. "I'll follow your lead, my friend."

They entered the showroom and began walking around the display of vehicles. Within moments, a well-dressed, young salesman approached the women, his eye taken obviously by the petite blonde. "Is there anything that I could help you with, Ladies?" He turned to the young woman, studying her intently. "Hmm, I can see you driving that bright red Corvette convertible over there. Would you like me to get the keys and we'll take it for a test drive?"

She gave a coy smile and let go with a nervous laugh. "No, I really don't think that is my style," she said with her nose wrinkling up slightly. "I figure myself more of a sunset on the beach at Malibu." She turned to look at Garrett, "While my friend here is more of the dark, sleek trailblazing kind."

The salesman's eyes grew in size as his mind grasped the metaphor.

The surgeon leaned up against a car and watched as the young nurse played with the salesman's ego. She was ruthless in her negotiating tactics, using anything she could to make this poor man offer her the world just to be able to be close to her. The exchange of information between the two was something to be seen. Each one played the seducer in this dance of dissent, the advantage swaying between the two with each round of banter. The tall woman was completely amazed by her younger friend's ability to steadily gain the advantage in this unorthodox sales negotiation.

Danni stepped over to her silent friend as the young man retreated into an office cubicle. "So Garrett, I guess you're going to have to get some insurance before we pick up our new cars tomorrow," she said nonchalantly.

"Yeah, I guess I'll have..." the tall woman's mouth was suddenly agape, as her brain had finally registered what her young friend had implied. The surgeon's eyes widened as she gulped, "you mean, it's a done deal? I've got the Black Chevy Blazer with 4-wheel drive? Hey, you said ***our*** *new cars...plural. I thought..."*

The young woman rubbed her fingernails in a mock polishing effort against her blouse saying, "I was able to work out a better deal if I traded in the Geo and we bought two vehicles at once."

"What did...when did..." Garrett was confused. She thought she had been following the conversation; obviously she had not picked up on something. Shaking her head, she queried, "I didn't know that you were looking to buy a new car. Did I miss something here?"

"Shh! He is coming back, just play along. Okay?"

The surgeon slowly nodded her head, totally amazed at her petite friend. She was definitely going to find out what she had missed in the negotiations.

Again, she did what she was told and remained silent as the salesman joined them.

"It's all set. If we could get some financial information from the two of you, your vehicles will be ready to be picked up tomorrow at 5 P.M." He looked first at the tall, dark-haired woman then to the perky, little blonde. "If that's all right with you?" He hesitated, shifting his gaze from woman to woman, a look of apprehension on his face.

Danni smiled at the salesman, "Yes, that will be just fine."

The salesman nodded, "Now, if you follow me over to my office." He was grinning from ear to ear, proud of the deal that he had struck up with the beautiful blonde. "We'll get all the paper work out of the way."

A half-hour later, the women were walking out of the dealership headed for Danni's Geo Metro. They were brimming with enthusiasm over the deal that had just been made for the new vehicles but knew that they had to wait to discuss what had just happened until they were in the car.

Garrett was getting good at folding herself into the small car of her friend. She waited for the younger woman to settle herself into the driver's seat before asking, "So, Danni, what car did you purchase? If you don't mind me asking." She gave her friend a sidelong glance.

"A gold Chevy Malibu," she stated. "Sorry, but it will be bigger than you're used to in this one." She let out a laugh, her eyes quickly taking in the accordion-like form of her tall companion.

The surgeon started to chuckle and nodded her head carefully as it abutted the interior of the roof. "I think I could get used to that."

"What do you say we celebrate our good fortune? Milkshakes?" she asked.

The older woman suddenly turned very serious. "Danni, can I ask you something?" She looked at her friend and asked, "You didn't agree to go out with him or anything, did you?" There was a look of real concern on her face as she awaited her friend's answer.

The small blonde shot a glance over to her passenger; her eyes registered her friend's concern. "No, maybe Rosie would do something like that, but not me. I just let him flirt with me. While his mind was preoccupied with his thoughts I just out haggled him. Honest."

"Mom told me that you were good at bargaining, but I never thought..." the surgeon trailed off. She looked over at her friend, "Thanks for doing that for me, Danni." A lop-sided grin showed on her face.

"You're welcome, Garrett. I'm just glad that I could help." The nurse pulled into the parking lot of the ice cream shop. "Now, are we going to celebrate or what?"

The sound of birds chirping floated lightly on the gentle breeze that was coming in through the open window. The nights were not as hot or humid anymore and the thought of sleeping in the fresh air was so stimulating to the surgeon. She had forgotten about the noise of the birds in the early morning, after all, you didn't get that close to land on a ship or in air-conditioned hotels. Garrett made a mental note about the morning noise and open windows for the next time she had the luxury of sleeping in. But for now, she gathered her pillow and pulled it over her head to drown out the energetic noise, determined to enjoy more time in the land of Morpheus.

Blue haze from the cigarette smoke was creeping out of the doorway to the bar and gliding along the ceiling. The room appeared to be clean and orderly but somewhat aged for the faded posters that covered the walls. The light was focused low from the hanging fixtures that advertised locally brewed alcoholic beverages, each one strategically placed above a small round table. It was definitely not an upper class establishment but the nurses had assured her that it served some of the best ethnic food in the "Burgh". She followed the group of nurses as they ventured into the backroom of what they had called a typical corner bar. Soon they were seated around one of the tables with their eyes intent on finding a waitress.

"I got one!" Danni exclaimed as she motioned with her hand for the waitress in the far corner to come over to their table. Pleased with herself, she settled into her chair and waited. "So, Garrett, what do you think of the place?"

The surgeon looked startled as she was called upon to make a judgement of the atmosphere already. "Ah, I think I'll defer any comments until after the meal," her eyes wandered around the room and to each of her companions.

"Ah, come on Doc, we know that it's not the number one pick of the Yuppies across the country, but the food is really the best around." Rosie looked to her co-workers for support.

"I hate to say it, but she's right." Karen nodded her head in approval. "Do you think we'll see anybody that we know tonight?" she joked.

Rosie smiled, "Gee, Mom, why do you always have to bring up work when we go out?"

"Now, ladies, let's just have a nice time with good food and pleasant company." Danni tried to mediate the conversation, "Let's just forget about work and have some fun, shall we?"

Mom looked over at the small blonde nurse and let out a laugh, "And how do you propose that I forget work when I look at the motley crew that I'm with? Jeez, Danni, we just spent the last twelve hours together at work."

"Can I take your order?" The waitress impatiently tapped her foot as she looked from patron to patron at the table. Looking for someone in authority, she picked on Garrett, "So, what can I bring you?"

The tall woman was startled. "Ah... ah," and she looked over to Danni pleading with her eyes for help.

"Why don't we get a sampler platter of perogies for the table to start off with? The blonde nurse quickly did a visual poll of her friends, "Yes, a sampler platter of pierogies for the table. I'll have an IC Lite to drink."

"Yeah, IC Lite for me, too," Rosie nodded her head in agreement.

Karen thought for a moment then slowly motioned with her head her head and verbalized, "Same for me."

Not wanting to be an odd ball in the group of her new friends, Garrett nonchalantly looked up at the waitress saying, "Make that IC Lite all the way around."

Rosie reached out to grab at the waitress' arm. "Hey, you have that on draft, right? Then how about a pitcher of IC Lite for the table."

"Okay, let's make that four glasses with one pitcher of IC Lite and one perogies sampler." The impatient waitress hastily looked around the table. Hearing no more orders she moved away in the direction of the bar.

"Garrett, we're glad that you could join us tonight. Maybe you would like to come along when we have our next ladies night out?" The older nurse was trying to help the surgeon adjust to her new city.

"Yeah, Doc, we could go down to the Strip District that night and you could get to see the Primanti Brothers up close and personal." Rosie offered enthusiastically as she winked at Danni.

The doctors' eyebrow steadily rose up into her hairline as she stared at Rosie then at her young friend. She wondered what kind of signals she had been giving for Rosie to suggest that she would enjoy strip clubs and local Chippendale-type shows.

Seeing the look on her new friend's face, Danni quickly offered, "They have the best sandwiches there at Primante's. They have everything except the kitchen sink on them. You remember me getting the watermelons for the picnic in the Strip District, don't you, Garrett?"

The surgeon thought a moment then slowly smiled as she began to understand the true meaning of Rosie's statement. "Yeah, I think that would be fun." She stole a quick look at the blonde and thanked any god that would listen to her for such a compassionate and caring friend. The surgeon thought for a moment and realized that the word was creeping more often into her thoughts and vocabulary since she had arrived in town. It felt good to be able to call someone friend. She marveled at her circumstance and for the first time, believed that it was fate that had brought her to this place in time and with these people, no...co-workers. No, they were more than that to her for she was slowly being accepted into their extended families. That was a funny sensation for her. She hadn't had a feeling of family for many years. It was something that she never thought she would feel again. She was beginning to see that they had accepted her for herself without needing to pry into her past life. That feeling of acceptance was not lost on the raven-haired woman.

"So, have you ever eaten perogies before?" Danni offered the first choice to Garrett. "These are potato and onion, sauerkraut, and potato and cheese," she pointed to each group in the assortment on the platter. "Help yourself."

The lopsided smile spread quickly across her face as she came out of her thoughts and back into the presence of her companions, "Thanks, they look and smell so good." She chose one of each and began tasting as the others helped themselves to the appetizers. "Hey, these are really good." Her eyes were looking from one member to the other of the group and back to the stuffed dough pockets on her plate.

The friendly chuckling of the group at her comment was only emphasized by the young blonde's toast. "Here's to Garrett," she raised her glass filled with the white-foam-headed beverage. "May she find Pittsburgh and all that it holds, to be to her liking."

The group followed suit, each raising their glass in acknowledgement to the tall surgeon in their midst and saying, "To Garrett!"

Her golden complexion was now showing signs of a blush as she accepted the toast. She nodded and raised her glass touching each of theirs lightly and then the group sipped their drinks. Garrett raised her glass again, "To Pittsburgh. May I come to know all that it holds with the help of my friends." The glasses were raised and clinked. The drinking of the golden liquid ended the toast and brought about the conversation that was so much a part of human nature among the small group of friends.

She could feel her facial muscles being stretched into a smile as the haze of sleep slowly eroded from her mind. The calming memory of joyous camaraderie was the last thing that she could remember about her dream.

Blue eyes slowly opened and began to focus on her surroundings. She allowed herself to fill her mind with the atmosphere that was present in the room. The soft rays of sunlight filtered in through the edges of the blinds, straining to give the room a golden glow. It brought a rich appearance to the sparse furnishings. A bed, dresser, and nightstand with a lamp on it were the contents of the room in its entirety. It wasn't much, but she could call it home. It had been several years since she had thought of any place as home. She pondered about the last three years that she had lived from one assigned bunk to another and her clothing that was stored in metal lockers onboard ship or the duffel bag that carried them between duty stations. The woman's time spent in the Navy was just a way to pay off her debts from medical school. She had realized that it was a temporary life, a means to the end of getting herself through the necessary schooling to become the doctor that she was today.

She rolled over, staring at the ceiling. Her senses were awakening and she could vaguely make out the aroma of bacon and coffee in the air. For the first time in many years she could actually smell food being made as she climbed the stairs out of Morpheus' realm. It was a pleasant sensation that stirred her memory with thoughts of home, family and belonging. Her mind went off on a tangent as she thought about the events that had led her to this place.

"So, I guess that you haven't be able to find anything yet."

She turned in recognition of the soft voice that seemed to come from behind her. "No," shaking her head in disappointment. "I'm going to have to do something soon, I've only got a week to find someplace."

The small blonde stood next to her, balancing a tray of breakfast foods in her hands. "Mind if I join you?" She motioned to the empty seat across from the surgeon.

"Ah...no," she was clearing the table for her friend. "I'd enjoy the company." Garrett looked up at the woman who was slowly creeping into her life. "You just getting done for the night?"

"Yeah, I thought that I'd grab a quick bite to eat before I head home. It always seems more relaxing to me to have other people around than to be by myself." Danni looked

around at the other people then settled her eyes on her friend. "You know, Garrett, any place good has already been taken before September at the latest, by the college students."

The surgeon nodded in agreement, "I'm beginning to realize that now. McMurray is going to flip when I tell him that I'm going to have to live out of the call room or my car until I find a place."

There was silence between the two as each sat quietly with their own thoughts. The young nurse slowed down her rhythmic chewing as she began to contemplate her friend's plight.

Garrett raised her cup for more of the aromatic, black brew. Coffee was always her drink of choice, her get-up and keep-going source when she contemplated a problem.

Swallowing, Danni drew in a breath and offered, "I have a spare bedroom in my house." She looked up into the clear, blue eyes across from her. "You could move in with me." There, she had said it.

The surgeon shifted in her seat, her eyes wandering off into the crowded cafeteria. "No, Danni, I don't want to impose on you."

"Aw, come on, Garrett, it would be an answer to both of our problems." She searched for any kind of emotion on the surgeon's face. "You need a place to stay for the rest of your Fellowship and it would be less lonely for me around the house when I'm not working. Besides, it would be safer for the both of us." She was smug with herself for thinking of this point to help win over her friend. "It would be like a buddy system for safety's sake. My sister has been on my case to get a roommate for some time now. What do you say?" The eager look of acceptance was displayed on her face. "If it doesn't work out, it will have at least given you more time to find a decent place."

The surgeon raised her eyebrow. "Okay, I'll stop by after clinic today and take a look at the place. But if I take it, I **will** *be paying you rent." She held up her hand to prevent any further discussion from the petite woman. "I expect that you* *will be able to come up with a fair price and any house rules that I will have to follow."*

Digging into her food with a renewed zeal, Danni smiled. "Great! I'll be expecting you about 5 or so."

Garrett gave her friend a lopsided grin and nodded her head. "This just might work out. After all, who knows where I'll be working after June when this Fellowship is through? I'll see you then." She stole a look at her watch and gathered her things together. "Hey, I've got to go. I'll just make it if I leave now."

"See you later." The blonde nurse called out to her. "Have a good morning."

"Good morning!"

"Huh…" One eyelid opened, the crystal blue iris franticly trying to get a fix on the sound that seemed to be echoing in her head. There it was again, that knocking sound. The raven-haired surgeon turned her head in the direction of the sound. She could barely raise both eyelids open when the cheerful sound came again.

"Good morning, Garrett." The door opened slightly and a partial head slid into the opening. "Hey, are you awake for your special breakfast yet? You don't want to let it get cold, do you?"

The surgeon drank in the aroma of the breakfast as her mind stumbled its way into the present. "Oh, yeah, I forgot about that." She raised her hand to wave a lone finger at the door signaling that she would be there in a minute.

"Just let me get some clothes on," her voice was husky from sleep. "I'll be right out." Covers were being thrown off in disarray.

The petite blonde caught a glimpse of muscled arms and the broad expanse of shoulders connecting into a well-defined back as the covers began to reveal the emerging body of the slumbering surgeon. She hastily closed the door to assure her new roommate her privacy. She smiled to herself and raised an eyebrow at the idea that her friend felt comfortable enough to sleep in the nude.

It was the first morning since Garrett had moved into Danni's extra room that they were both off. Several months had gone by since the softball game but a bet was a bet and the surgeon was ready to collect her prize.

"Yeah, breakfast in bed," she muttered. "That's the only way to enjoy it." She sat on the edge of the bed sluggishly pulling on a T-shirt and gym shorts. *Boy, Danni, I'm so glad that you made the addition of the winner getting to pick the place to have the breakfast to that bet. Come to think of it, I believe you really thought that you were going to win.* Her senses were being teased with the inviting smells of a homemade breakfast that wafted in even stronger when the door had been opened. *I wonder,* she thought to herself, *where would you have picked to have the breakfast had your team won?* After a brief trip to the bathroom she opened her door and called out, "I'm ready for my victory breakfast now."

"Okay, I'm coming with it," the younger woman answered, picking up the tray that she had just finished arranging. Her lips curled up at the corners of her mouth as she made her way to Garrett's bedroom. "I never thought that I would be serving my 'Amazon' breakfast in bed," she muttered to herself. *Heck, I never thought that we would lose that softball game to the Physicians. Well, not until I saw her play ball*, she mused. *Who would have guessed that she had so many skills?*

The physician plumped her pillows, aligning them against the headboard of the bed. She gracefully slipped under the covers and smoothed them around her long legs, waiting for her reward.

The sound of footsteps approaching caused the raven-haired woman to look over at the door as it opened into the mutely lit room. Soft rays of sunlight fell gently on the form carrying the tray, giving it a warm golden glow. A friendly smile accompanied the hopeful look in the radiant, green eyes as she entered the room. "I hope you like scrambled eggs and bacon."

"I do if they are real," the surgeon joked. Her blues eyes looked into the green veil of the small woman's soul and immediately knew that she was blessed with a glimpse of the true spirit of this heaven-sent being. She gazed for as long as she dared before letting the lopsided grin come to her face in acknowledgement of the shared moment.

Danni sat the tray down across the surgeon's lap. Beautifully arranged were the scrambled eggs with bacon strips garnished with a sprig of parsley and a thinly sliced orange round that was cut and twisted. A glass of orange juice, a mug of coffee and two pieces of toast were positioned on the tray with the utensils. Off to one corner was a small bud vase with the most delicate pink rose and bud in it. Garrett looked over the array of food and nodded her approval. Picking up the napkin to place on her lap, the surgeon stopped and looked over at the woman watching her intently.

"What?" Garrett was puzzled by the look on her friend.

"I brought home the quarterly news bulletin from the hospital last night. Want to read it?" She smiled coyly as she rocked back and forth on the balls of her feet in anticipation.

"Something tells me that you want me to see it. Right?" The surgeon was picking up her utensils, ready to eat. She sighed knowing that she couldn't enjoy her food with those green eyes watching every bite. "Say, did you eat yet?

The eyebrows raised on the blonde with that remark. "Why, no. I've been making your breakfast." She looked so cute as she turned her head slightly as if she were shy about what she was about to reveal. "But I did make enough for me. I left mine out in the kitchen."

"Well, go bring it in here and eat with me. There's no sense in us eating by ourselves when we are both here together." Her face turned into a scowl. "I'm sure not joining you in the kitchen. No way! The bet was breakfast wherever I wanted it. And here in bed is where I intend to eat it."

It was a decree straight from Garrett's mouth and there was no way that the blonde nurse was going to refuse a chance like this. *After all, wasn't that what I was going to request if I had won the game?* Danni quickly assembled her food on another tray and briskly walked down to Garrett's room. Save for the flowers, the trays were laid out almost identical. She rounded the corner of the bed and sat down on the far side. Nestling into the extra soft pillows she placed there, she made herself comfortable before she handed the small hospital news bulletin over to the woman beside her. "You may want to start out reading the story on page three. I think you might know some of the people."

Garrett took the paper and opened it to page three. There on the bottom of the page was an article about the annual E.R. Physician/Staff softball challenge. Off to the right of it was a photograph of Danni and Garrett sprawled on top of each other in the dirt with a caption that read, "Nurse and Physician get down and dirty to save lives."

Garrett's face turned red. "I don't remember any pictures being taken, do you?"

The petite nurse shook her head. "No, I don't but obviously there was. We have the proof of that right there."

"You know," Garrett kept cocking her head from side to side to look at it better. "It's not really a bad picture of either one of us. Maybe we could get a bigger one that we could frame and put on the wall. What do you think?"

Danni nodded in agreement. "I'll see what I can do. Now let's eat."

With that said, both women started eating the food before them as they contemplated the situation in their own minds.

I may have lost that game, but I still came out a winner. Danni thought that it could get no better than to be eating breakfast in bed with her raven-haired friend. Stealing glances at the person next to her, she kept a smile stretched across her face as she devoured the food on her tray.

Garrett had won a lot of softball games in her athletic years but this one was the sweetest of them all. No trophy had been awarded or records broken, but the feelings of accomplishment and teamwork overwhelmed her. Maybe that was because she felt a growing bond with the motley crew from the hospital emergency room who had opened their arms and taken her into their world, especially one small blonde nurse in particular. Her eyes glanced over casually at the photograph in the bulletin. *Besides, we kind of look like we belong together.*

Chapter 8

The weather was beginning to cool down and the first samplings of autumn colors were settling on the trees. The young nurse thought to herself as she put her key into the lock on the door. She was finding it difficult to relax when she came home from work with the sounds of the excited children playing outside all summer. It often brought back all of the childhood memories that she cared to muster. Her mind would think back on them but something was always missing, as if she was never really a part of the activity around her but rather a spectator in the game of life. It had made her feel uneasy, even unsettled, in her life just like she was now.

There's got to be something more to life. Some other kind of... she searched for the right word, *fulfillment. Yeah, that's it.* She shrugged her shoulders dejectedly. *Maybe someday....*

The noise of the neighborhood children could only be heard now in the late afternoons and on the weekends. It had not been keeping her from sleeping since every night seemed to drain her energy with the multitude of traumas that were coming into the E.R. There were seasons to everything, including trauma. Danni had been around long enough to know that each of the weather seasons brought on a rise in a particular kind of traumatic mishap that would befall her patients. The autumn of the year brought scholastic sports injuries with it as well as the falls from trees as people were preparing for the colder winter months ahead.

She pushed open the door and made her way into the comfortable looking living area. Her tired green eyes scanned the room until they detected the out of place duffel bag next to the coffee table. A grin came to her face as she thought about the owner of the bag and what a pleasant impact she was making on the life of the young nurse. It had been years since Danni had had a roommate. The several roommates back in her college days never seemed to work out. In fact, it was those horrible experiences that had made her promise herself not to be put into those circumstances again. She shook her head in amazement at her situation now. Who would have thought that two people as different as night and day could actually be so comfortable around each other? It was as though they had known each other for as long as they had been alive or even longer.

The petite blonde shivered as a chill ran down her spine at the thought. *I guess I just had to find the right roommate,* she reflected. *Too bad I'll probably lose her after next June. She'll have a ton of offers from the really big hospitals across the country with her talents.* At that thought a melancholy mood came over her.

Danni shook her head in an effort to rid herself of the possible reality. "Take each day as it comes and don't worry about the next until it is here," she whispered, as if saying a prayer. Danni mentally chastised herself for her thoughts. She knew that her time with the tall, dark surgeon was limited. Garrett had no reason to stay here, no ties that could hold her here. *I just wish...she could see how much better I am...ah...we are for her.*

Danni remembered the numerous times that she had been left behind as someone's choice, never really finding that true allegiance of spirit in her youth. It seemed like it just followed her no matter what she did or where she went. There was always something that made her feel isolated back then. The E.R. was the first real place that she had ever felt she belonged...well, except for her Grandfather and her days spent at his cabin. He never looked at her as different or lacking, but rather with the acceptance of an unconditional love that she had grown to cherish.

She wondered if the surgeon had changed on-call nights and forgotten her familiar duffel bag this morning. She looked over at the desk for a note but found none. "Well, only one way to find out. I'll just page her," the nurse assured herself as she placed the phone call to the paging operator at the hospital. She stole a quick glance at her watch. It was 0830. Her mind tried to remember Garrett's schedule but she found it next to impossible with her lack of sleep.

"Dr. Trivoli here." The voice was strong and clear.

Startled from her thoughts, Danni spoke hesitantly. "Ah, this is Danni."

The surgeon's voice now softened in tone, "Hey, how did your night go?"

"It was busy as usual, traumas don't wait for you when you're not on-call," she said with a laugh. "Thanks for asking anyway."

"I walked right into that one, didn't I? Sorry to hear it was so busy."

"Don't worry. I'll survive. Just think, after I sleep today, I get to come in and do it all over again tonight."

"Yeah, but this time you will have a real good time. I promise."

The nurse looked surprised, "...and just why is that?"

"Well, 'cause I'll be on-call tonight instead of Rene."

"Oh, did something come up?"

"No, more like something coming out," the surgeon teased. "Renee's wife is in labor. It's their first child, so it could take a while. He called me at 5 this morning," she laughed. "Right after he called the Obstetrician."

"Oh, so that explains the duffel bag in the living room."

Her voice reflected the blank expression on her face. "I guess I was so excited for Rene and his wife that I forgot it."

"Don't worry, I'll bring it with me when I come to work this evening."

"Thanks, Danni. I appreciate that and so will everyone around me tonight. It has all my toiletries and a change of clothes. Boy, I guess I'd be in a real bind if I didn't have a roommate, huh?"

"Well, consider it part of the roommate code. Rule # 7, I think."

"And that would be...?"

"Never let your roommate go without clean clothes and toiletries for an overnight outing." The petite woman was finding it hard to keep from laughing.

"One of these days, you are going to have to show me these codes that you quote, okay? I don't believe I ever received my copy of them."

Jokingly the blonde woman stated, "You have to be a roommate for a while before they give them out." She could hear a beeping coming over the phone. "Is that you?"

Garrett looked down at the annoying sound to see a number flashing across the pager. "Yeah, I've got to answer this. I'll see you later tonight and thanks for bringing that in for me. Now go and get some sleep."

"I'll page you when I get in. Bye!"

"See you later." She hung up the phone, pausing for a moment as she considered how lucky she was.

The brisk episodes of wind seemed to make the outside world alive with the ever-floating leaves in the air. It brought to mind the small snow globe that she had received as a child on a long-forgotten day. She was amazed at how obscure that gift and the circumstances surrounding it had come to her mind. Continuing to gaze out of the window, her mind replayed the events. The cherished thoughts made her feel warm and conjured up a feeling of love.

Her parents had given the globe to her. It was their way of explaining the bond that was to fill her life. The two snowmen inside of the globe stood side-by-side, one slightly larger than the other. They had told her about an unseen bond between the two figures.

Her father shook the globe vigorously and held it out for her to see. Her mother knelt down behind her to wrap her arms around the young girl. Pointing to the snowstorm of activity inside the globe she commented that the two snowmen were held together in their strength for each other and that nothing could separate the bond they shared, not even the cold, harsh winds of the snowstorm. At times it was hard to see the figures but then, the snow would die down and there the two were, standing side by side, as if nothing had ever happened.

"Which one am I?" the small child wondered out loud. She watched as her father pointed to the larger of the two.

"This one is you."

The girl looked up to her mother for confirmation of the choice. She was hugged gently as her mother's voice whispered in her ear.

"You are the older and bigger one, my love."

A puzzled look appeared on the youngster's face as she pulled back and looked from parent to parent.

Seeing this, her father winked at her mother and motioned his head to the other room. Her mother stood and left the room only to return a moment later carrying something in her arms. Her face was radiant as she looked at her daughter and husband. She sat down on the sofa, cooing gently into the blanket that was in her arms. Hand in hand the young girl and her father crossed the room to her mother. Together, they invited her to meet her new baby brother. She could still remember the exact words as though it was yesterday.

"This is your brother, Lucas. He will need you to look out for him and help him when the storms come. Do you think you can do that?"

The young girl's eyes grew to the size of saucers at the sight of her new brother. She nodded her head and asked. "He'll be with me always...forever and forever?"

"Yes, he will," was their simultaneous reply.

"Hey, Doc! You want in on the baby pool?"

The tall woman's concentration had been broken. She turned from the window in the trauma vestibule to see John, the E.R. nurse, standing with a long sheet of computer paper in his hands. "I take it this is for Dr. Chabot's baby?"

"Yep!" The smile was big across his face. "We're splitting it 50/50 with the baby. It's only two bucks, Doc. I just need you to guess a time and sex," his eyebrows seemed to vibrate as he said the last word.

Garrett chuckled as she thought of the stories she had heard of the young male from the other nurses and Danni. She was amused that even with the pending birth, this guy would find an angle to talk about sex. "Yeah, let me in on the pool." The ends of her mouth curled upward as she considered what time the baby would arrive. "Hmmm! It's 1845 now and they are still in labor," she mused. Her face twisted with thought, "Let's say 2115."

"Sex?" The word was said with more of an implication than a question. The look of anticipation at the dual meaning and purpose of the question was written all over the man's face. John waited for her answer to be a slip in a moment of Freudian thought.

The look on his face told the surgeon that he was thinking of more than what the baby would be. She held off saying anything until the look on his face was nearing one of ecstasy. "Girl!" The answer was crisp and clear, her eyebrow arching up under her dark bangs.

His dreams had come to a grinding halt. "What?" He snapped back.

"I said, Girl...and at 2115 to be exact. That's my guess for the birth of the Chabot baby." She smiled sexily, fully aware of the agony that she was putting the nurse through. Digging into her lab coat she produced two-dollar bills.

"Here!" She shoved them into his hand, just letting her touch linger long enough to add to his sense of lost dreams. "I'll trust you to mark me down." With that she winked and moved away.

John stood there in a dazed state of mind. He quickly ran through the conversation in his head. Where had he gone wrong? It had worked several times earlier today. Why not now? He shook his head for a moment then scratched his right scalp area. Letting go with a long, drawn-out sigh, his shoulders portrayed his defeat as he lost sight of the surgeon down the crowded hallway. Shrugging it off, he turned to look for his next body of conquest.

Exchanging her street clothes for a set of trauma scrubs, Danni found herself listening to the buzz of activity coming from the other occupants in the locker room. There was definitely an aura of excitement in the staff today. She shoved her purse into her locker and closed the door. Making several tugs here and there, she straightened her hospital-issued clothing. Just as she was about to leave, the locker room door swung open by a very upset Manager.

Nan looked as though steam was ready to come out of her ears as she scanned the occupants of the Staff locker room. The professional image that she always tried to project was on the edge of a losing battle.

"All right, has anybody seen John?" Her voice was full of intensity. "I swear, if I get my hands on that little snake, he'll wish he was somewhere else." Then she sighed loudly, crossing her arms in front of her chest, her right foot tapping nervously on the tile floor. "If anyone sees him, tell him to report to me immediately." She turned and stormed back through the doorway. "See if he makes a mockery out of that child's birth just to have a reason to solicit sex from unsuspecting staff members. They're going to think that we're all like that down here in the E.R. They already associate us with the seedier side of life anyway."

The small nurse had never seen her Manager so upset. She turned to look into the faces of the staff around her.

Shrugging her shoulders she asked, "What's up with John?"

The brown-haired young aide let out a long whistle. "Glad I'm not him."

Danni looked over at Marianna, "I don't ever think that I've ever seen Nan this upset. What happened on daylight shift?"

The tall blonde nurse seated on the bench in front of the lockers finished tying her shoestring and offered, "I heard it was something to do with a doctor's wife," Lori said shyly.

Everyone's eyes riveted to the girl showing her naivete as she blushed at what she had said.

"Lori, are you sure?" Danni asked, trying to stop any wild and unfound rumors.

"Well, I think that's what I overheard," she stated insecurely.

"I don't see what all the fuss is about," Marianna shrugged her shoulders. "It's not like he keeps his steamy little affairs under wraps. Sooner or later he's bound to end up in hot water."

"Well, just remember that he is a nurse and part of our department." Danni let her gaze advance slowly from one person to the next. "You know how rumors get blown out of proportion in a place like this. Next thing you know someone will be saying that he's sleeping with me."

Everyone chuckled at the thought of Danni sleeping with John. They all knew of her complete aversion to the male nurse.

"Nah, that was last week's rumor." Rosie stood at the doorway with a large smile on her face as she watched the petite blonde's mouth drop open. Then, with a serious look, she deadpanned, "Is it really true that you made it a threesome when Garrett came home?"

The riotous sound of laughter could be heard out into the hallway. The atmosphere was now one of mirth and camaraderie. It was a running joke with the E.R. Staff. They all knew how hard John was trying to get any action out of the roommates, always resulting in a brush off or a flat refusal to acknowledge his suggestions.

"Yeah, and you are the one that probably started it," Danni shook her head with a wry smile. The small nurse made her way over to the tall, auburn- haired woman. "Hey, how was vacation? It's nice to have you back."

Rosie rolled her eyes, "Too short! That's how vacations always are." She noticed her watch and gasped, "Geez, look at the time. We better get out into the department before Nan wants our heads, too." Motioning toward the door, she turned her head to whisper so only Danni could hear, "I'll tell you later."

Standing in front of the assignment board, the petite nurse slowly looked over the list of names that would staff the E.R. tonight. It was nice to have Rosie back on shift again she thought, the regulars always worked better together. Next, she studied the list of Doctors that would be with her, Jamie for the E.R. Attending and Garrett for Trauma Fellow. Tonight was stacked in their favor. No matter what could be thrown in their direction, Danni felt comfortable that this staff was the best the hospital had to offer. A smile came slowly to her as she looked over the assignment that was hers, Trauma Nurse. She liked being in that position, especially if the Fellow was Garrett. There was just something about the two of them working together that always brought a good feeling with it. It always seemed like the patients had a better than average chance to survive when the two worked jointly. The young nurse made a mental note to check into that notion. Just what **was** their survival rate, she wondered?

Danni thought back over her days as a young graduate nurse when all things were new and wonderful. She stood in awe of the things that had changed or improved over the course of time till now. She had grown to be a well-seasoned and established veteran of the nursing profession. She had made her mark with most of the doctors who passed through this E.R. Rarely did she find one that balked at her better judgement, at least where compassion was involved. She never tried to tell a physician their job, but she was not above trying to dissuade them out of a wrong or hurtful encounter with either a patient or family members. If ever there was an advocate for the patient, it was she.

"Phssst! Danni!"

Her concentration broken, the petite nurse looked around for the source of the hushed beckoning.

"Hey! Danni, over here." The muffled voice called out.

She turned abruptly to see the door to the supply room ajar with someone peering out of the opening. Trying to get a better look at the concealed features, she moved closer to the doorway. Pausing, she looked around the hallway before entering the room. Once inside, the door was promptly closed revealing the tall, blonde-haired, male nurse. Nervously he looked out of the small window built into the door. Seeing no one approaching, John let a sigh escape, trying to calm himself.

The young nurse was weighing in her own mind about how wise of an idea it was to be in the small supply room with John. "You know that Nan is looking for you," she stated, "don't you?" She kept her distance from the man, relieved that the room was on a well-traveled hallway and that the door had an unshaded window in it that brought her into view of anyone outside of the small room.

"Yeah, I got that impression." He paused to look out of the window again.. "I just wanted to give you report."

"Is there a reason for being in this supply closet, other than you trying to avoid Nan?" *Don't even think of trying anything, Mister. I may be small, but I can be tough when I have to be.*

The man swallowed hard, shaking his head. He stammered at first, "There's… There's nothing going on in Trauma right now. Hasn't been all day in fact." He handed over the beeper to his relief. "That's why I was asking everyone if they would like to get in on making the baby pool."

"Making the baby pool?" She looked at him with raised eyebrows, her arms protectively crossing over her chest. She was leery of anything having to do in any way with sex where this man was involved. *Jeez! I knew it.*

"Come on, Danni, join in on the fun." He smiled sweetly, "I've already got Garrett pencilled in for nine fifteen..." leaning in towards the smaller nurse he confided, "...and she's hoping for a girl."

The young woman's mind was thrown into a quandary. Images of her tall, dark-haired friend in the arms of this man raced through her head. *No, Garrett would never. She hates his sexist attitude as much as I do. There has to be something that I'm missing.* She let her eyes stare directly into his, hoping for some sign to disprove what he had implied. Her mind raced with a little green-eyed monster darting recklessly around it. *Why would she choose him? She could have anyone. She could even have...* then her thoughts were interrupted.

"You know, I realize that you two are close, so why don't I just put you down for nine fifteen also. I figure, being a doctor that she will probably have the best time." He winked at the blonde woman. "You're roommates. I know that you're okay with sharing. I guess you'll want a boy, that way all your bases will be covered." His look was one of hopefulness.

Stunned, Danni blurted out, "I can't believe this. Garrett..." she reiterated, "Garrett Trivoli is going along with this?"

"Sure, why not? It's a fifty-fifty deal. Everybody can walk away happy." He smiled at her. "It makes you feel good, it makes a deposit towards the baby bank, and me," his smile broadened. "I just walk away feeling damn good about the whole thing for doing my part."

Danni was appalled at the ease with which this man talked about the intimate acts that he was suggesting to her. *He acts as if it's nothing to bring a life into the world. This is disgusting, and he wants me to do it with him and Garrett at the same time? He has finally crossed over that imaginary line of good taste, not to mention the code of roommates.*

Her eyes darted from him to the door and back again. She had all she was going to take. Danni stepped in the direction of the door, reaching for the handle. Before she could grasp the knob, the door flung open. It was Rosie.

"Have you seen John?" the well-relaxed nurse asked.

Danni's eye riveted to the tall, male nurse standing off to one side. "He's in here," she spat out.

"Great! Hey, John, put me down for nine twenty-eight and it better be a boy." The auburn-haired nurse held out her hand with two crisp dollar bills in it. "I can't believe that I made it back in time for the birth of Rene's baby." The bubbly nurse looked at her friend, "So, what time did you guess the baby's delivery would be?"

The young blonde nurse stood looking from Rosie to John and back again. Her mouth opened several times trying to form words but couldn't. Suddenly it hit her. She thought about the phone conversation with Garrett earlier that morning and remembered the duffel bag in her locker. *Jeez, he's been talking about Rene's baby. That's what the baby pool is about.* She mentally chastised herself. Nervously she gulped and reached into the back pocket of her scrub pants. Retrieving her money, she meekly held out two, rumpled dollar bills to John. Smiling weakly and scrunching up her nose she said, "Put me down for that roommate thing. Okay?"

John took the money, "Sure!" He noticed the puzzled look on Rosie's face and shrugged his shoulders as the embarrassed nurse slinked out of the room.

Karen sat at the desk studying the computer screen that listed the patient assignments. She marveled at how good it felt to have all of her girls together again. It was like having the pieces of a puzzle all in the right spots. The charge nurse had acted like a second mother for both Danni and Rosie for so long that she felt the symptoms of the "empty nest" syndrome when either one was on vacation. She smiled at the concept of enlarging her family with the addition of the strong and brilliant surgeon, Garrett Trivoli. The doctor that had started out as Danni's "Amazon" very easily became just one of the daughters in the older nurse's extended family. There was something about the interaction between the young nurse and the trauma surgeon that complemented the other. It was going to be a fine night with all of her girls here together, the older woman thought. Resigning herself to the fact that there was business to attend to, she sighed and willed her mind back to the task of running the emergency room.

"Well, Mom, did you miss me?" Rosie stood peering over the desk at the older nurse.

Putting her hand on her hip, Karen cocked her head to a side and gave the nurse an uninterested look. "I can't say that I did. You went somewhere?"

Rosie was thrown by what the older nurse said. Her mouth dropped open as she stood there. Looking over the desk at Karen, she studied the facial expression. Suddenly the tight-lipped nurse broke into laughter. It was truly a work of art the way she was able to tease and elicit the young nurse into believing that she was not missed.

"You did miss me," the nurse proclaimed. "Mom, you really know how to hurt a nurse, now don't you?"

"Miss you, Rosie, she was counting the days until you got back. She said that it was too quiet with you gone." Dr. Potter added to their conversation as she came up behind Karen. "Now, enough of this joking around." The red-haired physician was teasing both of the nurses. She winked at Rosie as she tapped the charge nurse on the shoulder.

"Hey, did I miss something?" Danni seated herself in a chair and slid it over to the desk.

"Nothing special, Dan, just these two being their normal selves," said Jamie as she pushed her glasses up on her nose and tossed her head in the direction of the other nurses at the desk. "Hey, has anyone heard how the delivery is going for Rene and his wife?"

Rosie looked down at her watch; it was almost 8 o'clock in the evening. "Yeah, how **is** that baby coming? I hope it waits for my time."

Everyone at the desk began to chuckle. Danni reached over to pick up the phone and punch in a sequence of numbers. "Maybe Dr. Trivoli will know. I'll ask her when she calls back."

"I'm glad that Garrett is covering for Rene tonight. I like it when she's on my shift. It makes the traumas more bearable." The E.R. attending physician was confiding in the small group of friends. "She'd be the one that I would want to see working on me if **I** ever ended up as a trauma."

An almost inaudible, "Me, too!" was heard coming from each of the nurses as they all stared off into space with the same thought, attesting to the skills of the capable surgeon.

Making the sign of the cross, Rosie offered a small prayer to any god that may be listening. "From our lips to your ears, please don't let any one of us ever need her skills in such a manner."

"I don't know, Rosie. I've seen your driving." The blonde nurse chuckled as she grabbed for the phone that had begun ringing. "E.R., Danni speaking."

"Hey, Danni. What can I do for you?" A familiar voice on the other end of the receiver asked.

The nurse's eyes brightened at the recognition of the voice. It was Garrett. "Don't forget that I brought in that duffel bag for you. Any word on the Chabot baby yet?"

"No, nothing yet, but I think that she's getting close. I'm betting that she has it before the end of your shift."

"Well, thanks for that non-committal update on her condition," the roommate chided.

"Hey, I don't have the stork listed as one of my office partners." The surgeon cleared her throat. "I'm into saving lives not bringing new ones into the world."

The gentle laughter coming through the phone sounded good to the nurse's ear. "Okay, Trauma Fellow Trivoli, I guess you are right. So, when are you going to pick up the duffel that you forgot at home this morning?"

The surgeon sighed. She had forgotten all about the bag and the request she had made of her roommate to bring it in with her this evening. "I'll be down in a few minutes for it. Where will I find you?"

"I'm at the front desk right now. If I'm not there, I'll be in the trauma rooms getting them ready for some action with you later."

"Okay, see you in a bit," the surgeon ended the conversation wondering why she had never allowed herself to have friends before. It was so nice to be able to rely on someone to be there when you needed a hand. She smiled silently to herself feeling an inner peace, one that she had not felt for most of her life.

The night was going to be a long one at the rate that patients trickled into the emergency room for treatment. Most of the injuries were scholastic sports related, the running injuries associated with Soccer, Football, Track and Field events. The ages and genders of the participants varied, as did the degree with which they dealt with the injuries.

The surgeon cast an eye of scrutiny over the waiting room as she made her way to the entrance of the Emergency Department. Satisfied that none of the waiting patients looked to be of a surgical nature, she breathed a sigh of relief as she thanked the gods that she had decided against a career in the practice of orthopedic medicine. One of her professors in medical school had tried to push her in that direction because of her physical stature. It was times like these she was glad that she had been so driven to achieve her goal and not be so easily dissuaded.

Opening the door to the department, she noticed the large round clock hanging on the wall. It was 2000 hours and her thoughts drifted off to her colleague Rene and his wife. *That baby has got to be a girl,* she mused, *or at least a procrastinator.* The tall woman offered a prayer for the safe delivery and good health of the baby and mother as she let her gaze wander over the nurse's station.

Sauntering up behind Rosie, Garrett lowered her voice and spoke directly into her ear. "What's the matter? Didn't you find anyone to latch onto during your vacation?"

The tall nurse's eyes widened with each word as she tried to imagine who could be so bold as to tease her. She spun in the direction of the voice, ready to give a verbal ear beating to the culprit. Seeing Garrett standing there with a lopsided grin, her eyes twinkling mischievously, the nurse gulped and quickly changed her mind. "I should have known it would be you," she accused, as she gave the surgeon's shoulder a tap.

"Hey, careful where you go tapping," the raven-haired woman raised her arms in caution. "These are the arms of a surgeon. Can't afford any injuries, you know."

Both broke into gentle laughter as the nurse shook her head in disbelief of the easy nature the surgeon was allowing her to see. It was only a few months ago on their first meeting, that the nurse was ready to throttle her for her rude and arrogant nature. Rosie made a mental note to thank Danni for not letting her do that. The 'Amazon' label that the tall nurse had given her that first day now seemed so inappropriate.

"Seriously, Rosie, it's good to have you back." Looking around quickly, Garrett asked, "Have you seen Danni? I need to get my duffel bag from her."

As if on cue, the loud shrill tones of the Trauma Team pager went off in a steady stream of beeps. "Trauma Team Page, Trauma Team Page" the crackling sound of the voice being emitted sounded of urgency. "Multiple vehicle accident, three possibly four victims transporting via helicopters with an eight minute ETA. This is a Level One Trauma Team Page."

"Guess you'll find her in the trauma room, Doc."

Garrett nodded her head, "But I won't need that duffel bag now. Looks like I'm not going to get any sleep tonight."

In unison the pair turned and headed toward the trauma rooms in the back hallway. The calm, cool demeanor of the professionals that they were was now replacing the laughter they had shared only a few minutes ago. Reaching the hallway, they quickly donned the lead aprons and trauma gowns, each mentally preparing themselves for the worse case scenario before the patients' arrival. Garrett watched from the hall as Rosie strode off into the second trauma room, the first trauma room being already manned by the petite, blonde nurse.

Scanning over the rooms, Garrett allowed her gaze to settle on Danni. The young nurse, sensing the attention, turned to look at the surgeon. The brief visual exchange between the two roommates, as they acknowledged each other, brought the slightest hint of a smile under their protective masks. It was as if they had spoken volumes of words of encouragement as the green eyes locked onto blue.

The scurry of activity in the hallway increased as the other members of the Trauma Team arrived. Quickly, Garrett sized up the available resources and began plotting a course of action. It was hectic enough when one severely traumatized patient arrived, but now she had the possibility of three or four arriving within minutes of each other. Her Chief Resident for the night was Kreger, whom she knew to be capable in the trauma setting. He was eager to learn and had demonstrated that to her time and again.

"Rob," the surgeon called out. "You take the first one. Use room # 2."

Kreger nodded in approval as he moved into the second trauma room where he positioned himself opposite Rosie. He waited patiently for the first trauma to arrive.

The Trauma Fellow thought about her next move in this game of chess. Her team tonight was not as deep as she would have liked it to be. The experience of the members was not of a surgical nature, and she pondered over the choice of team leader for the next patient. The surgeon thought of Dr. Rene Chabot up in the delivery suite, resigning herself to call upon the impending father-to-be as a very last resort. She viewed the members of her team again. The sight of a lone, red-haired, bespectacled figure came into her view. *There's my answer,* she thought. The young E.R. Attending physician would be able to handle any life-threatening emergency until one of the surgeons could break away from their own patient.

The tall surgeon moved in a path to intersect that of the E.R. Attending physician. She acknowledging her colleague with a slight nod of her head, "Dr. Potter, would you be so kind as to be team leader for patient #3?"

The physician pushed her glasses up as she grabbed one of the lead aprons that hung outside of the trauma rooms, "Don't mind if I do." She accepted the surgeon's offer as she completed her preparations for the job of team leader in the end room.

Everyone snapped into attention as the loudspeaker overhead blared out, "Trauma's in the department, Trauma's in the department." The patients started to arrive, one at a time.

"All right, people, let's do our jobs." The commanding voice of the Trauma Fellow was heard throughout the hallway.

The first patient-laden stretcher accompanied by the helicopter crew turned the corner and was met by Garrett who motioned them into the trauma room where Dr. Rob Kreger waited. Advancing speedily into the room, the Flight Medic gave a brief report of the patient's obvious injuries and vital signs. The blood-splattered and twisted body belted onto the backboard was swiftly lifted from the stretcher and placed carefully onto the gurney. Each member of the team with his or her own tasks at hand began their work. Garrett watched approvingly from the foot of the bed at the skills that the team leader was demonstrating, her smile shielded by the mask. Dr. Kreger was proving himself in her eyes. His quick assessment of the patient's airway, breathing, and circulation began to reveal the critical nature of the injuries that the patient had sustained.

"I need a chest X-ray now," Rob commanded. His eyes glanced over to the Trauma Fellow at the foot of the gurney. Garrett subtly nodded. In the brief moment that the two surgeons locked eyes, Dr. Kreger had her approval of his actions and an exchange of confidence occurred. She had inspired him from that first day in the O.R. and now he felt as though he had taken another step up on the ladder that brought him closer to being her equal.

It was obvious to all in the trauma room that the woman was seriously injured. Her breathing was labored, and the large discolored area along the middle of her chest, stretching from right shoulder to left abdomen, was a sign of significant seatbelt injury, specifically that of a restrained passenger. The chest X-ray would be a guide to the appropriate treatment.

Rob Kreger decided to utilize the precious time that he needed to see the X-ray. "Let's set up for bilateral chest tubes. Type and cross for six units of blood. Alert CT Scan that we will need to scan the head, and chest, abdomen, pelvis."

Garrett watched the electronic screen as the patient's chest X-ray appeared. Her eyes turned a steely blue color as she studied it. Her voice came out tense, "Looks like she has a lot of broken ribs and bilateral pneumothorax." She peered at the X-ray again, letting her fingers measure out something on the screen display. "The aortic knob looks pretty wide."

"That's what I was afraid of," the team leader shook his head. "What's her pressure?"

Rosie looked up at the monitor to her right. "Eighty over fifty and the heart rate is 126."

Rob's eyes snapped up to the heart monitor, "Damn, look at those irregular complexes." His eyes quickly fell back onto the chest wall that he was inserting the tube into. "Call the O.R. and tell them to have a room ready for a ruptured aorta." Kreger hurried to finish placing the tube into the left chest and secure it from falling out. Blood now escaped from the chest via the tube as it drained into the holding container. "Damn!" He bit off the word, "No time for the other side to be placed. Call the O.R. We're coming NOW."

As if on cue, the overhead speaker squawked again, "Trauma's in the Department. Trauma's in the Department."

Garrett turned to face the hallway leading from the door of the trauma rooms. Her eyes could barely see the patient through all of the bulky dressing wrapped around his head, soaked through with blood. The only thing that she was sure of was that the patient was being assisted in his respirations by the medic who was bagging him. She motioned for the crew to follow her into Trauma Room #1.

Danni looked at the stretcher with the seemingly lifeless body on it. She noted the small, chalky- white hand that stuck out from under the insulated cover that the flight crew had used to control his body temperature during the flight. Her heart sank as it always did when confronted with the ravages of trauma on a young person. Her thoughts drifted briefly to her own younger brother and she said her well-rehearsed prayer for his safekeeping. She quickly drew the soft cloth of the trauma gown sleeve across the side of her face, catching the single tear that lingered at the corner of her eye.

Danni started to reminisce about her brother. He had always been such a vivacious child, getting into trouble at the drop of a hat. It wasn't that he was bad or ill mannered; trouble just seemed to follow him around. During one incident that she recalled, Matt was with her visiting with their grandfather at his cabin. She would have been ten that year and he had just turned five. Being the older sister, she always felt responsible for him, especially when he got injured. That was the first time she could remember having to tell her parents of Matt's misfortune. He had fallen out of a tree while trying to get an egg out of a bird's nest. His grip had let go as he stretched out for it, thus resulting in a broken arm. After a while it became standard policy that Danni possessed in her hands a letter of parental consent for emergency care, just in case Matt had to be rushed to the hospital. She thought about how it felt to be in charge of her sibling, watching out over him like a mother hen. Perhaps that is when she first felt the urge to start collecting and helping lost, injured or wayward animals. It made her feel important, at least for a little while.

It was there, the first emergency room that her brother was in, that she had made her mind up to be a nurse. Not just any old nurse, but the best and most skilled one that she could possibly be. She always thought that she owed her brother a thank you for introducing her to the profession she loved and had brought so much joy to her. In fact, Danni made a mental note to thank him the next time she talked to him, but who would know when that would be. They were older now and with lives of their own. Twenty years had flown by and now they were both adults and living in separate cities. It wasn't just the years that had them growing apart, but rather Danni's choice of life at the cabin, out of the reach of all the materialistic goals that her mother tried setting for her, that had lost most of the ties of their teen years. She found the simple life with her Grandfather during the summer months to be so much more enjoyable than the loneliness of the city and her family for that matter. Her mother was always trying to push her daughters into meeting only the most promising young men from well-to-do families, thinking that only money could buy them happiness. She wanted a life of success for her daughters and, in her mind, that meant running a house and raising a family. Danni's parents had always gauged their children's success by the status that they had been lavished with on the social circuit. Unfortunately, she was never one to rise to the occasion of parties and dating with her classmates. She left that to her younger sister, Breanna, who was seen as more favorable and brilliant in their eyes with her many interested suitors, all vying to wear her on their arms. The bond of sisterhood was still between them, but each had always listened to their own hearts. Now, they all had grown up and gone there separate ways. Matt was with his friends now, all working in law firms, Breanna with her boyfriend, Marc who eventually became her husband, fathering her first child on their wedding night and Danni, mostly by herself, always wanting something that would make her feel whole.

Her mother never approved of her choice in careers, saying that it was beneath someone of her upbringing to be a servant to sick people. Her mother never understood her or her needs: to be giving and compassionate to a total stranger. That would always be a bone of contention between them. Her mother viewed this job as one without rewards or a decent income. Thinking that she needed more time to come into her own with men, her mother agreed to let her go to Nursing School but only if it were at a college that was attractive to the right elements, namely males of good breeding and money. Secretly, she feared that her mother still prayed that it would lead to her rightful position in society, by landing her a well-established physician to marry. Danni could never see herself as the arm piece of anyone, nor would she flourish being treated as someone's lesser half.

The blonde nurse was brought back from her thoughts by the voice of the woman across from her, commanding the placement of the patient. Once the stretcher was in position beside the gurney, the Trauma Fellow disconnected the bag from the tube that was securing the patient's airway. "Okay, on my count," her eyes sweeping the length of the patient for any possible problems with the move. "One, two, three!" The size of the patient was evident by the ease of the move as he was lifted on the long board over to the trauma room gurney. The mechanical act of breathing was again resumed for the patient by the respiratory therapist positioned at the head of the bed.

Extending her arm, Garrett arched her body overtop of the now patientless stretcher as she adjusted the earpieces of her stethoscope, listening for lung sounds to assure her that the breathing tube was in the proper place. She moved the sensitive device from one side of his chest to the other.

"I want a chest X-ray now," the surgeon bellowed out as she rose to her full height. Stepping back slightly to allow the flight crew to depart with their equipment, she caught the harried pace of Dr. Kreger and his patient being moved briskly through the hallway to the elevators. Their eyes met for a second. The silent exchange was acknowledged by the slightest of nods on each of their parts and each one's attention quickly returning to their own patient at hand.

Garrett moved closer to her patient as she reached over to the neck area to check for a carotid pulse. She glanced over to the tracing on the heart monitor, assuring herself that the weak pulse she felt under her fingertips was indeed the patient's and not her own. "Let's get blood hung on the rapid infuser." The surgeon's gaze riveted to the medic at the end of the bed, "What the hell happened?"

The exasperated medic snapped back, "He was a rear seat passenger, that was partially ejected through the windshield of the SUV. It was a head-on with a tractor trailer; that's what stopped him, Doc." The medic grew pale as he gulped and continued. "We had to get his head out of the truck's grille."

An eyebrow arched high under the dark hair of the tall surgeon. "Karen, get me…"

Her words were cut off. "I have Neurosurgery called already."

"Then get me a…"

"Scanner's ready and waiting, Doc." The charge nurse motioned to the CT Tech standing patiently in the hallway outside of the trauma room.

"Chest X-ray is out," the technologist informed anyone that was listening.

Garrett stepped back, "finish up on that blood work. X-ray, get me a lateral C-spine and abdomen." She turned and walked into the hallway and then over to the electronic viewer. She carefully studied the chest X-ray that was displayed on the screen. *The tube is in a good location, no apparent fractures or pneumothorax,* she pondered over the X-ray a little more. She sidestepped and looked back into the trauma room.

"Dr. Trivoli," the CT Tech tried to get her attention.

"HMMMM," she muttered as she turned her head toward the voice, while her eyes remained observant of the activity around the patient.

"Head, chest and abdomen scans?" She asked staring up at the doctor's face, full of concern.

Nodding her head in agreement Garrett responded, "Yes, but that may change after we see the head."

"Okay, Doc, whenever you're ready."

"Just give us enough time for those X-rays and we'll be right over," the surgeon glanced at the technologist who was walking back to her scanner. *It's nice to have experienced people to work with,* she thought as her eyes moved between the two nurses in her room.

The sound of the loud speaker again was heard, "Trauma's in the Department, Trauma's in the Department."

Within seconds of the announcement, a stretcher was whisked around the corner and toward the beckoning motion of the E.R. Physician in front of the third trauma room. Jamie Potter, red hair flaring out from around the mask/shield combination that she wore, stood there waiting for them to traverse the distance to her. The young doctor's attention stayed solely on the patient lying on the stretcher. Her assessment began with that initial moment. The experiences that she had gained in the few short years of being an attending in the metropolitan city hospital setting were evident. Her attention was on the patient as she absorbed the exchange of information from the medic. The cries of pain not only attested to the anguish of the patient's torment, but also assured her that his airway was patent. With the blanket removed from the lower extremities, Dr. Potter could see the evidence of trauma to the man's legs. The odd angularity of his right ankle caused her to wince at the sight of it.

"Call Ortho down," she commanded as she readied the team for the careful transfer of the injured patient. "Okay, nice and gentle now. One, two, three."

The patient was settled on the gurney, as a string of curses rolled off of his lips that would make a sailor blush. The anger and the intensity of his pain were fully realized by the facial expressions that he displayed to convey his emotions. His hands reached out as if to soothe and steady his aching limb, only to find them restrained by the belts that secured him to the long board he was lying on. Breathing hard and ragged in an effort to control his pain, the patient's right hand grasped the gloved hand of the nurse as she released the board. His terror-filled eyes shifted to lock onto hers.

"Give me something for the fucking pain, will ya? You've got drugs here."

His gaze seemed to burn a hole through the insecure nurse as she attempted to remove her hand from his grasp. Lori looked over to Jamie, her eyes silently pleading for help.

The physician leaned into the patient's line of sight to get his attention. "Sir, we know that you are in pain, just give us a minute to find out what all hurts. I need to know where you hurt first before I can give you something to take the edge off that pain." Her left hand slowly traveled down the man's arm until her gentle touch conveyed her sincerity as she held onto his hand. "Now let us do our jobs. Okay?" She asked.

With that the man's grip weakened, allowing the slender hand to withdraw. The tall, blonde nurse gently rubbed her hand, trying to forget the memory of the vice-like grip that had held onto it.

The tension and strain of the situation was evident on the faces of the Flight Crew as they made their way back down the hallway to finish their report. The short, thin medic walked over to the Trauma Fellow who was now studying the X-rays displayed on the viewer.

"Dr. Trivoli," he started as she looked over at him. "We thought you might like to know that the forth victim was DOA." He unzipped one of the cargo pockets on his nomex flight suit. Fishing out a Polaroid, he offered it to her.

Garrett accepted the picture for closer observation. Her keen, azure eyes scanned the images; quickly noting the victim pinned behind the steering wheel. The classic signs of upper body and extremity engorgement and the distinct purple discoloration of the skin along with the animated fully thrust tongue and bulging eyes screamed only one thing in her mind. "Hmmm," she nodded. "Looks like traumatic asphyxiation, wouldn't you say?" Her eyes were raised to his in question as she handed the Polaroid back to him.

"Yeah, I've read about it but never saw it before," his tone was sober. "Maybe, I hoped that I never would," his voice trailing off to a whisper.

The surgeon reached out and touched his shoulder; "None of us should ever have to." Her voice was reassuring, "Thank you for sharing that with me." She looked directly into his eyes saying, "If you need to talk about it…."

Closing his eyes, he simply nodded and slowly moved away from her, letting her hand slowly slide off of him. "Thanks, Doc," he whispered.

"Dr. Trivoli, we're ready to go," Danni informed her as the entourage of medical personnel slowly rounded the corner of the trauma room into the hallway, escorting the gurney.

"Yeah, I'm with you." The tall woman pulled herself away from her thoughts that the Polaroid had brought to her mind and once again assumed her role as Trauma Fellow. "Let's see what's going on in that head." She turned and popped her head into the nearly vacant trauma room, "Karen, when Neuro..."

"When Neurosurgery shows, I'll send them to CT," the older nurse cut her off. "Now, go do your job and I'll take care of mine," she said teasingly, and winked at the surgeon.

Letting a lopsided grin show, the raven-haired woman stated, "Mom, you're the best." *I guess these nurses are quick learners. They seem to anticipate my thoughts before I can voice them.* She was relieved that they had followed her way and not fought her demands. *I wonder if they know that they joined my team?* She smirked at the thought of how McMurray would view this when he reviewed the tapes.

The painful screams that she heard coming from behind her made her think of Dr. Potter and the third trauma patient. She made quick, mental note to check on them as soon as she reviewed the head scan on her patient. Then using her long strides, she made off to the CT Scanner and her patient.

The air was thick with tension as the surgical team fought desperately to save the life of the woman lying on the table. The heat from the bright lights illuminating the field of operation and the anxiety of the surgeon were enough to bring a sheen of perspiration to his brow. He turned his head to the circulating nurse who hastily wiped his forehead free of the gathering sweat. His eyes never left his patient as his nimble fingers deftly worked to suture the jagged tear through the woman's aorta. The flap of vessel was evidence to the traumatic nature of the head-on crash. It was a typical injury in an abrupt deceleration scenario. The effect on the large vessel that had been filled with blood during the sudden impact was similar to that of a balloon filled with water. The continued kinetic energy in the forward motion had nowhere to go once the outside casing was halted, thus resulting in enough force to cause the walls to give way at their weakest points.

Kreger thought about what might be able to tip the scales into his patient's favor. His mind trying to emulate that of his mentor, Trauma Fellow Garrett Trivoli, he considered all of the tricks she had taught him that could possibly help in the circumstance that he now found himself. He did not want to fail his patient and let down the trust that was placed into his hands by the Trauma Fellow.

"Damn!" His voice was sharp. "This flap is so flimsy, it just continues to tear the more I try to repair it." He blinked several times in succession as though trying to clear his view. "It looks like the weakened area is extending up into the carotid artery as it branches off the aorta."

What had started as only a small tear was now becoming more unmanageable as the seconds ticked on. He was losing precious time that would ultimately result in the demise of his patient.

Kerger bit at his lip nervously. His decision was being made for him and there was nothing he could do about it. Clearing his throat, he barked out, "Page Dr. Trivoli to the O.R., STAT!"

The small form lay silent on the cradle of the CT Scanner. The only sounds coming from the room were that of the rhythmic cycling of the mechanical ventilator that forced air into his lungs and the whirring of the circling X-ray tube within the gantry of the scanner itself. The saying that "a picture is worth a thousand words" came to mind as Danni watched the grim faces of the doctors. The CT Technologist shifted her position to reach for some paperwork allowing the petite nurse to maneuver herself to get a look at the images that were appearing on the monitor screen. The nurse had seen enough scans in her career to know something was definitely wrong. The image that she saw on the screen was nothing like what she was used to seeing. Her eyes traveled to the patient's electronic monitoring devices as she jotted down their readings onto the patient flow sheet, making sure to note the time. It was 2047.

Michelle Payo, the Neurosurgery resident on-call for the night had arrived and was watching the last few images come up on the screen. She was of medium height and her pregnancy was obvious, compared with her rather small body frame, her white lab coat hanging open around the protruding belly. Shaking her short brown hair, she let out a deep sigh. "May I see?" She asked as she pointed to the screen.

"Sure, Doc," the CT Technologist began cueing up the first image and slowly ran through them all.

"Well, what do you think, Michelle?" The surgeon was sure that the answer would not be good.

Looking up from the screen and out to the patient, the Neurosurgeon asked, "Did you give him any paralytics?"

"No, he hasn't had any."

"How about the initial neuro exam, any stimulus?"

"No, nothing, not even decorticate posturing." The surgeon's voice reflected the severity of the young man's injuries.

Pursing her lips as she gently patted her pregnant belly, the small woman sighed deeply. "I don't know of anything that we could do. It already appears that he has sustained an anoxic injury to the brain." She shifted her weight to the other foot, "With the extent of the skull fractures, I'd have to say that the only thing to do now is see if the next of kin will consent for him to be a donor." The young woman looked up to the tall Trauma Fellow; "There is really no hope for this kind of injury. The respirator will keep his body alive, but the brain will have no function whatsoever. I'd be pretty certain to say that he is brain dead."

Garrett looked away. Her face took on a disgusted scowl as she sucked in on her lips. Letting out a soft, snorting sound, she shook her head. "Scan his chest and abdomen. Let's see if there is anything going on with the vital organs."

The petite blonde nurse wrinkled her nose, giving her a questioning look.

"Have the Social Worker find out if there is any family and contact C.O.R.E." The surgeon was disappointed, "There is nothing more we can do for him, Danni," she offered, "but maybe we can help someone else."

The nurse blinked her eyes to catch the small tear that was forming, "All right, I'll let the Social Worker know. I think that I saw Alex earlier tonight." She turned to the right and reached for the wall phone.

"Dr. Trivoli, Please report to O.R. #1 STAT!" The loud speaker blared, paused, and repeated again.

Garrett's attention was grabbed as though someone had reached out and vigorously shook her without any warning. Almost immediately her pocket came to life with the sound of the pager beeping. She looked down and studied the number that was imprinted across the display screen. She looked over to Danni, "It's the O.R., call them and tell them I'm on my way." The tall, athletic body of the surgeon was being propelled though the doorway by her long, powerful legs even as she was speaking. She quickly made her way to the stairwell and taking the steps two at a time, she pushed herself up the two flights of stairs. The metal door at the landing slammed open as she launched herself down the hall in the direction of the O.R. entrance. Nearing the doorway, she peeled off her trauma gown as she sidestepped her way past an X-ray Tech with a slow moving portable machine. Yanking the right side half of the double doors, she entered into the main desk area. She slowed only long enough to grab a blue hair bonnet and shoe covers, while dropping the lead apron to the floor. Snapping the bonnet down over her shoulder length hair with one hand, she leaned on the desk for balance. "What's going on?" Her words were punctuated by heavy breathing. She leaned over and slid her foot inside of the covers. The older woman at the desk looked up only to see the back of the surgeon as she vaulted down the hall.

Through the window in the door, she could see the scurry of activity in the operating suite. Hastily she picked up a facemask and placing it on her face, pinched the small metal piece over the bridge of her nose. Pushing open the doors, she entered the surgical arena. The circulating nurse was holding a gown that Garrett thrust her arms through, then spun around in, so as to have the gown tied shut by the nurse while maintaining sterility. The surgeon reached for the pair of sterile gloves that had been laid out for her use as the nurse swiftly tied the loose ends of the facemask to secure it in place.

Striding over to the operating table, the surgeon snapped her gloves into place. "What's going on, Rob? What can I do to help?"

"She's bleeding out." His speech was fast and frank. "For every piece of the tear that I get sewn up, another area rips more." He quickly glanced over at Garrett. "I'm losing ground here," he confided.

"Hemostats! Suture!" The instruments were promptly placed into her outstretched hands as she entered into the life or death battle allied with Dr. Kreger.

The screams of anguish heard earlier were now turning into whimpers of discomfort as the medication began to take effect. Having thoroughly examined the man and ascertaining that his only apparent injuries were indeed the multiple fracture sights of both his legs, Dr. Potter felt obligated to ease the patient's pain. A thought brought a smile to the freckled face of the physician, ***'I wonder if I gave him that to relieve his pain or more to relieve the pain we are experiencing from listening to his screaming.'*** Much to the pleasure of all concerned, the medication was doing its job. A quiet peace was once again coming to the trauma hallway and the staff that still remained with the patient in Trauma Room #3.

Jamie stepped outside of the room to look at the X-rays that had already been done. She cued the viewer and began studying the routine films that were part of the trauma protocol. Having seen nothing to alarm or concern her on the cervical spine, chest or abdomen films, she felt good about her choice in pain control for the patient. Her job was just about done, and now it would clearly be an orthopedic case. Still, with the severity of the accident and knowing the fact that one person had been killed at the scene, she thought that it would be best to at least get a CT Scan of his abdomen, just to be on the safe side. She pondered only momentarily the wrath that she might incur from the tall, gorgeous, and demanding trauma surgeon if she didn't.

"Lori, call CT and tell them we'll need an abdomen scan for this patient," she said, leaning into the doorway of the trauma room.

"Sure thing, Dr. Potter." The insecure nurse was beginning to regain her composure. Her shyness was something that she had had trouble with all of her life. She loved being a nurse, but felt at times somewhat overwhelmed by the emotional demands of her patients. Her conservatively styled blonde hair and tall shapely body made her look older, but when she smiled, the illusion was gone in an instant as the youthful appearance of braces glistened in the light.

Jamie was now watching as the X-rays of the lower extremities were becoming available. Shaking her head at the multiple fractures that were very evident on the X-rays, she advised the young nurse, "It may be a while until Ortho has all of the splinting done. You may want to let them know in CT."

The nurse reached for the phone and did the doctor's bidding. Hanging up, she informed the physician, "They're just finishing up that second trauma now, so whenever we're ready will be all right with them."

"Good, and here comes Ortho now." She waited for the tall, lanky form to come closer to her before addressing him. "Hi! I don't believe we've met," she held out her hand to him.

His large hand was gentle at the touch of the handshake. "I'm Dr. Armando Selep, I'm covering for your regulars tonight." His eyes held her in his gaze.

"Jamie Potter, E.R. Attending." She smiled pleasantly at him, her hand lingering in his grasp.

The young nurse looked at the two, feeling embarrassed by her intrusion on the intimate moment. She nervously coughed, trying to bring them back to the realization of where they were. "Dr. Potter," Lori spoke softly. "CT Scan is waiting for the patient," she reminded her.

Surprised at her reactions to the tall dark-haired man, the physician could feel her face begin to flush. Trying as hard as she might to subdue her inner feelings, she quickly started rattling off a brief report of the patient's mode of trauma and her findings. "Thirty year old male, unrestrained driver of a tractor trailer that was involved in a head-on crash with an SUV. Obvious deformity to the right leg and ankle, complaining of severe pain in both lower extremities." She pointed to the viewer where the X-rays of his legs were displayed. Clearing her throat, she continued. "There was a reported death in the SUV. We would like to have those legs splinted before he goes to CT Scan to check out his abdomen."

The tall doctor stood with his hand rubbing his face and the barely visible growth of beard, studying the X-rays. Blinking several times as he compared one view of the leg to the other, he began to shake his head. "Those are some pretty bad fractures." He paused and looked into the trauma room at the patient. "Seems pretty quiet for the likes of **those** injuries," he mused.

"Well, you should have been here when he first came in." Jamie chuckled, "We snowed him pretty good. He was disturbing the entire E.R. with his screaming."

"Yeah, I bet." Armando smiled down at the physician. "Let me get started splinting then," he said. "While he's in the scanner, I'll notify my Attending. I'm sure he'll want to take him to the O.R. tonight."

"All right, then." The red-haired doctor nodded in agreement. Adjusting her glasses on her face, Jamie watched as the orthopedic surgeon assembled his supplies to splint the legs.

The long, eerie-toned note was all that was heard, as the surgical team stood transfixed to the electronic monitoring devices. Garrett sniffed as she looked over to the large clock on the wall, "Time of death, 2113."

The Anesthesiologist slowly turned off his monitoring devices. Suddenly the room became deafeningly loud with the silence.

Stepping back from the lifeless body on the operating table, she snapped her gloves as she ripped them off of her hands and threw them into the waste bucket on the floor. Next, she pulled at the mask on her face, ripping the ties with a strong yank of her hand. She spat into the waste bucket, using the mask to wipe her mouth and discarded it. Death always left a bad taste in her mouth, even if there was nothing she could do to prevent it.

Rob Kreger let his eyes fall into the gaping chest cavity that had been his center of attention for the last hour or so. He reviewed his actions as he questioned the reason for his patient's outcome. Perhaps he should have called sooner for the talented surgeon to assist him. Would that have made a difference? Had he allowed himself to become arrogant in thinking that he could do the job himself? Alone?

Slowly his hands busied themselves with the task of removing the rib spreaders that were used to gain access to the chest cavity and its contents. The draping was being removed from the face of the woman and he felt compelled to look at her features. He studied them intently, so as to burn them into his memory. This was the face of his first patient lost during an operation that he would call to mind during the rest of his career. He owed it to her and to all the patients he would treat in his lifetime. The lesson he learned and would remember from this day forward was to keep his ego in check, never to hesitate to ask for help, not just for him, but also for his patient.

Long dark hair moved gently with the breeze as the tall form stood staring at the landing sight for the helicopter. The marker lights in the darkening twilight hours illuminated the helipad. Her back faced the trauma doors to the emergency area of the hospital, but she could somehow feel the presence of another human walking towards her. Sensing no danger, she remained absorbed in her thoughts.

The small hand reached out to touch her arm. "Gar…I mean, Dr. Trivoli, Mom told me you were out here," Danni used her most comforting tone of voice.

"You were right the first time. I don't feel much like a doctor right about now." She nodded absent-mindedly to herself.

"I'm sorry."

"No need to be, Danni." The surgeon turned to face her friend. "Some things just happen. We all tried the best we could." She shrugged her shoulders, "It just wasn't meant to be."

Danni looked off into the distance, "I know that, but it's hard knowing that you lost two from the same vehicle."

The surgeon cleared her throat, "Ah… actually it was all three that were in the same vehicle."

Danni's head snapped around to peer into the blue eyes of her roommate, "What do you mean, all three?"

"The driver of the vehicle was the one dead on the scene. The last flight crew showed me a Polaroid of him." She licked her teeth, making a disatisfied expression, "It looked like a classic traumatic asphyxiation. He was dead before he knew what hit him."

"Oh," was all that the petite woman said, nodding her head knowingly. Her gaze fell to the ground as she stood there, pondering the results of the catastrophic accident. Her gentle nature was always thinking about the victim or the effect the trauma would have on the survivors. She closed her eyes and prayed for the strength to carry her through until morning when her shift would end.

Garrett broke the silence, "Any word yet on family?"

"No, but Alex said that she would let us know."

"She'll notify C.O.R.E. then, when she finds out?" Garrett looked away.

The nurse nodded, "Yes, she thought that would be best, just in case there is no one with the authority to deal with the situation."

"Good," the surgeon nodded. "Maybe we'll be able to salvage some good out of the tragedy and give someone a second chance with organ donation."

They stood there for several moments, each absorbed in their own thoughts. The air was turning colder and brought a shiver to the small blonde nurse. Danni rubbed her arms to get warm. "I'm going back in." She turned, taking several steps, then stopped abruptly, "Garrett?"

"Hmmm?"

"Would you like your duffel bag now, before we get too busy again?"

"Yeah, I guess I could use something to freshen up with right about now," her voice was teasing as she sniffed at her scrub top. "Whew!"

This action brought a smile to both of them as they headed back inside. The two roommates nudging one another with their elbows and giggling as they walked along was letting the tension of the last few hours ease on both of them. For a minute or two, they were able to act as though they still possessed the innocence of childhood.

Entering the E.R., the two were meet by an agitated charge nurse. "Oh, so there you are!" The older nurse shook her finger at the pair. "I've been looking all over for you two. You're the hardest people I know of to find when there is good news."

Danni and Garrett exchanged glances with each other, shrugging their shoulders in unison, and then slowly both looked down at the pagers on their clothing.

"Gee, Mom, it's not like you couldn't page us or something," Danni teased.

"Yeah, there for a while tonight, you were reading my thoughts like you were inside of my head. What happened?" An eyebrow raised as Garrett looked in her direction.

"Well, next time, short of setting off those darn trauma pagers again, I just might do that," she was becoming flustered.

"So, what's the good news, Mom?" The petite nurse tried to help Karen get back on track with her thoughts.

"Ah…oh! Yeah, you won the baby pool."

"Which one of us, Mom?" She glanced up at Garrett. "We both guessed nine fifteen."

"Well apparently you both won, Rene and his wife had twins; a girl at nine sixteen and a boy at nine eighteen. Surprised everyone including themselves," she chuckled. "They finally took her for a C-section. Seems you two were the closest to the actual times."

Danni looked up to the surgeon, noticing the lopsided grin on her face, "Well, how about that, roommate?" She winked. "We make a pretty good team, you and I," and her soft chuckle became infectious for all three.

The surgeon was taken by surprise at her permutation into a team player, even if that team only consisted of two. She chuckled along with them, but her laugh was more on the side of nervousness at this odd sensation that was binding her to the small nurse.

Garrett thought about the time of delivery. "You know, it only seems fitting that those babies be born around that time."

"Why is that?" Danni had a half laugh sound to her voice.

"I pronounced the woman in the O.R. at 2113." The surgeon's voice was somber with the reflection.

"Oh, I see." There was silence for a moment of reverent thought before the young nurse spoke. "You know, they say that when one spirit leaves this earth, another one comes to take its place." She shrugged her shoulders. "Life goes on."

"Hmm…interesting thought, Danni. Interesting in a lot of ways." Garrett pondered that concept for a moment. *So who do you suppose is to take your place, Lucas? Would I even know them if they were standing right next to me?* She closed her eyes to still her own lingering pain. *This is too painful to think about right now.* Sighing, she gave her had a subtle shake and dropped the whole idea. She'd have to give this idea more thought when she had the time. Right now, she was just too tired to put forth the effort.

Chapter 9

The aroma of the strongly brewed coffee acted like a homing device to the sleep-deprived surgeon as she made her way to the Doctors' Lounge, adjacent to the O.R. locker room. She knew this was the most powerful coffee within the entire complex and she was desperate to stay awake after the long night of monitoring the critically injured trauma patient. It was close to noon and still there was no word of any family members or next of kin for her patient. She hated to think that there was no one in the world that would care whether or not the young man even existed. She made a mental note to get in touch with the Social Worker and see if there was any progress in the case, but first she would get her cup of caffeine-enriched coffee. Her mind drifted to thoughts of her bed at Danni's house and she found herself envying the nurse for only having to work twelve-hour shifts, unlike the thirty-six hours that her night of call held for her. *She'll be fast asleep by now.* She looked at her watch. It registered as eleven hundred hours in her military mind.

She reached out for the door handle only to have it swing open towards her. Her forward momentum halted as she saw a haggard figure before her. The rumpled and unshaven man was none other than her colleague, Rene Chabot. With his eyelids barely open, he tilted his head back to view the obstacle in front of him. After a long moment, he recognized the tall, raven-haired figure as his replacement for the trauma team the previous day. Too tired to speak he grinned from ear to ear, the way all new fathers do, and held up his hand showing two fingers raised side by side. His nervous giggle was all that was needed to realize that the arrival of twins had taken him by surprise also. So much for modern medicine and being able to predict with any certainty the number and gender of the fetuses, but then again, it may have been their choice not to know ahead of time.

Garrett found herself grinning at the man, nodding her head approvingly. Reaching out, she patted his shoulder, "Everybody is healthy?" The man's head nodded in affirmation. "If your wife is resting comfortably upstairs, Rene, what are you still doing here?"

"I just don't want to leave them. My family," his smile grew in size. "I have a family to watch over." He grasped her free hand with one of his, while placing the other around her waist. Suddenly he was humming a lullaby and dancing with her right in the hallway. For his tired looking condition, he was light on his feet, moving them swiftly around the corridor. When his humming stopped, he bowed to his dance partner. Looking directly into her eyes, Rene spoke. "You have no idea what it's like having an instant family. My world is finally complete and full of joy. How can I ever thank you for allowing me the pleasure of seeing my children being born into the world?"

Her mind flashed memories of the last time she had seen her parents and a tear began to form in her eyes. Struggling to keep the tears at bay, she leaned toward the man while whispering into his ear. "Don't let a day go by without telling them that you love them, Rene. That'll be enough payment for me." She moved back from him physically while her eyes continued to convey her message.

The new father could sense that her words were spoken from the realm of her heart and he let her know that he would indeed heed them. "I will, Garrett. Not a day will go by without all the members of my family knowing the love that I have for them."

She coughed, trying to clear her throat, "Now you better get some sleep so that you can see them grow big and strong." She stepped back to allow him to pass by. Advancing once again to the door and opening it she could hear him call out to her, "Thanks, again."

Her eyes quickly checked the small lounge for signs of any inhabitants. Seeing no one, the emotionally drained woman stood with her head buried in her hands. It wasn't often that she felt like this, but with the lack of sleep and the loss of several patients in the last 24 hours it could be expected. Her thoughts turned to Rene and his new family as she offered a prayer to keep them safe from any misfortune the world could throw at them. She reached out, taking a Styrofoam cup in her hand.

Damn you and your babies Rene. You should have been the one last night to get those traumas. Her hand flexed then contracted sharply, smashing the cup in her hand. *Why me? I've already had my fill.*

Her eyes narrowed and she crumpled the cup even more before she threw it at the trashcan next to the table. She walked away from the table and stood staring at the ceiling, trying to calm herself. Finally pulling herself together, she returned to the table with the coffee urn and filled another cup. Coddling it in her hands, she made her way over to the soft, leather couch. Sipping the black, unsweetened coffee, she tried to bring her mind back to the problems at hand. Perhaps if she closed her eyes, the task would become easier. Much to her surprise, all it brought to her was some very needed sleep. She allowed herself to go willingly into its arms as the dreams of a much simpler life overtook her.

"I love you," the woman bent down and kissed the young boy on the cheek. She adjusted his sweater and winked at him. Then, turning to her daughter, "and you, young lady, watch after your brother. He's the only one you have," she teased. The woman tucked a strand of loose hair behind her

daughter's ear. "I love you, too!" She leaned in to kiss the girl's forehead. "Now, off to school, the both of you."

"Come on," the girl coaxed. "Keep up with me or we'll be late again like yesterday." The pace was already being set as her long legs carried her down the walk. The small boy struggled in double time to match her strides.

"Garrett! Garrett! You keep up that pace and you'll end up carrying him most of the way," her mother cautioned.

The tall child turned around with a lopsided grin at the words her mother had spoken. "I'm strong, I can carry him. I'll never leave him behind."

The woman shook her head in delight at the playful nature of her daughter. "Garrett, wait up for him. Garrett, do you hear me?"

"Garrett, wake up." Dr. Kreger spoke again, "Garrett, do you hear me?"

One heavy eyelid slid open to the harsh assault of the light that filled the room. Her mind had to be playing tricks on her. She could have sworn that her mother was calling out her name.

"Garrett!" Rob's voice became a little harsher as he tried to rouse the woman out of sleep. "We've been looking all over for you. We have some family members that want to see you." His hand gently shook her arm. "Garrett!" Deciding that it was time for drastic measures, he yelled and nudged her violently, **"Your patient is crashing!"**

Dark eyebrows shot sky high on her forehead pulling her eyelids wide open, revealing intense blue orbs. With a move as swift as a bolt of lightning, she was standing next to him, her hand grasping the material of his lab coat. "Which one?" The adrenaline pumping at maximum capacity through her body was like that of a caged panther waiting for the gate to open.

He now rethought his decision. By the look of intensity on the tall surgeon's face, Rob knew immediately that he had chosen the wrong manner with which to awaken the sleeping woman. This woman was definitely someone who could scare the living daylights out of the most virile of men. He closed his eyes and gulped as he made a mental note to check his shorts for soilage after he calmed her down. That was, **if** he could calm her down. Wincing, he readied himself for her wrath. "No one. No one is crashing," he uttered.

The surging electric blue of her eyes searched deep into the windows of his soul. "What do you mean, no one is crashing? You just said that my patient…"

"I lied!" He was unable to return her gaze. "I had to get you to wake up. I'm sorry but nothing else seemed to arouse you." He sighed as her hold released. "I'll know better next time." He assured her. "It's just that we have been trying to get a hold of you for a while now."

Garrett looked down at her pager. She must have slept through the pages, and by the number of them she guessed that it had been a long time that she had been dead to the world. "I must have fallen asleep." She remembered vaguely sipping on the cup of coffee. She looked down on the nearly full cup of black coffee waiting for her return on the small table next to the couch where she had placed it. "So what's up that you've been trying to reach me?" She tried to wipe the sleepiness from her tired eyes as she twisted and turned her neck as if to work a kink out of it.

"The Social Worker was finally able to get in touch with a family member for that young boy from last night." Rob bit at his lip thoughtfully. "I knew that you would want to be the one to talk with them."

The somber look on her face and the slight nod of her head was enough of a reply for Dr. Kreger. "They should be here any minute. I told them that we would meet them in the Family Room outside of the Neuro-ICU."

She glanced at her watch. "Let me just splash some water on my face and I'll meet you there in a few minutes." Garrett turned to move toward the locker room area.

"I am sorry that I had to wake you like that." Rob felt compelled to apologize again. "I'll see you up there in a few."

"It's okay, Rob, you did what you had to do. Given the situation, I would have done the same thing. Don't ever apologize if it helps the patient."

He looked at her funny saying, "But how can we help the patient? He's brain dead."

Her eyes once again pinned him. "We'll help the patient through the family's understanding and coming to terms with the loss. Sometimes that is all you can do."

Kreger accepted her words, knowing that she was right. Dealing with the family could very well be considered part of the healing process. It was times like these that he thought about how very little he did know, but he was glad to have been placed in the presence of such a remarkable teacher. His head nodded in agreement. "I'll see you upstairs," he said as he made his way to the door.

****

The hallway outside of the Neuro-ICU was silent reflecting the serious nature of the area. Most patients here were immediately post-operative, remaining only a day or two until they would be transferred to a regular Neurosurgical floor. Then, there were the others. Those who were not well enough to be weaned off of a ventilator or those who would soon die from the total lack of brain function. The color scheme of the area reflected the neutrality. It was an area that could run the gamut of emotions from extreme happiness to that of severe depression all hinging on the words spoken.

The Social Worker stood waiting in the hall, her brown unruly hair constantly getting in her way. It was not long enough to put behind her ears and too long not to fall into her vision or face with each movement of her head. The suit that she wore gave her an air of business as she presented herself, standing to her full five foot seven inches of height. She glanced at her watch only to check on the time. It was 3:58 P.M. and once again her hopes were rising with the sound of the elevator's alerting ding.

With the doors opening slowly, the figure of a man departing the elevator became apparent. The crisp white lab coat had a military look to it with the finely detailed starched lines running down the sleeves. He checked his lapel to assure that his I.D. was in place. In his hand he carried a manila envelope full of forms that would be needed for the family's signature, if they would decide to donate the usable organs for transplantation. He slowed as he came upon the Social Worker and introduced himself. "Hi! My name is Mark Crawford. I'm with C.O.R.E." He offered her his hand.

"Alexia," she shook his hand. "I'm the Social Worker. Nice to meet you, Mr. Crawford." She smiled at him to conceal the eerie feeling she always got when meeting with anyone from the Organ Recovery Team. It always made her think she was dealing with someone out of a Frankenstein novel, the grave robbers to be truthful. Alexia never gave these people her full name, nor would she let them call her by the name that her friends did. It was her mechanism of distancing herself from them.

He smiled courteously at her as his eyes strayed over to the door of the Family Room. "Have the doctors spoken to them yet?" His head motioned toward the door, his eyes eager for her answer.

"No, that's who I'm waiting on now." Her face tensed a little. "Dr. Trivoli was tied up in a case for a while. She should be here any minute."

He looked at her with a puzzled face. "Trivoli, she must be new. I don't recognize her name."

Alex was pleased that her friend Danni's roommate was not one who would make Crawford's presence necessary that often. For that, she was thankful. "No, actually she's been here since July. She's one of our Trauma Fellows."

"She must be pretty good or just lucky to be on when the traumas are not that bad," he joked.

"I think that I would bet on good, Mr. Crawford." The voice was confident as Rob Kreger walked over to them from the Neuro-ICU. "If I were you, I'd enjoy this meeting with her today."

"And why is that?" Crawford demanded.

"I don't believe you will be seeing a lot of her in the future. That's why." Rob let his face show a smug appearance. Hearing the elevator announcing its arrival to the floor, he gazed over to the opening doors. "Here she is now."

The tall, stalwart figure appeared to have an aura around her when the bright fluorescent lighting of the elevator contrasted to that of the muted mood lighting of the hallway as she stood in the doorway. Her facial features remained undistinguishable until the doors closed behind her, allowing the dim lighting to give her well-defined features a softened appearance. The power and grace of her moves as she walked down the hall towards them brought to mind the stalking qualities of a panther. If she had meant to impress anyone, she was indeed fulfilling that wish.

Rob and Alex both watched as the surgeon cast a spell over Mark Crawford. They saw his look go from one of utter annoyance with her luck, to that of disbelief at her ability to bring him to his knees. Glistening beads of perspiration were gathering across his forehead the closer to him that she came. His lower lip was noticeably quivering, as his mouth became agape. The man's eyes seemed to be the only things moving on him with any purpose at all as they wandered up and down her long body. Yes, he was definitely hers for the asking.

Alex's voice broke the solemn exchange of stares as she introduced the two to each other. "Dr. Trivoli, this is Mark Crawford from the Organ Recovery Team, C.O.R.E.," she paused momentarily. "Mr. Crawford, this is Trauma Fellow Garrett Trivoli."

Garrett eyed the lecherous man. "Mr. Crawford," she greeted him, offering her hand that she'd just drawn out of her lab coat pocket.

His hand nervously smoothed the buttons of his lab jacket. Gulping audibly as he took her hand in his. "The pleasure is definitely all mine." Bringing her hand towards his mouth he gingerly placed a kiss on the back of it as he held her fingers in his.

The surgeon's eyebrow edged upward into her hairline as her eyes narrowed. If looks could indeed kill the cold, steel blue color of her eyes would have penetrated his heart, and this man in front of her would be the next trauma page going off on her beeper. She tugged at her hand, not wanting him to think that she was actually enjoying his attempt at flirting with her.

"I believe you said that the family was here?" Garrett was professional in her manner as she addressed Alex. She withdrew her hand, placing it in her lab coat pocket, trying as she might to position it in such a way as to allow the absorbent material to erase the moisture of his kiss. "Yes, the only family member that we could find is here." Alex turned to face Garrett directly. "I found out the man that was D.O.A. was David Morgan, the woman who died in the O.R. was his wife, Rita."

"The boy in ICU now, was he related to them?" Crawford was obviously edgy, waiting for her reply.

"Their son, Bradley," was all that she said, seeing the disappointment in his face.

"How old was he? Did he have a driver's license on him?" His only concern was that the young man had checked off the Organ Donor box on his driver's license.

"Sorry, he isn't old enough to even have a learner's permit," Alex said apologetically.

"Hmmm! Is it a grandparent then?" His tone was insistent. "The one we're to meet," he pointed toward the door of the Family Room. "I'd like to know so that I can gear my request toward their level of understanding."

Tired of the interrogation that the Social Worker was under, Dr. Trivoli spoke up. "Why don't you introduce me to the family member. I'd like to discuss my patient's," she paused to correct herself, "Bradley's condition with them."

Alex was appreciative for the intrusion in the line of questioning. "Allow me to do that right now. Dr. Kreger, Dr.

Trivoli, if you would come with me." She purposely ushered them to the door of the Family Room, leaving a disappointed but still hopeful Mark Crawford standing alone.

Garrett looked through the narrow panel of glass in the door viewing the occupants of the Family Room. There was a woman, who she guessed to be in her early forties, and two teenage girls.

With her hand on the doorknob, Alex looked at Garrett, then at Rob; "You ready for this?"

Rob's eyes flashed to his mentor. Seeing the calmness in her, he nodded his head. The surgeon inhaled deeply and nodded saying, "As ready as I'll ever be."

The door opened and the three walked single file into the small room.

There was an incredible tenseness in the air as the hospital personnel formed a tight semi-circle in front of the three women. The emotionless faces were nothing but a mask for the pleading eyes of hopefulness that watched them intently, waiting for the deafening silence to be broken. The older woman rested her arm on the shoulder of the smaller teen while the other teen quickly flanked the girl on the opposite side.

Alex cleared her throat and began. "My name is Alexia, I'm the Social Worker that you spoke to on the phone. This is Dr.Trivoli and Dr. Kreger." She motioned to each as she said their name.

"Hello, I'm Marianne Gryphon," the older woman introduced herself. She gently touched the far teen with her hand saying, "This is my daughter, Kristen and her friend Diana Morgan."

Garrett studied the small teen. She couldn't be any older than perhaps seventeen. Her brown hair pulled back into a barrette accentuated the worried look on her face. She looked like the typical girl next door, young and full of life although her eyes reflected more worry then they ever should at this age.

"When we took Diana home from the sleep-over last night, we found the message on the answering machine. We thought that it was kind of funny that the rest of the family wasn't at home. Are they all right?" The woman was genuinely concerned.

"Are you a relative, Ms. Gryphon?" The Social Worker so desperately hoped that she was.

Sighing loudly, the woman replied, "No. No, I am not." She looked at the teen. "Diana is the only relative that I know of."

Struggling to control her emotions, Garrett blinked back a tear as she reached out to the small girl. *Rene, you owe me big time for this.* "Diana, why don't we have a seat over here." She moved them in the direction of the comfortable looking couch along the far wall. Once seated she continued, "Does your family own a sports utility vehicle?"

The young girl stared at her, "Yes." Her eyes were searching the doctor's face for some indication of her loved ones' conditions. The build up of tears was like that of a dam ready to overflow.

Garrett glanced at her co-workers briefly before she took the young girl's hands in hers. "Your parents and your brother were involved in a very serious motor vehicle accident last night. Your mother and brother were brought to this hospital by helicopter straight from the accident scene. Diana, the rescue workers at the scene, Dr. Kreger, and myself did everything that we possibly could to save your parents but their injuries were just too extensive to sustain life."

"NO!" The girl cried out in anguish. "They can't be. They just haven't come home yet. It's not them!" She turned, pulling her hands away from Garrett's and then balled them into fists. She lunged at the surgeon next to her while her arms flung wildly in denial. "You…you let them die!" The torment of her soul was evident. "You didn't even try to help them, did you?"

Garrett backed away, her mind reeling from the sudden outburst of anger shown toward her. Ms. Gryphon came from behind Diana and tried to stop her emotional display. The sobbing soon took over the girl as her words became more garbled and unintelligible. Diana stood up. She turned into her friend's mother and clung to her body for support. She needed to be comforted and by the intensity of the outburst in Garrett's direction, that would not come from the doctor. The surprised surgeon never liked doing the sensitive things connected with her job, but now, this was even worse. *I don't know how to deal with this. I...I...S*he thought about all of the many times she had witnessed the rich flow of compassion oozing forth from Danni in the trauma suite or with the members of a family in the hallway. *God, I wish she was here doing this. She'd know how to handle this girl.* Garrett was afraid that the situation would escalate into one of sheer hostility, all directed at her.

Diana stared into space, tears spilling over her eyelashes and rolling down her cheeks. After several moments, the words slowly came to her voice. "My brother, Brad…is he okay?" Her eyes now stared into the doctor's, looking for the truth. "Or are you going to kill him, too?"

"Your brother is in the Neuro-ICU with head injuries. The assault on his brain from the impact of the vehicles has left him unable to breathe on his own. We are breathing for him with the help of a mechanical respirator." Garrett held her eyes fixed to Diana's as she allowed time for this information to sink in. *She doesn't trust me. I can see it in her eyes.*

"Will he get any better?" she asked, almost knowing what the answer would be.

The surgeon lowered her eyes to the ground and very quietly said, "No, we believe his injuries to be fatal in nature."

"Do all of the doctors believe this, or just you?" Her voice was like venom spat in Garrett's direction.

Rob Kreger now spoke up. "If you don't think that Dr. Trivoli or myself gave every effort…"

Garrett turned abruptly, her eyes sending forth a message of complete control when they locked onto the vocal Chief

Resident. "I'm sure if Ms. Morgan wants to talk to another Doctor, we can arrange that." Her eyes flashed anger at her outspoken colleague. She was trying hard not to provoke any more confrontation than was necessary.

Diana's head dropped and the sobbing began. She broke away from her friend's mother. She strode over to the couch, falling into it and slowly curled into a ball, her body shaking relentlessly with each round of tears. Her world, as she had known it, was at an end, never to be the same again.

Marianne held onto her own daughter now, fearing that if she let go she would somehow disappear. The color drained out of her face and the look of desolation was in her eyes. "They're gone," she muttered and shook her head in disbelief as she clutched onto her own daughter even tighter than before. Her eyes closed in thanksgiving that it was not Kristen living through this tragedy. She looked to Alex, "What is going to happen to Diana now?" Biting at her lower lip she pondered the thought. "She doesn't have any living relatives, at least that we know of." She looked at her daughter for reassurance. Kristen's reply was a slow shake of her head.

Garrett sat down again next to the grief-stricken girl. Pulling a tissue from her pocket, she offered it to Diana and waited for the sobbing to diminish. The girl pulled away further into the corner of the couch, not wanting to have any physical connection with the surgeon. In Garrett's own mind, scenes from her life tugged at her emotions as she remembered how things had been for her so many years ago.

The surgeon's vivid memory recalled the small, antiseptic smelling room where the lighting had been just as harsh as the words that the doctor had said to her, "They're dead," engulfing her senses. The words echoed in her brain over and over again. Everywhere she turned, the people around her all had the same, somnolent faces. No one offered her any reasons or causes, not even an excuse, just nothing but the stark fact that they were gone forever.

She found herself leaning in toward the teen to speak, "Would you like to see your brother?" Her words were kind as her eyes searched for an answer in the red, swollen orbs that peered up at her. The hate in the young girl's eyes was evident. "He has a tube in his mouth that goes down his throat to breathe for him. There will be a lot of intravenous lines that are giving him fluids and medicine. The electrical devices that enable us to monitor his body functions take up the better part of the room." Garrett attempted to paint a reasonable picture of what the girl would see. The last thing that she wanted was to be frightened even more or to be giving her any false hope regarding his condition.

The young girl wiped her eyes, "Could I, please?" Her voice was shaky and weak but pleading like a child's.

"Dr. Kreger, would you call into the ICU and tell them that Diana would like to visit her brother?"

Rob set about to his task of clearing the way for the entourage to enter the ICU without being subjected to any undue strain from viewing the other patients or procedures that might be going on. When everything was set, he called into the Family Room on the dedicated phone line, informing the Social Worker of the time available for visitation.

The group made their way into the unit. Stopping at the nurse's station right inside the door, Dr. Trivoli reviewed Bradley Morgan's chart. His condition had remained the same. There were no voluntary movements or responses to deep painful stimulus. The extent of his injuries was quite clear in her mind. She would be talking to the Neurosurgeon after Diana was done visiting, and ask that a brain death protocol be ordered. Putting the chart down, she motioned for them to follow her to his bedside.

The young girl walked over to the tall surgeon who held out a gown for her to put on. Donning her own gown quickly, she accompanied Diana across the room to the cubicle where her brother's body lay, supported by a multitude of machines. The roaming eyes of the teen took in every detail of the room, her eyes darting from one noise to another as the machines did their job.

Garrett watched as the teen finally settled in on her brother's face, a tear rolling down her own cheek. "You can talk to him if you'd like, Diana."

Her voice was barely above a whisper, "Could I touch his hand?" She looked up to the surgeon, her eyes showing her true feelings and need for approval of her request.

"I think he would like that." Her head motioned to the body laying in repose. She watched as Diana made her way to the bedside. She hesitated as she reached out for his hand, looking over her shoulder for encouragement. Garrett nodded in approval. The young girl stroked his small hand with her own. Soon she was leaning over to talk ever so softly into his ear.

The surgeon studied the scene intently, looking for any sign of recognition on Brad's part. His eyes never fluttered, the muscles in his face never twitched, the hand remained still as if it had never been touched. Her keen sense of hearing listened for any change in the rhythm of the beeping noise emitted from the heart monitor, but there was none. In essence, the body before her was nothing more than an empty shell devoid of all the nuances that denote life.

After several minutes, she bent over and kissed her brother's forehead. Slowly she backed away from the bed until she was standing next to the tall woman. Her eyes never wavered from watching him. "He looks so peaceful."

A minute or two passed by before the silence was broken. "Does he feel anything?" Diana looked up at Garrett, "He's not in pain, I mean?"

"No, we're giving him some medication to make sure of that," she responded.

"So, what's next?" Her young voice had vagueness about it. "Does he just go on like this forever?"

The surgeon thought about what to say. "There is a group of tests that we will do on your brother that will tell us whether or not there is any activity going on in his brain. If they result in showing no brain function then we can declare him brain dead and remove the ventilator. After a few minutes, his heart will stop beating and his other organs will cease to function." She tried to lessen the impact as much as she could.

"When?" She stuttered, "W…when will that happen?"

"We should know by tomorrow around noon," Garrett projected. "If you would like, you could be here with him, if that is what we need to do."

The girl nodded her head in agreement. Sighing, she hung her head and muttered. "Will you be here too? Yeah, I bet you like seeing people die." Her eyes flashed at the surgeon with all the hatred that she could muster. Her attitude toward Garrett had completely changed. The surgeon was aware of the normal stages of grieving and Diana was beginning the process with this harsh language. Knowing not to take it personally, Garrett allowed the girl to verbalize her emotions. "I bet you just love to see people's whole lives get thrown right in the toilet before your eyes. It makes you feel all high and mighty, doesn't it? You all think that you're gods."

The surgeon grasped tightly onto the bed rail with both her hands. She really wanted to lash out at this girl for her taunting ways but knew that it would only provoke more of the same. "I will be here, but only because I have to be. He's my patient, Diana, not some experiment."

Diana turned to face her. "Well, at least you realize that he's my brother and I'm not going to just throw him away." She saw her friend off in the distance behind the doctor. "I'd better get back with my friend now. I have some things that I need to sort out." She turned to look at her brother for a moment, and then turning back to the surgeon she glared. The two stood that way for a moment before Diana slowly walked in the direction of Kristen and her mother, continuing to pass them on her way out the door.

Garrett watched her leave with the Gryphons following right behind her. Cursing to herself for not being able to save the girl from the pain and anguish she was going through, she ran her fingers through her long raven hair in desperation.

Danni, why couldn't you have been here?

****

The sound of the front door opening caught Danni's attention. She placed her plate in the dishwasher and made her way into the living room.

"Garrett, is that you?" She came around the corner of the hall to see the haggard appearance of her roommate. "Want happened to you?" She came over to her and took the duffel bag from her hand. "Didn't you get any sleep at all?" Concern was written all over her face.

"Yeah, a few hours," she leaned against the couch to take off her shoes. "But not very comfortable, to say the least. I fell asleep in the Doctor's Lounge in the O.R." Her hand rubbed at her lower back to ease the soreness. "I think I'm just going to take a hot bath and go to bed."

The petite woman could not believe how tired her Amazon looked. "You want something to eat?"

"Thanks, but no, I ate at the hospital. I just need to relax and get a lot of sleep."

"Well, let me start your bath for you." Danni went into the bathroom and turned on the water for the tub. Emerging from the doorway, she came back into the living room. "How about I fix you a nice cup of tea, hmmm?"

Garrett nodded and muttered the word, "Thanks," as Danni passed by on her way to the kitchen, her energy waning.

Calling in from the kitchen, Danni asked, "Did they find any family for that young trauma patient yet?"

Garrett waited for her return, too tired to yell back. "Yeah, turns out the only family so far is his sister." She looked up at her roommate. "She's only seventeen."

"Oh, by the gods," Danni sank down onto the couch. "She must be devastated."

"She's doing better than some that I've seen. Tomorrow's going to be the hard one."

Danni looked puzzled.

"I ordered the brain death protocol. We'll know for sure by noon tomorrow." The surgeon rolled her tongue across her teeth. "I told her that I would be there with her tomorrow when it's time."

The blonde sighed. "I wish I could have been there with you today. I know how much you like doing the sensitive chats."

"Yeah, well..." Garrett nodded as her eyes roamed about the room. "It's part of the job, too."

"Garrett, I'm off for the next two days. Let me be there with you tomorrow?"

"Thanks, but you don't have to, Danni." The surgeon rose to her feet. "I better get that bath before I fall asleep right here." She thought about the offer as she walked to the bathroom. Pausing at the door, she turned back toward the nurse. "Maybe that might not be a bad idea. Could you meet us about noon tomorrow in the Neuro-ICU?"

Danni nodded, "Anything to help. Now go and take a long hot soak. Let it get all the aches out, Gar. I'll see you tomorrow at noon."

"Thanks Danni, I think I will." The surgeon slowly looked toward the stairs and headed for the tub.

After the time spent soothing her tired muscles with the heat of the water, the tall woman stole herself quietly into her bedroom. There, on the corner of her nightstand was a cup of hot tea. *I'll have to remember to thank her for this. I guess it's nice to have someone who cares around.*

Letting her robe fall off of her body into a heap on the floor, she slid under the covers that had been neatly turned down for her. Taking a few sips of tea from the cup, she placed it back on the table and readied herself for sleep.

****

She had always prided herself on keeping her word and now, as she mulled over the events of the last two days, the surgeon was not looking forward to what was about to take place within the next hour or so. It was her day off technically, but she had promised to be here with Brad's sister Diana when the time came. Sure, she could have put it off for another day, but somehow that just didn't seem right, to make the poor girl agonize over the potential outcome of the tests. Besides, she didn't want to add to the young girl's burden by causing any hassles over payment of the hospital bills by the insurance company.

Garrett sipped at her cup of black coffee as she was looking over the reports of the tests that she had ordered on Bradley Morgan. The EEG test, which measured the activity of the brain, was plain and to the point; no activity found. The other test reports were all in alignment with the Neurosurgeon's prognosis at the sight of the initial CT Scan. Now it was going to be her job to help Diana grasp the concept that her brother didn't really inhabit the body that was being kept alive in the ICU. There really was no life force present, only the mechanical initiative that preserved the body in its vegetative state.

The surgeon rested her head in her hands as she contemplated the course of changes that the life of Diana Morgan was going to encounter. She sighed knowing full well that this was not the way her parents would have wished for her life to be. Unfortunately, there was nothing Garrett could do about it except to give the support and guidance that she would need in the next few hours. The surgeon felt absolutely helpless at the outcome of her efforts.

The small, windowless office seemed to be closing in on her as she raised her head out of her hands and looked around. She had been so preoccupied with her thoughts that she had not heard the knock at the door. The motion of the door slowly opening and the appearance of the blonde hair brought her back to reality.

Knocking again on the open door, Danni peered in at the woman seated behind the desk. "Hey," she smiled, "mind if I come in?"

The answer was evident by the lopsided smile on the surgeon's face at the sight of her friend. "Yeah, I was hoping that you'd be a little early."

The petite woman slipped in the door as she studied the room. "I guess you don't spend too much time in here." The nurse knew how claustrophobic the tall woman could be at times.

Garrett chuckled slightly, "Every free minute that I get." She was being sarcastic with her reply. "Have a seat." She motioned to the small chair that was behind the door. While waiting for the door to close all the way, she gathered the papers that were spread out across her desk and offered them to the nurse. "Care to read the results?"

"By the look on your face when I stuck my head in, I don't think that I have to." Danni shifted her position in the chair. "Did you tell his sister yet?"

"No, I just got done reviewing them myself." She placed the stack of reports on the desk. "Danni," she hesitated, biting her lower lip, "I'd appreciate it if you would help me with this one."

The nurse sensed the apprehension in Garrett's voice. Something about this case was really bothering her but Danni knew enough about her friend not to push for answers. "Sure, anything that I can do to help, just let me know." She watched as the tense look on the surgeon's face relaxed.

"Thanks, I really want to be as gentle and considerate as I can on this one. She's got a lot on her plate right now and being so young..." she took a deep breath, "well, it could affect her for the rest of her life. I don't want to let her feel any remorse about what has to be done. She doesn't need to be haunted with this tragedy any more than she is already." Garrett closed her eyes at the thought, a pained look over taking her face.

Danni felt compelled to reach out to her friend. She was certain that this was affecting the surgeon more than usual. She knew that Garrett was not one for talking about herself or her childhood, and now seeing this, she was sure that there was a reason why. She let her hand gently rest on the edge of the desk with her fingers flexing. "Do you want to talk about it?"

Crystal blue eyes shot to attention as her lids opened wide then slowly narrowed, settling on Danni. "There's nothing to talk about," she snapped. Her face had taken on a new hard look to her usually pleasant features.

Sensing that she had touched on an exposed nerve, Danni backed off. "Sorry, I only meant to help," she apologized. "If you ever..." her voice trailed off abruptly with the intense look that she was receiving from her friend.

The surgeon cleared her throat, trying to choke back the cry that was readying to escape from her. She let her gaze drift away from her friend to hide the well of tears that were threatening to overflow. Having successfully reigned in her emotions she pushed herself away from the desk and stood up.

"Let's get this over with," Garrett's face expressed no emotion as she rounded the corner of the desk, advancing toward the door.

Danni watched in amazement as she witnessed the surgeon fighting back her emotional turmoil and reinstating her mask of professional facade. This sight saddened the young woman's heart. Her friend was hurting and she could do nothing but be ready for the time when Garrett would allow her into that secret place where her tortured soul dwelled.

The nurse followed her friend, reluctantly, out of the office. Pausing as she closed the door, she offered up a silent prayer. *She's hurting so badly. Please, if there is any god that ameliorates the healers, let me act as your instrument to help her soul find peace within herself.* Sighing deeply, she turned and followed the surgeon to the Neuro-ICU area.

****

A young girl peered out of the safety window in the door of the Family Room, her sullen eyes reflecting the scene before them. "Mom," she whispered to the woman who had just joined her there. "I don't think it's good news." She looked up to her mother for support.

Mrs. Gryphon observed the three women in the hall. She recognized Alexia and Dr. Trivoli from the day before. The third woman was new to her. She watched the grim looks that each one had on their faces and prepared for the worst. Resting her arm around her daughter's shoulders, she glanced over at Diana sitting on the couch with her head buried in her hands. Sniffing back a tear, she squeezed Kristen and whispered gently in her ear, "I love you." The young girl smiled up at her and nodded. "We have to be strong for Diana now. Can you do that?" She nodded again then went to sit beside her friend. Moving away from the door, Marianne took up a position nearer to the two young girls and waited for the trio to enter the room.

A few moments later the door opened with Alex leading the procession of sober faced professionals. Diana's raised her head when she heard the sound of heels walking across the polished tile floor. The hopeful eyes of the young girl searched the faces as each one entered the room for the answer to the question ripping at her heart. Her mood went spiraling out of control as the petite blonde stepped in, closing the door behind her. Tears were streaking down her cheeks as Alexia greeted them. All her mind could think about was her brother and how he had been so full of life the last time she saw him outside of the hospital. Her eyes grew large as she picked out the tall surgeon and stared directly into her crystal orbs. The girl shivered seeing eyes staring back at her that were devoid of any emotion. Before any one had even spoken to her, Diana knew what was about to happen. Her hopes and dreams of the future were about to change for the rest of her life, for the second time in the last two days.

Garrett cleared her throat and began to slowly approach the young girl. "Diana," she paused motioning the petite nurse to come forward. "Let me introduce one of our trauma nurses to you. This is Danni, she was Brad's nurse when he first arrived here the night before last." The surgeon's eyes were gauging her response to the nurse. "Danni, this is Diana Morgan, Brad's sister, and her friend Kristen and Kristen's mother Marianne Gryphon." She pointed to them as they were introduced.

The nurse used all of her skills as she came forward to greet the young girl. She brought herself to sit on the couch next to her and spoke in a soft, quiet manner. "I hope you don't mind, Diana, but I asked my friend, Dr. Trivoli, if I could meet you today." She waited for a response but the young girl's eyes were blank. Danni looked around the room to the mother and her daughter, each one with only true concern written on their faces. The nurse tried a slightly different approach this time. "You know, little brothers can be a challenge to their older sisters, but deep within our hearts we love them dearly. When I was growing up, my brother was always teasing me and…"

The girl suddenly focused on the nurse sitting next to her. "You have a little brother too?" Her eyes were now coming to life as a common ground was found, linking the two women together.

"Yes," her warm smile bridged the invisible gap between them. "I know you love your brother just like I do mine, and that you only want the best of everything for him." She gently laid her hand on top of the arm. "That's why I would like you to listen to what Dr. Trivoli has to tell you. Okay?"

Diana sniffed as she wiped a tear from her cheek with the back of her hand. She blinked several times trying to contain the tears that were waiting for release and nodded in affirmation. Her attention now turned to the tall figure in front of her.

"We've gotten the results from the tests back." Garrett paused as she looked at the nurse for support. "They proved what we had speculated about the night he came in." Her eye caught Kristen glancing at her mother in anticipation. "I've studied the reports and have spoken with several colleagues of mine in reference to Brad's prognosis. I'm sorry to say but there is no evidence of a recovery at this point in time. His body is not able to function on its own without the assistance of the machines. I was hoping that there would be some small chance, but I can't even give you any glimmer of hope that he will ever be anything more than what you see in that bed today."

The young girl bit down on her lip. She looked over to Kristen and then slowly lifted her gaze to Mrs. Gryphon. "What..." she stuttered, "What happens now?" She turned to the nurse beside her, pleading for guidance. "How do I take care of my brother now?" A large tear found its way over her cheek as her hand reached out to grasp the hand of the nurse.

"You have to think of what is best for your brother now. How he would like his life to be." She held onto the girl's hand, letting the compassion show in her face. Studying the young girl's face intently, Danni added, "Would your brother have enjoyed his life like it is now?"

Her gaze drifted to the floor, as she answered shakily, "No." Then, without warning her body stiffened and she rose abruptly. "But he's my brother, damn it!" Her head turned quickly as she looked at the people around her. "I can't just kill..." her voice trail off into a whisper, "him."

"Nobody is asking you to kill him, dear." Mrs. Gryphon spoke up.

Kristen tried helping, "You know that's not really Brad in there."

Danni drew her attention back by touching the young girl's arm. "They're right, Diana. Your brother's life force," she paused searching for a better explanation of it, "the essence that makes Brad different from anybody else just isn't there any longer. All that you see is his body, the shell that housed his soul and gave direction to the energy that he was." Danni gazed into the young girl's eyes and then slowly directed her to look over to the surgeon.

Sensing that it was her time to speak, Garrett started. "We just need to let his body go, Diana."

"But how…who?" Diana's eyes grew bigger as her mind raced with the possibilities. "You don't expect me to…" her eyes now darted around the room, the tears welling up and starting to fall. "You're asking too much. I couldn't…"

"Me," Garrett fought hard so that the break that came to her voice wasn't that noticeable. "I'll be the one to turn the machines off," the surgeon reassured her.

The girl thought about it for a moment. Looking to her friend's mother for approval, she slowly nodded her head in agreement. Garrett closed her eyes and sighed. The decision was made. Now all she had to do was carry out the task.

"Would you like to see him before…?" Danni waited for her answer. The girl only shrugged her shoulders, then after thinking on it, shook her head. "That's all right, Diana. If it were my brother, I think I would want to remember him at his happiest moment, full of life and loving everything in it. What did your brother love to do best?"

The girl thought for only a second. "It would be riding his bicycle. With his racing helmet on, streaking across the top of the hill at the end of our street, the late afternoon sun at his back…that's how I'll remember him." A faint smile played upon her lips at the thought.

"Then, that is the way you will see him. Remember him like that and you will never be far from his spirit." Danni instinctively meet the azure eyes of the surgeon and felt that her words had helped more than just Diana.

The subdued voice of the nurse seemed to wrap itself around Garrett's soul. The silences of the moment allowed a fleeting glimpse of a tasseled haired boy come to Garrett's mind. His youthful features were covered with a smattering of sweat and dirt as he laughed holding up his prize catch, a rainbow trout.

The nurse watched as a serene look came over the face of the surgeon. She wasn't sure what her friend was thinking about, but at least what she had said was helping her cope with the situation at hand, if not what she possibly held in her past.

Alex breathed a sigh of relief knowing that the hard part, if only for her, was over. She had feared the worst out of the young girl who was being dealt a hard slap in the face by reality. The intense emotional scene that she expected had been averted by the combined effort of Danni and Garrett. For this she was truly grateful.

Diana walked over to Mrs. Gryphon. “I’d like to leave now.” Her voice was even and unwavering.

The woman gathered both girls into her arms and hugged them equally. Looking back to the medical professionals she mouthed the words, “Thank You.” She watched as each one accepted her appreciation. “Come on, let’s go home.” With that, the small group made their way to the door and out of the hospital.

Danni sidled up to the tall surgeon who seemed to still be absorbed by her thoughts. She watched the expression on her friend change to one of confused questioning, as the surgeon became aware of her. “Ah…I’d like to be with you when you take him off.” Her green eyes locked onto the blue orbs in a knowing plea to allow her to share this last service to her patient.

Garrett acquiesced. There was something about the petite nurse that made her feel better about the whole situation. Rubbing her chin in thought, she nodded. “Let’s go see to our patient’s needs one last time.”

They left the confines of the small room. The slow procession traveled down the hall into the Neuro-ICU without a single word spoken. The anguish on each of their faces was the only lament to the task they were about to do. As they passed the nurses’ station, Alex left the formation to review the arrangements for the destination of Bradley Morgan’s remains.

With the tall woman in the lead, the healthcare professionals walked with purposeful strides through the unit to the cubicle where the young boy’s body was being maintained. Garrett stood observing the array of mechanical support systems and sighed. *This is all that modern medicine can do. We can duplicate and maintain the bodily functions but we can't give him back his soul,* she mused. *I didn't want this to ever happen to anyone else.*

Garrett was presented with the boy's chart. Taking it, the surgeon flipped it open reading the latest entry in the nurses' charting area. 'No new observations of any physical activity on the part of the patient noted.' That one sentence said it all along with the results of the battery of tests she had received earlier. She handed the chart to the petite nurse, allowing her eyes to view that all-encompassing declaration, announcing the futility of any further hope for Bradley's survival.

The surgeon closed her eyes in an effort to calm the anger that was building within her. Her mind was in a quandary as she remembered what her goal had been when she decided to become a doctor. The suffering was soon to be over for Brad, but in her mind she had been able to do nothing for his sister, Diana. It was happening again and she had no control over it this time, either.

Her mind was forced back to her present physical surroundings, as she felt a warm touch upon her back, the heat of which seemed to bring comfort to her. Garrett looked down at Danni trying to hide all of the emotions that were raging inside of her head. "Would you like to give it one last try?"

The green eyes twinkled with the thought. Hesitantly she nodded saying; "I'd like that. Thank you." The nurse went to the boy's bedside talking to him in the same gentle manner as when he had first arrived in the trauma room. She placed his hand into hers and delicately stroked the back of it. Squeezing his hand with hers she watched for any signs of response. Looking over her shoulder at Garrett, Danni shook her head, a disappointed look crossing her face. She laid his hand back down and once again stared at his angelic face. The nurse brushed back a straying lock of hair on his forehead as she leaned in to place a light kiss on his cheek before coming back to stand with her friend.

Garrett looked around the unit and motioned for the nurse to close the drapery, shutting the cubicle off from view. It was time to let the young boy's body take its leave without the stares of any visitors or other patients to distract from his final moments in human form. The surgeon swallowed hard, trying to settle her nervous stomach. Walking over to the ventilator, she reached out and pressed the toggle switch to the off position. The healer pressed her eyelids together and inhaled deeply, trying to keep the scene of a distant time from reappearing in her mind. Exhaling, she opened her eyes and watched the electronic devices showing the deterioration of the human body lying before her.

The patient's nurse stood off to the side recording the time and vital signs prior to the termination of mechanical support as Danni braced herself for the events to come. It was always sad to watch the passing of a life before your very eyes, but Danni was no stranger to death, it went with the job of being a trauma nurse. The sadness today seemed to come from her friend and the demons that Garrett was wrestling with. Something in this woman's past had really affected her. Wishing that she would be able to help ease the surgeon's mind, Danni resigned herself to the fact that she could do no more than to just be here for her. With that thought in mind, the golden haired nurse watched the tall woman for any clue as to how she might help her deal with that pain.

It was a few moments now since the rhythmic sound of the respirator filled the room. The steady rise and fall of the boy's chest had ceased and his form remained motionless. The constant beeping of the heart monitor was beginning to slow; the electronic tracing on the screen became wider and more irregular in its pattern. The reading of the recycling blood pressure monitor revealed a steady drop in his pressure.

The minutes ticked by. Garrett was transfixed on the devices watching the progressive widening complexes of the heartbeat. Long drawn out pauses of inactivity with only a single pattern was now showing across the screen, the single beep randomly breaking the silence of the room. Her eyes took on a new intensity as a rapid flurry of patterned activity shot across the screen, the beeping coming one right after the other, almost without pause. The jagged, erratic tracing soon ceased, followed by the telltale warning sound of the flat line tracing that floated across the monitor. They all stood just watching for another moment or two. Assured that it was over, Dr. Trivoli blinked back a tear as she glanced over to the large clock on the wall opposite her.

In a monotone voice she uttered, "Time of death, 1310." She cleared her throat and looked at the two nurses. "Thank you for you help," her voice was only slightly louder than a whisper. Silently, the surgeon left the room.

"Is she okay?" The nurse moved toward the bed to begin removing the connections of the machines to the lifeless body.

Danni had to think about that herself. "I hope so," she uttered under her breath.

****

The rest of the day was spent in solitude as Garrett opted to drive out to the countryside. She needed time to think and did so, as she walked through the leaves that graced the woodland floor. Her mind kept conjuring up familiar faces from her past. Each figure came back to haunt her in their own way. With dusk approaching, she drew her walk to a close and began the long drive back home.

Time to go home, she mused. *Even my thoughts are haunting me. Home,* she laughed to herself, *I'll never have a place that feels like home, or anyone that feels like family ever again.* The words bit into her, tearing at her soul.

The image of the petite blonde came to her mind. This image was different from the rest that had visited her today. It did not haunt her, but instead brought with it a feeling of warmth and compassion. A feeling that made her yearn for the sights and smells that reminded her of the nurse. No one had ever stood out in her mind like that, not even her…. She paused at the thought. Her face took on a surprised look as her brow raised at the concept.

Chapter 10

Staring out into the early morning sky, the young woman sat motionless enjoying the crisp October air. Danni watched the hues of the sky turn to shades of red as the first hints of a new day dawned. Her mind wandered through a list of nursery rhymes and other assorted phrases that one kept from their childhood, looking for the reference of a red sky at morning. She thought for a few moments, and then the fleeting phrases came to her mind. *Red sky in the morning shepherds take warning. Red sky at night, shepherds' delight.* Chuckling to herself she thought aloud. "I wonder if there is any truth to that?"

"Any truth to what, Danni?" The motherly charge nurse was standing a few feet away from her, clutching at her lab jacket to keep the crisp air from invading the warmth of her clothing.

"Oh...Hi Mom! I didn't realize you were standing there." Her voice was whimsical as she continued. "You know, the saying about the red sky in the morning."

"Sailors take warning," Karen chimed in. "That one you mean?"

"Sailors?" The blonde shook her head. "I thought it was shepherds," she wrinkled up her nose.

"Shepherds, sailors does it really make a difference? They are both waiting for the storm that's starting to brew around them." Mom chuckled, "I guess it was what time period that you grew up in."

"Yeah, I guess so." She gazed out at the deepening hue of the sky, mesmerized by the changing patterns in the morning light. "Do you really think that they take warning?"

"I think there has to be some truth to it, otherwise why would it be passed down from one generation to the next?" Karen walked over to the bench that Danni was sitting on. "Mind if I sit down?" She pointed to the other half of the bench.

"No, go right ahead."

The two women sat watching the ever-changing sky turn from night into dawn, each lost in their own thoughts. Mom looked intently at the petite nurse. Her mood was very introspective. Karen had noticed a change in the vivacious woman. She seemed to keep a little more to herself these last few weeks. She wondered if there was something troubling her.

Pondering the thought, she made her decision to act. "Danni, is there anything that you want to talk about? I've noticed that you have been in the doldrums lately."

The young woman sighed; leaning forward she worked her hands under her thighs, locking her elbows. She looked down to the ground in front of her and then back to the concerned friend beside her. "I wish there was," she whispered, "then I could do something to help."

Karen was puzzled. "I'm not following you."

"I'm worried about Garrett, Mom. There is something going on and it's tormenting her. I just don't know what it is or how to help her."

The charge nurse let the mother instinct in her take over. "You live with her, I'm sure that you would notice before any of us would. Has she given you any clue as to what it might be? Maybe she is just worried about her work or where she will be next year," she offered.

Danni looked at her, "I don't think it's her work, Mom. She's one of the best Trauma Fellows that I've seen." The nurse became a little sullen at her next thought. "She could go anywhere she wants next year. A hospital would be crazy not to want someone like her on their staff."

Picking up a note of regret at the possible loss of a friend, Karen tried to change the subject. "What makes you think that something is tormenting her?"

Shrugging her shoulders, she looked back out to the sky's first light. "I've noticed that she hasn't been sleeping. Last weekend we were both off together. I could hear her mumbling and tossing and turning in her bed," she said, showing signs of embarrassment. "It sounds like the same nightmare every time, all weekend long. I almost went and knocked on her bedroom door Sunday night to see if she was all right."

"Have you offered to talk about it?" She held up her hand in a halting motion, "forget that I asked that." Karen smiled, she knew that would be the first thing the young woman would do. She thought about how Danni always looked after her friends; always more concerned about their welfare than her own. Just like the parable of the shepherd and his flock. What a match the shepherd and the sailor were becoming!

"She says that nothing is wrong. At least that's what she said when I asked her over breakfast on Sunday morning. I tried to bring it up in the conversation but she just kept changing the subject." Pressing her lips tightly together and inhaling deeply she shook her head. "Mom, she's been like this since that night she covered call for Rene...when his kids were born."

Karen placed her hand on Danni's back, letting it move in a soothing circling motion. "Sometimes you have to let people work out their own problems first. All you can do is let her know that you are there for her and wait." She paused to think about the talented surgeon. "She's an intelligent woman, she'll talk when she's ready." Danni turned her head to look at Karen with her mouth opening to speak. "Shhh!" She whispered, stopping the young woman. "Just be ready to listen when she is ready to talk."

"I will," Danni said softly as she wiped at the single tear that had escaped her eye. *I only wish that I could help Gar if she'd let me.*

Mom rubbed her arms feigning a shiver. "It's too cold for me out here, I'm going in. Why don't you take a minute to pull yourself together before you come back inside?"

Danni nodded, "Thanks, Mom."

The charge nurse got up and moved towards the door. Opening it, she turned and looked at the solitary figure. She thought about the question concerning the truth to the red sky in the morning and considered her two pseudo-daughters. "I hope this time, both the shepherd and the sailor will heed the warning," she muttered to herself as she went inside.

Sitting there in the cool air, the nurse looked up into the heavens and realized that she was just a speck in the workings of the universe. Sighing, she closed her eyes and offered a prayer for strength and the wisdom to be able to help her friend when the time came.

****

Sleep had not come easily to her this night. Her dreams had been filled with nightmarish visions of what she had hoped would be her forgotten past. She cursed her memory, begging for a night of amnesic bliss. Forcing her eyelids open, she searched the blackness of the room for the neon numbers of the digital clock on the nightstand. It read 0437. She snorted in disbelief, "Well, that's a half an hour more than I had at 0400." She reached over and turned off the alarm before it went off at her usual wake up time: 0445. "No sense in trying to go back to sleep now," she mumbled.

Throwing off her covers, she let her long legs slide over the edge of the bed. Pulling her torso up to a sitting position, she stared blurry-eyed into the darkness of the room, trying to get her thoughts organized for the day ahead. She shook her head in an attempt to clear her mind but it didn't seem to help. She sat there motionless and, for the first time since she moved in, she noticed how quiet the house was without the small blonde in the next room. It had felt so comfortable the past weekend with both of them home at the same time. The dead quiet was almost unnerving to her now, making her feel even more alone.

What I wouldn't give to hear Danni stirring out in the kitchen right now. Sighing, she planted her feet on the floor, pushing herself up off of the bed and began to make her way to the bathroom down the hall.

Garrett felt her body reacting to the cooler temperature of the house with a shiver. The goose bumps on her flesh reminded her of a plucked chicken. She smirked and thought about how much like a chicken she really was. She had always met any problem head-on, but this was something else. Problems, she could deal with, but the actions of the past jumping back into her life were more than she could contend with. Her mind drifted back to the past weekend. She had hoped for a relaxing one but those damn nightmares would not let up. She was going to have to do something about them. They evidently were not just keeping **her** from sleep, but Danni also.

The thought of the small blonde's action filled Garrett's mind. Danni had delicately tried to open the pathway for discussion about what was troubling the surgeon. *I can't believe her, always worrying about everyone else.* The surgeon remembered the concerned look on the face of the nurse as she sat across from her. *You'd think she would have more regard about her life than mine. I just don't understand her.*

Garrett had remained the same toward Danni, stoic as ever. She didn't need to pass her nightmares on to anyone. They were hers alone.

"Alone," she mumbled under her breath. "It all stems back to the same thing." The surgeon could see no sense in burdening someone else with her demons. What good would that do anyway, except to allow them to haunt more than just her. *No, I did the right thing by evading her questions. She doesn't need to know any of this.* She tried to chase the image of the blonde imp out of her mind and get on with her morning ritual, but it kept fading into view like it never wanted to let her go. "I definitely need more sleep," she verbalized as she stumbled into the bathroom doorway.

Squinting to shield her eyes, Garrett flicked on the bathroom light. Slowly her eyes adjusted to the coruscating light bouncing off of the white walls and fixtures. The mirror before her reflected an image that she couldn't believe was one that she knew. Dark hair stood out from her head in a wild, sleep-deprived manner and lackluster shadows under her eyes added to the scary reflection. *Jeez, I've got to get some sleep tonight,* she thought.

"Shit!" She hung her head with a sigh of disappointment, realizing that she was on-call for the next 24 hours. "I guess a little make-up might help me to look a little less zombie-like." She winced at the thought. *I really hate that stuff on me. It's a good thing I don't need to use it everyday.*

She stepped into the shower and turned it on, hoping that the cold water would wake her body up and stimulate her mind. Realizing that she was hoping for the impossible, she pushed herself to complete her morning ritual as soon moved out of the shower and over to the vanity.

"Why am I doing this?" Garret stopped in the middle of putting blush to her cheek. She looked into the mirror and cringed.

It was as though the mirror had a life of its own. Suddenly she saw her own reflection talking back to her. *Because you look like a crazed lunatic without it, that's why. What do you think your patients would say if they saw you looking like that? Hmm?*

The eyebrow of the image slowly raised in speculation, daring her to answer. She wrinkled her nose, sticking her tongue out at the mirror. "All right," she continued the finishing touches mumbling, "but I still don't have to like it."

Now she was really worried, the hallucination of her talking to herself only proved how much she desperately needed sleep. She looked into the mirror, appraising her efforts. Not too bad, if she had to admit it. At least she resembled a human being. "Satisfied?" She challenged her image to answer. She waited for a moment, then turned, shutting off the light and left to begin her day.

She paused at the door, taking stock of the possessions that filled her arms. Her mind was in such a disorganized quandary that she knew she would have to make a determined effort with any task that she did. She ran down the list of items necessary to sustain her for the next 24 to 36 hours, checking to make sure that they were packed. "Daily planner, toiletries, change of clothes, money, car keys, house key, pager, I.D. badge. Check," she sighed. "Now, all I have to do is to get through the next day without any trouble." She crossed her fingers, figuring that it couldn't hurt, and made a silent wish.

The surgeon left the house and made her way to the Chevy Blazer parked at the curb. Loading her necessities into the open tailgate, she marveled at the gorgeous red hues of the morning sky. *Just my luck, looks like there is a storm brewing on the horizon. It figures.*

"So much for a good day." With that thought in mind, she climbed into the driver's seat and set her course for the inner city trauma center.

****

The daylight shift had begun to receive report on the remaining patients in the emergency room when the loud, shrill beeps of the trauma pager went off. With a sigh of relief, Rosie handed Steve the pager saying, "Here's your report. It's the only thing I was handling last night." She smiled and began to walk away.

"Trauma page, trauma page. Level 1 Trauma, MVA, car into pole. Female unrestrained driver complaining of shortness of breath. ETA to your facility is 4 minutes. Level 1 trauma page."

Steve closed his eyes murmuring, "It's going to be one of those days, I can tell." His eyes drifted over to the assignment board to see whom he would be working with. "Dr. Trivoli! Well, it can't be that bad now." He took off down the hall to the trauma room to get ready.

Rosie waited for her friend to finish giving report to the oncoming nurse as she watched the activity around the desk. Out of the corner of her eye, the nurse saw a flurry of excitement. In the center of it was the E.R. Attending, Ian McCormick. He was trying to fight his way through the gathering of staff clogging the hallway. Without warning he stopped, throwing his hands up in the air. "Will everyone **please** clear the hallway!" His face grew red as the decibels were raised with his thundering voice. As if by magic, the sea of human bodies parted and a clear path was made the entire length of the hallway leading to the trauma rooms in the rear. Seeing that his words were heeded and a little embarrassed about the fact that he yelled, Ian sheepishly repeated his appreciation for the path as he made his way hurriedly to the trauma room. Reaching the area, he quickly searched for the formidable, Dr. Trivoli. He had made his mind up after that first day never to let her beat him to the O.R. without seeing a trauma patient in his emergency room first.

The door at the end of the hall opened and the tall surgeon emerged, her presence immediately was felt in the hallway. The hectic ritual of dressing for the trauma became a relaxed routine when she was there. The staff had come to respect and appreciate her quiet but commanding demeanor.

Ian eyed her closely as she made her way towards him. Slipping his hand to his head, he wiped his baldhead with a handkerchief trying not to be obvious. He thought of her as strikingly beautiful as well as a damn good surgeon. She definitely didn't need to be someone's 'little woman' to feel good about herself. His past choices in the women were less commanding. None had been strong or self-sufficient like Garrett Trivoli. Instead, they had all looked up to him as the great and all-knowing doctor. Well, that was until they divorced him. Three failed marriages and he had little to show for it. The only thing that was a constant reminder of his past copulations was the huge amount that was missing from his paychecks each month. Besides the alimony payments and child support receipts, the only things he had to show for the few short years of combined marriages were two worn photographs. The first one being his son, Jonathan, who lived with his third wife in New Jersey and the other one his daughter, Elaine, in Florida, who was now attending college. He hadn't been a strong fixture in her life but was proud that she was following in his footsteps with a major in Pre-Med.

He first wife had been so frail and quiet until the night she caught him with another woman, walking into his office at the hospital. She had packed and taken the small baby girl with her before he could get off of his shift. He closed his eyes and breathed deeply. Perhaps, if he were different, he would not be a three-time loser in love. You learn from your mistakes and now, Ian realized that marriage for him was nothing but that, a mistake. What he needed was someone who didn't need to be in a committed relationship, or who didn't have time to worry about the infidelities of a partner. He let his eyes wander about the tall surgeon, sizing her up for her playing ability. There would be only one way to find out, and that was to see for himself.

She strode past the Chairman of the Emergency Department and over to the rack of lead aprons. Choosing one, she began putting it on as she walked over in his direction. She said, smiling coyly at him, "So, I see you come a little faster these days, Dr. McCormick." She adjusted the Velcro closure to secure the apron in place.

He tipped his head in her direction, a slight smile tugging at his lips. "I like to get the most out of my efforts, Dr. Trivoli. Sometimes that means you have to adjust your approach." He watched her pick up a gown and thrust her arms down into the sleeves. "Perhaps we could discuss it over lunch."

She looked at him with an eyebrow hovering upwards, as her hands secured the gown. She opened her mouth to speak, but the overhead page alerting everyone that the trauma was in the department broke the silence. "Maybe another time, I'm a little busy at the moment."

He watched her smile become masked by the protective shield that she tied in place. He was fascinated by the agility with which her hands eased into the gloves, his mind wondering what they would feel like on his body. He looked around to see if anyone had noticed the smirk on his face, but the arrival of the trauma patient had captured everyone's undivided attention.

****

Steve sat bleary-eyed as he stared down at the papers in front of him. It was late afternoon but he felt as though he had been there in the trauma room for days on end. The constant bombardment of injured patients from various scenarios of accidents was taking its toll on him. He was glad that his shift would soon be over and the remainder of the night would be his for rest and relaxation.

The nurse looked over to the tall woman leaning against the wall. Her body appeared to be begging for the support of the immovable structure to keep her upright. She had seen every patient that Steve had taken care of and the four others that had been picked up by the back-up trauma nurse, Lori, when he was unavailable. It seemed to be taking its toll on the doctor as she started to be a little on edge and quick to snap with a reply when asked a question. He wondered what made her do it, to willingly punish her body with the long hours and grueling conditions. Then he remembered the look on her face when she was able to tell the patient that the injuries would heal and not to worry. That was the driving force behind the surgeon, the patient's recovery. He admired her for her unselfishness, her urge to put the welfare of others above her own.

Steve rubbed his eyes in an attempt to see the writing better, to complete his paper work before yet another trauma patient could come in. All hope was banished as the beeper once again engaged in alerting the team for yet another trauma before he could finish compiling all of the needed paperwork into the trauma folder. It was as though some god was playing a cruel joke on them. The nurse dropped his head, breathed in deeply, and then with an exaggerated sigh, pushed himself forward and into an upright position. He staggered over to the rack of lead aprons and began the process all over again.

Steve spun around to see Dr. Trivoli next to him, reaching for a lead apron. "Looks like we're going for a record today."

The surgeon looked at him with one eyebrow raised. "Just my luck, too." She was tired from lack of sleep and, by the looks of things, the prospect of her getting any shut-eye tonight was nonexistent. For once in her life, Garrett wished that there would be nothing more to do and no patients in need of her skills. Mindlessly she performed the well-rehearsed ritual of dressing in the gown, mask, and gloves to anticipate the arrival of the next traumatized patient.

"Trauma's in the department, Trauma's in the department."

The squawking of the overhead voice brought her back to the present. The surgeon shot a questioning look at the nurse next to her.

Noting the bewildered look on her face, Steve leaned in toward her, nodding his head and jogging her memory with the whispered words, "Multiple stab wounds."

She nodded her head, now remembering the report that was given with the trauma alert. Mentally she prepared herself for another grueling session in the O.R. suite. She looked up at the clock on the wall. It was only 1752. *Only twelve more hours to go,* she thought. *How many more can we possibly get?*

****

Danni lingered at her computer, reading through her E-mails. It was close to the time that she should be leaving for work, but she wanted to leave a note for Garrett just in case the night became too hectic. She thought about her roommate and her troubled sleep, wanting to help her in any way that she could.

Garrett,

I'm off on the weekend and would like to spend some time relaxing. If you are able to, we could take in a movie or go for a drive out in the country to look at the fall foliage. I know some great roads that offer wonderful scenery this time of the year. I'd love to show them to you. Let me know if this is possible.

Danni

"There, that should make it sound like I need the rest and relaxation." Her nose wrinkled as she smiled. "The only way to get **her** to take it easy is to make her think that **I** need it. Well, so be it." With only her friend's best interest at heart, she struck the enter key, sending the E-mail on its way.

Danni noticed the time on her computer. "Damn, it's 1815. I'm going to be late if I don't hurry." Quickly she shut down her terminal and gathered her knapsack and keys. To make up for lost time she walked briskly through the house as she pulled her coat on.

Opening the door, her eyes scanned the horizon. *Well, it doesn't look like any storm hit today while I slept. Hmmm...I wonder if it passed us by.* The small woman shrugged her shoulders, then made her way to her car parked several spaces down the street. She entered it, and turned the key in the ignition. Using the moment to check her appearance in the vanity mirror, she let the engine warm up. Securing her seatbelt in place, the young woman looked up and down the street then hastily pulled out of the parking space on her way to work.

****

Rosie stood adjusting her scrubs as the door opened and a small blonde figure darted in hurriedly, making her way to the locker that housed her apparel for work. The nurse had finished putting the stethoscope around her neck when she eyed her friend's rushed mannerisms. "You running late or just that anxious to get in to work?" She shook her head. "You got time. Besides, I understand that Garrett just took a trauma patient up to surgery about half an hour ago."

"Oh," She cleared her throat. "You **are** just coming on, right?" Danni wondered how Rosie had known about Garrett's whereabouts.

"Yep, but I ducked in and looked at the assignment board first. That's when I heard them talking about how bad it's been with traumas today." She closed her locker door and turned to face her friend. "You and me in trauma, it should be a good night," she smiled.

The petite nurse quickly dressed then pulled her necessary accessories off of the shelf, and closed the locker. "So, I guess I'm Trauma One, huh?"

Rosie laughed, "You better believe it. I was that last night, remember?"

Danni slid her feet into her shoes. "Yeah, I hope the night isn't too busy." She hoped with all her heart for her roommate's sake. She stood upright and made a final adjustment to her pants. "Well, let's get out there."

The taller nurse sauntered over to the door, holding it open she motioned for the woman to advance through it. "Age before beauty…er…I mean…after you," she joked. Danni just smiled and shook her head.

They went down the hall through the main entrance of the E.R. where a stern-looking charge nurse met them. Karen sat at the desk peering over her reading glasses at the two nurses. She motioned to her watch and gave a dissatisfied frown. That was all she did, as words were unnecessary to convey her meaning.

"We must be a minute late," Rosie whispered.

"Shh! She'll hear you," Danni turned and whispered back. "Sorry, Mom." Her face full of innocence as she watched Karen begin to smile, causing them all to giggle.

"You two like to push it to the last second, don't you?" Karen shuffled the papers on the desk. "I've been waiting to see you two."

The bewildered nurses looked at each other, each one trying to think of what they could have possibly done wrong. They approached the older nurse cautiously. "You wanted to see us about what? Dear, sweet Mom." Rosie frequently used exaggerated terms of endearment when she wanted to lessen any possible problems.

The charge nurse sighed. "Why do you always think that it's something bad? Hmmm? Is there something you need to worry about?" She eyeballed the taller nurse, waiting to see if she offered any information.

"No, nothing to worry about. Honest!" The answer came back quickly from the small blonde.

"Yeah, right. What she said," the auburn-haired nurse said, pointing to the blonde. The look on her face was one of complete, forced innocence.

Karen rolled her eyes, "You two are going to be the death of me." Each of the nurses smiled trying her best not to laugh. "I just wanted you to help Steve finish up his paperwork on the traumas, so that he can get out of here at a reasonable time. He's had a pretty busy day." She used her hands to shoo them along. "He's in the back, now go. Danni…"

"I know, Mom, I'm Trauma One, I'll get report too." She smiled at the older nurse, then turned and headed down the hall.

Karen winked, "That's my girls!" She watched them with the loving eyes of a mother.

They rounded the corner to see Steve sitting at the long desk, mounds of papers stacked in neat piles lining its length. The male nurse looked as though he had waged a long and tiring battle with the gods that controlled the flow of traumas. The expression on his face was one of relief when he saw his co-workers coming over to him.

"Thank God!" He clasped his hands together in mock prayer. "My prayers have been answered. Finally this day from hell is over." He made no attempt to conceal his disdain for the last 12 hours of work.

"I'm your actual relief. Anything I need to know about?" The petite blonde studied his face. It was drawn and tired looking. Danni wondered how badly her roommate looked at this point. She accepted the trauma team pager from him and clipped it to her scrub pants after she cleared the previously issued pages.

Exhausted, Steve shook his head. "Nothing coming in at this time. I just have to send off all of the paper work." He motioned to the desk full of piled papers. "It's been so busy, I haven't had the time to get to it." He sighed deeply. "I hate to stick you with it."

Holding her hand up, Danni spoke. "We'll take care of it. You just go and head home."

Steve got up to leave. "Really? Thanks, I appreciate it." He slowly started down the hall to the locker room.

"Hey, Steve! Be careful on your way home, we wouldn't want you coming in as a trauma now, would we?" Rosie yelled after him to get his attention. The tired man just kept on walking, glad to have a chance to go home to relax. She turned to her fellow nurse, "I guess he can't take a joke." They laughed openly and started in on the task at hand.

****

The tall surgeon trudged from the doctor's lounge with a cup of dark, black coffee in her hand. She slowly brought it up to her mouth, praying with each sip that it would keep her awake. She was amused that last night when she could sleep, she hadn't been able to, and now, when it was imperative that she be awake, able to function at a moment's notice, she could barely keep her eyes open. She could try for some shut-eye but she was afraid that she would not wake up when the trauma pager went off. "By the gods!" She looked down at the beeping pager. "Not again!"

The crackling voice began its recital. "Trauma page, Trauma page. Twenty-year-old male patient unrestrained passenger involved in a minor MVA. Level 2 trauma page. ETA 5 minutes to your facility via ambulance."

Glancing at her watch, she shook her head and wondered when it would all stop. It was only 1953 and already she had seen a total of 15 traumas since 0600. She could feel herself becoming tired and irritable. *Perhaps this night will be over soon,* she thought. *Yeah, fat chance of that.* With that thought in mind she chugged down the remainder of the coffee, praying that it would do the job. She paused only long enough to dispose of the now empty Styrofoam cup before making her way down to the Trauma Room to await the next patient's arrival.

The team was moving sluggishly as they donned the trauma apparel. The lead aprons seemed to weigh twice as much as when they had started thirteen hours ago. The medical school students appeared to be the ones showing the lack of energy the worst. It was their inexperience with the long, grueling hours that was their undoing.

Garrett had dressed at her usual pace, and took her position on the left side of the empty stretcher. She leaned stiff-armed on the bed, trying to take some of the weight off of her back and legs. She closed her eyes in an effort to summon all of her strength to make it through the remainder of the night. She could hear the lively talking and joking of the fresh set of nurses as they waited for the patient to arrive. The only energy in any abundance seemed to be held by them. She thanked the gods for sending her a team of nurses that she knew and worked well with. As she saw it, this would be the only saving grace to the rest of the night.

Danni studied the surgeon intently as the patient was wheeled into the room with the medics giving their hasty report. She could see the deeply furrowed brow that shadowed the lusterless blue orbs of her roommate. This was so unlike her friend. Her eyes had always held an air of excitement about them. She thought back to the first time she had gazed into those crystal blue pools of emotion and the feeling of déjà vu that had come over her. For some reason, the spark in those eyes had set off a feeling so powerful that it had caused the young nurse to stand in awe of the figure in front of her.

Somewhere in time she had known this woman before. Where or when, it didn't matter. What did matter was that there was an undeniable bond between them, a bond that would become recognizant to them both in time. Danni put aside her thoughts when she heard the familiar tones of the surgeon signaling the transference of the patient to the hospital stretcher.

"Ready? On my count, one, two, three." The tall woman stepped back allowing the ambulance stretcher enough clearance to be removed, as the rest of the team converged on the patient, each with his or her own task to perform.

The initial examination assuring the patient's airway, breathing, and circulation was completed to the surgeon's satisfaction. She then began her secondary survey of the young man before her. She explained what she was doing to him as she moved from body part to body part to ascertain whether or not he had sustained any injuries in the minor MVA. Working her way down his long body, it became obvious to her that the medical student on the right side was standing motionless with his hands resting on the young man's groin. She followed the arms up until the face of the student was clearly visible. His eyes were closed and if she didn't know better, she would have to say that he was asleep. It couldn't have been worse if he had been a sentry caught sleeping on guard duty. He was going to be made an example of. There was no sleeping when duty called! No, in her book there wasn't.

"You," she pointed to the Resident standing next to the dozing team member. "Take him out into the hallway." Her voice was low as it rumbled across the room, commanding immediate obedience. "Then step in here and take his place."

The surgeon finished her examination of the injured man, finding only a few broken ribs to be the reason for his breathing problem. The chest X-ray had confirmed it. She felt justified in ordering the patient a twenty-three hour observation bed. She wanted to watch him overnight just to make sure that a pneumothorax did not develop.

Danni called in a report on the patient to the assigned floor that would be taking him. Then the nurse readied his chart and made arrangements for him to be transported to his designated bed while Garrett addressed the medical student.

The raven-haired woman removed her mask, gloves, and gown as she stormed out of the room. The rest of the team had disbursed, leaving the lonely-looking figure standing in the hall. His face grew pale as the surgeon came closer to him. She motioned for him to enter the conference room ahead of her. She followed him in and closed the door. Pacing back and forth as she removed the lead apron, she gathered her thoughts. Relieved of its weight, the surgeon stood to her full height, slowly inhaling before she spoke. Her eyes surveyed the form before her.

"I'm sorry…I was trying to concentrate…" his thoughts were in pieces as he nervously tried to excuse his actions. "I didn't mean to…I haven't stopped all day."

Her brow rose as she listened to his jumbled attempt to justify his action. Each attempt only added to her anger. Her feelings were screaming deep inside of her to rid the medical profession of this poor excuse for a doctor wannabe before he truly endangered a patient's life. She held up her hand trying to put an end to his ramblings. "You'd do yourself more of a service if you would stop talking now." Her voice was low and unwavering.

His mouth dropped open as he stared at her menacing form.

"And just what field of specialty is it that you propose to be interested in, when and if you do become a physician?" Her steel blue eyes were narrowed at him.

He gulped. His throat was dry, and he found it hard to speak. "Radiology, like my…my father," he stammered.

"I should have guessed as much!" She thought about the cushy job of a Radiologist, where, once out of Residency and Fellowship years, the only tough subspecialty was that of an Angiographer. They were often referred to as the "bankers" of medicine in their comfortable 9 to 5 work hours, where every night was filled with sleep. "You've got a long way to go before you can enjoy that lifestyle. I suggest that you **not** fall asleep again in my presence during a trauma or I'll personally see to it that you never get that title of Doctor." Her words were harsh and without feeling, like the metal of a sword cutting deep to the bone.

He opened his mouth but thought more wisely not to meet her threat with a rebuttal, simply nodding his head in understanding. Disgustedly, she waved her hand, dismissing him from her presence. After he had left, the tall surgeon leaned on the conference table, hanging her head in disbelief.

The petite blonde nurse had kept a cautious watch of her friend through the large glass panels that lined the hallway, allowing her a view of the conference room. She could see the tension on the surgeon's face and in the movements of her body as she addressed the medical student. She waited until the confrontation was over before getting her patient underway to his final destination for the remainder of the night.

****

Danni arrived back to the trauma room to find Rosie restocking the supplies that were greatly depleted due to the overabundance of trauma patients. She put the stretcher in place and readied it with fresh linen. By the time she had replaced the heart monitor batteries with new ones, the trauma pager was again crying for attention.

"Trauma page, trauma page. Twenty-five year old female assaulted with a brick. Severe facial damage. The patient has an unsecured airway at this time. ETA four minutes via helicopter. This is a Level One trauma page."

The two nurses flew out of the room, grabbing lead aprons and securing them quickly to their bodies. It was as though the two were in a race, as each moved efficiently to dress in the trauma gowns and masks. The overhead page now was breaking their concentration. "The Flight Crew is requesting a Physician on the helipad for intubation."

Danni grabbed a set of gloves and made for the door leading to the helipad. Converging on the door from the opposite end of the hall was the E.R. Attending for the evening, Dr. Potter, with her coat tails trailing behind her. Marianne, the Aide, had met them at the door with the bright orange intubation supply bag that they would need. Without hesitation, the door slid open and the trio stood outside, watching the helicopter gently touch down on the ground. Crouched over and shielding their eyes from the dust and debris that the propeller blades kicked up, they made their way to the aircraft. The long, red hair of the physician whipped wildly about her head as the crew door opened to the ship. Battling to keep the hair out of her face, Dr. Potter quickly climbed onboard.

The blood-soaked, swollen face of the women was barely recognizable as that of a human. The nurse and aide worked hastily to assemble the necessary equipment out of the bag. Jamie positioned herself as she pulled on a pair of gloves. She held out her hand in anticipation of the laryngoscope and the endotracheal tube. The blade on the handle was snapped into place producing a bright white ray of light to guide her once inside of the patient's mouth. The welled-up pool of blood visualized inside of the oral cavity was making it impossible to place the tube.

"Give me some suction," the physician yelled above the noise of the slowing overhead blades. The flight medic immediately complied, evacuating the bright red liquid.

Knowing that time would be short before the build-up would occur again, Dr. Potter acted with confidence as she positioned the tube into the woman's trachea and inflated the cuff at the end of it, securing the patient's lungs from further liquid impingement. The flight medic attached the ambu bag to the end of the tube, enabling the patient to be oxygenated with artificial breaths. Danni offered the physician her stethoscope to assure the proper placement of the tube inside of the patient's trachea. Jamie listened intently for the sound of air rushing in and out of the patient's lungs. Checking both sides of her chest, the physician gave a thumbs-up sign and the tube was secured in place.

Marianne hastily repacked the equipment into the orange bag and found herself breathing a little bit easier now. She was relieved that the patient was successfully intubated but she was even more ecstatic that the blades of the helicopter's propeller were slowing down to a stop. The whirling 'blades of death', as she called them, had always scared her from the first day of the flight safety class. She loved the emergency medical setting but she didn't want to lose her head over it either.

The physician climbed out of the crew area. She was concerned about the patient and the possible long-term effects the difficult intubation could have further down the road in the patient's recovery. She handed the stethoscope back to Danni as they made their way to the rear of the helicopter to assist with unloading the patient. The pilot had already opened the doors and begun the removal of the stretcher onto the hospital gurney, which the security personnel had standing by. Dr. Potter quickly got into position at the head of the patient and accepted the ambu bag as it was handed out to her. Falling in step as the flight crew made their way to the trauma doors with their precious cargo, Danni offered up a silent prayer on the injured woman's behalf.

Inside, the team of trauma personnel awaited the arrival of the patient, each going over the duties of their positions and praying that they would be able to do everything right. It was evident to them that the night was going to be a long, hard battle of conscious effort if the traumas continued to come in the quantity and severity they had all day long.

Once again, the blaring of the overhead speakers broke the silence of the emergency room. "Trauma's in the department, Trauma's in the department."

The Trauma Fellow rolled her head from shoulder to shoulder, trying her best to loosen the tense muscles of her neck and upper back. "Okay, people, let's just do our jobs and sooner or later this night will be over." Her gaze passed from one to the next around the roomful of people. As if on cue, she turned and looked at the entrance to the trauma room just as the assembly of Flight Crew and E.R. staff came into sight. An arched eyebrow appeared on her face at the sight of the unruly, red hair of Dr. Potter.

Looking up from her position at the patient's head, their eyes met in a moment of silent communication, transmitting the concern that Jamie had for the patient she was administering to. As fast as the gaze had locked with the surgeon, it was now gone, as the Flight Crew turned the stretcher to advance into the trauma room headfirst.

The well-rehearsed ease with which the patient was transferred onto the trauma room gurney was not lost on the unsuspecting eyes of the Social Worker, who waited patiently outside of the room in the hall. It would be her job to try to find the family or a friend of the battered woman. Alex sighed as she thought about the pain and suffering that the patient would go through to recover from the assault. Absent-mindedly she shook her head at the sight of the intubated woman as her clothing was efficiently removed to allow the trauma team to examine her body for any further injuries.

Alex quietly accepted the remnants of discarded clothing and began rummaging through them with her gloved hands in search of any form of identification. The only clue to the woman's identity was the small nametag that simply read, 'Sunshine'. The Social Worker closed her eyes and sighed in disappointment, then turned to find the members of the Flight Crew.

"Do any of you know her name?" Alex prayed that they could help her find a starting ground for the search into the woman's relatives or friends.

They looked at each other and slowly shrugged their shoulders, almost in unison. "All we can tell you is that she was found next to a building in a small alley in Washington County. We picked her up at an "LZ" a couple of blocks away. Sorry, but there was nobody that recognized her and we didn't find a purse, either." The Flight Medic hung his head slightly. "They were questioning whether it was a simple assault or a possible rape at the scene."

The Social Worker's eyes opened wide at this last revelation. "Thanks for you help," she hastily retreated and propelled her body back toward the trauma room. "Dr. Trivoli…Dr.Trivoli!" She gasped for a breath as she waited for the surgeon to look her way. In a low voice that was professionally driven, Alex stated, "There is a question of rape at the scene."

The tall surgeon closed her eyes momentarily, in self-condemnation. *Damn, I should have thought of that possibility.* Regrouping her thoughts, Garrett began firing off orders. "Can you put each article of clothing in a separate bag?" The Social Worker nodded in agreement. "Thanks, Alex." The surgeon turned to the right, getting the attention of the nurses. "Rosie, Danni, we'll need to bag her hands for possible evidence. Mom, we'll need a rape kit and camera."

"Gotcha one already coming," Karen replied.

"Dr. Potter, did you suction her mouth before you intubated?" The surgeon was looking steely-eyed at the E.R.

Attending.

"Why…yes, there was too much blood and fluids to see the cords." The look of realization flashed across her face. "It could have contained possible evidence," Jamie rubbed her forehead in thought. "I'd better get the Flight Crew to retrieve it from the helicopter and label it." She left to find the Flight Medic who had handled the task of suctioning for her.

Garrett's attention now turned back to the exposed body before her. The skilled eyes of the observant surgeon slowly studied the woman's body, noting any small scrapes, lacerations, or signs of discoloration that she could find. Burning into her memory anything that could possibly be a sign of force, she verbalized what she saw for the videotape that recorded the events in the trauma room. The upper torso appeared to be pristine until she gently raised the woman's voluptuous left breast to see all aspects of it.

"Shine that light over here." The surgeon motioned with her head to the lateral aspect of the body. Rosie quickly reached up and positioned the large operating room light to illuminate the area. Moving closer to get a better look, Garrett began to describe what she saw. "There appears to be a faint purple discoloration in the shape of a semi-circle…no, make that two semi-circles, opening to each other. I get the impression of a possible human bite mark with no visible break in the skin."

Out of the corner of her eye she could see the medical student fussing with his gloves as he began to go toward the patient's upper thigh. "Everybody freeze right where you are!" Her low, throaty growl was ominous. She straightened to her full height as she turned to stare directly at the medical student, "And what are you about to do?" Her eyes were like a swirling blue ocean readying to unleash a raging storm at the thought of a man invading this patient's private area once more. **"Answer me!"** The anger in her voice was evident as the people around the medical student now edged away from him, trying as they might not to evoke her rage on themselves also.

His eyes grew big as he became aware of the attention he had drawn to himself once again. He had pissed her off but good this time. He tried to swallow, but he was so scared that his mouth could produce no saliva. He looked down at his hands, then back up to the surgeon. "I…I …was just going to put in the …the Foley Catheter," he stuttered meekly. Then he defended his action in a slightly bolder tone. "It's my job."

"Get out of my eyesight. I want you to think about what you were attempting to do." Her voice was cold and edged with disgust. Her steely-eyed gaze followed him as he slowly retreated out of the trauma room. Once out in the hallway, he snapped off his gloves and reached for the mask covering his face, ripping it off in anger. Then, grabbing the gown with both hands at his chest, tore it from his body, and cast it to the floor as he strode down the hall, away from the menacing surgeon.

"Any more bright ideas here?" Garrett looked around the room at the shocked team.

"Rape kit is here, Dr. Trivoli," Karen's soft-spoken words seemed to put an end to the tense situation. She handed the package to Danni.

The surgeon paused to review the electronic monitoring devices showing the patient's vital signs. The woman was holding her own. "Karen, call CT Scan and see how long before we can get in. We'll need a head and abdomen." She let out a breath as she tried to calm herself.

"Already did. It will be another 20 minutes before there is an open scanner."

Garrett nodded her head, "Danni, set up the Rape Kit." She stripped the gloves from her hands, and walked over to the waste receptacle for hazardous materials by the entrance where she disposed of them. Reaching for the curtain that shielded the trauma room from the rest of the E.R., she bowed slightly, showing the way out, "Now, if you will excuse us…."

The team of medical people filed out into the hallway, not wanting to see a replay of the surgeon's wrath.

The last one in line was an Intern who paused and questioned the dismissal. "How are we supposed to learn, this way?" He motioned to the group standing in the hall.

The surgeon's eyebrow rose in warning. "By reviewing the tape at Trauma Conference," her voice was barely above a whisper. She looked down on the smaller stature of the man, "Think about how you would feel if this were your mother, daughter, or significant other. Hmmm?"

His eyes registered the terror of the thought as he looked back to the patient lying on the gurney. Nodding to the surgeon, he joined the group in the hall.

The trio of nurses and the surgeon proceeded to take samples from the various orifices of the patient's body, making sure to label them appropriately. Each one was silently standing vigil to the serious nature of their job. The act of the rape alone was degrading and demoralizing to a woman, but now, to have to emphasize each area of possible contact or penetration for clinical inspection and sampling could be just as psychologically traumatic. The surgeon kept a professional demeanor in her voice as she stated her findings for the videotape to record.

During this entire time Danni spoke softly into the injured woman's ear, advising her of what they were doing and soothing her of any fears of a repeated attack. It seemed to be working, as the monitors showing the vital signs never wavered from normal with each new probing of her exposed body. She watched intently at the actions of her friends. She could see the tired and drawn look in the surgeon's face.

The last intrusion into the patient's privacy was the combing of any body hair for stray pieces of evidence. The surgeon carefully ran the comb over the sensitive body parts, gathering any loose strands of hair or fibers into the plastic bags that Rosie held open. The nurse sealed the bag and marked it with the site of the collection. Having completed the examination and evidence gathering, Garrett finished the trauma protocol by placing a urinary catheter and probing the patient's rectum with her gloved and lubricated digit for any signs of internal bowel trauma and bleeding.

"Hemoccult negative," she reported for the record as she disposed of the soiled gloves and testing kit. She turned to see Rosie unfolding a fresh, warmed blanket over the patient's body as the sound of the respirator kept a steady rhythm in the background. The curtain had been opened and the exiled trauma team now ventured back into the room. The touch on her arm caught her attention as Garrett turned to see the petite nurse standing next to her.

"Don't you think you were a little rough on that Med Student?" She wrinkled her nose and looked up into the blue pools of the surgeon's eyes. "He was only doing what he thought you wanted him to do..." the nurse was trying to smooth over the earlier confrontation, "…after all, it's not like he fell asleep again."

All eyes were on the pair, watching for the tall surgeon's response. Garrett finished removing her mask and gown, letting the full impact of Danni's speech sink in. Graciously looking around the room at the many shocked faces staring back at her in awe, the surgeon smiled politely. "Ah…Danni, could I see you in the conference room, please?" Her voice was sickeningly sweet, as the smile never left her face. "Rosie, can you keep an eye on the patient?" Garrett looked over to Rosie enlisting her approval.

"Yeah, go ahead. I got you covered here." The nurse made herself busy, preparing the patient for the upcoming CT Scan.

"Thank you." The surgeon started out of the trauma room into the hall, only to stop suddenly and lean back into the room, "You know where I'll be if you need me for anything. This should really only take a minute or two." Turning briskly, her determined stride carried her into the conference room.

The petite nurse stood, looking dumfounded. She quickly gazed from Karen to Rosie, as if looking for some kind of answer to Garrett's behavior. Each one shrugged at the other as their eyes made contact, not knowing what to expect from the surgeon. *Why do I feel like I'm a sheep being lead to the slaughter?* Taking a deep breath, Danni walked into the conference room as she quietly exhaled, trying as she might to settle her nerves.

The surgeon stood facing the large audio-visual cart at the opposite end of the room, her face a stoic mask as she looked blankly out of one of the windows that lined the hallway. Sensing that the young nurse had stepped into the room, the surgeon turned just slightly, "Come in. Oh, and close the door, will you?" The nurse obliged and moved further into the room, her eyes never leaving the tall woman's figure.

Garrett didn't like what she was going to have to do, but she could not afford a breach in command, not in front of the team. She sniffed as she thought of how military her thoughts were. *By the gods, I guess some of the Navy actually rubbed off on me over the last three years.* She swept her tongue over the front of her teeth as she readied herself, her eyes closing momentarily at the thought of disciplining a friend.

"Danni," she started then turned to face the nurse. "What were you doing in there just now?" Her face remained a stoic mask as she waited for an answer.

The petite nurse looked into the face of the woman in front of her. "I…I just thought that maybe…" she now stared at the floor, "…maybe you were a little tired and didn't realize how the Med Student felt."

"No, what you don't realize is that you tried to use our friendship to supersede me in a professional setting." Garrett sighed, took up a position on the opposite side of the conference table. "I can't have that outside bond invade and undermine **my** chain of command."

Danni looked at her friend in a different light as she locked onto the steely gaze coming at her.

During her reprimand of the nurse, the surgeon emphasized her involvement and responsibility by stressing the singular pronoun louder than the last one. "**I'm** dealing with a patient's life in that room and **my** words have to stand as the bottom line. Not only does that one single patient rely on **me** to make the correct decisions now, but every patient that any member of that team treats in a later trauma setting depends on **me**, and what **I** was able to teach them in there today."

Her crystal orbs had not left the shimmering green eyes of the nurse. Garrett leaned over the table with both her tightly fisted hands resting on it. The hard lines of her face gave her stare even more intensity to the words that she spoke. "If you were in the Navy, **I'd** be having you up on charges of insubordination. Damn it! **I'd** have to do it, too! You questioned **my** authority in front of **my** team."

At first Danni had tried to make excuses for the actions of her friend, but with each new acclamation of total responsibility, the nurse became more defensive with both her posture and thinking. This was not the friend and roommate that she thought she knew, but rather some egotistical tyrant that had descended from some lofty throne to lay claim to her territory. *How dare she think that without **her**, we would not be able to treat this patient or the ones to follow! By the gods, how does she think we took care of the patients before she came here?*

Garrett sighed heavily. "Do you think I like the idea of singling out that Med Student for his actions? Someone has to show them what the reality of this profession is. If they can't handle the job now, then they need to think about getting out before they waste their lives and a lot of everyone else's time trying to teach them. And we can't forget about the patients and the lives that they could really screw-up now, can we? It's easier to get a bad seed out now, than to wait until they become a licensed physician. I can't see him going into debt, trying to be something that he was never cut out to be."

By now the young nurse had crossed her arms over her chest and began tapping her foot nervously, waiting for the verbal rampage to end. She bit the inside of her lip so as not to blurt out a rebuttal until the surgeon had ended her litany of self-exoneration for her earlier actions.

Momentarily, Danni's gaze had been distracted by the figure of Dr. Potter as she walked down the hall past the window behind Garrett. It had given her enough pause to think of her co-workers over the years and of all the people who had been seen as patients through the trauma suite. She was more determined than ever to let this newcomer know just how she thought. Her green eyes turned into a churning sea of emotions as she narrowed her gaze into the surgeon's blue pools.

Not being one to yell and scream in anger, Danni initiated her rebuttal in a calm, orderly fashion. Letting her hands go down to her sides, the young nurse asked, "Can you spell the word 'trauma' for me?"

This had completely taken the surgeon off her guard. "What?" Her eyes expressing a puzzled look as she regarded the nurse.

The petite woman smiled coyly at her adversary; "I asked how do **you** spell the word 'trauma'." She paused, waiting to hear the answer.

"What does that have to do with…"

"No, I want to see if you spell it the same way as we do. Please, humor me."

The tall woman grimaced, rolling her eyes and curtly replied, "T-R-A-U-M-A. But I don't see…."

"HMMM, just as I thought." The nurse crossed her abdomen with one arm as she allowed her chin to rest in a thoughtful pose with the other arm. "You know how to spell the word, but you really don't see what it's all about, now do you?" Her pose once again relaxed at the startled look on the surgeon's face.

"What do you mean by that? I know all about…." The surgeon's gaze narrowed as her eyes took on an ice-like appearance.

"NO! You ***think*** you know all about trauma, but let me tell you what trauma really means." The nurse placed her hands on her hips in a defiant manner. "Let me spell the word out for you in the manner that we understand it here." Her right hand began ticking off the letters as she said them. "**T** stands for **Teamwork** in a tense setting. **R** stands for **Respect** of not only the patient's life and privacy, but also that of the staff you're teamed with. **A** takes into consideration the feeling of **Achievement** in the patient's physical and emotional outcome. **U** reminds us of our need to be in **Unison** when dealing with the matters at hand. **M** brings to mind that the **Mortality** of the patient is as fragile as our own." Her right hand being completely used she brought her left one up, extending her thumb. "And finally, **A** leads us to **Anticipate** the needs of the family in response to the patient's injured state." The young woman's face tightened into a hard and calculating stare. She had gradually made her way closer to the table while she was spelling out the list of letters in the word.

"There doesn't seem to be any **'I'** in the word trauma when you think of it in that respect, hmmm? Is there?" Before she knew it, the nurse was leaning on the table giving the appearance of a mirror image of Garrett's aggressive stance.

The face-off came as a surprise. Garrett had never considered that the young woman would be so adamant about the surgeon's possessive and controlling nature. It was something that had always come so naturally to her that she had never given it very much thought. Besides, everyone had always assumed that she would take charge just by her physical appearance alone. *What is it about this slip of a girl that makes her think she can stand up to me?* She fought hard to control her raging anger at her friend. *No. Friendship had no place in this argument,* she thought, *this is totally on a professional level.* The ice blue of her eyes turned even colder as she smashed her fist against the table. "Damn it, Danni. You're going to **make** me do this, aren't you?"

The nurse caught the motion of the surgeon's arm as it brought all the force that it could muster into the downward slam, impacting the table. She never flinched at the sound or the vibrations that emanated throughout the piece of furniture, advancing up into her hands. She had made her stand. There would be no backing down now. She thought of how her mother had always warned her when she was growing up that her stubbornness, in the defense of others, would be her downfall.

"Do what you have to…you will anyway." The spitfire of a nurse spat back at the menacing figure before her with the turmoil of emotions building deep within her small frame.

Garrett's voice lowered an octave and the rumble of it over her lips caused the hair to rise on the young woman's neck. "You're out of **my** traumas starting now!" She inched even closer to the blonde's face with her own. "I don't care if you go home, go to lunch, or just hang out for the rest of your shift." She audibly filled her lungs with air. "I…don't…want…to… see…you," saying each word singularly for emphasis, "in **my** trauma rooms for the **rest** of the night." She paused. "Do you…" she drew the word out, "understand **me**?"

The electricity of the moment charged the air around the pair, as they faced nose to nose across the table. The hair on their arms was standing on end as if they had been in close proximity to a lightning strike. They were in their own microcosm, unaware of the stunned expressions on the faces of the people that lined the hall outside of the trauma room, staring in at them through the window.

The charge nurse made the sign of the cross on her body, praying that one of her pseudo-daughters would not be the next trauma as she headed toward the conference room's closed door. She couldn't believe what she was seeing, especially from her non-confrontational friend.

As if to add further emphasis to her proclamation, the raven-haired woman gritted her teeth, showing the stark whiteness of them saying, "I call the shots here, not the nurses."

Seeing that they had reached a standoff, Danni acquiesced, "Fine!" Then turned with the speed of a tornado and stormed out of the now-opened conference room door.

Karen stepped back, releasing the doorknob, her mouth agape. She watched as the blonde spitfire brushed past her and headed down the hall, cutting a wide path from all that she passed by.

Without stopping or slowing down, the young nurse called back, "I'll be going to lunch now, Mom." The tasseled blonde locks of hair moved with the shaking of her head. She had left, walked right out of the area before she would regret anything she might do. She needed time to think and definitely to cool down her hot temper. It didn't manifest itself often, but when it did...well, she'd rather not think about that. She may be small but her mind could hold its own against the likes of anyone ten times her size, whether that was stature or ego.

Garrett knew that the older nurse was quietly studying her solemn figure, which still occupied the room. The drain of energy from the surgeon's spent emotions was evident as she hung her head in disbelief at what had just transpired between her and the person she had thought of as a friend. *If only she hadn't pushed me so hard.* The surgeon closed her eyes and shook her head. *It wouldn't have come to this.* The woman brought her eyes up to see Karen standing in the doorway. "Yes?" she inquired distractedly.

"They're ready for your patient in CT Scan now," she struggled to keep her voice calm.

Garrett nodded her head, "Tell Rosie that she's now Trauma One for the rest of the night. Oh, ...and Mom," she paused to look directly at the Charge Nurse. "You're going to have to find someone else to take up the Trauma Two position."

"Okay," the nurse speculated for a moment. "Dr. Trivoli," the older nurse deliberated about offering help, but then thought better of it as she saw the distant look in the surgeon's eye. "We'll take the patient down to CT. You can meet up with us there."

The tall woman raised her hand in a motion of her approval, and then stood with her eyes closed, just trying to reign in her feelings toward the emotional outburst that she had just been a part of. She knew that the sleep-deprived state she was in had helped to set her on edge. Her fury had rapidly turned into a full-fledged, "batten down your hatches" storm front. Now, she would just have to ride out the swell of the waves that were sure to be gathering around her. It would be imperative for her to keep on course, especially in the state she was in. *By the gods, I hate emotions. I never felt like this before.*

The Charge Nurse looked down at her wrist, noticing the time. Smiling in recognition, she jotted down 2210 in the patient's chart as the time of departure for the scanner. It was still the same day as when she and Danni had watched the magnificent red hues in the morning sky. "I guess neither one heeded the warning," she mumbled under her breath, as if in answer to the earlier question.

Chapter 11

The small office reverberated with the sounds of muffled snores as the dim light, afforded by the screen saver, cast a dancing rainbow of colors from the rippling bezel pattern that illuminated the monitor. Next to the computer terminal the slumped-over form lay sprawled across the metal desktop, the head nestled into the long muscular arm folded around it as if it were a cradle, its face covered by cascading lengths of raven hair. It certainly was not the most comfortable of places to choose to sleep but, when the realms of Morpheus did finally entreat the weary surgeon, she could barely refuse. The depleted body needed to rest and heal the wounds that the previous weeks of unsatisfying sleep had languished on her. It didn't matter where or how, just that sleep was the ultimate goal. She hadn't fought it when it came but instead gave into it willingly, letting her mind embrace it, allowing it to soothe her tortured soul.

The subdued noises coming from the beeper that rested on the waist of her scrub pants was all that was needed to cause a half-lidded eye to stir. The covering slowly rose with each reminding tone until the entire eyelid had retreated from sight. It took several minutes, but gradually the blurred perception seen out of the lone eye began to clear, bringing her vision and mind into focus. She hesitantly pushed her body off of the desk, allowing the muscles in her shoulders and back time to work out any kinks found along the way. *Jeez, I feel like I've done battle with an equally matched opponent.* Her mind flashed with thoughts of Danni standing her down across the conference table. Once sitting fully erect, she stretched her long arms out to the sides. *Well, I guess that's one **friend** you can say you lost before you knew them. I can't believe that I can be so bull-headed.* As if to grasp something that was passing her by, she contracted her fingers, then hands and arms crossing her chest trying to hold on to what had been a moment ago, evading her. *You're just never going to learn are you, Garrett. Empty as usual.*

"BEEP!" There it was again only louder this time.

The surgeon took the pager off her waistband and pressed the button to reveal the numeric message. She breathed a sigh of relief, seeing the symbol for the alarm across the tiny display screen. *Well, at least it's not another trauma,* she thought to herself. *Rounds in half an hour with the new team and then, just two O.R. cases with Dr. McMurray,* she thought.

She looked around at the contents of the small room to gently jog her mind. This was not a room that she cared to hang out in, with walls that always made her feel as though they were closing in on her. Scrubbing her face with her hands, Garrett thought about the previous day's events and how they had played out. The hours after midnight had finally ended the onslaught of traumas and she had stolen away to her office to catch up on some paperwork.

Paperwork, huh, she laughed. *It's all computerized now.* "Hmmm…Let's see what I was working on," she spoke aloud trying to jar her memory.

Long, sinewy fingers caressed the mouse, moving it slightly. The monitor screen quickly changed from the roaming bezel pattern to one of letters and words. To her surprise it was E-mail. Most of the correspondence she received electronically was work related, but this one was different. Her eyes quickly read over the lines of text, as a smile began to tug at the corners of her lips. It read:

Garrett,

I'm off on the weekend and would like to spend some time relaxing. If you are able to, we could take in a movie or go for a drive out to the country looking at the fall foliage. I know some great roads that offer wonderful scenery this time of the year. I'd love to show them to you. Let me know if this is possible.

Danni

She contemplated how nice it would be to spend some much needed time relaxing with her friend. Then, with a sudden feeling of urgency, the surgeon looked desperately to the date and time that the E-mail was sent. Seeing that it had been dated yesterday before her friend had come on shift, the tall woman cursed under her breath. "Son of a…" she let her head hang as the instant replay of the prior evening was rapidly viewed in her mind. She closed her eyelids tightly and shook her head, but the images would not stop. Her fingers nervously raked through her raven hair. Finally, resigning herself to the inevitable, she sighed. "What were you thinking?" She chastised herself. "Hmmpf! Maybe that's the problem, you weren't thinking."

Her mind gave a fleeting tally of all of the wonderful moments that she had encountered in the presence of the small blonde. In less than four months, there were more than she could count using both hands. This surprised her, considering that during the last twenty years of her life she could barely come up with five or six memorable times shared with another person, and even all of those were not shared with the same person. She thought about the fact that for the first time in her adult life, she let someone get close enough to her to have finally made a friend, only now to have possibly thrown it all away with one tyrannical outburst.

Her thoughts turned to her young companion and she wondered if Danni would be able to discern the professional reprimand, not taking it personally to heart. The surgeon bit down on her lip as she thought about the force with which she had repelled the young nurse, banning her from trauma rooms for the rest of the night. It had to be the lack of sleep that had caused her to act the way she did. *The best Trauma Nurse I've ever met and I throw her out of my traumas.* She shook her head in disbelief. *I must not have been thinking clearly at all.*

She replayed the scene of confrontation with Danni, cringing as she remembered her words. The surgeon sank back into her chair, her shoulders slumping in defeat. *Well, that's what you get for letting someone get close to you.* She taunted herself even more, *Hurts, doesn't it?* She closed her eyes as she remembered the anger and frustration that had been written all over the nurse's face when she locked into that nose-to-nose standoff. Garrett wasn't sure what had upset her more last night, the fact that she was snapping out at every little thing because of her lack of sleep, or that Danni knew more about her than the surgeon knew herself. *Danni was right. I did lash out at him unmercifully.* The corner of Garrett's mouth twitched into a smirk when she thought of how much courage her non-confrontational friend had shown. "I like that," she mindlessly said aloud.

"Like what?" The accented voice came from the direction of the open door; an almost inaudible knock was heard as he stuck his head into the room.

Startled at the sound of another voice, the surgeon's eyes opened wide; she looked up from the screen that she had been absently staring at, while she was deep in thought. "I…I…" she stuttered. "I like the sight of my relief," she said, trying to quickly reorganize her thoughts, grasping at the first thing to come to her head. "You just startled me, that's all."

She glanced at her watch. It was 0545 and as always, Dr. Rene Chabot was in early, ready to begin a new day. "I guess I lost track of the time."

The thin man looked cautiously around the tiny speck of an office that the three Trauma Fellows shared. "I'm not disturbing anything, am I?" His face took on a hopeful look that he had interrupted a private moment. He often worried about the all too serious surgeon, and had even casually dropped hints about her finding someone to share her life with. He had always been a good judge of character, that was why Rene was able to see the gentle, loving heart of the woman most people steered clear of.

"Rene, you expect too much," she shook her head at his implied thought. "I'm a Trauma Surgeon. Nobody wants to put up with that kind of lifestyle, not even for a little while."

"Ah, but you forget, I'm the one with newborn twins and a loving wife at home. Things like that don't happen overnight. Eh?" A sly smile crossed his lips, "So, you see, it's not impossible. You just have to open yourself up to the thought. I'm sure that there is at least one someone out there that would enjoy the chance to know you and share a life with you. Or are you so terrible that no one would have you? I think not." He answered his own question.

"You're never going to give up, are you?" Garrett's hand moved the mouse into position letting the cursor find its mark and closed the window of the E-mail from sight, not wanting to give the man any more ammunition to use. *Besides,* she thought, *I probably lost that thread of friendship with Danni after last night.*

Shaking his head he smiled saying, "I have the rest of the year to still work on it. You will see, one day it will happen. Then you will think back on ol' Rene and smile." He winked at her as he held out his hand for the pager sitting on the desk.

The woman smiled at his conviction to her happiness. "Why is it that all happily married people think about is getting all of the unattached people around them paired up?"

She handed him the pager. "If I didn't know better, Dr. Chabot, I would guess that you have a little Jewish Yenta in you," she teased him knowing all too well of his French-Canadian ancestry.

Rene cocked his head to one side, "If it will help to go visit a Synagogue, or wear a prayer shawl, then perhaps…"

Garrett held up her hands in quiet protest. "All right, enough." She chuckled at the thought of her colleague wearing a prayer shawl just to ensure her happiness. "I get the idea. I promise to leave myself open to the thought, how's that? Okay?"

He looked deep into her eyes, seeing the crystal blue pools reflect the melancholy of her soul. He wondered what troubles had befallen her in the past to render such a deep hurt. He thought to ask her, but realized that he had probably pushed her far enough for one day. Nodding in acceptance of her offer, "For now, Garrett, but one day you will see that someone will step out from behind you and capture your heart. It happened to me," he said proudly. "But let's get down to business. You look worse than me with two babies to take care of during the night." He had only now noticed her haggard appearance. "You look like you haven't gotten more than a couple of hours sleep in the last week or so," he teased her.

She looked at the man who felt comfortable with her, knowing that she probably looked worse than what he was letting on to. *I have to remember to put some make-up on before meeting up with McMurray.* She made a mental note, not wanting the Chief of Trauma Surgery to think her unable to withstand the long, grueling hours that the job dictated. She had fought long and hard for this chance to accomplish her life's goal, and she wasn't about to let anybody think that she wasn't capable of doing the job, whatever it took.

"Come on, Rene, I'll tell you all about the patients while we make our rounds." She pushed herself away from the desk and got up, heading for the door. "After you," she motioned with her hand toward the open door behind him. He nodded and turned, advancing into the hall from the tiny room.

^^^^^^^^^^^^^

Karen watched as the petite nurse finished stocking the last of the specialty carts that were used by the different disciplines of medicine that frequented their area. She wondered where the nurse was getting all the energy. Not only had she busied herself with most of the aide's duties, but she had also volunteered to take every transport from the regular emergency room to the floors during the remainder of the night. Each time, making sure not to pass anywhere near the trauma rooms if she thought that the raven-haired surgeon would be in attendance. It was almost as if she needed to be working off her pent-up emotions.

Finding nothing more to use her energy on, she took a seat next to the charge nurse. "So, Mom, anything else that I can do?" The blonde tried to hide her emotions from the older nurse.

Playing along with the game, Karen feigned a disinterested attitude as she studied the computer screen in front of her. She so wanted to help the young nurse deal with the emotions that plagued her, but knew that if they were not dealt with in the proper manner, she would never get the nurse to bare her soul.

"Mom, did you hear me?" Danni tugged at the Charge Nurse's sleeve. "Anything," she reiterated, "just tell me anything and I'll do it."

The older nurse smiled to herself, as the opening that she was waiting for had just jumped into her lap. "Anything?"

Without hesitation, the petite nurse nodded her head in mock eagerness, "Yes, anything!"

Karen cleared her throat as she turned toward the impish figure next to her. "You could let me know what that was all about earlier with you and Garrett. I mean, so that if I'm called on the carpet by Nan, I'll have some idea as to at least what it was about." She watched as Danni's nose wrinkled up at the realization that she had been tricked.

"I guess you got me there." Her words were slow and thoughtful as she tried to find a way out of this. "I…I…" she tossed her head from side to side, "I guess I thought that she was being too hard on that poor medical student. I realize now that I let my self-righteous pride step right into it, when she told me that it was **her** trauma to run as she saw fit." She shrugged her shoulders. "I just kept thinking that we had always done our best with the traumas, working as a team before she came. I assumed that I knew better and questioned her authority."

Raising a skeptical eyebrow at the young nurse, Karen waited.

"Okay, I was wrong. I flew off the handle and just let my emotions take control. I'm sorry, Mom." She sighed, "I know that it wasn't very professional of me but…"

"But you were determined to show her just how strong-willed you were. Right?"

"Yeah, you're right." Her fingers nervously played with the cord on the nearby phone. "Do you think she'll listen to an apology?"

"I think that depends on what your apology will be for, stepping on her authority or your concern for her as a friend." The older woman reached over and patted the small hand with her own. "If you believe your disagreement stemmed from something other than a personal nature, then treat it that way." She smiled at the thoughtful expression on Danni's face. "She's a professional, I'm sure she will listen to reason."

"I don't know, Mom. We weren't exactly on speaking terms when I left that room." The nurse shrugged her shoulders, "Maybe…"

Karen caught sight of the first daylight employees entering the doors to the emergency room. "Maybe," she interrupted, "you need to go home now and sleep on it for a while."

"Thanks Mom, I will." Danni pulled her emotionally drained body up from the chair and started making her way to the locker room, contemplating the thought of sleep. In a passing moment, she prayed that the gods would look after her sleepless friend for the rest of the day until Garrett also, made her way safely home.

Watching as Danni trudged away Karen quietly spoke what was on her mind. "The way I see it, my young friend, you were right in trying to get her to admit that she wasn't thinking clearly with that medical student."

****

The make-up did little to keep her dulled senses from showing to the Chief of Trauma Services. She blinked repeatedly, trying to keep from falling asleep as she assisted the burly "Ol' Cutter" as he called himself. It was nearly 1100 and she still had the other O.R. case to assist him with.

"Rough night, Dr. Trivoli?" His speech was mellow, conversing with her as he continued to request instruments from the Scrub Nurse. "Hemostat. Thank you."

"I think we were trying for a record, Sir." She sucked in a mouthful of air in a feeble attempt to stimulate her mind. "Twenty-one in all, and we didn't lose a single one."

"Suture." He sniffed loudly. "Thank you. Not any patients, but I understand that by midnight, you were down two members of your team. Care to tell me about those?" He looked over his half spectacles at the tall surgeon across from him. "Gauze. Thank you." His eyes shifted back to the opened abdomen that was before him.

She sighed as she considered that the medical student had probably waited for him at the door of his office this morning. *That would account for one that he would know about, but how did he find out about Danni? Surely she hadn't....*

"Dr. Trivoli, if you are trying to figure out how I know about what goes on in my service after hours, I'll tell you." He continued working on the patient. "After Mr. Keithe came to me this morning, you do know who Mr. Keithe is, don't you?" He shifted his eyes to catch her nod of affirmation to his question. "I watched the tape from the trauma room. I noticed that after you asked to speak with Nurse Bossard, she never reappeared in the room for the rest of the night. Although I did hear her voice, quite loudly I must admit, state that she was going to lunch."

The tall woman prepared herself, waiting for the ranting and raving to start. Much to her surprise, it didn't. The "Ol' Cutter" just kept on course with the operation as they had previously discussed.

"Seems like you know just about everything already, Sir." She held the retractor steady as he finished examining the glistening junction of the small intestine with the larger bowel.

"Count," he demanded, signaling that he was ready to close. "Sometimes those nurses take care of us and our patients more than we care to think about."

Garrett thought about what Dr. McMurray was saying in his unique, cryptic fashion. *That's what Danni was trying to do last night...take care of me.* It startled her to think that someone would be looking out for her.

The high-pitched voice of the Circulating Nurse offered, "Sixteen gauze, and three needles."

The Scrub Nurse countered in response, "Correct, sixteen gauze and three needles used. Clear to close Dr. McMurray."

The gruff voice took command once again. "Okay," he winked at Garrett, "Let's get this operation over with before I grow too old to sew in straight lines anymore and have to turn it over to you young snips." He chuckled.

Garrett nodded in approval and thought about the interesting lesson that the wise "Ol' Cutter" had taught her during this all but mundane appendectomy. She had heard him loud and clear, letting his words of wisdom impart upon her. She knew what she needed to do. "Thanks, Dr. McMurray." She looked at the surgeon, busy at his work. "I've learned a lot from you today."

His eyes glanced up at her, "And the year's not over yet." He winked and continued on with the suturing. "Wait until we get a really tough case, Dr. Trivoli, then we'll see how quickly you can learn."

****

Her day was finally over. The tall surgeon slid the key into the lock on the office door and opened it. She walked around the desk and sat down in the chair. Gathering her things from her one allotted drawer that each of the Fellows were granted, she thought about the E-mail from Danni.

Looking up at the sound of the soft knocking, her eyes met the flash of blonde hair as it pushed in through the door that had been left ajar. A lopsided grin painted itself on her face as she recognized the features of the nurse that she had just been thinking about. "You're in early, aren't you?"

The small blonde wrinkled her nose up, "Yeah, I was hoping to catch you before you left for the day." She motioned to be allowed in, "May I?"

"Oh, excuse me…come on in. Have a seat, Danni." The surgeon was befuddled by her roommate's appearance at her office.

There was a moment or two of uneasy silence, each of them trying to muster up the courage to address the issue of last night. Their eyes avoided each other's gaze by looking all around the small room so as not to settle on the other. Without warning, they both started to speak at the same time.

"I want to…"

"About last night…"

Then both looked at one another as the nervous round of giggling began.

Garrett was the first to regain her composure, "Please, you first." She bowed to the nurse.

Danni held a single index finger up in the air as she drew her giggling to a halt. She thought about how different her roommate seemed now, as opposed to last night. It was almost as if the surgeon was two completely different people. This one was definitely the Garrett that the nurse had looked upon as a friend.

"I want to tell you that I'm sorry for questioning your judgement in front of the team last evening." The nurse held her hand up to stop any rebuttal from her friend. "I was wrong. I should have talked to you in private. I'm sorry for not doing that." She let her hand come down to rest at her side. "I'll understand if you don't want me to be on your team."

The azure pools searched the young blonde's face until they met the quiet green orbs, locking on to them. The words came from her mouth, but the emotion was spoken directly from her heart. "If I had to pick only one Trauma Nurse to work with, Danni, it would be you." The surgeon shifted her gaze, not wanting the nurse to feel uncomfortable. "I guess I fell into the "God Trap" last night."

Squinting, she allowed the wrinkles to play across her nose, "God Trap? I don't understand."

"In medical school they warned us about "The God Trap", it's when the doctor feels that the world is revolving around him. That he is the center of all necessary attention." She dropped her head, feeling the guilt of her actions. "My lack of sleep made it easy for me to become confused about who was really the center of attention. It should have been the patient. I'm sorry for rattling my saber so loudly." Then, looking up into a sea of green, she continued, "I'm sorry for everything that I said to you. You didn't deserve it."

"That's okay, we both learned from our mistakes." "Yeah, only I like your version of the word Trauma, more then the one that they taught us."

The blonde raised an eyebrow at this acknowledgement, "How was yours spelled?"

"Well, remember, they were teaching us to be doctors." The tall woman shrugged her shoulders and began, "Tyrannical, Rude, Abrupt, Ubermensch, Meticulous, and

Arrogant. That's what they told us we had to have in order to become good Trauma Surgeons. Honest," she quickly crossed her heart, then held her hand up with two fingers crossed.

Seeing the laughter in Danni's eyes, the surgeon let her smile settle in for good. She marveled at how good it felt to laugh with this person, even if it was just about some silly, nonsense phrase. She decided right then and there that it was a feeling that she wanted to have more often.

Garrett was mesmerized as the small slip of a girl let the most beautiful smile come across her face. Her eyes felt as though they were transfixed on that smile for an eternity. Suddenly, the tired surgeon became self-conscious about the reason her friend was smiling. Looking over herself quickly and briefly into the monitor screen to see her own reflection, the surgeon could find nothing out of place. "What…?" Her eyes were searching still for a clue.

"I was just thinking. You're the best Trauma Surgeon that I know, but you still don't meet all the designated attributes."

"Huh?" The surgeon felt awkward for the first time in many years. A small amount of color started over the woman's face as she began to blush.

"It's just that you're not rude. I can definitely say that at times you can be tyrannical, abrupt, ubermensch, meticulous, and arrogant, but rude is not one that I've seen…at least not just yet."

"Thanks, I think," the surgeon let her eyes roll and ever so slowly let her characteristic lopsided grin show.

Danni closed her eyes and bowed her head in acceptance. "You're welcome." It was nice to see her friend respond to her in this manner, especially after the words that they had exchanged the night before. She had gone home this morning thinking that all hopes of a friendship with the woman had been thrown right out the window. Now it felt like the bond of their friendship had just grown, tenfold. They had weathered the storm and the outlook ahead was one of clear sailing.

There was a moment of quiet, acceptable peace that both of the women felt comfortable with, their eyes drinking in the other's warm, silent, outpouring of love.

Garrett knew now what it felt like, when she had seen that look so many times on her mother's face as she watched her children play. It made her a little sad to think that finally, after all these years; she knew just how much she and her brother had been loved.

Not wanting to bring the moment to an end, but realizing that her time was short, Danni hesitantly began to speak. "Did you get my E-mail?"

Shaken out of her thoughts, Garrett cleared her throat. "Yes, I did. I have the entire weekend off so…are you still interested?"

"You better believe I am! Let me plan the weekend, if that's all right with you, I mean." The young woman waited for approval. "After all, I'm not the one who's been up and on-call twice this week. Okay?"

"Be my guest," she chuckled. "All that I'm interested in right now is going home and sleeping until tomorrow morning." The surgeon stood up, grasping her small duffel bag and daily planner in hand. "Come on, I'll walk you down to the E.R. on my way out." She tapped her coat pocket in search of her keys and followed the nurse out of the small office.

Seeing her colleague, Dr. Chabot, coming down the hall, she held the door open for him to enter the office. "I'm going home Rene, the office is all yours." She smiled at him politely. "I hope you have a good night."

"Thank you for the kind thought," he tipped his head towards the two women as he passed by and partially entered the open office door. He turned and watched as they made their way down the deserted hall. He studied the relaxed stature of his tall, fellow surgeon and enjoyed the friendly banter that he could hear coming from the pair as they waited for the elevator. A smile slowly crept across his face. His whispered words were in his native language, " Ouvre toi a l'idec, Mon Amie, l'amour trouvera son chemin." He stepped back so as not to be seen watching. "You will see, love always finds a way in," he said under his breath, as he resumed his journey into the office where he finally spoke the words in English. "Let yourself be open to the thought, my friend, love will find its way in."

****

The auburn-haired nurse had just caught up to Karen, as she reached for the door leading into the hospital. "Gee, thanks Mom!" She smiled and walked into the lobby bustling with visitors at this hour.

"Don't mention it," the older nurse came back with, as she entered the building. Her eyes roamed over the activity of the lobby and stopped dead at the sight of a certain pair coming off of the elevator. "Look!" She tugged at Rosie's sleeve and, once she got her attention, motioned with her chin in the direction of two women. "I hope everything went all right," she whispered.

After watching for a few seconds, she witnessed the close proximity of her two pseudo-daughters. As their steps brought them closer to her, she could hear their gentle banter.

Putting her stern, motherly face on for the occasion, Karen waited only a few seconds before calling out to her fair-haired nurse. "Well, you going to come to work or lollygag with friends all night? Hmmm, young lady? You've got a job to do, you know."

Danni scanned the lobby filled with moving bodies for the source of the familiar voice. Upon seeing Karen and Rosie, both in a crossed-armed glaring stance, the petite nurse could feel the flush rise up her neck and spread across her face. "I should have known it would be you," she aimed her speech at the Charge Nurse.

Garrett altered her course to go in their direction, gently nudging Danni along with her. "Hi, Mom, Rosie!" Her voice sounded playful as she continued. "I'd make her be Trauma One for the rest of the week if I were you, Mom," she winked, "especially for the way she bailed out on us last night." The surgeon coughed as Danni slapped her stomach with the backside of her hand.

"That's enough out of you, my friend." The blonde countered. "It's time for all good surgeons to go home and get some sleep." Her tone turned full of concern. "Garrett, be careful and call me when you get in, okay?"

"What..." The surgeon looked at the trio of concerned faces staring back at her. "What am I...five or something?" Seeing that she was outnumbered, she tipped her head from side to side, "Oh, all right." She kicked her foot at an imaginary stone, "but I don't have to like it." She looked at them again and found that each one in their own manner was shooing her towards the door and home. "Okay, I get the picture. See you guys in the morning."

The nurses stood there daring her to head anywhere but home.

"And we'll be timing you. We know where you live." Rosie voiced as the surgeon turned to walk away. Garrett nodded in assent and raised her free hand to wave weakly, as she walked out through the door and into the chilly, fall air.

When the tall surgeon was no longer in sight, the sound of laughter filled the air around the trio of friends.

"I guess she accepted your apology," the older nurse inquired, wiping a tear from her eye.

"Well, we accepted each other's and decided to learn from our mistakes." She smiled and gazed back to where she had last seen her tall friend. "It feels good not being at odds with her." She turned and looked at Karen.

"Thanks, Mom, for your advice."

The Charge Nurse winked at Danni. "Any time, little one." Glancing at the huge clock in the lobby, she attempted to hurry them along. "We'd better get moving or I'm going to have to have a talk with all three of us for being late." With that thought in mind, the three women scurried into the locker room.

****

The week passed by rather quickly with each of the roommates anticipating the relaxing weekend awaiting them. Garrett had no idea of what to expect from her friend, but was sure that it would be delightful for them both. After all, Danni had grown up around this part of the country and probably knew some very interesting and picturesque places. The tall surgeon found herself willing to follow her friend just about anywhere, especially if it didn't have beepers or a paging system involved. She definitely knew that she needed a break from her routine and hoped that this weekend would help her regain control of her life.

It was almost a month now since that night when the past had come rushing headlong back at her. The taunting dreams that crept into her mind while she slept would never let her go on with her life. They always reminded her of her inability to hold on to anyone that she cared for. For the longest time, she had given up and chosen not to allow her heart or hopes to be placed on any one person in particular. That had seemed to work for the most part, but proved to take its toll, as the surgeon walled off the exposures of her heart. It had made her a better surgeon, being so independent of others and able to stand on her own two feet when those around her seemed to be floundering. But the skills that she lacked because of it would take a long time to nurture.

She had thought enough about her past. It was time to live in the present and dream of the future instead. With that thought in her mind, Garrett threw back the covers and greeted the new day. The chill of the early morning air inside of the house exhilarated her as she made her way around her room, taking the time to cover her naked form with her long, silk robe as she headed toward the bathroom.

The small blonde was already busy in the kitchen getting things ready for the day that she had planned. By the time she was done packing the cooler with the necessary supplies, the tall surgeon was standing in the doorway, dressed and ready to go. Looking up from her position seated on top of the large cooler, the nurse noticed that she was being watched. “Hey! You been standing there long?”

“Just long enough to see you sit on the lid to get it to close.” She shook her head in disbelief. “I hope that is not just for lunch.” She teased the small woman, knowing her ravenous appetite.

“Nope, it’s our food for the weekend, two lunches, one dinner and one breakfast.” She fastened the latch on the cooler to keep it closed.

“I take it we are spending the weekend somewhere that food is not easily obtained,” she questioned.

The blonde woman lifted her head from her task and winked at her friend. “You’re just going to have to come along for the ride to find out now, aren’t you?” A sly smile shone across her face. She stepped back and looked at the cooler. “Hey, Gar…do you think we could take your Blazer? I don’t think this is going to fit in my car.”

“Sure, but you are going to direct me, aren’t you?” She teased. “Do I need to take anything with me? Clothes, toiletries, anything in particular?”

Danni stood beaming, “Nope, already taken care of. I hope you don’t mind, but I packed your stuff yesterday while you were at work.”

One dark eyebrow of the raven-haired woman rose at this tidbit of information. “So let me get this straight. I’m driving my Blazer to some place I don’t know, taking enough food to feed a small army, wearing outfits that you have chosen for me, leaving myself at your mercy for an entertaining weekend, and that’s suppose to help me to relax. Right?”

Nodding her head up and down emphatically, Danni agreed, “Yep, you got it.”

Garrett shrugged her shoulders. Putting her complete trust in the younger woman, she stated, “Sounds like a plan to me.”

****

Garrett felt like she was on shore leave, setting her sights for new and foreign lands as she made her way up the twisted road. The scenery was beautiful and intrigued her just as much as any port that she had seen during her time in the Navy. The only thing that was different was, for the first time in her adult life, she was sharing the ride and looking forward to sharing the entire weekend of living and laughing with someone that she could call "friend." It was funny now, but the word no longer brought a dreaded fear to her. Instead, it felt like a breath of fresh air that had seeped into her world.

Stealing glances as she drove, she saw glimpses of the awed expression on her companion's face as each turn in the road opened up another new world of color and whimsical fantasy in the showcase that Mother Nature was presenting to their very eyes.

Even though the young woman had planned out the course of travel, the beautiful colors and her good fortune to pick the peak time for viewing, the seasonal changing of the foliage stunned her. Danni silently thanked the gods who were watching over her and her 'Amazon,' for not only giving them this beautiful and wondrous day to enjoy, but for allowing their friendship to weather the storm that had swept over them in such a fury.

The petite nurse had opened her heart to many doctors as they drifted through her work area during the course of their duties as Interns, Residents, and or Fellows, but none had ever touched her in such a way as this one in particular. It was as if she had some hidden bond with the tall surgeon, tying the two together.

"So, are we almost there?"

The question brought her back from her revelry. She looked down at the piece of paper in her hand, her eyes going over the cryptic notes that were scribbled on it. "Yep," she agreed, "just one more turn and we should be there."

"Is that turn in this state or the next?" Garrett teased her companion.

"Hey, you were the one that wanted to be far away from any beeper or paging system. I can't help it if this was how far we had to go to get out of the hospital's range." The blonde's retort was filled with easy flowing laughter. "I think that's it! Up there on the left, where the sign is." Her attention was directed from the road, as she leaned forward again, checking the note. The Blazer moved steadily forward as the seconds clicked by, each one bringing them closer to their destination. With an assured smile on her face, Danni pointed to the small dirt road just passed the sign saying, "Turn here."

The surgeon studied the rutted, dirt path that her friend had been calling a road, as she stopped before crossing the two lane black top to turn onto it. "Hmmm…I can see why taking my SUV made good sense. Hang on, it looks like it maybe a little bumpy."

The half-mile trek on the trail had been well worth it. There, ahead of them, in an area of cleared out trees, was a small cabin nestled into the midst of the forest. Pulling up to the structure, Danni was eager to get out, undoing her seatbelt before the vehicle had come to a complete stop. Her eyes flashed with the light of recognition, as she surveyed her surroundings. "It hasn't changed one bit. It's just like I remembered it," she declared. She opened the passenger door and sprang from the seat. She ran up to the porch steps and turned around with both her arms outstretched.

The sight of the young woman, her blonde hair being tussled by the breeze and an incredible smile showing from her radiant face, made the surgeon think she was intruding upon some long-lost, private memory. The surgeon's keen eyesight followed the dancing figure as it glided from one point to the next, spinning and laughing until she finally stood very still and hugged herself, trying to hold on to those things she had just experienced in her mind.

The small woman looked up into the distant, calming, azure pools, a soft shade of crimson now spreading over her skin, as she realized she was being watched. It was as though she was a young girl caught playing at make-believe. But this time it was different. This time it was for real and she had the friend with her that her heart had always longed for, who would be the one that touched her very soul to its hidden depths. Danni could not help but be a little embarrassed at her unbridled actions pouring forth from her childhood, manifesting now in front of her friend.

She slowed her pace to a standstill and gazed back at the tall woman emerging from the opened driver's door of the vehicle. The long, raven locks moved gently with the forest's natural air current, beckoning to them as she moved away from the vehicle and closer to Danni. The small woman stood mesmerized as she watched Garrett come to within just a few feet of her. Reaching out to her friend, she touched her arm, just ever so lightly, to make sure that this was not just another of her dreams. Wrinkling her nose, she cocked her head to one side and spoke softly. "I guess you think that I'm silly."

"Nope," the word was deliberately drawn out. "I think you look cute." She looked around the clearing and then back to her friend. "You must have had some wonderful times here in the past to feel this way."

The blonde was speechless at the surgeon's words, nodding in agreement. Closing her eyes, she willed her emotions to yield once again to her control.

A warm smile tugged at her lips as she began to speak. "I used to spend time here with my grandfather when I was growing up. My brother and sister never really enjoyed it like I did." A single tear rolled down her check as she remembered. "I haven't been up here since I was sixteen, right before he died." She wiped her cheek with the back of her hand. "By the gods, I don't know whether I missed him or this place more," she confided.

The older woman was curious about what had kept her friend from coming back sooner than now. "So, why did you wait so long to come back?"

Reflecting inwardly, she sighed. "I guess I just got too busy with school, friends, and all the stuff that goes along with becoming an adult. Besides, my uncle inherited it but never spent more than a week or two here each year." She shrugged her shoulders, "No one to enjoy it with mostly. It was never one of the 'in' places to go when I was a teenager. You'd say Sandy Lake to someone and they would look at you like you were from Mars." She was quiet for a moment before continuing. "There is something about the beauty of nature that you just can't enjoy unless you share it with someone."

"But surely you had friends that you could bring…"

"I'm friendly, Garrett, but that doesn't always mean that I had friends to share quiet moments with, or who would understand and appreciate the solitude of the forest."

Her words seemed profound to the surgeon's ears. She looked at her companion, as if seeing her for the first time in this new light. Here, in front of her, was not the social butterfly one thought that she was originally, but rather the lone pine tree that stood ever vigilant against the changing weather patterns, offering shelter to all who sought it. A sense of pride came over the woman, realizing that she was thought of as someone special and deserving to share in the beauty of this place. It felt good to be thought of in that way and she let her small friend know it by the lopsided grin stretched across her face. She choked on the words at first, but finally got them out. "Thanks for thinking enough of me to share this with you."

Danni smiled back at her, too scared to let her know what she was thinking.

****

The remainder of the day, after unpacking the supplies, was spent on exploring the area and enjoying the natural beauty of the land. The two grown women frolicked and played like children in the piles of fallen leaves that had accumulated on the ground, first gathering them and then taking turns jumping into them. Anyone watching would not have considered them capable of holding the highly disciplined and demanding careers that they had. The sounds of laughter and giggling were like music to their ears, as each delighted in the closeness of this budding friendship.

With the light of day drawing to a close, thoughts of food and a warm fire soon came to their minds. Each one chipped in to the common goal. Garrett stacked the small branches and kindling, starting a fire in the fireplace, as Danni prepared their food for dinner. By the time they were done eating, darkness had fallen outside making the glowing embers of the fire even more inviting. They sporadically conversed about the day's events. Their thoughts often left long moments of comfortable silence as they sat in front of the fireplace, soothed by its warmth and their full bellies.

The fresh country air had taken its toll, as Danni began to find it hard to keep her drooping eyelids from closing almost completely. Shaking her head to try to fight off the ensuing sleep, the blonde yawned as she slowly made motions of getting up from her chair. "I guess I'm more tired than I thought." She stretched and yawned again. "I better turn in before you have to carry me to bed," she teased innocently.

The dark-haired woman looked into the fire, studying it. "Hmmm…sounds like a plan to me." She smiled at the young woman. "Maybe I should bank up the fire so it will last 'til the morning."

Danni nodded, making her way over to the beds. "Does it matter to you," she pointed to the two bunk beds against the wall, "upper or lower?"

"You take what you want," she chuckled, "I'll sleep in whatever is left empty."

The small woman grabbed her nightclothes out of her bag and headed for the bathroom to change. Stopping at the door she looked over to Garrett who was strategically placing more logs on the fire. "Hey Gar, I couldn't find your pajamas when I looked for them yesterday, so I packed a pair of sweats for you to sleep in. I hope that's okay?"

Garrett held onto the log she was about to place and began chuckling, "Yeah, that's okay." She watched the perplexed look on the blonde's face.

"Where do you keep them anyway?" She shyly asked, then offered, "for future reference, I mean."

"Ahh...Danni, I don't really have pajamas per se, that's why you couldn't find any."

"Oh! A boxer and T-shirt kind of girl, eh?"

A lone eyebrow arched as she answered with all sincerity. "Not really, I sleep in the buff when I'm not on call."

Mouthing the word 'Oh' she went into the bathroom with visions of a tall, raven-haired, stalwart, unencumbered body being carefully caressed between the sheets on the bed. She closed the door and fell back into it. She fanned herself with her hand in an attempt to cool her raging thoughts. "That was more than I needed to know," she said under her breath as she contemplated taking a cold shower.

****

The pristine sound of silence was deafening to the ears of the city dwellers as each lay in their bunk. The combination of full bellies, a day full of fresh air, not to mention the warmth and smells of the wood-burning fireplace, had quickly dulled their senses enough to allow each woman to drift off happily into the land of slumber.

Thinking back about her younger days spent here, Danni had prayed that her strong friend would easily succumb to the deep and relaxing sleep that she had always experienced when she stayed here. The mountain air was different than the city air. It had a way of cleansing your thoughts of worries and troubles. At least that is what her grandfather had always told her. The small blonde had surfaced from her sleep just long enough to hear the slow, rhythmic breathing of her friend. She smiled, then turning onto her side she pulled the blanket under her chin as she nestled into the pillow, drifting off swiftly once again.

The occasional popping and crackling of the logs on the fire had given way over time to the gentle even glow of burning embers. The night was edging over the apex of its nigritude into the softening light of early morning when Danni could feel herself being slowly aroused from sleep by the irregular rocking sensation of her body. Her mind strained to make sense of it, thinking that she had just relived a somewhat humiliating ambulance ride that she had once had in her now-forgotten dream. The harder that she tried to bring order to her mind, the more she was able to actually feel the rocking and bouncing of the bed beneath her. Her external senses were now coming to life with the surging adrenaline that sped through her body. The audible noises of thrashing and turning from the bed underneath hers filled her ears.

"What?" Danni mumbled sleepily as she tried to push her head up off of the pillow. "Garrett, do you feel that?" She was now leaning up on her elbow, rubbing her eyes with her fingers. "Are you all right?"

The sudden movement of the body below had sent a rippling tremble throughout the bed frame as she quickly sat up, throwing her long legs over the edge and on to the floor. Garrett sat there with her fingers clenched tightly onto the mattress, her body rocking back and forth as she tried desperately to regain her breathing.

The sounds of gasping sent alarms through the nurse's brain as she scurried to the end of the bed and started down the ladder that was attached to the frame. Blinking her eyes in rapid succession to accustom them to the dim light, Danni stepped around from the bed and gazed at the sight before her. Seeing the long hair draped forward on the downcast face, hiding it from view, and the tall body tense with fear, the young woman reached out to place a gentle hand on her shoulder. The soft touch on her skin drew an abrupt, uplifting turn of the shadowed head, allowing large, pleading eyes to be seen staring back at her in the dim glow given off by the smoldering embers. The look touched the very depth of Danni's soul with its need to be comforted. Words were not exchanged as the small woman stepped closer, wrapping her arm around Garrett's shoulders, pulling her in toward her welcoming body.

With her head resting on her young friend's chest, Garrett let the tears slowly find their way out, escaping the prison that housed them for so long. Soon, it became a hard, soul-cleansing cry that had overtaken her. Her fingers released the mattress, only to allow her long, muscular arms to wrap themselves around the small waist of the nurses.

The gentling touch of Danni's hand stroking her friend's dark hair was accompanied by the soothing sound of her voice. "It's okay…I'm here…I'm with you now…nothing can hurt you," she whispered. Brushing her lips against the top of the crying woman's head, she tenderly rested her cheek on it, her eyes closed in meditation. "I won't let it."

Garrett found herself being comforted with tears rolling down her face as her mind fought to regain control. The vulnerability of the normally strong, stoic woman had been shown to the petite nurse without any reserve. There for her to see, the surgeon subconsciously had bared herself, both body and soul, for scrutiny.

The effortless ease that the pair had in their friendship was evident, as both the comforted and the comforter relished in the moment. Each soul either getting or giving what was needed most, unselfishly.

With her tears subsiding, the once thought of strong woman began to speak, her voice quivering as she tried to get the words out. "I…I…can't change a thing." Garrett shook her head in defeat. "It just keeps coming…keeps repeating itself over and over again." She bit her lip to stop it from trembling, "I can't prevent it, or change its outcome."

Maintaining a soothing voice, the younger woman asked, "What can't you change, Gar?" Then offered, "Maybe I can help you."

Crystal blue eyes pierced through the dimly lit room with such intensity that they shook the very soul of the young nurse. The hurt and pain transmitted between the two was immeasurable. With that single gaze, Danni had become privy to the driving force of the surgeon's life.

The nurse's mind began gathering the pieces of the puzzle, searching desperately for the one key element that would tie it all together. The sounds that had awakened her this night were the same as the ones she had heard on their nights off together for the last several weeks. Danni thought back, trying to remember exactly when the surgeon had first shown signs suggesting her lack of sleep. Green lamps blazed with the realization that it had all started around the time of the birth of Rene's children, the night of the horrific family tragedy and the days of dealing with the single-family member that had been left.

Danni closed her eyes tightly and prayed. *Please, don't let me be right. Don't let that have happened to her.* Her mind raced for any reference that her roommate had ever made as to family and came up empty. It was as though they had been wiped out of the surgeon's memory. Images of a serene-looking Garrett entered her mind. The scene quickly playing in her head, they were talking to Diana Morgan about how she wanted to remember her brother, Brad. Then the nurse could hear the sound of her friend's voice talking in the distance. It was a conversation she had had with Danni, enlisting her aid in the situation. *...It could affect her for the rest of her life. I don't want to let her feel any remorse about what has to be done. She doesn't need to be haunted with this tragedy any more than she is already.* She could still see the pained look on Garrett's face from that day.

"By the gods!" Danni exclaimed under her breath. She had found the single, elusive piece that completed the puzzle. Tears began to roll down her cheek as she felt the rage of her anger build within her. The fates could be cruel indeed. Had it not been for Rene needing to be off that night, her friend would never have been in a position to see history repeat itself firsthand and all too personally. Her heart cried out in anguish for the surgeon.

With renewed concern, the young woman held on to her friend. "I'm here…shhh, I'm right here with you." Sensing the chilled touch of the skin under her hand, Danni reached down to the rumpled ball of blankets, pulling one around to cover the trembling form. "I think we better get you warm," she whispered into the sulking woman's ear, proceeding to rub her hands on top of the blanket to hasten the warmth into the shivering body. "Garrett, I'm going to put some more wood on the fire." She tugged at the surgeon's hand that was now clutching the blanket together in front of her. "Let's get you closer to the fireplace. Come on…you can sit up here in the chair."

Blue eyes rose to meet the warmth of the loving green that acted like the beacon of a lighthouse, guiding the ships away from the rocky traps of a jagged shoreline. With the promise of safety guiding her motions, she nodded her head and rose to follow the smaller woman. There was shelter in those eyes and the sailor was sure that for now, she had found her safe harbor.

Danni patiently waited, not wanting to push her friend before she was ready to share her past life experiences. She made herself busy replenishing the wood in the fireplace, and coaxing the glowing embers into igniting the kindling. Her mind tried to think of how her friend had been able to live for so long without having anyone close to her. The young woman thought about her siblings and how much she enjoyed and took pride in their lives and loves. Danni looked over her shoulder at the ghastly form that filled the chair. She could feel her heart tugging at her to give comfort, but knew that what her friend needed now was warmth and time to deal with her feelings.

The nurse got up from the fireplace and ventured into the small kitchen area of the cabin. She had provided warmth for the exterior of the tall woman, now it was time to think of something for the inside. The blonde rummaged through the bag of provisions that they had brought with them until she found the box of tea bags. A slight smile came across her lips as she remembered her mother's favorite saying when troubled times would reach one of her offspring, *Share some tea with me and I'll share in your troubles.* Danni had always marveled that by the time the cup or two of tea would be gone, the troubles seemed to be also.

Sighing, she reverently whispered as if it were some kind of prayer, "Well, Mom, let's hope that I paid attention all those times." She reached for the teakettle on the stove and filled it with water, placing in it back on the now-lit burner. An occasional gaze in on her friend only prolonged the task of readying the cups for the steaming liquid that would steep the tea of its flavor. Sooner than she anticipated, the teakettle began to whistle, drawing attention to its timely readiness. Stealing a brief look in Garrett's direction proved only to be disheartening, as the bleak woman sat unaware of the shrill whistling that the excited teakettle was producing.

Carrying the two cups over to the fireplace area, she placed one down on the table next to the empty chair. The nurse gently placed the other cup next to the surgeon's sinewy fingers, "Garrett, I made us some tea. Would you like to have a cup?"

She waited to see if the words would get any type of response from her friend. They didn't. The huddled figure still clutched onto the blanket, her eyes staring straight ahead of her. The petite blonde wasn't about to give up on her friend, though. Instead, she carefully pried the fingers of one hand away from the blanket, replacing it with the handle of the cup. "Careful now, it's hot. We've got to get some warmth going on the inside, Gar. Take a sip or two for me, will you?" The blonde watched patiently as the cup slowly made its way to the lips of her friend. With each sip a little more of the warm liquid reached its destination. The combination of the warmth, both inside and out, was beginning to soothe the ragged woman, easing her with as much gentleness as was being shown by her small friend.

Danni took solace that her words were getting through to her sullen friend. The simple act of sipping tea had been as long awaited as a baby's first step. The nurse smiled, knowing that it was the first step for her friend in her battle to learn to love and be loved. Pleased that she was a part of the healing that was beginning to take place, Danni lavished in the thought. She bent her head to gently brush her lips on top of the contemplative woman's head, then slowly moved away to tend to the fire.

The petite woman stood before the fireplace, her mind consumed with thoughts of her friend as she absently watched the flames dancing along the logs. After a few moments, her train of thought was interrupted by the sound of a voice coming from behind her. Startled by it, she turned to see her friend, still mesmerized but slowly moving her mouth in speech.

"You need to know…." The words were rough in coming out. "I never wanted..." her eyes fell on the woman tending the fire. "I never needed…"

Danni rose, moving closer to her friend. "Garrett, you don't need to explain anything if you don't want to."

The firelight that reflected in the tortured globes made them shimmer as they followed the movement towards her. "Please, I want to tell you. You deserve to know what's going on." She got a far away look in her eye as she thought for a moment. "I never dreamed that I would want to talk about it, ever again."

The nurse braced herself for what was about to unfold. Pulling the empty chair closer to her friend, she sat down, calmly waiting for Garrett to begin.

The surgeon pressed her eyelids closed as she concentrated on her breathing, trying to slow it down to a rhythmic pattern. Biting her lip, she jerked her head into a nod, before turning to look directly into the love-drenched green fields that were her friend's eyes. Pursing her lips, the woman cautiously began her tale.

"I know exactly what Diana Morgan is going through. I'm a lone surviving family member, too." She held her hand up, not wanting to be interrupted. "I was out with a group of school chums at a movie when it happened. My parents and my younger brother were coming home from one of his baseball games when the accident occurred. They were going through an intersection when they were broadsided and pushed into a telephone pole. I didn't find out until I came home. The house was empty when I arrived. I thought that they were just out for a celebratory ice cream cone after Lucas' game. Then the phone rang, changing my life forever. I got the next door neighbor to drive me over to the hospital and that's where, in no uncertain words, I was informed that my parents were dead." Pausing momentarily to choke back a tear, the woman continued. "They told me that my brother was critically injured and that it would be better if he were to die. He was so badly hurt that it would be impossible for me to take care of him then, or possibly even for the rest of my life. They had me sign a release for the bodies, they told me it was necessary to let them be removed by the funeral home. I found out years later that what I had really signed was the consent to remove Lucas from all life support." She gazed deeply into the misting green reflection pools of her friend. "I trusted them, Danni, I didn't know any better."

The nurse could feel her heart breaking for Garrett. How she wished she had been there beside her then. But it was the present now, and she would do her best to comfort and support her in any way that she could. "You were just a child then, you weren't expected to know any better. Why, I wish I knew who that physician was today. I'd like to give him a piece of my mind, taking advantage of the situation and you." She could feel her anger growing, deciding that now was not the time to explode.

"I was devastated with the loss. I had no one to really look after me and since I was only seventeen, I was still considered a minor in the eyes of the law. I was shuffled between the three relatives that I had left in the world, for the next year and a half, until I went to college." She sniffed back a tear that was trying to escape. "I never realized how much I took them for granted until they were gone. That's when I vowed never to let anyone hurt me again…that's when I decided to not let anyone get close to me. The hurt was just too much when they left me. I pretty much succeeded," she looked away, shyly admitting, "until I came here to Pittsburgh and couldn't help myself." The dark haired woman coughed, trying to clear her throat. "I told myself that I could make a difference and not let what happened to me, happen to someone else. I found out that I was wrong…dead wrong."

"Gar, there was nothing you could have done to prevent the accident. In fact, you did everything within your powers to give that family a fighting chance," she sighed. "It just wasn't in the cards. Don't let yourself think that you can stop the fates in their tracks." She reached out to touch the surgeon's cheek, catching an isolated tear in its path. "I realize that it wasn't your original call night, but everything happens for a reason. I think the Chabot twins chose that time to come into the world so that you could be in the right place, at the right time."

"I just know what that girl is going to live through, the torment, the wondering, the pain." The surgeon bit down on her lip in anguish. "I've been there, Danni, it's not a nice place. You wonder if you had been in the car with them…if it had taken another minute longer to leave…would your family still be intact."

She closed her eyelids, letting the tears flow as they may. She was in too deep to try pulling back into that stoic protectiveness that she had used for so many years. She felt the gentle cupping of her cheek by the small hand of her friend and leaned into it. She could not believe that she was doing this, talking about her life, her family, after all these years. The events of the past few weeks had really shaken her world into the realization that she could no longer hold everything inside.

The comfort that she felt with the petite nurse was undeniable. She had felt it from the first day that Danni talked to her. It was as if she had known her for years, but yet only met her then. The only other person that she had ever felt that close to was her brother and look what had happened to him. For a moment she was seriously scared to let the young woman into her private arena of emotions, or anywhere near her, terrified that some horrible tragedy would befall her also, if left to become too close to the ill-fated surgeon.

Sensing the grief and turbulence in her friend's soul, Danni felt compelled to speak. "I know what you're thinking, Garrett, and I don't accept it. You are not responsible for the fates of the people you love." She raised the forlorn woman's head so that their eyes met. The radiance of the gaze filled her soul and overflowed into the azure pools, giving new life to the still and murky waters within her. "You have done nothing but treat people with kindness and love. I see it every time that you're in the trauma rooms. There is a special aura around you, I know, I can feel it. You have a wonderful gift to give, Garrett, don't shut the world out. Please…don't shut me out, not now."

The voice was almost inaudible, "How can you say that? The people I love only end up dead."

"We all will die someday, it's just a matter of time. Why not enjoy life and each other until that day comes and then be thankful for the chance to have known that kind of bond?" Danni's eyes stayed pinned to the surgeon. She was not about to let go of this friendship, not now. It took too long to find.

"I still can't do anything to help Diana…" Garrett countered.

"You could be there for her; let her lean on you." Danni winked, "I bet she'd jump at the chance to have someone in her life that she could relate to right now. Think of how you would have felt if you would have been able to talk to someone years ago." Danni paused, gauging the effects of her words on her friend. "You could help each other to heal."

The surgeon contemplated the idea. It would have been nice to talk to someone, anyone, before she had so completely walled herself off from the closeness of people in general. "Maybe, you're right. Maybe I could help her adjust to her new life or just be there for her." Garrett looked at the blonde in front of her with renewed interest. "Thanks for helping me turn this around. I appreciate that."

It amazed her, this new feeling. Yes, for the first time in so many years, Garrett Trivoli reached out and actually embraced the person who had slipped right under her defenses and into her heart.

Danni wiped a tear from her own eye with the back of her hand, the outer corners of her lips turning up into a smile as she tried to hold back her body's need to cry. "That's okay, Gar, that's what friends are for, to help in any way they can. You'll see, just give it a chance, give us a chance."

The tall woman nodded her head, "I think I just may." She winked and both women proceeded to giggle in acceptance of the newfound bond between them.

Garrett looked around the cabin; the soft rays of morning's first light were gently creeping in through the windows. "I guess we didn't get too much sleep last night. I'm sorry that you…that I kept you awake."

"I'm not. I'm glad that I was able to be here for you. You might as well get used to it, Dr. Trivoli, you've got a friend here in Pennsylvania." The last part was a direct mocking of the state motto, and they both knew it as the laughter began. "I don't know about you, but I sure could use a few more hours of restful sleep, what do you say?"

"Sounds like a plan to me." Garrett rose from the chair and started over towards her bunk. "First one up makes breakfast, right?"

"Right! Now let's get back to sleep." The nurse watched as the bundled woman straightened the remaining covers on the bed and settled herself under them. It had been a long night, but if it had helped her new friend, it will have been worth it.

****

The outcome that the last few hours of sleep had on her was in effect, a cleansing of the soul. The normally stoic woman woke up feeling a sense of inner peace and, for the first time in her adult life, she welcomed it with open arms. Letting her eyes take in their surroundings, she let her senses imbibe in the warmth and friendliness of the cabin and its furnishings. The comfortable rustic appearance had a charm and pleasantness all its own. She put her head back down on the pillow, staring at the underside of the bunk above her. Her thoughts drifted to the young blonde, who was becoming so much more to her than just another passing acquaintance. Her life had been filled with acquaintances, now it was time to make a friend. No, rather to it was time to **be** a friend.

She wondered when the walls of thick black stone had been removed from around her heart. She contemplated over the past night of soul searching, gut twisting, stare you in the face reality of her life, and concluded that she knew exactly when the wall had disappeared. It was when she had gazed into those wondrous green eyes, filled with nothing but love.

With a creak from the wood frame of the bunk beds, tussled blonde hair that was attached to an upside-down face come tumbling over the side of the bed.

"Hey, you're awake!" Her eyes lit up seeing that the surgeon was lying silently in bed. "Get enough sleep?"

"Hmmm," the dark-haired woman let one eye open wide. "Guess so, I've been up for a few minutes."

"What do you say to getting up, now? I'll make breakfast right after I use the bathroom, okay?" Danni scampered down from the upper bunk. She started walking in the direction of the bathroom when her body was captured by a long drawn-out yawn; her arms stretching up and out as far as they could. When the yawn had dissipated, she shook her head, rubbing her upper arms with her hands to chase the chill away. "I'll be out in a minute or two," she stated as she entered the small room, closing the door.

The surgeon was caught completely off guard, her voice allowing small chuckles to rise from her mouth. Her life was definitely not going to be the same as before, that was for sure. Garrett threw back the covers and slid her long legs out of the bunk, reaching for the sweats that Danni had packed; she began pulling them on. *I bared enough for one morning,* she thought, getting the sweatshirt over her head. *I don't think she could take much more.*

The breakfast had been a simple one that was shared by the two women, easy conversation being interspersed along the way. No mention was made to the tormentuous early morning hours by either one. Both thought only of the other's comfort level with the past events, knowing that when the time was right, they would breech the subject again.

"If we hurry, we'll have time to hike down to the lake," the small blonde offered. "You like to fish?" Her eyebrows jumped up and down in anticipation.

"Fish? Yeah, I like to fish." The surgeon stopped, thinking back to the last time that she had been fishing. A smile tugged at the corners of her mouth. "I haven't been fishing since..." she gulped, paused and then continued on. "Since the last vacation with my family." She looked over to the gentle face of her friend. Taking comfort there gave her the ability to speak about them for the first time in many years. "Lucas and I would fish all day long, Dad would clean them and Mom would fry them up for the family dinner that evening."

Danni could feel her emotions surfacing. Thinking that she was going to cry, the nurse blinked back the tear forming in her eye. She couldn't believe that the stoic surgeon had just let her in to the secret world of her youth. This small gesture of sharing was a definite sign that the healing process for her friend was becoming a reality.

"Do you think we could do just a little fishing today, I mean, the two of us?" Garrett looked at the petite woman, hope written all over her face.

Speechless, the blonde hair moved freely on top of the nodding head, while a dazzling smile swept across her face. Her voice was unsteady at first, taken aback by the emotion of the moment. "Sure thing! I'll get the rods and gear." She pushed back from the table and went to the small closet on the far wall. "Grampa always had them ready to go. I bet…yep! They're still here." She pulled out a rather dated set of rods and a small tackle box. Holding them up, she proceeded to ask, "Shall we?"

"Sounds like a plan to me."

They hurriedly grabbed their jackets and took off with thoughts of fishing both now and in the past racing through each of their minds.

The day quickly sped by as they filled it with exploration of the area that Danni had grown up in. It was easy to fall in love with it all over again. The petite woman was amazed at how natural it felt to have the surgeon at her side as they roamed the many trails she had used as a girl. The pleasure brought to them in the time spent fishing had been soothing to both of their souls. Garrett was finding it easy to open up to the younger woman, while Danni lavished in the acceptance of herself by another living being, one who would willingly share with her unconditionally. Any scars remaining from the past days of loneliness in her youth now became insignificant.

With the sun now slowly starting its descent, the pair packed up their belongings and readied themselves for the ride home. The relaxed feeling of quiet camaraderie allowed each occupant of the homeward bound Blazer to reevaluate her outlooks on life in the light of the newly, bonded friendship.

Chapter 12

Danni marveled at the occurrences of the past few days. There had been a roller coaster ride full of emotions, ranging from the deepest depths of self-inflicted depression to the elated joys of finding a kindred spirit. Something was different about her. She couldn't quite put her finger on it, but she knew it to be true. For the first time in her life she had slept with no jumbled dreams, no pieces of a puzzle left lingering to haunt her first waking moments of the new day.

Sighing, she lazily rolled over in the large bed, basking in the afterglow of her mind's delight. Once on her back, she nestled into the soft pillow as she let her right arm sweep the expanse of the bedding, feeling the rumpled sheets that had formed into small mounds and valleys, only to find the object of her desire seemingly just out of her reach. Opening a sleepy eyelid as she raised her head, the petite woman started to survey the bed.

"Danni," the voice was muffled. "Danni, I thought you wanted to ride in together today?" The sounds of footsteps were in the hall. "Hey, sleepy head, are you going to stay in bed all day?" The voice was much louder now as the silk-robed form of the tall woman stood in the doorway. She busied herself with the towel that was wrapped around the wet hair on top of her head.

"Argggh! Now I know why I hate daylight. How come

the nights never pass this fast when I **work** them?" The nurse shook her head trying to rid herself of the last remnants of sleep. Danni reached out, fingering the journal that lay on her nightstand.

"Dan, it's getting late, I don't think you have time for that this morning." The surgeon eyed the book that her friend was toying with.

"Oh, this? No, I'm just so used to writing in it every time that I wake up, it's become a habit I guess." She let a smirk play across her face as she realized that for once, she had nothing to write in it. "Funny thing is, I don't have any bits or pieces to put into it today. I figured that sooner or later the pieces of the puzzle would come together, that's why I documented them."

"Hmmm, I always liked puzzles. Maybe you should let me look at it sometime." She offered, hoping that she was not being too presumptuous. "Maybe you are just too close to the clues to see what they are all about?"

"I never thought of that. You might be on to something there." The blonde hair tossed from side to side as the young woman stretched first this way and then that way, trying to limber up her muscles before using them. "Okay, I'm up now." Her body betrayed her with a yawn. "Excuse me," she rolled her eyes shyly. "How long before we leave?"

Without hesitation she beamed, "0530 sharp! That gives you a little under 45 minutes to get ready." She began moving down the hallway, still toweling her hair dry. "The trail blazer leaves on time, I've got an O.R. time at 0700 with McMurray."

"Okay, I'm going..." she slid out of the warm bed and padded off to the bathroom. "And I'll be waiting for you." Danni yelled out as she closed the door to her room.

****

True to her word, Danni was leaning against the side of the Blazer when Garrett came out of the front door of the house. With her arms folded across her chest, she watched as the surgeon made her way to the vehicle. Flicking her remote key device to unlock the doors, she shook her head saying, "I can't believe that you're ready. You couldn't have eaten."

Shrugging her shoulders, the nurse nonchalantly replied. "You're right. I opted to have breakfast in the cafeteria." The coy smile played across her face as she turned to open the passenger door.

The pair quietly took up their positions in the front seat of the SUV and belted themselves in for the journey to work. Casually Danni looked at the digital display on the dashboard. It was 0529 as Garrett turned the key, bringing the lumbering engine to life. After taking a cautious look up and down the quiet street, Garrett eased on the gas pedal and pulled away from the curb. The nurse smiled as the display of numbers now changed to 0530.

Danni marveled at the punctuality of her friend. Now, here was someone that she could count on, right down to the second.

The short drive to the hospital was quiet as each occupant of the vehicle thought about her day to come. The ride was at an end as Garrett pulled the oversized vehicle into the special section of the parking garage, startling the thought-absorbed nurse when her eyes focused on a concrete pillar in front of the now parked vehicle.

"Are we there already?" The blonde head turned, looking at her surroundings.

"Ah…yeah, Danni, it's not like the ride back from Sandy Lake yesterday." She thought about the long drive and how relaxed she felt from the weekend trip.

"Oh, yeah…right!" She climbed down from the seat and gathered up her knapsack and gloves. She closed the door and met the surgeon in the rear of the vehicle to start the walk over to the hospital entrance. "Gar," she spoke softly. "Are you going to talk to McMurray today?"

"Well, of course, I'll be assisting him in surgery. Why

wouldn't I be talking to him?" She looked puzzled.

The petite woman reached out to touch her friend's coat sleeve saying, "I mean about your idea, you know, Diana Morgan..." Her brows were furrowed as she looked up into the stoic face.

"Yeah, but I think I'll do that later today. I want to do a little research first. See what resources might be available to us." She nodded her head. "Are you still interested in helping?"

One look was all that it took to know the answer. The beaming smile and twinkling eyes said it all. The blonde suddenly bowed her head as if becoming shy and very reserved. "If you still want me to," she kept her voice barely above a whisper.

"I do! I want this to be a team effort; no more soaring out there on my own." There was a pause as the words settled on both their ears. Realizing what she had just verbalized to her friend surprised her a little... no, a whole lot. But it felt good and she was ready to take the next step into that warming smile of friendship. "I think that we can make a good team, you and I. What do you say?" She held her breath in anticipation of the young woman's answer.

"Yeah, I think we would make an excellent team. I wouldn't want it any other way." The blonde looked up to her tall companion, her nose wrinkling in thought. "Maybe we should see what McMurray will say?"

"What could he say? He's always pushing to get the spotlight for his Trauma Services. I think this will be a step in the right direction, at least from my standpoint." Garrett opened the door to the emergency area entrance, holding it for Danni to pass through ahead of her.

"I'll just feel better when you know for sure. Call me when you do. Okay?"

The surgeon nodded and began to walk towards the elevators. "Hey, Danni!" She turned to speak to the nurse once more. "Page me when you're done with work. I may spend some time doing some research after I've spoken with him."

"All right, I know how you get. You'll lose track of all time and forget about going home." She started to turn, "Have a good day, Gar, and good luck."

The surgeon stood and watched as Danni went down the hall towards the locker room. *How does she do that? She knows me so well. Humph, better than I know myself sometimes.* She shook her head in amazement, and then, stepping onto the next available elevator, continued on her way.

****

The morning hours were dragging for the young nurse. With every ring of the telephone at the nurses' station her anticipation rose. Every free minute she found herself beseeching any god that might be listening to have them smile down with favor on her friend's good intentions. Danni knew how much this project meant to the surgeon, not only for her own healing process to continue, but also for the help that it would give to others in the same situation like Diana Morgan. She had wished that she knew what kind of surgical case it was that Garrett was involved in, and then she would have some idea of when her phone call might come. Deciding to put it out of her mind for a while, she quickly fell into a nice steady pace triaging the onslaught of patients waiting to be seen.

****

The time seemed to be moving quickly. Before Garrett knew it, her scheduled surgical time with McMurray had come and gone. During the operation she had asked to see him later in the day to discuss something that was on her mind. Now, she waited patiently for the prearranged time to come. Studying the computer screen in front of her, she made several last minute notes to bolster support for her case. She didn't want anything to be overlooked. This was something that she felt compelled to do. If not here then somewhere at another time, but she knew she would do it. She had suffered far too long and too much to sit back watching the same thing happen to others who were just like she was all those many years ago. The loss of family could be so devastating as to wipe out your essence of identity. The bond of family transcends all others. Without it you are left alone and afraid that no one is like you in the world. You lose your self-worth because there is no one like you to measure it up against. The trauma didn't just stop with the loss of the family but continued on throughout your entire life. This is what she had to convey to McMurray. She had to make him realize that it was something that they could do to stop the trauma from continuing. She looked up at the clock on the wall. It was 1430. Time to present her case to the man down the hall who held all the cards.

Garrett gathered up her notes and shoved them into her pocket. Then, making her way down the hall, she stopped in front of Dr. McMurray's office. Arriving there, she ventured inside of the closed door where the older woman, the Department of Trauma Services' Secretary, greeted her. Having her appointment time confirmed, the Trauma Fellow knocked on Dr. McMurray's door.

Never being one for offering prayers to the gods above, something deep within the surgeon made her stop and lift her eyes heavenward. "Okay," Garrett sighed. *I need all the help I can get. I know that Danni would be asking for your help if she were here with me. So maybe you could pretend that it's her asking for it and not me. Please, let him go along with this proposal.*

Garrett raised her hand and knocked on the door to his office. When she heard the command to enter, she took a deep breath and paused. It had been a long time since she had prayed, but suddenly she remembered the only formal thing about prayer from her youth. As a final measure of her sincerity to her belief in her cause, she glanced upward and whispered. "Oh, I almost forgot…Amen." With that done, she nodded politely to the secretary at her desk before she entered into the realm of authority, the Chief of Trauma Services' office.

She scanned the room, letting her memory stir with tidbits of information that she had learned about the numerous photographs that graced the room over her many meetings with her mentor. Each time Garrett had come away with a new fact or two that would relate to the stories behind one of the photos. It was almost like part of her time in his office was dedicated to those pictures. They were reminders of his life, not hers, but they always seemed to hold her interest. It was almost like he was trying to convey some special knowledge to her each time he chose a photo to talk about.

She turned her attention to the man seated in the high-backed chair that swiveled freely behind the desk opposite her. The smug look upon his face almost made her think that he had been expecting this session with her for a long time. It was only a little over four months since she had started her year of Fellowship here, but it seemed like she had spent her whole learning experience inside of this office. Some of her most valued learning experiences always seemed to involve this man and his unique outlook on life.

"Come on in, Dr. Trivoli, have a seat." The Ol'Cutter motioned to the chair in front of his desk. "I've been waiting to hear what you have to talk about."

Garrett crossed the room and sat down, as she pushed her hand into her pocket to touch the notes she had jotted down. She smiled at him and nodded in his direction, "Thanks, sir."

There was a silence as she collected her thoughts, trying to decide just where to start with her proposal. "Sir, I've been thinking about the way we handle the families of the trauma patients. I've had the occasion to take care of a family where all the patients expired, except for a lone family member. I was wondering if there wasn't something that we could offer or do to help the trauma stop with the loss of the relatives and not continue on to the survivor."

"What? You want to take them to surgery, remove their

heart or memories so that they won't grieve or miss them?" His voice was gruff and taunting.

"Why, no sir! That would be ridiculous, absurd even." Her eyes were wide with shock at what he was saying. "I was thinking more in the line of counseling and support groups that would let them know that they're not the only ones to have gone through such a horrific experience." She watched for any sign of consideration in his bulldogish face. Seeing none, the surgeon continued. "It could eventually take the place of the family that they would be lacking. Not in any real sense, but rather in the means of mental support, that they are not as alone as they think they are."

McMurray eyed her. He could see that for some reason this was of particular interest to the fellow whom he had taken under his wing. There was finally something more than a stoic mask on her face, could it be the first stirrings of human emotion?

"Dr. McMurray, I've been researching the resources and think that with a little cooperation from some of the other Departments in the hospital, we could really do something good for these people." Garrett's face was earnest and full of conviction to her cause.

The Ol' Cutter's eyes darted to her. His full attention settled on her face. "What did you say?" His voice snapped in retort, "Did I just hear you use a pleural pronoun?" He leaned forward, squinting hard at her. "Who put you up to something like this?"

"Why, no one, sir." Her body took on a defensive position and she returned his stare. "I came up with the idea while Danni…er…I mean, Nurse Bossard and I were discussing a situation that we were both very familiar with. We thought that it might be an extension of the trauma services that we now offer."

He rose abruptly from his seated position and pushed off of the desk. The Chief of Trauma strode out from around his desk and started looking at the wall full of photographs with his hands clasped behind his back. Several moments went by before he stood frozen to one picture. His hands slowly came around from behind his body as he reached out to grab the photograph on the wall. His breath was slow and labored as he mulled over his thoughts, his fingers sweeping the expanse of the large, framed, group photo. With his attention still glued to the picture in front of him, McMurray began to speak. "Garrett, have I ever told you about my days in the Appalachian Foothills?"

" No sir, you haven't." She turned to look at him. His arm was motioning for her to come over to where he was standing. She rose and moved closer to where he stood transfixed to the photograph.

"I went up to the Appalachian Foothills on a bet with a buddy of mine in surgery. My wife told me that things were different in the backwoods but I was a damn bullhead and took the bet, sure that I would win. Back in those days a fifty-dollar bet was nothing to walk away from, especially if you knew it was a cinch to win. Heck, that was my monthly payment on the loans from medical school," he reminisced. Glancing over at her he said, "So, what's the going monthly rate now on that education?"

"I'm sorry sir, I wouldn't know. I enlisted in the Navy for the three years and they took care of the debt."

"Hmm...Wish I'd thought of that. Three years...is that all?"

"Well, I'm on inactive reserve. My chances of being called back would be only in an declaration of war."

"Oh, I see." He grunted. "How long are you at the government's beck and call?"

She thought about what he was asking. "A little less then three years now. Is there a problem with that?"

"No, I knew you were smart. That's one way to cover your debt." He turned back to the photograph. "See that guy there," he pointed to a slim boy with oversized clothing, his eyes gaunt and lifeless. "He was one of the most knowledgeable people I have ever met. He doesn't look it, but he would pick-up anything that I offered in a teaching session, trying to bring their level of personal hygiene out of the dark ages." He reached out to touch his image, then hesitated. "He never had the chance to go to school or learn the ways of the world as we know it. The purpose of his daily chores was just to stay alive and have something to eat."

"Did you try to help him break out of the lifestyle?" She watched the older surgeon as he thought about the boy. His face was a mixture of regret and self-inflicted pain.

"I tried, but the week after I came home he died from a ruptured appendix. They don't have doctors up there on any regular basis, at least not then." He paused and sniffed, trying to collect his emotions before continuing. "I found out a month later when I went back to give him the books that I had gathered for him to learn how to read. I was devastated at what had transpired while I was gone."

"I'm sorry to hear that. How were you to know what might happen?"

McMurray was back in control again, his voice crisp and clear. "My wife told me to never pass up an opportunity to help someone when it came along." He looked Garrett straight in the eye. "She's right, you know. Women like her are always right. Better learn that now, Dr. Trivoli."

"Yes, sir. I think I am already." She thought back to the early morning hours that nightmarish Sunday, back at the cabin. Danni had been the one to suggest that she try to help Diana Morgan. *I'm learning to rely on her judgment more and more.* "So does that mean you'll consider our idea?"

The Ol'Cutter looked her over as she stood with her hand still pressed inside of her pocket. "I don't see any formally written proposal. Do you want me to go to bat for you and your idea with nothing to show but a few words to speak to the committee? Don't you think that would be a problem?"

She fingered the notes in her pocket. "Why no, I haven't written a proposal."

"Then do it," he snapped. "I want every aspect of this idea worked out on paper. I'll need all the facts, the who, the where, the how, everything." McMurray smiled coyly. "That damn leech of an E.R. Chief, Ian McCormick is always hounding me to do a joint project with his department. Do you think that you could figure someone in from the E.R. too? Say, maybe that Nurse Bossard, or haven't you allowed her back into your trauma rooms yet?"

Garrett could sense the teasing in his voice. She knew he watched those trauma room videotapes every morning. She had learned her lesson from him more than once about that night. The image of the blonde nurse crept into her mind from this morning when she voiced her wish to help in this project. "Yes, sir. She's back. I was a fool that night and I told her so later. I…I think that she would be happy to work with me on this project." The surgeon smiled at her confidence of Danni's interest.

McMurray thought for a moment then went with his gut reaction. "Okay, but Nurse Bossard and you are a **team**. I expect you both to work equally on this. Now get moving on that proposal. I want it on my desk no later than the Monday before Thanksgiving. That will give me a day to go over it before I present the idea to the Board of Directors for hospital approval." He turned and walked back to his desk.

"Thank you. I'll get to work on it right away." Excitement was in Garrett's voice at the thought of her plans venturing forward.

"Trivoli!"

"Yes." Garrett stopped herself from snapping to attention.

"I'll talk to McCormick tonight. You and Bossard should use work time for this proposal. Take a day or two out of surgery if you have to. I expect it to be good. No loopholes, mind you. I want everything to be spelled out, including who will be involved and how much money it will take to run the program."

"Yes, sir." She started to turn towards the door, eager to tell Danni the news. "Permission to be excused, sir," she voiced in a military manner.

"Permission granted, sailor," he chuckled at her ingrained Navy background coming forth as she saluted before she realized what she was doing. The older man returned the salute, shaking his head at her evident enthusiasm for the project.

Embarrassed, Garrett just shook her head at her own incredible military reaction and hurriedly took off out the door.

For the first time since she had arrived at the hospital, McMurray saw new life come to her eyes. They weren't condescending, angry, or even annoyed, as they were when she had been summoned into his office her first day. His plan was working. She was learning to be a real person and not just some robotic surgeon that only tolerated other humans. She cared about this project. He could see it in her demeanor towards him and the enthusiasm that carried over in her voice and eyes when she spoke of the ideas. Whatever it was that had spurred her into caring, he was sure that Nurse Bossard had a hand in it.

He looked down to the picture on the desk of his loving wife, the woman that had made him see life for the first time. "*Maybe she's found a nurse that will help her along the way, just like I found you," he whispered under his breath and then grinned at the picture of his wife before him.* "Not bad at teaching, am I?"

He felt good that his hard work was paying off. He liked that stoic woman more than he cared to admit. There was just something about her that made him think of himself and his own start as a young surgeon when he looked at her. The Ol'Cutter was sure that his wife would see it too. After all, she was the one who had helped him realize what potential his life held.

"Mrs. Weber," he called out for his secretary through the open door. Within seconds she appeared in the doorway. "Get me Dr. McCormick, would you, please? I need to talk to him about an important development."

"Yes, Dr. McMurray. Right away." She set out to make contact with the requested physician.

The Chief of Trauma Services settled in to his high-backed leather chair. He sat there with his elbows resting on the padded arms of the chair, the fingertips of one hand pressed and flexing against the other. "Well, my dear Dr. McCormick, let's see how you react to this idea. You always want to get your nose into my projects and grab some of the glory. I wonder how you'll view this proposal?"

****

The raven-haired woman let her long legs carry her down the hallway towards her office. The look of determination mixed with happiness was an unusual one, especially for her, drawing stares from those who she traveled by. As she made her way further down the hall, she was oblivious to the hushed whispers that came filtering back from the passing groups of nurses and residents. They were not used to seeing anything but the stoic façade that she had worn daily since her arrival, the first day of her Fellowship. The surgeon was eager to get started on the proposal, but she needed to get to Danni. *I can't wait to tell her.* She imagined the face of the petite nurse, thinking about Danni's normally radiant glow of enthusiasm.

I bet it will be intensified ten...no, twenty times with the news that I'm going to tell her. Garrett was finding it hard not to let her mouth spread into that seldom seen brilliant smile of hers and her mind thought back to her father and his teasing.

It was a game that all parents and children play with each other, but Garrett loved it, especially with her father. He was a tall man with enormous hands with which he would hold her and slowly start to tickle her until she produced a smile that was so brilliant it could outshine a light bulb. Well, at least that's how her father described it. The best part of the game was not the tickling and squirming to get away, but rather the warm feeling that she would have once that smile was produced and her father would acknowledge it. Her usual response was to put her small arms around his neck and hug him until he would whisk her up in his arms, twirling her with him as they danced across the floor, her laughter mixing ever so sweetly with his.

Then as she grew older, playful teasing and the making of faces replaced the tickling as he tried hard to get her to laugh. Somehow he was always able to do it. No matter how hard she tried to keep that stoic mask in place, she could not do it when he was around. Now the reward for that smile would be a loving pat on the arm or a quick hug as he gently kissed her forehead, whispering words of encouragement to her. She had always thought of the game as something special between them.

She thought about her father, pulling from deep in her memory to conjure up an image of him in her head. Then the image began transforming, soon being replaced by the radiant, smiling one of Danni. It was funny that one smile from out of her past lifetime could equal another in her present life today. She chuckled to herself as she entered her office. *I never thought I'd be able to smile in response to someone like that again.*

The small room didn't seem to bother her today as she sat at her desk waiting for the computer booting up in front of her. She glanced at her watch, taking note of the time. It was 1500 hours. She drummed her fingers as she tried to make her mind up as to what to do. Finally, she had made her decision. Pushing off of her desk with her out-stretched fingers, she swiveled the rickety chair away from the desk and moved fluidly to her feet. A step or two of her long strides brought her to the door that she readily opened. As she prepared to advance through the doorway, she looked up to see the thin build of her colleague who appeared out of nowhere.

"Rene!" Her voice sounded startled.

Looking at her with large eyes of surprise was Dr. Chabot. "Oh my dear…Garrett!" His feet started backing up to get out of her way. "Is there something wrong, some kind of emergency?" Concern filled his eyes.

"Sorry," she apologized as she reached out to stop his retreat. She paused only momentarily, then started edging her way down the hall toward the elevators. "No, nothing bad. In fact, you could say that it was something very right." That smile was spreading across her face again, with each word, as her mind thought about where she wanted to be right at that moment and with whom she wanted to be telling her news to.

Rene winked and called out. "Must be something pretty good to make you smile." A sly smile came to Dr. Chabot's face as he thoughtfully scratched his chin while thinking aloud. "Maybe all of my prayers for this one have not been wasted, no?" He watched her get into the elevator, noting the spring in her step and the anxiousness to get to her destination shown by her fidgety fingers tapping away at the button trying to hasten the slowly closing doors. "Perhaps she **has** opened her heart to someone." Rene smiled smugly. He was satisfied that his attempts to get the stoic and reserved woman to embrace life had finally worked. He shrugged his shoulders and continued into his office. "Well, whoever or whatever it is…it sure is making her happy."

****

The ride had only been a short one but still seemed too long. The trauma surgeon's pace was quick, but not rushed, as she moved through the still-opening doors of the elevator when it came to a stop. Her body language alone cleared a path in her intended direction as it always had. In the little over four months since her arrival, the staff had learned how best to stay out of her way. Today not being any exception to that rule. Only a few, slow moving visitors obscured her path, which she easily moved around, never altering the rhythm of her steps.

As her hands came in contact with the large Emergency Room doors, she remembered her first trip through them. Her eyes roved the hall on the other side as they swung open, looking for the same three people in a déjà vu effort of that first encounter. She sighed when she realized that the only occupants of the long hallway now were an empty stretcher or two and an occasional I.V. pole littering the way. Garrett turned her head in the direction of the nurse's desk, her eyes moving constantly to find the familiar faces that she had come to rely on. Then she remembered. It was still the daylight shift. Two of the three faces that she was hoping to see would not be here. The only one that would be possible to find now was the petite blonde nurse, Danni.

Seeing the tall surgeon come into her E.R. with such enthusiasm in her step, Dr. Potter hurriedly ran through the list of patients, trying to find anyone that could possibly be a candidate for surgery. There was none. Jamie quickly checked the computer monitors for any indication of an impending trauma. Again, there was none. Resolving to find out why the surgeon was here, Dr. Potter leaned on the counter with her elbow and greeted the Trauma Fellow.

"Dr. Trivoli, anything that I can help you with or is this just a social call?"

Hearing the name of one of the women with whom he would love to get closer to, John peered up over the monitor screen that he was sitting at. The adventuresome nurse had to admit that with the smile on her face, Garrett Trivoli never looked more appealing to him. He could see her blue eyes searching for someone and passing right over him and moving on down the hall. He held his breath when the surgeon started to speak then quickly realized that it wasn't he that Garrett was looking for.

"Actually, Dr. Potter, I'm looking for one of the nurses, Danni to be exact." Garrett looked around. "Do you have any idea where I could find her?"

Jamie shrugged her shoulders, looking over to John for help. She knew that John had a habit of keeping tabs on the whereabouts of his potential conquests when they worked with him, just in case their need for him arose. "John, any idea where Danni might be?"

Resigning to the fact that he would probably never have

either of his two most sought-after women, the male nurse rolled his eyes and answered. "She's in the back Conference Room working on some report or research of some kind." Garrett started moving in the direction of the Conference Room. "Hey, I wanted to help her but she said she didn't need any help," he offered to the now disappearing back of the tall surgeon.

Garrett made her way down the long hallway, nodding acknowledgement to staff members that she encountered along the way. Her stride slowed as she came upon the bank of windows that lined the Conference Room. Inside she could see the lone, blonde nurse mulling over the data on a computer screen. As she moved along the hall, closer to the door leading into the room itself, the surgeon could see the intense look on Danni's face. She was now pointing to the screen and intent on the particular line that was being revealed to her. The tall surgeon stopped at the last window briefly, just to study the woman inside the room. She couldn't help but be impressed by the dedication that this nurse showed to any task that she undertook. *Yes, she'll make an excellent addition to this team.* Garrett tried hard to fight back the full-face smile that was so desperately trying to be seen. She didn't want to shock the poor woman. After all, she was known for her stoicism, not her glowing personality. Turning the doorknob with her outstretched hand, the surgeon toned down her excitement and the expression on her face.

The gentle sound of tapping came from the direction of the door as it drew the young blonde's attention away from the monitor. Danni looked up in time to see the reserved face of her roommate as it peered into the room. "Hey, Dr. Trivoli, come on in." Her voice was smooth and welcoming.

Garrett looked around the room as if she was searching for something. "Is there a patient in there that I'm not seeing?"

Danni quickly looked around herself then shook her head. "No, why do you ask?" The curiosity of the woman was now peaked as she watched the tall surgeon enter the room, advancing toward her.

"Oh, I don't know…I thought you were only going to call me 'Dr. Trivoli' when patients were around. I mean, Danni, we do live in the same house together. Besides, I thought that friends usually used first names when they talked to one another."

Danni smiled, nodding her head in agreement. "You're right. I guess I'm just used to that old Trauma Fellow who used to occupy that tall, dark form of yours." She chuckled at the thought, "That would never fly with her. I'll see if I can't remember that, Dr. Tri…Garrett, I mean." She winked at the surgeon and began laughing at the confusion showing on the face of the surgeon.

"That's enough talking about me. Now, what were you so interested in on the computer screen when I disturbed you?" She made the motions of trying to see what was on the screen as a playful gesture to her friend's interest in the information that was displayed. Garrett tried to change the subject, as she had always felt uncomfortable when any conversation revolved around her.

The nurse's eyes flicked from the blue eyes of the surgeon to the monitor then back again. Cocking her head to the side, she wrinkled up her nose saying, "You're not going to believe me when I tell you."

"Okay," Garrett nodded, "try me?" She let her leg drape over the end of the conference table as she halfway sat on it with her arms extended and her hands clasped on her scrub pants at the knee. The head tilt suggested that she was daring Danni to continue.

"Okay, you asked for it." Danni warned her. "I was curious about the survival rate we have." She looked up at the puzzled face watching her, then quickly let her eyes return to the screen. Clearing her throat first, she continued. "It seems that when you pair up all of the Trauma Fellows with the different Trauma Nurses the different combinations all have varying percentages of survival rates."

"Oh?" Garrett's eyebrow now edged upward with her interest, wondering just how well her percentages were. "So who is my best pairing...ah...I mean...what is the best survival rate team for the patients?" Her face flushed with embarrassment as she stumbled through her thoughts, not wanting to let on as if she was personally interested.

"Well, that's what I was just looking at when you came in. Give me a minute here and I'll tell you."

The surgeon sat waiting, confident in herself that it surely would be her as the Trauma Fellow. She thought about Rene Chabot and knew that he would be close but the third Fellow in this year's group was not even entering her mind as a source of competition. The question was which nurse was best with her. *By the gods, I hope it's Danni.* Garrett thought back over the last several months. Most of her nights on call she had found that the endlessly enthused blonde nurse in front of her seemed to pull the Trauma Nurse One position a lot. Her mind wondered if that was purely coincidence alone. She watched as the petite nurse slowly looked up to her.

Danni's eyes grew wide in astonishment. The green seas of her soul were reflecting the churning thoughts in her mind as she stared at the screen. Blinking slowly several times, she raised her head to look at Garrett. "I don't believe it," she muttered.

"What?" Concern edged through the surgeon's voice. "What don't you believe?" *Jeez, don't tell me that Nathaniel Hostetler beat out both Rene and I? I don't mind being second to Chabot but...* The surgeon's face grew very intense. "Let me see," she moved quickly around the corner of the table, standing behind the nurse. "Where?" Her eyes searched the screen frantically.

Danni lifted her hand and pointed to the line of deciphered information. She waited a moment then looked up at the face of the tall surgeon looming above her as she quietly read the screen. *I can't believe it. I knew that there was a good feeling, but never anything like that.*

Garrett's mouth opened slightly as she let out a low

whistle. It startled her to think that she had such an impact on the outcome of the patients. Her numbers were consistently higher with all of the nurses that were involved in trauma. One number stood out above the rest. Her gaze narrowed as she read over the line a second, and then a third time.

"Can you believe that?" The nurse asked the tall woman who was still mesmerized by the numbers on the screen. "It's got to be wrong. I'll bet someone forgot to add all of the data into the equation."

"Hmmm…maybe it's just reiterating the fact that we make a good team." She nodded in affirmation. "It does always feel kind of better when we work together, don't you think?"

Danni thought for a moment. "Yeah, I'd have to say that you're right. It does feel kind of natural, that way." The blonde pushed her chair back from the table. "So, what do you think it means?"

The surgeon looked over to the blonde, studying her face for any misgivings. "I think we shouldn't look a gift horse in the mouth." With that said, they both looked intently into each other's eyes, trying to read the thoughts of the other. The clear, blue crystals of truth shone forth like a beacon that had been lit for the first time. It had been more than half of her lifetime in coming, but now the openness to extend herself allowed those chains that had bound her to loosen. Feeling slightly uncomfortable with the situation, Garrett chose to look back to the monitor screen. There was a moment of hushed stillness in the room as each woman came to grips with her own thoughts.

"I guess McMurray was right when he insisted that you and I work on the formal proposal for the support group." She used the information to tease at the nurse's inquisitiveness.

"Support group?" Danni's eyes riveted to the form of the surgeon as she stood looking over the information on the screen in a nonchalant manner.

The surgeon used her best poker face, playing with the

nurse's mind. When she felt she could contain her excitement no more, she slowly let her lopsided smile take hold. "Yeah," she nodded her head. "We have to have it in his hands the Monday before Thanksgiving. Then he'll review it and present it at the Board of Directors meeting that Wednesday."

"He's willing to back the idea? Did he have any suggestions? You know, if we include counseling, we could…" her mouth was going as fast as her mind could think.

The bombardment of questions was more than Garrett could comprehend. She just stood there, amazed at the obvious excitement of the petite woman. *I don't even think she realizes that she's involved yet.* Garrett shook her head and smiled politely. *I think we'll need to use a tape recorder for the idea session. I'm never going to remember everything that she's saying.* The surgeon chuckled to herself as she made the effort to stop the rambling woman. "Slow down, Danni. One thought at a time, please."

"Oh…sorry, I guess I got carried away." She admitted to her friend. "I'm glad you'll have the chance to do some good with your idea."

"**My** idea? If I remember correctly it was your idea." She looked the nurse straight in the eye, blue meeting green and holding it there. "McMurray is insisting that both of us…me **and** you are involved in this project from start to finish."

The nurse remained motionless, wondering if she had heard right. *Did she just say 'both of us'? McMurray is insisting that I be involved too?* "I…I don't know what to say." The blonde woman blinked in astonishment.

"That'll be a first," referring to her speechlessness, " So, when do you want to start putting it all together?"

"Garrett, you said that he wants it the Monday before Thanksgiving, right?"

"Yeah, and your problem with that is…?" The surgeon raised her eyebrow in question to the young nurse.

Danni hurriedly scrambled with the mouse to pull up a calendar on the computer screen. Seeing it, she froze, then quickly came back to life, her voice full of fear. "That's less than a week away!"

"I know. McMurray wants us to utilize work time to get it done. He's going to talk to Dr. McCormick and Nan and get your time cleared with them." Garrett looked around to make sure no one was watching or within earshot before she continued. "He said that Ian is always trying to squeeze his way into Trauma Service's special projects and that he'll probably jump at the chance to have **you** on the team."

"When do you think he'll…"?

The intra-departmental intercom crackled to life, interrupting Danni's thought, causing her hand to reach for her trauma beeper. "Nurse Bossard, please report to the Manager's office immediately."

Blue eyes flashed at green, locking on them for a brief second. "I'd say that McMurray already has. You better get going."

The nurse nodded her head and showed two entwined fingers, "Wish me luck." She stood up and proceeded down the hall to Nan's office.

****

The young nurse paused outside the closed door of her Manager's office. She took in a deep breath, trying to settle herself and her nerves. *I can't believe that I'm this nervous. It's not like this proposal is going to alter the rest of my life.* Then she took one more breath and exhaled it slowly. *I mean, it will probably only last the next six months…til Garrett leaves.* Danni didn't want to think about that. She was finding the tall, stoic at times, woman much more to her liking than she ever felt possible. *God, I'm going to miss her. Maybe we could still keep in touch with one another.* When her body finally calmed enough to appear eager without being over enthused, she gently knocked on the door.

Danni didn't have to wait long before the door was opened and the smartly dressed woman in her mid forties was showing her to a seat. Nan always gave off a professional image, even in her worst moments. She was a difficult book cover to read in that perspective. The petite blonde walked through the doorway, noticing that Dr. McCormick was also seated in the room. Stopping abruptly and motioning in the direction of the already occupied chair, Danni started apologizing. "I'm sorry. I didn't know that you had someone here. I thought that the overhead said, 'immediately.' I'll…I'll come back later." Her legs were edging her back into the hallway as she attempted to leave.

Ian McCormick jumped up from his chair, his face full of eagerness. "Danni, we're both here to talk to you." He motioned to Nan. "Now, come on in and have a seat."

She moved into the room and shook Ian's offered hand. Danni thought back to the last time she had seen that look in his eyes. Her mind showed a brief glimpse of the man in an outdoor setting. Now, she recognized it. *The softball game, right before the ambulance arrived.* She watched the eagerness changed to an appreciative look in his eyes. *Well, at least he's not angry about something.* She released his grip and stepped in front of the chair that her Manager was now motioning to.

Nan quickly moved to the seat behind her desk as the other two sat down. Folding her hands on her desk, she looked over to the Chief of the Emergency Department. Seeing his slight nod, Nan turned to address the young nurse directly. "Nurse Bossard," she smiled, then restarted. "Danni," the Manager wanted to keep the impromptu meeting as informal and friendly as she could. "Dr. McCormick approached me about the possibility of adding you to a task force that is being formed jointly between the Department of Trauma Services and our own."

"Oh?" Danni fought hard not to laugh, thinking back about what Garrett had revealed to her about McCormick and how Dr. McMurray viewed him. "I didn't know that there was any kind of 'task force' being assembled." With her air of naivete being aided by her youthful appearance, she pushed on for more information. "What will the task force be dealing with and why do you think that I would be interested in it?"

Ian took over now. He attempted to explain how he had gone to the Chief of Trauma Services, Dr. McMurray, with the proposition and they had both agreed that it would be best for a task force to be put into place. Then he dropped the bombshell. He announced that a proposal would have to be drawn up and since it was so close to the quarterly Board Meeting, it would have to be done within the next few days. He offered some "I'm too busy to do it myself" excuse, then proceeded to tell her that it was his idea to use the best and the brightest from each department to be the work horses. He was coming to an end of his long explanation when he reached out and placed his hand on top of her's as it resting on the arm of the chair. "That's why we thought, since the staff all felt that the two of you work so well together, that it would be no problem for either of you."

Danni looked at him, then at Nan. "Work well…with whom?" *I just love seeing what he's going to offer as the excuse for picking Garrett and myself for this project.* The petite nurse played with them as she eyed the balding man skeptically. She didn't want to seem too eager. Besides, it was fun watching him sweat a little. The gods knew that he made the staff all sweat occasionally with his egomania about competing with other departments within the hospital.

"Well," he brought his handkerchief out of his pocket to wipe the isolated bead or two of perspiration now forming on his forehead, "with Dr. Trivoli, of course." He sounded shocked that she would not have already figured this out.

"You have to admit it, Danni, you two do have a natural feel for each other. It's like you communicate on some level that none of us are aware of." Nan shocked herself at her own astute observation of the pair. "In all of my years, I've never seen someone be able to do that with all of the hostility **that** woman can give off. It's been hell trying to keep nurses from refusing to work under her demands all around the hospital. The other managers are all receiving complaints about her from their staff." Nan shook her head. "Thank God, for some odd reason I'm not one of them. The staff here views her differently in the E.R. Maybe it's because we don't see her for that long of a time." She paused to take a breath, and then continued. "You seem to be able to bring out a side of her that no one else could see. For that, I'm grateful."

The young nurse sat dumbfounded. She didn't realize it was that noticeable to those around her. The "taming of the shrew," as some had termed her attempt at having a friendship with the perfectionistic surgeon behind her back. She had ignored them and rightfully so. She could see the faint image of the real Garrett Trivoli, even as early as that first morning run in. It was something that she believed in, just like now. She believed in Garrett's idea, knowing full well that she had a stake in it also. The eventual healing of the surgeon's own traumatized soul. Her thoughts were interrupted by the sound of the deeper male voice.

"I'd like to see this project get all the support that it needs. What do you say, Danni?" He winked and looked encouragingly at her. "You're the best one to work with her on this." The disgruntled look of envy was written all over his face.

Danni's mind had been made up before she ever entered the office some thirty minutes earlier. Now, it was time to voice her belief in the project...and Garrett also. She turned her gaze now to Nan. "You do realize that if I take this assignment, I'll have very little time to concentrate on it with my present scheduling?" Her face was serious and very business-like.

"Yes, that's why we are taking you off of your assigned nursing duties for the rest of the week." Nan was confident that the small nurse would go to bat for them now, just like she always had. "You'll be reassigned to them starting next Monday evening. Is that all right with you?"

The nurse nodded and stood up to leave. "Well, if you'll excuse me, I have some things to get done before I dig into that proposal."

Dr. McCormick stood and cupped his hand on her shoulder. "I knew that you would come through for us, Danni."

The nurse looked up to see a far off look in the physician's eye. His mind definitely was on something else that brought a rather blissful look to his face.

"Ah...heaven," he muttered softly under his breath.

"What?" Danni asked as her eyes searched his face.

"Heaven, that's what it would be to work with Dr. Trivoli," his words came without thinking. Coughing to clear his throat and his lewd visions, McCormick asked, "Haven't you wasted enough time in this office already?" He hoped that his face was not reflecting his daydreams to be with the Trauma Fellow, but he couldn't put her out of his mind.

"You're right, Dr. McCormick. I'd better get going." She nodded at her Manager across from her and turned, leaving the office. Once on the other side of the door, Danni's face was one of sheer joy.

She made her way back to the Conference Room where she had been talking to Garrett when the ominous overhead announcement had summoned her. The room was empty. *I guess she couldn't wait that long.* She glanced down at her watch, noticing that a significant amount of time had passed. *Well, at least the day is almost over.*

****

The news traveled fast once the changes where made to the week's work schedule. The occasional rude and thoughtless comments were being made by some of the staff as to why Danni had been so privileged, until none other than Nan filtered the true reason down through the ranks. Once they found out that the project was to be in close workings with the perfectionistic surgeon, all bidders quickly stopped their grumbling. The staff liked the strong-willed Trauma Fellow, but not that much to be saddled solely with her for the next six days.

Danni waited for the last hour of her shift to pass by filling her time with the paperwork that seldom got attention. The nurse had not noticed her friend standing a few feet away when her thoughts were interrupted.

"So, I hear that you got a big job during the next week." Rosie was teasing her. "Must be nice, not having to leave home to work."

"Rosie!" Danni sat shaking her head. "I wish it was going to be that easy. Everyone around here thinks that besides the fact that I have to work with Dr. Trivoli, it's going to be a cinch job."

"Well, isn't it? How hard can writing a project proposal be?"

The blonde nurse didn't know what to say to that. *If you only knew why this proposal is so important, you would understand. I'd love to be able to tell you but I'm not sure Garrett wants the world to know, at least not yet.* "I guess it could be worse. No, you're right, with the two of us working on it, it shouldn't be that difficult." She chose the easy way out, knowing that Rosie would never understand her allegiance with the Trauma Fellow. "Say, what are you doing in so early, anyway?"

"Early?" Rosie looked puzzled. "Danni, I hate to tell you this, but it's just about time for you to head on home. Your shift's just about done."

"Jeez, I must have lost track of all time." Her head turned from side to side as she scanned the visible parts of the E.R. "You haven't seen Dr. Trivoli anywhere, have you?"

"Nope, all's quiet on the trauma front." Rosie laughed. "Why? Did you misplace her?"

Danni made a silly face at the sassy nurse. "No, we drove in together. I'd better page her or she'll forget all about going home." *Better yet, I think I'll pick up some food in the cafeteria and maybe we can start to work on that proposal now.* The nurse got up and headed toward the elevators. "I'll see you later, Rosie."

"Hey, I thought you were going to page Garrett?"

"I'm not ready to go home just yet. Besides, I have a better idea." Danni waved and resumed her forward motion, only to be stopped by Karen as she came through the E.R.'s main doors. "Hey, Mom!"

"Hey, yourself." Karen sidestepped as the blonde made her way through the doorway. The older nurse turned and watched as Danni headed over to the first available elevator and got on. "Must be on a mission,"she laughed and turned to face the auburn-haired nurse at the desk. "What's up with the little one?" Karen motioned her head at Danni's last sighting.

"She's been reassigned for a week to work with Garrett on a special project, some kind of proposal for a joint venture between us and Trauma Services. Lucky, huh?"

Mom thought for a moment before even trying to answer Rosie's question. "Yeah, well, I guess that all depends on how easy that project is to tackle. Somehow with Garrett involved...I wouldn't exactly say it's 'lucky' to be with her for a week." Mom ambled over to the Charge Nurse desk and sat down. "All right, now get to work." She looked sternly at Rosie, then began to laugh. It was going to be another night shift as usual but without two of her "daughters" at her side.

****

The soft knock followed by a slightly louder one gradually stirred the surgeon from her thoughts as she poured over the computer screen. "Come on in." She called out, not losing her place on the data filled screen. Upon hearing the door swing open she started talking. "Rene, you don't have to knock. It's as much your office..." Only when she finished the line of data did she look up. Seeing that it was Danni and not her colleague, she chuckled apologetically. "Sorry, you're not Rene. Hi," she winced, "I guess I forgot about going home, huh?"

The nurse shook her head and smiled. Holding up the tray of food, she offered. "I figured that you would be up to your elbows in research anyway, so I picked up some dinner for us." Setting the tray down on the desk, she looked over the jotted notes on the pad in front of the tall surgeon. "You found more lone survivors?" Danni's eyes flashed up and caught the surgeon's blue orbs.

"Yeah, and I've only gone back two years so far." Garrett sniffed at the air, a faintly familiar aroma drifted on the air. "You got any tea on that tray? I could sure go for some."

"Spiced Apple or Mandarin Orange? I think maybe orange might be just what you need to refresh you, Doc." Danni handed over the cup of tea. "I thought that we could finish up on some of the research tonight. I mean, since you've already been wading through it all day. We could finish it off then move on to planning out the proposal tomorrow."

"Thanks." Garrett sipped at the warming liquid. "I'm almost done here, anyway. It shouldn't take us too much longer."

"So, how many have you found so far?"

"Only three more, but if you think of all of the Trauma Centers in the state, that number could easily grow." The look on the woman's face was one of pensiveness as she wondered why no one else had ever thought to look at the numbers. *I guess they only look at the accident victims themselves and not the families.*

Picking up on her friend's sadness, the nurse tried to turn it into a positive thought. "Things happen for a reason. I think that you were meant to address this. You're one of them and who else would have even thought about it?"

"I'm afraid that I'm not the one that thought of it...you were. For that, I'm grateful."

"Garrett, I truly believe that each of us are put on this earth with a direct mission in mind from some higher being. Sometimes it takes somebody else to make us aware of that plan and they help us achieve our goals. That's all." Her voice became soft as she cast her eyes down in a reflective manner. "I guess I'm that person for you."

The surgeon thought about it for several minutes. The quiet office felt comfortable; words were no longer a necessity between the two women. She had spent all of her adult life subconsciously looking for a feeling of home that had been ripped away from her as a teen. Now, here in this tiny office, in a town on the opposite side of the country, she was feeling very much at home with the nurse who was sharing her life with her, one thought at a time.

Reflective in nature, Garrett came to her conclusions. *I'm going to have to give this more thought. Yes, after the proposal is written, I'll think this whole thing over. She just may be right.*

****

Time passed quickly as both the nurse and the trauma surgeon worked diligently over the information they had gathered that first day. The labor of love was not lost on either of them as they put together the pieces of a project that would help those it was designed for, the lone survivors of traumatic injury. With Garrett pouring her knowledge of what it is like to be the lone survivor, Danni became absorbed in finding ways to help ease the wounds of a lifetime of desiring to belong.

As one day turned into the next, the two women found that not only were they working on the project together, but also each was coming away from it with more insight into themselves and each other. Each new day brought with it a renewed sense of homecoming as the two worked side by side, the aloof and demanding surgeon finding it easier now to talk and share her life with the nurse. If ever a project had been designed for anyone specifically, it was this one for Danni and Garrett both.

Along the way, the small nurse began to understand her own repressed need for belonging that had been so evident, now that she looked back on her life. She found her circumstances much different from that of the surgeon's, but still, she felt that she had never fit into her family's mold. Although still alive and around her, they had never given her that sense of home. Never quite putting her finger on it, that was something she was in search of.

The time and effort that they had put forth to develop their brainchild into a successful program of recovery and support seemed to be working on them before it was even officially started. Now, with the task almost completed, each stood back and evaluated their own lives and their own needs to be whole.

They soon found themselves at the crossroads of completion, each one eager to finish the task but yet hesitant to see it end. The time that they had spent together seemed effortless, as each was reluctant to go back to their normal daily grind.

Danni sat reading over the information on the computer screen as they put the finishing touches on the proposal that was due in McMurray's hands by the morning. Garrett's tall body was unceremoniously draped over the armed chair as she watched in anticipation. Working at Danni's house had given them the needed privacy to concentrate solely on the proposal without any unwanted interruptions. It had helped in her final closure and the plea for the support program had taken much out of her in its writing. Her face was gaunt and her mood one of near defeat as she stared off into space. She had never opened up her soul like this before and she wasn't quite sure that she would ever want to again. She thought of the wisp of a woman who had helped her reach this point, knowing that she would have never made it without her calm and comforting ways. "Hmm…?" Her mind was drawn out of its thoughts by the sound of a voice directed towards her.

"I said," Danni began again as she looked over to Garrett. "I think it reads pretty clear and concise. I don't think that we can improve it any more than we already have."

"You don't think that it sounds like the ranting of a mad woman, do you?" She tried to joke at herself, but the look in her eyes told of her concern at how it would be perceived.

"No, I don't. You should be proud of this, Gar. I am." The nurse's positive attitude was ever present, as always. "You know something?"

"Hmm…what?" She drew herself into a more humanly seated form.

"I'm going to miss this last week once we hand this over to your boss in the morning."

"**My** boss? Danni, you're still on this team and he's **our** boss right now." That drew an arched eyebrow from the tall surgeon as she dared her friend to repudiate it.

"Okay, **our** boss." She rolled her eyes and then bit at her lip pensively. "Well, do you want the honors of hitting the print key? After all, it is all **your** work." *I don't really want this to be over. I've never felt so good about anything as I have this.*

"No, it was **your** idea, you get the honor." The surgeon forced a smile, nodding in assent. "Tomorrow, we'll both take it to McMurray." She tried to reason with herself the benefits that the project could have for those who needed it, but all she really felt was remorse that the time spent putting it together was over. *Together,* the word seemed to echo in her head as she reviewed the last six days. *I've never felt so together as I did during this last week. Well…up until now.*

Danni nodded as she hit the print key causing the inkjet to come to life. *At least it won't be over for another day. I'll just have to hope that this project becomes a reality.* Her thoughts drifted to every known god that she could remember as she offered a prayer in the proposal's behalf.

Within a minute or two the sound of the printer stopped, both women sat motionless as their eyes stared at the completed work lying there in its bin. Neither one wanted to make the first move to retrieve it.

****

Crisp white sheets of paper lay neatly arranged in the official looking folder with the insignia of the hospital on the front cover. The small hands held it tightly in her grasp as she sat waiting for her team member to arrive. The waiting area of the small outer office of Dr. McMurray was friendly, but carried an air of dignity about it. Danni's eyes roamed across the paneled walls, taking in all of the photographs and distinguished looking certificates that adorned them. Her eyes flicked from one photo to another, studying them intently as she tried to pass the time.

She looked down at her watch only to see that her new interest in being early had taken on a different edge this morning. *Perhaps it's the anticipation that made me get here so soon. I can't wait to hear what Dr. McMurray is going think of our proposal.* She lifted her eyes up to the heavens. *God, I hope he likes it. I'd hate for Garrett to have gone through all this and nothing to come of it.* She looked down to her hands, taking note of the slight tremor in them stemming from her nervousness. Her thoughts drifted to the tall surgeon as she imagined her trying to do surgery right now. *Jeez, I hope she's not this nervous.* She repositioned her hands, holding onto the proposal a little tighter to steady them.

Danni smiled pleasantly at the secretary when their eyes met as she began to look around the room once more. Then she offered an attempt at making small talk, trying to hide her nervousness. "Nice waiting room," the nurse motioned to the walls filled with framed pieces.

The older woman nodded and spoke softly, "Yes, Dr. McMurray is as particular about what gets hung out here as he is about the ones in his own office. He thinks that they all tell a story about the Trauma Services Department."

"Oh! I'll have to take a better look then."

The secretary smiled politely and resumed her work at the computer keyboard in front of her.

Danni gazed from photograph to photograph, paying much more attention to them now. In each of them she was able to pick out the familiar face of the Head of the Department, Dr. McMurray. She studied them again, this time noting the different stages of the man's career displayed across the room. It was as though his chronological timeline was in view for all to see, starting at the left side of the doorway from the hall and progressing to its right side.

Then, an odd thing struck the nurse's thoughts. She glanced quickly around the room again. *Yep, I was right. There is another face that is in almost every picture.* She concentrated on the woman always off to the side and behind the ever-present surgeon. "Hmmm…I wonder who she is?" Her voice was barely audible as she brought her right hand up to her chin, striking a thoughtful pose.

The older woman looked up from her computer screen, "Excuse me?" The question was directed at Danni.

"Sorry, I guess I was just wondering out loud," the nurse apologized. "The woman in the pictures, I don't recognize her. Who is she?"

"Why that's Mrs. McMurray. The doctor thinks of her as his good luck piece." She shook her head in disbelief. "He attributes her with his success and always insists that she be a part of the picture."

"Hmmm…I guess that makes her feel like she's a part of his work then."

"You might be right. The doctor is always saying that behind every good physician is a nurse guiding them." The secretary smiled as she got up from her desk with a bundle of papers in her hand. "He shouldn't be too much longer in surgery. I'll be back in a few minutes." Then she left through the doorway into the hall.

The petite nurse got up, taking the opportunity to get a closer look at the photographs without being observed. She had just about made it full circle around the room studying each picture more intently than before, only this time looking for the story that each of the photos was revealing. She glanced at her watch when she heard someone enter the room. It was 10 A.M. and a smile slowly stretched across her face. She knew that it would be her team member and friend, Garrett. She could sense her presence. *Her punctuality is phenomenal. How does she do that?* Danni caught a glimpse of the tall surgeon as she turned her attention toward the door.

"Hey! You're here already." The surgeon sounded a little surprised at seeing Danni waiting for both her and McMurray to arrive.

"I guess you're rubbing off on me," she chuckled. Then, motioning to the inner office she continued, "He's not in yet."

"I know..." she adjusted her collar and straightened her lab coat, "he's still in surgery, just finishing up."

"Did everything go all right with your patient in surgery? You look a little..." Danni searched for the right word to use before settling on one, "edgy."

The eyebrow of the raven-haired woman slowly rose to new heights as she contemplated the idea of her patient being in jeopardy. "Why would you think...? I'm just anxious to get this presentation done with and hear what the Ol' Cutter thinks about it."

The nurse moved closer to the surgeon and rested her hand on the taller woman's shoulder in a comforting manner. "He'll like it, Gar. I know he will. When he sees all the work and thought that you've put into it..."

"**We**." The surgeon corrected her. "That **we've** put into it." She let her eyes meet and linger on the petite nurse's in a silent exchange of thoughts.

For the first time in a long while, she realized the importance of working together as a committed team and the feeling that it brought with it. *Déjà vu.* The surgeon thought. It wasn't new to her, just long forgotten.

Her thoughts raced back to a time when the world was all fresh and new. There were so many times that she felt like this, when the combined effort of some plan that she and her brother put into action had turned into one of accomplishment. Often it had come as a surprise to her parents. When all was said and done, her brother would always reach up, cupping her shoulder in victory, while communicating as only close siblings do...with a meeting of the eyes.

Dr. McMurray stood silently in the doorway, watching the unfolding scene knowing that the bonding of one human to another was of more importance then any meeting could ever be. It was something that his wife had taught him and he was grateful for it. The world always seemed to put more importance to things concerning money or prosperity instead of matters of the heart.

"Without the heart, one has no need of a soul," he spoke the words of his wife under his breath. He was pleased that he was now witnessing the true awakening of a heart that had been lost in an abyss of everyday life. Yes, his plan was working.

Danni was the first to notice the man standing in the doorway. Her face blushed with the embarrassment of being watched. She retracted her hand from its comfortable position while her eyes changed their point of focus. "He's here," she whispered to Garrett as she felt a renewed sensation of butterflies in her stomach.

The tall surgeon swallowed hard with the gulping sound almost filling the room. Her palms began to sweat as a sudden need to empty her bladder overtook her body. *Nerves? I thought I had you under control a long time ago.* She cursed her body for its reactions, willing herself to regain her composure. Then, with a faint smile, she nodded in his direction saying, "Dr. McMurray, we have that proposal ready for you."

"Good! Did you two just work it out this morning or did you spend all week on it like I suggested?" He took off striding into his office. "Well, you don't expect me to listen to it out there in the waiting room, do you?"

"No! No, Sir." The voices of the team members piped in, one over top of the other. The nurse stood mesmerized at the view of the Chief of Trauma Services' office as the door opened wide. Garrett nudged her gently from behind in an effort to advance into his office but the blonde was frozen in place. Bending over, she whispered into her ear, "The view gets better once you get inside." Then she pushed her again, this time with a little more force. "Go on."

Danni suddenly realized her fear and looked back for support from the tall surgeon behind her. Blinking several times to help her mind register what she needed her body to do, the nurse slowly began to move forward toward the open office door, her hand wrapped tightly around the bound proposal. The gentle touches of the large hand on her back helped to ease the fear of rejection that was racing through her body with each step. Before she knew it, she was standing in front of the large desk, with McMurray seated at it. *Please, God. Please.* She offered up one last quick plea on their behalf as she handed the proposal over to him. Then stepping blindly backward, Danni bumped into the woman behind her. "Sorry, I…"

"So this is the other half of your team, Dr. Trivoli?" His voice sounded slightly bemused at the nervousness that he was evoking in the small blonde. He began to look over the bound proposal, opening its cover to go deeper.

"Yes, Sir. Let me introduce Nurse Danni Bossard to you, Danni this is Dr. McM…"

"Damn it, Trivoli. She knows who I am. I'm the Chief of the Department," his voice was coarse and gruff. He shot her a glance, then let his eyes fall back upon the nurse, watching for her reaction. "Nice package you have here." He nodded to the nurse as he motioned to the document before him. "Looks like you spent quite a bit of time putting it together."

"Yes, we worked all week on it. The time that we put into the research alone was the better part of that week."

Danni's voice took on a bit of a defensive tone to it to show her resentment of the words that were directed to her friend. "Sir, I'd like to just say that, Dr. Trivoli was only trying to be polite and follow proper etiquette when she..."

He lifted his eyes from the page he was reading. "You're right. I should have let her finish, but then I wouldn't know if you two were really a cohesive unit or not. Now, would I?" McMurray half laughed and half-grunted. "I like what I see. I can tell by this report," he held it up, "that you're working together, at least on paper. It's evident that Trivoli didn't write this. It doesn't sound like surgical dictation." He glanced at the wide-eyed look on the surgeon's face in front of him.

"Why, sir, is there something that you don't like about the way I document my operative records?" Garrett narrowed her gaze at him, trying to read the body language that he was displaying.

He sat back in the comfortable-looking chair. "No, doctor, there isn't. It's just that this document will need to reach out and grab at the heart of that cold, calculating bunch that sit on the Board of Directors here. To do that, we'll need something with more feeling and emotion in it than any surgical report." He returned to his reading as he skimmed swiftly through the rest of the proposal.

The two women stood side by side now as they waited for him to finish. Each one prayed, in her own manner, for the proposal to meet with his approval. With every change of his facial expression, Danni could feel her heart either rise or fall in anticipation of his words, while Garrett seemed unscathed by it all. The tall surgeon had pulled out one of her stoic masks from the dark recesses of her heart and used it to cover her emotions as she waited for his reaction.

Turning the last page of the document to show the back cover of the packet, the Ol' Cutter sat there, his face somewhat expressionless as he thought about the proposal that he had just finished reading. He speculated whether or not to tell them of the fine job they had done, letting them know of his pride in their efforts or letting them learn it for themselves, and from each other. He mulled over the possible effects that it could have on them, then closed the cover of the proposal, holding it in his hands in a playful motion.

"Well, what are you waiting around in here for? The Board won't meet until Wednesday, I'll present it to them then." His lips pressed together tightly for a moment and then, as an afterthought, he threw out,"It should be enough to do the trick." He waved the proposal at them and then threw it off to the side of his desk. "Don't you two have work to be doing?"

Garrett's eyebrow rose in question to their dismissal, her body standing straighter now, if that were at all possible. The nurse could sense the impending reaction as she reached out, tugging at the surgeon's sleeve.

"Why, I ought to..." the tall woman leaned forward, to which Danni's tugging became more exaggerated.

"We ought to go back to work now, Dr. Trivoli. Thank you for your time, Dr. McMurray." She pulled her friend with her as she made her way backwards toward the door. "It was nice meeting you and getting to see your office." She quickly looked around it and smiled wryly. "Very nice. I'll have to see it a little more closely next time." She pushed the raven-haired woman through the now open door and once outside of it, reached back to draw it shut. "Thanks, again. You have a good day, okay?"

She breathed a sigh of relief when the door finally met its frame and she could hear the clicking sound of the lock as it fell into place. She looked up to see the face of her friend. At first her expression was one of being startled, then it gradually changed for the better, showing that trademark lopsided grin of hers. "What?" Danni looked at her for an answer.

"I would have said something stupid in there if it wasn't for you. Probably would have ruined our chances of ever getting that proposal through to the Board, too."

"Well, let's just hope that hasn't already happened." The two looked at each other and started to head out of the waiting room. Once in the hall Danni started to giggle, trying to hide it behind her hand.

"What's so funny?" Garrett stopped, placing her hands on her hips for emphasis.

"I was just thinking." She reached up and cupped the surgeon's shoulder. "We make a pretty good team. You had to push **me** into his office, while I had to pull **you** out of it." Her eyes flickered with the laughter in her voice. "You can't get any closer to teamwork than that, now can you?"

The surgeon thought for a moment, then answered, "No, I guess you can't." Nodding in agreement she concluded her thought, "Thanks."

****

As fast as the days that they worked together on the proposal had passed by, the days waiting to hear of its approval dragged ever so slowly by. The hospital staff was all caught up in a state of anticipation for the upcoming holiday on Thursday. Even Danni seemed to be excited about it as she prepared her offering for the Thanksgiving Day feast to come. She had labored with love over the Pumpkin Roll Desert she was preparing for the next day, trying as she might to forget about the Board Meeting that was going on. There was nothing more she could do to get the proposal passed than what she had already done. It was all up to the fates now.

She thought about her family and how lucky they were to be able to spend time together. Her siblings would be there and of course, her parents. She had tried to talk her roommate into going with her but sensed her desire not to dampen anyone else's holiday, her excuse being that she was working so that Rene could be with his new family. *If only I could get her to realize that she's part of a family too.* The nurse set about making that idea become a reality. After a few quick phone calls, she was smiling again. Her plan was being put into motion.

****

It was going to be another one of those family holidays that Dr. Trivoli shied away from, always volunteering to work for someone else so that the other person could enjoy it. The truth of the matter was that she had no one to enjoy it with, let alone be thankful. Her only feeling of belonging was her work and there is where she chose to be as she had for all of her adult life.

Why should this year be any different? Garrett pondered as she sat in front of the window that overlooked the helipad. She couldn't even get excited about work, there wasn't any. Sure, there were still patients on the floors and in the units to take care of, but nothing that would get her mind off the outcome of the Board Meeting the night before. The Ol' Cutter hadn't gotten in touch with her yet about the Board's decision. She had to assume that their proposal had been rejected.

The weather had turned colder now and the small flakes of snow coming down seemed to glisten in the late afternoon sun, the wind swirling them around and around on their way toward the ground. She stared out into nothing, yet her eyes looked at everything that came into view.

There, in the distance was a small figure trudging across the parking area, its form bundled tightly with heavy clothing and its arms laden with boxes and bags. The swirling snow kept sticking to it as it moved closer. The surgeon's mind drifted briefly to that small snow globe of her youth as the images outside stirred her memory to life. She tried to place it but there was no larger figure coming into view.

She watched as each step brought it nearer to the hospital and her. When the figure had reached the illuminated helipad, Garrett sensed that she was familiar with the form. Straining her eyes against the falling snow she tried to make out who the person was. *I swear, that looks like Danni.* She blinked and looked again, seeing a tassel of blonde hair coming out from underneath the knit cap. For a brief second, their eyes met. "It

is Danni."

Garrett was up in a flash, making her way to the trauma bay doors leading to the helipad. Without any concern for the cold and snow, the surgeon went outside, meeting her friend halfway. Relieving her of some of the packages, the surgeon was puzzled by her presence. "Why are you here? You're supposed to be at a family dinner."

Danni pulled at the scarf that was covering her mouth, "I decided to be with my real family. The ones who accept me for who I am, not just because I share their blood." She smiled and nodded toward the door. "Besides, who else was going to bring dinner."

The surgeon shivered as the wind swept the clinging snow into her thin scrub attire, while the white lab coat acted like a magnet for the snow. "Jeez, it's colder out here then I thought. Let's get inside."

The several minutes that it had taken for them to get to the door was more than enough to cover the two women with snow, causing them to look very much like two snow people, one small snow-covered figure with a larger one right beside it, matching step for step. Mom stood at the door, watching as they came nearer. "If I didn't know any better, I'd say that might make a nice snow globe scene." She mused, "Wonder if I should mention it to them?" When they were a few steps away, Karen triggered the automatic door to open.

The two snow-covered forms stepped inside, trying to shed the remnants of the snow squall from their bodies. Karen watched with awe her two pseudo-daughters, as they slowly warmed up not only to the temperature inside but also to each other with their quiet bantering.

"Jesus, Mary and Joseph!" The older nurse was blessing herself. "What are you trying to do, give our Trauma Fellow a death of a cold?" She shook her head with her hands perched on top of her hips, her right foot tapping to some unknown melody. "You'd think you two were some little street urchins the way you get into trouble." Her voice was now strained as she tried to keep from laughing. "Hey, Rosie!" She called out. "Look what the wind just blew into our midst."

"Yeah, I see that." Rosie had just turned the corner, coming down from the trauma hallway. "It's about time, I'm starved. One of those boxes better have a turkey in it."

"Come on, let's get dinner set up." Danni shook her clothing one last time before she started down the hall. "If we're lucky, it should still be warm enough to eat." She looked behind her at the surprised surgeon.

"You had this planned, didn't you?" Garrett let Rosie slide some of the bags from out of her arms, then stepped lively to follow behind the spirited blonde.

"Yep! From nuts to desert." Danni led the way into the already-prepared, secluded exam room. "We're a family here. Whether you like it or not, you're now part of it."

"But…but…" Garrett stammered.

"No buts about it, Doc. I've…er…we've adopted you, just like everyone else in our little family here."

Karen looked at the surgeon challengingly. "You better learn to accept it. We're even worse come the real family holidays. Don't even think about trying to get out of **those** celebrations." She winked at the surgeon just to prove that her bark was worse than her bite.

"All right, but you could have at least let me contribute something to this meal." Garrett was slowly resigning herself to the idea of this adoptive family.

"Oh, but you are contributing, Doc. Who do you think is going to carve up this wonderful bird?" Mom stepped back from the table with a large carving knife in her hand, presenting it to the surgeon. "Since you're the newest member of our family here," she looked at the motley crew of the E.R. staff, "it's your honor to offer up a prayer in our behalf and then use those surgical skills of yours and carve away."

A look of panic flashed across the surgeon's face. Sure, she would have no problem slicing up the turkey, but she wasn't accustomed to praying. How was she going to do it now, in front of everyone assembled there? She could feel the spittle in her mouth turning to paste. *'Why me? Why not...'* She looked up into Danni's gaze like a deer that was caught in headlights.

"Mom, I wouldn't mind doing the prayer for Garrett." Danni's voice was strong. "I'm sure that I've had more practice than the good doctor here."

"Next holiday, Garrett." Mom warned her, shaking her finger. "You're not getting off the hook that easy." Then she turned to the petite nurse. "Okay, Danni, let's get this going before everybody else's dinner is over."

Danni looked around the assembled group of doctors, nurses, aides, technologists, housekeepers, and security personnel. One thing drew her attention as all the different shades of skin hues had come together on this holiday to give medical coverage to the rest of the world as they celebrated at home with their families. *Medicine truly is a diversified field! No one country or ethnic group or gender is in control of it.*

The petite nurse bowed her head and the group followed suit, anxious to move on to the food. After collecting her thoughts for a moment, Danni began her prayer of thanksgiving for all of those gathered.

"Lord, look down upon us, your servants. Whether we are here to learn or to teach, it is in your name that we serve the sick and injured. In this time of global communication, we are thankful that you have chosen us to learn from one another, to act in friendship and fellowship. Both technology and our strong will to reach out to each other have breached the barriers that have kept us distant from one another in the past, isolated in a world of our own. For this, we are truly thankful."

Garrett let the words sink in, knowing that they were especially meant for her. She raised her eyes to view the tiny blonde that was making landmark changes in her life. She didn't hear the rest of the prayer, as her mind took off on its own tangent. The past suddenly became intermingled with the present. Scenes came back to her of her brother Lucas, but were suddenly superimposed with those of Danni in his place.

Her mind raced with thoughts of the snow globe and what her parents had told her.

Her parents had given the globe to her. It was their way of explaining the bond that was to fill her life. The two snowmen inside of the globe stood side-by-side, one slightly larger than the other. They had told her about an unseen bond between the two figures. Her mother knelt down behind her to wrap her arms around the young girl. Pointing to the snowstorm of activity inside the globe, she commented that the two snowmen were held together in their strength for each other and that nothing could separate the bond they shared, not even the cold, harsh winds of the snowstorm. At times it was hard to see the figures, but then, the snow would die down and there the two were, standing side by side, as if nothing had ever happened. The small child wondered which snowman she was. The girl looked up to her mother for confirmation of the choice. She was hugged gently as her mother whispered, "You are the older and bigger one, my love."

Then she thought of how Danni had looked when she viewed her through the window not less than half an hour ago.

The weather had turned colder now and the small flakes of snow coming down seemed to glisten in the late afternoon sun, the wind swirling them around and around on their way toward the ground. There, in the distance was a small figure trudging across the parking area, its form bundled tightly with heavy clothing and its arms laden with boxes and bags. The swirling snow kept sticking to it as it moved closer. The surgeon's mind drifted briefly to that small snow globe of her youth as the images outside stirred her memory to life. She remembered looking down at the both of them, thinking how they resembled the snowmen of her globe by the time they entered the trauma bay doors. She, of course, **was** the larger one.

'No, It's just my body trying to warm up from being

outside. I'm just trying to think too hard, making some sense of things.' She shook her head and looked once more at the demure nurse deep in her thoughts. Before she realized it, another scene stole into her thoughts. The silences of the moment allowed a fleeting glimpse of a tasseled-haired boy come to Garrett's mind. His youthful features were covered with a smattering of sweat and dirt as he laughed, holding up his prize catch, a rainbow trout.

Garrett's mind recalled the joy of fishing in her younger sibling, then twisted and turned until the tasseled-haired boy turned into a petite blonde.

"If we hurry, we'll have time to hike down to the lake," the small blonde offered. "You like to fish?" Her eyebrows jumped up and down in anticipation.

"Fish? Yeah, I like to fish." The surgeon stopped, thinking back to the last time that she had been fishing. A smile tugged at the corners of her mouth.

"Do you think we could do just a little fishing today, I mean, the two of us?" Garrett looked at the petite woman, hope written all over her face.

Speechless, the blonde hair moved freely on top of the nodding head, while a dazzling smile swept across her face. Her voice was unsteady at first, taken aback by the emotion of the moment. "Sure thing, I'll get the rods and gear."

Her thoughts were wild with abandon now, drawing more to her attention.

There were so many times that she felt like this, when the combined effort of some plan that she and her brother put into action had turned into one of accomplishment. Often it had come as a surprise to her parents. When all was said and done, her brother would always reach up, cupping her shoulder in victory, while communicating as only close siblings do, with a meeting of the eyes.

Then the surgeon's mind flashed to earlier this week, bringing the petite blonde back into the picture.

"I was just thinking." She reached up and cupped the surgeon's shoulder. "We make a pretty good team. You had

to push me **into** *his office, while I had to pull you* **out** *of it." Her eyes flickered with the laughter in her voice. "You can't get any closer to teamwork than that now, can you?"*

Her mind was changing its stance. Reasoning was giving way to wanting it to be so. She had loved her brother and missed that bond of fellowship. She thought about how easy it was to talk to him, to tell him of her dreams and what was eating at her soul. *'If only I could have him back. I'd never let go of that fellowship again.'*

The image of the dimly lit cabin came floating back into her mind. The warmth of the tea and the fire as she spilled her soul out for Danni to see. Now that she thought about it, she wasn't sure that it wasn't Danni's presence that had warmed her, not the other sources. That night had been like a breath of fresh air to her soul; one that it had needed and waited on for a long time, like the birth of a long awaited child.

Garrett's mind flashed to the night Rene's babies was born.

"Oh, I see." There was silence for a moment of reverent thought before the young nurse spoke. "You know, they say that when one spirit leaves this earth, another one comes to take its place." She shrugged her shoulders. "Life goes on."

"Hmm...interesting thought, Danni. Interesting in a lot of ways." Garrett wondered who would be the one to take over the place that was vacated in her life. She'd have to give this concept more thought when she had the time.

Her eyes flashed brightly with the final realization, *Could it be? Could this blonde nurse be the one to replace my brother in my life?* Her gaze fell upon Danni's as she ended her prayer. The life that showed forth in that moment was phenomenal, her blue eyes twinkling in delight. *Have you been trying to show this to me the entire time?* She thought of her brother and knew it to be true. "I love you," she whispered under her breath, knowing that the one it was meant for would hear.

Danni raised her head with the final word of her prayer, "Amen." Her gaze fell upon the vision of a dark-haired woman, holding a large sharp object in front of her. There was something about her eyes that made the nurse take a closer look. She could see that the fiery blue crystals had come to life. *They're twinkling like they are full of life. I've never seen her so alive before. I wonder if it was something that I said.* The nurse tried to think what it could have been, but the same nagging image kept coming into her head. *Jeez, why would that darn journal of mine pop into my thoughts, now of all times?*

Then her thoughts took in the periphery of her vision and she saw the glistening edge of the carving knife, calling to mind her first time in trauma with Garrett.

Looking across her patient, Danni could see the dark-haired surgeon standing with the Trocar clenched in both hands. Danni's mind thought back to her dream, startling the young nurse. Her eyes opened wider as she looked at the surgeon poised, ready to send the long blunt- tipped rod into the patient's side. The surgeon began the insertion of the chest tube, her face taut with concentration; the confident blue eyes focused on the job at hand. All of a sudden there was a feeling of déjà vu, as a chill ran down the young nurse's spine. It was an all too familiar scene but something was missing. Everything seemed so mechanical and devoid of emotion that it reminded Danni of a cyberspace movie. Her mind recalled her dream almost instantly, flashing it across her brain.

Then her mind wondered if she had had some part in the now-glowing figure before her. *Could I have made that much of a difference in her life? God knows, she has made a difference in mine.*

Then, as if from out of nowhere, while everyone else was responding with their own form of "Amen" to hers, she thought that she heard the gentle whisper of 'I love you' come floating on the air, causing her heart to skip a beat. It brought with it a warm feeling that she grabbed onto and cherished. *I'm not sure where that came from,* Danni's eyes immediately riveted up to the raven-haired surgeon who was addressing the heavens with her mouth pursed in a vowel-like ending. She quickly surveyed the others in the room, then settled once again on the surgeon across from her. *...But it's just made this one of the best Thanksgivings ever.* She felt her face grow warm with the soft blush that was creeping up her neck and face as she realized the depth of her love for the members of her menagerie.

"All right, Doc, it's your turn in the spotlight now. You'd better get on with that carving. There's lots of hungry people here." Mom was nudging the surgeon, being careful of the knife.

"Huh? Oh, yeah!" Garrett let her mind come back to the present and all of the people around her. The surgeon started carving the golden brown bird as she thought about her life in Pittsburgh. She had only been here just short of five months, but the feeling of fellowship and love that surrounded her had given new meaning to her life. For the first time in a long while, she finally felt that she had come home. Garrett turned slightly, holding out the first slice of turkey and there, to take it on the offered plate, was the woman she attributed her new life to...Danni.

"Happy Thanksgiving, Gar. Thank you." The nurse smiled at her friend.

"No, I have to thank you, Danni. You've really given me something to be thankful for." The lopsided smile was showing now for all to see. There was a silent moment as blue eyes met green and the exchange of sentiments was conveyed. Then, pulling herself back to the reality of time, she motioned toward the steaming turkey. "Now let me get this bird carved up before they grab this knife and turn it on me." She eyed the hungry line behind the nurse.

The blonde reached up and cupped the surgeon's shoulder, "Okay, my friend, I'll be here."

"I know, that's what I'm counting on." Garrett drew in a deep breath as Danni left her side. *Thanks to you, too.* Her eyes lifted momentarily to heaven, thinking of her brother and then, quickly resumed her role in the family that she was now a part of. She looked to the next person in line for turkey, "Okay, John, will that be a piece of breast or leg for you? Or perhaps a little piece of tail?" Her face was coy with the implied innuendo.

The group chuckled at her questions to the ever-obsessed-with-sex nurse as he hesitated to answer. The laughter was pleasant and the taunting was quick to follow, just like any family get-together. Yes, this indeed was her new family.

****

The E.R. was quiet and most of the staff had found rooms and cubbyholes to their liking. Danni and Garrett had found themselves huddled in a corner of the Conference Room with Rosie and Karen, listening and sharing stories of past holiday gatherings as they finished their dessert. With their bellies full and the good mood of friends and family around them, they each secretly hoped that the world would forget about the part that they had to play in it tonight.

Garrett listened to those around her, letting the warmth of their stories soak in. She wished that she had a story to share with them out of her past, but knew that next year would be another story. As the surgeon reached to put her used paper plate into the wastebasket, she caught sight of a snow-covered figure walking towards the Conference Room. "Jeez, tell me we have a walk-in," she muttered under her breath.

Danni looked out the opened door. "Must have come in the trauma doors."

The group began to rise in response to the approaching figure, each knowing their part in the well-rehearsed scenario. They watched as the figure stopped outside of the door and began brushing the snow off of its coat. It didn't appear to be injured or sick, but one could not always tell from a distance. The figure reached up, removing its hat and scarf to reveal none other than the Chief of Trauma Services himself.

"Dr. McMurray, what are you doing out on a day like this?" Garrett sounded a little startled that something might have slipped by her watchful eye.

The group was a little relieved to see a familiar face, but they all knew that something had to be up to have this man here on a holiday.

"Oh, nothing really. I just didn't want you to find out about the Board Meeting last night from someone else."

Danni viewed her friend, both showing the disappointment in their eyes. "Oh?" They groaned in an unrehearsed unison.

"You two always this cheerful or is it just the holiday?" He was being sarcastic. "I could always go back home and let you wait until Monday." He made a motion towards the door.

"No, Sir. You can tell us now." Garrett shrugged her shoulders as she felt the clasp of the small hand on her elbow. "We're ready to hear what they decided." Danni nodded in agreement as she tightened her grip on Garrett.

"Well, it took some doing. I had to just about beat it into that knucklehead accountant who sits on that Board that services are needed even if they don't bring money into the coffers, but the Board finally approved it. In fact, they want it up and running by the first of the New Year. Think your team can do that, Trivoli?"

"They approved it?" Garrett's mouth was now agape. "But I thought when I didn't hear from you last night…"

Danni began to shake the surgeon's arm, her face filled with emotion. "They approved it!" She began tugging at the arm of the surgeon.

The Ol' Cutter smirked and flashed a smile at her. "Hell, I wanted to. It's the wife who wouldn't let me. She figured that if you knew, you wouldn't be able to sleep. Can't have a tired Trauma Fellow on for a holiday now, can we?" He winked. "So, think you can bring it into being before January first?"

"Yes, yes, sir!" The answer came in complete unison.

"Good! That's what I told them. I'll see you two first thing Monday morning and fill you in on all of the details." He listened to the enthusiastic good wishes of their friends as he turned to leave. “Oh, Nurse Bossard, Dr. Trivoli,” he turned his head to them, “I’d get some rest if I were you. They have a lot more planned for your team after they took a look at that proposal of yours.” He began walking out of the room only to throw out a seasonal greeting as he left. “Happy Thanksgiving.”

A hush fell over the group as the petite blonde and the tall surgeon turned to face each other muttering out loud, “They have a lot more planned for us?” Danni wrinkled her nose as she watched the lone raised eyebrow reaching high on Garrett’s forehead, each woman trying to think of the vast possibilities of things that the Board could have in mind for them.

The silence of the moment was shattered by the sound of the trauma pager going off. “Trauma Team Page, Trauma Team Page. Inbound via ambulance, male approximately 47 years of age. Multiple penetrating wounds and an impaled object in the abdomen believed to have been made by a carving fork. ETA 5 minutes. This is a Level One Trauma Team Page.”

The E.R. was awakening once again in the knowledge that life goes on.

About the Author

Deeply rooted in the Western Pennsylvania area, K. Darblyne has spent years observing people both on and off the job. Her schooling in the physical sciences may be the foundation for her analytical thinking, but it's her time spent in the fields of E.M.S., Firefighting, and Health Care that give life to her stories. Trauma is second nature to her after having been involved in all aspects of the human emotions that a crisis evokes. It is with this commitment to the spirit of survival, for both victim and rescuer alike, that she writes from the heart.

Order These Great Books Directly From Limitless, Dare 2 Dream Publishing		
The Amazon Queen by L M Townsend	20.00	
Define Destiny by J M Dragon	20.00	The one that started it all…
Desert Hawk,revised by Katherine E. Standelll	18.00	Many new scenes
Golden Gate by Erin Jennifer Mar	18.00	
The Brass Ring **By Mavis Applewater**	18.00	HOT
Haunting Shadows by J M Dragon	18.00	
Spirit Harvest by Trish Shields	15.00	
PWP: Plot? What Plot? by Mavis Applewater	18.00	HOT
Journeys **By Anne Azel**	18.00	NEW
Memories Kill By S. B. Zarben	20.00	
Up The River, revised **By Sam Ruskin**	18.00	Many new scenes
	Total	

South Carolina residents add 5% sales tax.
Domestic shipping is $3.50 per book

Visit our website at: http://limitlessd2d.net

Please mail your orders with credit card info, check or money order to:

Limitless, Dare 2 Dream Publishing
100 Pin Oak Ct.
Lexington, SC 29073-7911

Please make checks or money orders payable to: Limitless.

Order More Great Books Directly From Limitless, Dare 2 Dream Publishing		
Daughters of Artemis by L M Townsend	18.00	
Connecting Hearts By Val Brown and MJ Walker	18.00	
Mysti: Mistress of Dreams By Sam Ruskin	18.00	HOT
Family Connections By Val Brown & MJ Walker	18.00	Sequel to Connecting Hearts
A Thousand Shades of Feeling by Carolyn McBride	18.00	
The Amazon Nation By Carla Osborne	18.00	Great for research
Poetry from the Featherbed By pinfeather	18.00	If you think you hate poetry you haven't read this
None So Blind, 3rd Edition By LJ Maas	16.00	NEW
A Saving Solace By DS Bauden	18.00	NEW
Return of the Warrior By Katherine E. Standell	20.00	Sequel to Desert Hawk
Journey's End By LJ Maas	18.00	NEW
	Total	

South Carolina residents add 5% sales tax.
Domestic shipping is $3.50 per book

Please mail your orders with credit card info, check or money order to:

Limitless, Dare 2 Dream Publishing
100 Pin Oak Ct.
Lexington, SC 29073-7911

Please make checks or money orders payable to: Limitless.

Name:
Address:
Address:
City/State/Zip:
Country:
Phone:
Credit Card Type:
CC Number:
EXP Date:
List Items Ordered and Retail Prices:

List Items Ordered and Retail Prices:

You may also send a money order or check. Please make payments out to: Limitless Corporation.
You may Fax this form to us at: 803-359-2881 or mail it to:

Limitless Corporation
100 Pin Oak Court
Lexington, SC 29073-7911

South Carolina residents add 5% sales tax.
Domestic shipping is $3.50 per book

Visit our website at: http://limitlessd2d.net

Printed in the United States
23179LVS00003B/175

9 780974 103464